Ulick Ralph Burke

A Life of Benito Juarez

Constitutional President of Mexico

Ulick Ralph Burke

A Life of Benito Juarez
Constitutional President of Mexico

ISBN/EAN: 9783337415082

Printed in Europe, USA, Canada, Australia, Japan

Cover: Foto ©Raphael Reischuk / pixelio.de

More available books at **www.hansebooks.com**

A LIFE

OF

BENITO JUAREZ

CONSTITUTIONAL PRESIDENT OF MEXICO.

BY

ULICK RALPH BURKE, M.A.,

Author of " A Life of Gonsalvo de Cordova,"
" Sancho Panza's Proverbs," Etc.

REMINGTON AND COMPANY, LIMITED,

LONDON AND SYDNEY.

1894.

PREFATORY NOTE.

The following publications, constantly consulted by me in the course of my work, will be referred to as a rule under the abbreviated titles as hereafter noted.

1.—Le Comte Emil de Kératry. " L'Empereur Maximilien: son élévation et sa chute," 1 vol., Leipzig, 1867. [*Kératry.*]

2.—Le Comte Emil de Kératry. " La Créance Jecker," 1 vol., Paris, 1868. [*Kératry—Jecker.*]

3.—Gustavo Baz. "Vida de Benito Juarez," 1 vol., Mexico, 1874. [*Baz.*]

4.—Arrangoiz: "Historia de Mexico, desde 1808 hasta 1867," 4 volumes, Madrid, 1871. [*Arrangoiz.*]

5.—Le Capitaine Niox. "L'Expédition du Mexique," 1 vol., Paris, 1874.   [*Niox.*]

6.—Paul Gaulot. "Rève d'Empire," 1 volume, Paris, 1889.   [*Gaulot—Rève.*]

„   "L'Empire de Maximilien," 1 vol. Paris, 1890.   [*Gaulot—Maximilien.*]

„   "Fin d'Empire," 1 vol., Paris, 1891.   [*Gaulot—Fin.*]

7.—" Correspondance de Juarez et de Montluc," 1 vol., Paris, 1885.   [*Montluc.*]

8.—E. Masseras. "Essai d' Empire au Mexique," 1 vol., Paris, 1879.   [*Masseras.*]

9.—Prince Félix Salm-Salm. "My Diary in Mexico," 2 volumes, Bentley, 1868.   [*Salm-Salm.*]

[Note.—Volume II. contains the Diary of the Princess.]

10.—Emmanuel Domenech. "Histoire du Mexique: Juarez et Maximilien: Correspondances inédites, etc., etc.," Paris, 1868, 3 vols.   [*Domenech—Hist.*]

11.—D. Vicente Riva Palacio, and D. José M. Vigil. "Mexico à Traves de los Siglos," 5 vols., Mexico and Barcelona, 1889.   [*Mexico.*]

12.—" Directorio Estadistico de la Republica Mexicana." F. Navarro y Ca., Mexico., 1 vol., 1890.   [*Directorio.*]

TABLE OF CONTENTS.

A LIFE OF BENITO JUAREZ.

CHAPTER I.

INTRODUCTORY.—1810—1852.

For full fifty years of this Nineteenth Century the name of Mexico was almost synonymous with disorder and disgrace.

The home of sordid and never-ending revolutions, the prey of the most despicable adventurers, the cockpit of transatlantic swashbucklers, the country attained, even among other Spanish-American Republics, a pre-eminence of national abasement.

Amid the struggles of military bravos for the

B

control during a few days of an empty exchequer, and the plunder of a well-nigh bankrupt community, there was ever a recklessness in the conduct of those who found themselves in positions of national responsibility, unexampled in the history of civilised nations.[*]

A Mexican Bond was the type of financial worthlessness, a Mexican General was the type of military dishonour, a Mexican Statesman suggested recklessness, instability and fraud.

One of the master strokes of English policy in the earliest days of the existence of the new Republic (1823-5) was the establishment of diplomatic relations with the infant nation; and the dispatch of an accredited envoy from the Court of St. James to the Court of Mexico was hailed with acclamations on both sides of the Atlantic.

Yet in future years diplomatic relations were fruitless, if not actually impossible; not so much in that the Government of the Republic was faithless and shameless in its dealings; but in that there was no Government with which it was possible to deal.

An agreement concluded by the Minister of Monday was repudiated by the Minister of Wednesday,

---

* Brantz Mayer " Mexico," II, 146-150.
From 1821 to 1868 there are said to have been *three hundred* pronunciamientos.

after a sanguinary and apparently unmeaning revolution on the intervening Tuesday.*

Under such circumstances international comity was impossible.

But all this is now a matter of ancient history. When we say that things are made to move faster on the other side of the Atlantic than in the old home in Europe, we think, if we do not speak, of the United States of North America. But the change that has taken place in Mexico and its institutions within the last quarter of a century, is one of the most rapid as well as one of the most remarkable that is to be found in the history of nations, in the ancient or the modern world.

For of all the revolutions that have taken place in Mexico, the most astounding by far is that which has been accomplished during the last fifteen years, and is still in process of silent and hardly noticed development.

Mexico now † enjoys a well settled Government,

---

* From 1821 to 1853, Domenech ("L'Empire au Mexique" Paris, Dentu, 1862) gives a list of no less than 48 different forms of Government, which succeeded one another in the 32 years. The names of the various Presidents, Dictators, and other Chiefs, including one Emperor, are given, with the dates of their acquisition of and rejection from power.

† A fair account of the social and economic condition of Mexico in the year 1893, will be found in the *Revue de Deux Mondes* for 15th July, 1893, vol. cxviii., p. 305, in an article by Mr. Claudio Jannet.

respected not only at home but abroad. Her envoys are to be found residing in all civilised countries. Her public obligations are punctually met. Her foreign and domestic credit is excellent. Nearly seven thousand miles of railway traverse her rich and fertile country. Her commerce is daily increasing. The worthy, the wise, and the industrious of all nations are welcomed and protected by her rulers, as they help her to develop her vast and varied resources.*

Religion is absolutely free. Education is encouraged and endowed. The army is kept in honourable subjection. Law reigns supreme throughout the country. This marvellous, this magnificent change could hardly be the work of

———

So large a proportion of the French residents in Mexico have come from the valleys on the South Eastern Frontier of France, that the term Barcelonettes is commonly applied to them all.

An article by Señor Emilio Velasco upon the " Condition des Etranger au Mexique," printed in the *Bulletin de la Société de Legislation Comparée, for 1892*, is also of great interest.

* It could hardly be expected that public opinion in Europe should keep pace with the actual condition of things on the other side of the Atlantic.

In a play that I saw this year at the Garrick, the villain of the piece, a fraudulent trustee and bankrupt speculator, has a good post *in Mexico* awaiting the moment when he judges it fit to decamp, quite as a matter of course. Posts in Mexico are not very commonly heard of in England now, and would, as a matter of fact, be no doubt eagerly sought by first-rate men of business in London, who were capable of performing the duties attached to the position.

one man.   But one man contributed more than any
other to bring about this happy result.*

At the moment when things were at their worst,
Benito Juarez, an obscure lawyer in a country town,
the only man of pure Indian blood who has ever
achieved for himself a reputation among the great
leaders of the modern world, stood forth and shewed
that one righteous man was yet to be found in
Mexico.

A diligent student, a trustworthy official, a just
judge, a heaven-born administrator, he passed the
first forty years of his life almost unknown in his
native State, incorruptible, indefatigable, single-
minded, seeking first, and above all things, to do
his duty.

----

* The great decline in market value of Mexican securities
of every kind in the Autumn of this year—1893—is due, not
to any want of confidence in the stability or good faith of the
Government, but to the fall in the price of silver, all the world
over, and the possible effects of further complications upon a
country whose total exports consist in round figures
of

Silver—valued at..   ..   .. $45,000,000
All other commodities $30,000,000
                                                          ————————
Total, say $75,000,000

The honesty and vigour with which President Diaz has
faced the situation is worthy of all praise, and commands
universal respect, and may be fairly appreciated by a perusal
of his Presidential Speech on the opening of the Chambers,
September 16th, 1893.   See also Report of Mr. Lionel Carden,
H.B.M. Consul at Mexico, and an article thereupon of great
interest as regards the financial future of Mexico in *The Times*
of October 21st, 1893, p. 9.

For hard upon thirty years more he was found at all times when honour called him, where danger surrounded him ; neither puffed up by success, nor cast down by failure, striving with a noble simplicity to free his country from the foreigner, and to make her people worthy of independent life.

He was no soldier.   He was no orator.   He had none of the dazzling qualities that make a revolutionary hero or a popular idol, but he was essentially an honest man.

That his influence in Mexico should have been what it was, is a fact supremely encouraging to those who may be tempted to fear that in these days the clever sham is more potent than the honest reality ; the profusion of gilt pieces more effective than the sterling coin.

The first name on the long list of Mexican revolutionists is that of Miguel Hidalgo,* the Parish Priest of a little town near Guanajuato, in Central Mexico.

And on the 16th of September, 1810, after early mass in the parish church, the inhabitants of Dolores, docile in all things, but as yet unprepared for rebellion, were invited to range themselves by the side of their good priest and his military

----

* Domenech likens Hidalgo to Peter the Hermit. Hist. du Mexique : II., p. 3

associate,* Captain Allende of the Dragoons, under the banner and protection of the Most Holy Virgin of Guadalupe.†

Thus was the torch of revolution first lighted in Mexico.

The exact object of Hidalgo's rising is not quite apparent. It is, perhaps, sufficiently explained by the fact that revolution was in the air, and that the Mexicans were weary of the stupid if not very violent oppression of the Spanish Government.

But his war-cry or *Grito*, known as the *Grito de Dolores*, was certainly unlike anything that had ever been formulated by contemporary revolutionists in Europe. It was : "*May true Religion flourish and may false Governments be destroyed !*"

---

* A lawyer of the name of Aldama was also associated with them in the rising, as well as Morelos, of whom more hereafter. Hidalgo was at this time no less than 58 years of age.

† The Most Holy Virgin of Guadalupe is the patron Saint of Mexico, and her cult dates from December, 1531. A full account of the legend and of various miracles which bear witness to its authenticity will be found in Mayer's "Mexico as it was and as it is," p. 63. The Spaniards nick-named the Mexicans *Guadalupes ;* the Mexicans retorted by calling the Spaniards *Gachupines*.

A fierce rivalry, according to Mr. Tylor, ("Anahuac," p. 123) existed between Our Lady of Guadalupe and a Virgin of Spanish origin, Our Lady de los Remedios. It appears that the Aztecs, long before the arrival of the Spaniards, had been in the habit of worshipping in this very place a goddess known as Teotenantzin—the mother god.

There are many valuable notes on Aztec remains, customs, and names in Mr. Tylor's book.

The maintenance of Spanish Catholicism was a strange watchword for a modern Liberator. But even as three hundred years before in Old Castile, the Comuneros of 1520 had cried " Long live the King and down with his evil councillors," when they took up arms against Charles V., so the Mexican revolutionists of 1810 appear to have concerned themselves very little with religion in any form, even though they marched under the banner of the Blessed Virgin, held aloft by the sacred hands of a consecrated priest.

Hidalgo, indeed, was promptly excommunicated by the Bishops. His works and ways were denounced from every altar. He had incurred the censure of the Inquisition in the year 1800, and he was now adjudged not only a present rebel, but an *ex post facto* heretic. His true religion, whatever it was, was *anathema*.

But Hidalgo was at once an enthusiast and a man of action. The people were dissatisfied and impressionable ; and in less than a week fifty thousand armed Mexicans were marching upon the rich and important town of Guanajuato.

The era of revolution had begun in earnest.

For nearly three hundred years Mexico had been untouched by political troubles. Viceroys, good and bad, had come and gone—fifty-nine of them—from Antonio de Mendoza, Count of Tendilla, who

was sent by Charles V. in 1535, to his Excellency
Don Francisco de Venegas, who was commissioned
by the Spanish Council of Regency at Seville in
1810.*   But the good and the bad deeds of these
Spanish Pro-consuls are alike unrecorded in the
history of the world, and are long buried and
forgotten in the limbo of a dead past.

Of the vast extent of territory which was
included in their Government, it is well
that we should take some pains to remind
ourselves.

At the beginning of the present century,† the
Viceroy of his Most Catholic Majesty residing

---

* VICEROYS OF MEXICO DURING THE PRESENT CENTURY.

No.

54	Don Miguel José de Azanza	1798-1800
55	Don Felix Berenguer De Marquina ..	1800-1802
56	Don José Iturrigaray..	1803-1808
57	Field Marshal Don Pedro Garibay.. ..	1808
58	The Archbishop Francisco Xavier De Lianza	1809-1810
59	Lieutenant General Don Francisco Xavier	
	Venegas	1810-1813

"A traitor who, by his conduct in the army destined to co-operate
with Lord Wellington, rendered the victory of Talavera worse than a
defeat." "Encyclopædia Britannica" — Supplement, 1824—Sub Tit:
Mexico, p. 395.

60	Don Felix Maria Calleja	1813-1816
61	Don Juan Ruiz De Apodaca, Conde Del	
	Venadito	1816-1821
62	Don Juan O'Donoju	1821-1824

† The area of the Vice-royalty of Mexico or Nueva
España at the time of its greatest extent under the Spanish
monarchy (1763-1800) was about 2,850,000 square miles, or
about the same area as that of the entire U.S. of N. America.

at Mexico, ruled supreme over a great part of the entire continent of North America, from Guatemala to Vancouver's Island and from Florida to San Francisco.

His dominions included the whole of the modern Republic of Mexico, with the territory now comprised in the States of Louisiana, Arkansas, Missouri, Kansas, Iowa, Nebraska, Minnesota, North and South Dacota, Wyoming, Montana, Oregon, Washington, Idaho, Texas, New Mexico, Arizona, Colorado, Utah, Nevada, Florida and California. It was indeed a noble Pro-consulate.*

But Spain was unworthy of these vast possessions. Charles IV. was reckless of these noble opportunities. And the Bourbon basely and

at the present time. Of this immense territory no less than 2,100,000 square miles have since been acquired by treaty, by conquest, or by purchase, by the United States, leaving Mexico at the present day with about 750,000 square miles. For a detailed account of these transfers see post p. 43.

* By the Treaty of Paris in 1763, Spain gave up the Floridas to England, but obtained what was called Louisiana from France. Mexico, or New Spain, thus extended to the Mississippi and the Upper Missouri.

In October 1800, by the Secret Treaty of San Ildefonso, the whole of Louisiana, including the territory mentioned in the text, was ceded by Charles IV. to Napoleon, and by the Treaty of Paris, April 30th, 1803, the whole was handed over by France to the United States.

And the United States gave up at the same time all claim to Texas, which remained, as it had ever been, a part of New Spain.

ignorantly abandoned the greater part of his transatlantic Empire to his masterful neighbour in Europe, not as the spoil of open war, but as the price of a secret and a dishonourable peace. Within three years Napoleon had sold his plunder —known by the general name of " Louisiana," for a pitiful sum, to the United States of North America (in 1803) without even consulting his wretched ally.

Sixteen years later (in 1819) Ferdinand VII.— unworthy son of an unworthy father—sold the Peninsula of Florida and the adjacent districts which were still in the power of Spain, to the same willing purchasers; to whom also he abandoned all his Imperial rights over the Spanish possessions in the North West, an immense tract of country now included in the States of Oregon, Idaho, and Washington Territory, as far north as Vancouver's Island, and the borders of British Columbia, washed by the noble estuary that still bears its old Spanish name of San Juan de Fuca.

So much for royal abandonment.*

---

* It was in 1819 that Ferdinand VII. sold the Floridas, *i.e.*, Florida, and part of Alabama and Georgia, to the United States for $5,000,000, renouncing at the same time all claims to Spanish territory in the North West to the South of the 42nd parallel, *i.e.*, Oregon and Washington.

Texas declared its independence in 1836. New Mexico,

How closely the new Republic was clipped of the fair lands which she still possessed on her entrance into separate national life, in 1822, will be told in due season. But for hard upon three hundred years, the great Colony, of dimensions so vast that the loss or gain of a few hundred thousands of square miles was hardly counted either at Mexico or Madrid, was governed by Spain for the sole and simple advantage of the governors, Royal, Vice regal, and Spanish.

That the Civil Power was arbitrary, that the Ecclesiastical Power was uncompromising—so much was simply a matter of course. But beyond this, it was taken as the basis and rule of the entire government and administration of the country, that Mexico and the Mexicans alike existed only for the benefit of Old Spain.* Nothing that

Arizona, California, with part of Nevada, and Dakota were wrested from conquered Mexico by the Northern invaders, under the Treaty of Guadalupe Hidalgo in 1848.

* The income of New Spain in the year 1809 (according to Brantz Mayer "Mexico," 1852, vol. II., pp. 93 *et seq)* was $15,700,000, of which cock-fights produced $38,332 and bulls, not sporting but Papal, $271,888. Of this fifteen millions and threequarters of Dollars, say, £3,150,000, eight and a quarter millions, or, say, £1,250,000, was the balance transmitted to Spain.

The exports in the same year were :

Silver	..	..	..	..	..	..	$14,000,000
Indigo	..	..	..	..	..	..	$2,700,000
Cochineal	..	..	..	..	..	..	$1,715,000
Sugar	..	..	..	..	..	..	$1,500,000
Flour	..	..	..	..	..	..	$500,000

could be produced in the mother country was suffered even to grow in the Colony.   Even game cocks were heavily taxed.*   The cultivation of the grape and of the olive, for which the climate of many districts was peculiarly favourable, was altogether forbidden, lest the export of oil and wine should be diminished from Cadiz and Corunna.   And as with the fruits of the earth,† so with the

---

No other article of export reached the value of \$100,000.

A reviewer in *The Quarterly Review*, CXV., p. 362, gives the income in 1810 in round figures at £4,000,000, of which £2,000,000 was remitted to Spain. Under Maximilian the revenue fell to about £3,000,000, and in 1869, the worst year under Republican Government, to \$13,600,000, or about £2,500,000.

The revenue in 1892 amounted to about £8,000,000.

* Cock-fighting is a national amusement of great antiquity, and one that has been taken by the Spaniards with them into every one of their colonies, and it is still a cherished sport in Spain, in the Philippines, and in every part of Spanish South America.

The curious in such matters will find a full account of the rules and regulations of the sport, the mode of rearing and training the cocks, and much out-of-the-way information, set down with much authority in a little book published in the Philippine Islands—*Manual nang Sasabungin, en Castellano y en Tagolog, libro de Suma utilidad à toda el que tenga y cuidè gallos de pelea*, by V. M. de Abella, Manila, 1878, pp. 48. In Mexico, as we see, it was a source of public revenue. I do not know if this was the case in any other country. Bull fights in Spain at the present day contribute largely to the endowment of the hospitals. I am not aware that cock-fights minister to any charity.

† Just before the rising of Hidalgo in 1810, the vines and the mulberry trees that he had cultivated near Dolores were cut down by order of the Spanish authorities, as *wine* and *silk* were both prohibited productions in Mexico.—Domenech: Hist. du Mexique II., 13. Cf. Gen. Grant's Memoirs. I. 65.

children of the soil.   No office was at the disposal of any man who was not a native of Spain.   Not only every Mexican but every man born in the Colony, albeit of the purest Spanish blood, was ineligible for employment of any kind in the Colonial Service of his country.   And thus when, in the early days of national independence, we may marvel at the astounding incapacity for government, for administration, and for ordinary self-control, displayed alike by leaders and followers through dreary cycles of aimless revolution, it is well to remember the national education of the preceding three hundred years.

Only two ports were open for foreign commerce, Vera Cruz on the east, and Acapulco on the Pacific coast.

No stranger was allowed to enter the country without the special license of the Government at Madrid. Few Mexicans were permitted to travel abroad, or even to visit Spain.* Education was discouraged. No book could be introduced into the country without the sanction of the Inquisition.

----

* The members of the *Audiencia*, or Spanish Council of State, in Mexico, were not even allowed to marry in the Colony.

A Creole *(Criollo)* does not, as is sometimes supposed, signify a man or woman of mixed blood, but merely one born in the colony.

The issue of a Spaniard and a Mexican was called *Mestizo*, or half caste   The derivation of Creole is uncertain.

The best that can be said for such a state of things is, that it was pacific.

The State was convulsed by no wars. The Church was vexed by no opposition. The Inquisition,* indeed, existed; but it had no need to put forth its giant strength. The Commonwealth was troubled by neither political nor religious freethinkers. No preparation could possibly have been worse for the sudden leap into independent life that was taken in the Nineteenth Century.

The Viceroys kept things quiet in the Colony, and they remitted silver to Madrid. No more was asked of them.† The people were, of course, kept down; but they had no desire to rise.

---

* The Inquisition, indeed, was established in 1571. And we are told that at the first Auto da Fé in 1574 "twenty-one pestilent Lutherans were committed to the flames." But the Indians were exempted from the sphere of its operations, and there were not many European heretics for the Quemadero during the 17th and 18th Centuries.

Don Pedro de Contreras was appointed Inquisitor General in 1570, with headquarters in the City of Mexico.

The Quemadero, or burning-place, in the City of Mexico, on a spot now included in the Alameda, was a square platform in a large open space, where the spectacle could be witnessed by the entire population of the city.

† There seems to be no doubt that the Spaniards, both lay and ecclesiastical, were somewhat more reasonable in Mexico than the savage adventurers who plundered and destroyed millions of peaceful subjects in the West India Islands and in Peru. It is, perhaps, somewhat to the credit of the sixty-four Viceroys who bore rule in the city of Montezuma that we know so little about them.

The native races of Mexico, too, were doubtless hardier and more vigorous than their gentle congeners in South

Yet the wave of revolution that was passing over Europe at the end of the Eighteenth Century, at length made itself felt in Mexico. The great upheaval in France had been followed by a violent change of government in Spain. Ferdinand, Prince of Asturias, betraying his father to the French, was in his turn betrayed by Napoleon; and a Bonaparte was raised to the throne of the Spanish Bourbons. Thus, in absolutist Spain, resistance to authority came suddenly to be counted as a virtue. No revolution could have been more strange; no revulsion more complete. And in the year of Grace 1810, a Junta, at once patriotic and disloyal, at once constitutional and revolutionary, had been summoned to meet at Seville, upon the very day on which the band of transatlantic insurgents, under the leadership of a country priest, were marching upon the astonished city of Guanajuato.

For some weeks the cause of Hidalgo prevailed in Mexico. The war cry of Dolores had rallied fifty thousand fighting men to the standards of insurrection.

America. See Chapter II. and authorities there cited, especially H. H. Bancroft's "Native Races of the Pacific States."

But as to the cruelty of the Spaniards in Mexico, I have seen a very curious book entitled *Horribles Crueldades de los Conquistadores de Mexico por Fernando Alva de Ixtlilxuchixl.* Edited by Bustamente (Mexico, 1829), 1 vol. 4to.

Guanajuato was taken. Guadalajara was threatened. The Spanish authorities were for a time unable to make any head against the formidable and unprecedented outbreak. But the delay that ever dogs the path of military incompetence, proved fatal to the ill-disciplined hosts ; and Hidalgo and his friends having been beaten at Calderon, near Guadalajara, on the 16th of January, 1811, fled northwards, hoping to make their escape into the United States. They were captured,* however, near the Rio Grande, and promptly executed, just six months after their first success at Guanajuato.

The rebellion had, indeed, been suppressed. But the rapidity with which a large body of insurgents could be collected in a country which had so long slumbered in undisturbed peace, if not in contentment, was a disquieting feature in the situation,† even after the rebel armies had been satisfactorily dispersed or destroyed.

* Hidalgo was betrayed by a friend of his, one Elizondo. He was formally degraded and unfrocked by an Ecclesiastical Commissary, previous to being handed over to the Civil Power and shot.

Allende, Aldama, and Jimenez were shot at Chihuahua, in January, and Hidalgo on the 31st of July. The four heads were carried to Guanajuato and nailed upon the four corners of the Alhandega de las Granaditos.

† Hidalgo is said by the author of the remarkable article on Mexico—the supplement to the "Encyclopædia Britannica," published 1824, to have been a follower of Luther.

The *Grito de Dolores* is of interest, rather as being the first of so long a series of Cries, Plans, and *pronunciamientos* in a country unrivalled among modern States for the number and variety of its revolutions, than on account of any constitutional, or social, or military importance of its own. But before the blood of these protomartyrs of Mexican independence had been washed away by the northern rains, a new war cry had been raised by a new patriot in the south.

José Maria Morelos had been known in his youth and early manhood as an honest and hard working muleteer. Ambitious, intelligent, patriotic, he had, somewhat late in life, been admitted to Holy Orders,* had served under his fellow priest, Hidalgo, in the first days of his rising ; and had been despatched by him, some time before his defeat, to seek reinforcements on the Pacific coast.

More skilled in strategy than his old leader, he held his own against the Spanish troops for nearly three years,† until at length, in August, 1813, he

When at the height of his power at Zacatecas he caused money to be coined with the effigy of Ferdinand VII.—*Ibid* I have not seen any of the pieces.

* Morelos had actually studied at the Ecclesiastical College of San Nicolas with Hidalgo.

† Amongst the associates of Morelos was Father Matamoros, another priest, and a full-blooded Indian, whose name is honourably remembered in Mexico.

gained possession of Acapulco, the most important seaport on the western shores of Mexico, and the finest harbour on the entire Pacific coast from Vancouver to Cape Horn. And one month later, on the 14th of September, 1813, the first popular assembly in Mexico, met at Chilpancingo, with the title of The Junta of Anahuac.[*]

But the deliberation of this convention was far from harmonious: the military councils were no less divided: and the army of Morelos was completely routed [†] near Valladolid [‡] by the regular troops, under a young commander of the name of Agustin de Yturbide,[§] on Christmas Eve, 1813.

But Morelos himself escaped, and it was not until nearly two years later (November 5th, 1815), after he had proclaimed the first Mexican constitution, that he was betrayed by an officer who

---

[*] The old Mexican name for the entire tableland of Mexico.

[†] At Texuralaca.

[‡] Now called (*i.e.*, since 1828) in his honour, Morelia, the capital of the State of Michoacan, a town about 150 miles south west of the City of Mexico. A little province (1,650 square miles) immediately to the south of the capital has also been constituted and named after him, Morelos. The capital of this state is Cuernavaca.

[§] Yturbide, though actually born in Mexico, was of a good old Navarrese family. Of his wife and family we shall have more to say in connection with his unhappy successor on the Imperial throne, Maximilian of Hapsburg. His daughter, Princess Josefa, was still alive and residing in Mexico in 1892.

had formerly served under his command, and taken prisoner to Mexico.

Here, as a priest, he was handed over to the Inquisition, by whose orders he was put to the torture; and having been adjudged guilty on various counts, he was finally handed over to the secular arm, and shot at San Cristóbal Ecatepec, near the City of Mexico, on the 22nd of December, 1815.

Meanwhile, the French had been driven out of Old Spain. Ferdinand VII. had been restored to his crown by the success of the English arms; and having made his public entry into Madrid on March 20th, 1814, he proceeded at once to re-establish the Inquisition,* and to declare null and void all the acts of the National Assembly that had governed Spain from the time of his flight and abdication, just six years before. A comprehensive Edict of Proscription was issued on May 30th, 1814. The liberty of the Press was abolished in April, 1815. The Jesuits were brought back in the following May. Arbitrary arrests, military executions, savage decrees, succeeded each other with pitiful regularity. Nothing was left undone

---

* The Inquisition was also re-established in Mexico on the restoration of Ferdinand VII.—Cf. Alaman, "Historia de Mexico," lib. vi.

to alienate the loyal Spanish people from their wretched Sovereign.

In New Spain, as in Old Spain, from 1815 to 1820, revolution rather smouldered than slumbered. General Calleja, who had succeeded Venegas as Viceroy in March, 1813,* returned to Europe four years later, having fairly earned his title as Count of Calderon,† and was himself succeeded by the more amiable Apodaca, a naval officer of some distinction, who was sent out from Cadiz.

But amiability was powerless to stem the rising tide of disaffection in Mexico.

The arbitrary and odious Government of Ferdinand VII. resulted, after six years endurance, in revolution, not only in the Peninsula, but in every part of Spanish-America. And while George Canning, in England, was preparing to "call a new world into existence to redress the balance in the old," in Mexico the crisis was precipitated in a somewhat remarkable way.

A rising of the usual type having taken place in the Southern Provinces, under a local patriot of the name of Guerrero,‡ General Yturbide, the conqueror

---

* Venegas had resigned the Viceroyalty to Calleja on 4th March, 1813,

† The scene of his victory over Hidalgo.

‡ Guerrero was afterwards the third President of Mexico, and was shot, after a very brief term of office.

of Morelos, and one of the most trusted officers of the royal army, was despatched to quell this new insurrection.

But the overthrow of absolute government in Spain in 1820, not yet restored by French intervention in 1823, had powerfully affected the minds of men in Mexico. Yturbide, like many others, had dreamed of an Administration, not only liberal, but independent. And thus, instead of attacking the rebels whom he had been sent to destroy, he entered into friendly negotiations with their leader Guerrero; and he persuaded both his own troops and those of the enemy to acknowledge him as the leader of a new combined insurrection; and to adopt a scheme or plan of Mexican Independence, which became known as the *Plan de Iguala.**

Three essential articles made up this programme. 1.—The preservation of the Roman Catholic Church, with the exclusion of other forms of religion. 2.—The absolute independence of Mexico under the government of a moderate monarchy, with some member of the reigning house of Spain upon the throne. 3.—The amiable union of Spaniards and Mexicans. These three clauses were called the " three guarantees; " and when the

---

* This Plan or Charter, in twenty-four articles, and dated February 24th, 1821, is given in full in Domenech: Hist. du Mexique II. 36—38.

national Mexican flag was devised about the same time, its colours represented these three articles of the national faith : White, for religious purity, Green for union, and Red for independence. The army of Yturbide, known as the army of three guarantees, marched boldly upon Mexico.*

The Viceroy, taken completely by surprise, made such preparations as he could to check the insurrection. But the country was fairly roused. The Government troops could make no stand against the patriots. Apodaca was arrested in his own palace at Mexico, and ordered to return to Spain. In the meanwhile, a new Viceroy, whose name tells truly of his Irish origin, had been sent out to the great Colony from Madrid.

And Don Juan O'Donoju, having landed at Vera Cruz as Viceroy of King Ferdinand VII., and having taken the oath of office to uphold the dignity of that Sovereign, hastened, after brief negotiations with Yturbide, to recognise the new constitution. A Junta of thirty-eight members was speedily convoked, with a supreme Council of five Ministers, of whom the sixty-fourth and last Viceroy, Mr. O'Donoghue, was an important member, under the presidency of that most persuasive of rebels, Señor Don Agustin de Yturbide.†

---

* See Hale, " Mexico," p. 26.
† An Embassy was sent from Mexico in the Winter of 1821

But harmony was not found in the councils of the new Government.

The more respectable of the Mexican patriots were soon disgusted with the extravagances of the Administration ; while Yturbide, supported by the Clergy and the Army, was on the 18th of May, 1822, elected Emperor of Mexico under the title of Agustin I. The most elaborate provisions were made by the obedient Junta for the style and dignities to be accorded to the new Emperor; for the succession to the throne; and for the titles, precedence, and allowances of the several members of the Imperial Family.

On the 21st July, 1822, the Emperor and Empress were solemnly crowned, anointed, and blessed in the great Cathedral of Mexico; and on the 6th of the following December, a Republic was pro-claimed at Vera Cruz, and Señor Yturbide, with his wife and family, were politely requested to leave the country.

The hero of this new political development was a man whose name is known in every quarter of the world as the very flower and cream of revolutionary leaders, the incarnation of all that goes to make up the ideal of a modern Spanish-

---

to offer the Crown to Ferdinand of Spain ; but both he and his brother, Don Carlos, had too much prudence or too little pluck to accept it.

American adventurer. And it is to the reckless and venal ambition, the attractive daring, the shameless tergiversation, and the pertinacious incompetence of Antonio Lopez de Santa Anna that is largely attributable the immense load of loss and disaster which weighed upon Mexico during the greater portion of his long life.*

Born at Jalapa in 1795 or 1796, he entered the Spanish army as a cadet in 1810, served under Calleja against Hidalgo and Morelos, and took an active part in the operations at Vera Cruz in 1821, which contributed to the success of Yturbide, by whom he was appointed a Brigadier-General.

The first use that the young adventurer made of his new command was to conspire against his patron, and to procure his deposition, his banishment, and his condemnation to death should he at any time return to Mexico.

Yturbide sailed away to Europe in January, 1823, and on the 14th of July, 1824, he reappeared on the coast of Tamaulipas, and landed at Sota de la Marina, a small port to the north of Tampico. He was arrested within a few hours of his landing,

---

* Certainly from January, 1823, to 1848. Nor can his maleficent influence be said to have entirely died out until his death in 1872. From 1848 to 1872, indeed, he continued to organise revolution—but his plots were uniformly unsuccessful.

and promptly shot * as a conspirator, by virtue of the decree that had been promulgated some months before, at the suggestion of his friend Santa Anna, and of which, it is said, the ex-Emperor was entirely ignorant.

But those who play at bowls must proverbially look out for rubbers.

Yturbide, in the space of three years, had been a traitor to King Ferdinand and to his Viceroy Apodaca, to the Plan of Iguala, to the Treaty of Cordova, and to the National Junta of Mexico: and his hasty execution is chiefly to be regretted on the grounds that, had he been permitted to continue at large, he would in all probability have found some means of hoisting that versatile engineer, Santa Anna, with the petard that he had prepared for his patron. Meanwhile, a Constitution, truly admirable on paper, had been drawn up and accepted by a National Assembly convoked for that purpose; and Mexico became, on the 4th of October, 1824, a Federal Republic,†

---

* Had Santa Anna himself met a similar fate on any one of the many occasions of his own unexpected returns from banishment, it would undoubtedly have been far better for his country.

† A fair account of the Federal Constitution of 1824 will be found in Brantz Mayer: " Mexico," vol. II. pp. 146-149.

The Constitution was revised by the *Acta de reforma* in 1847. given by Mayer, p. 144.

under the Presidency of a successful General, Don Felix Fernandez Victoria, a man not unfriendly to Santa Anna. For Santa Anna, having sought and failed to obtain for himself the supreme power in the State, found it convenient to support a submissive President from his boasted retirement on his farm near Jalapa.*

†From 1824 to 1828 there was comparative peace‡ in Mexico ; but the Presidential election of 1828 led to the direst confusion, which continued unchecked for many years. Guerrero, the Liberal candidate, was shot at Acapulco ; Pedraza, the Conservative candidate, fled to New Orleans. The capital was

---

The present Constitution of Mexico is said to have been *proclaimed* on the 16th September, 1810, *y consumada el 27 de Setiembre de 1821*. It consists of 128 articles.

* The Province of Guatemala had revolted and declared itself independent of Mexico (September 15th, 1821). Its independence was recognised, after much fighting, by the Mexican Congress on December 1st, 1823, an independence maintained to this day.—See "Guatemala," by W. J. Brigham (1887).

† The first Treaty of Commerce between Great Britain and the United States of Mexico was signed at London on the 26th of December, 1826. It is printed in Vol. XXVII. of the Parliamentary State Papers, 1828, pp. 1—15. Cf. Domenech : Hist. II, cap. 2.

‡ On the first of January, 1825, the first *Chargé d' Affaires* accredited to the new Republic was sent by George Canning, from England. Alison's "History of Europe," Vol. II., 718, and Vol. III., 733.
And the Presidential message to the first Constituent Assembly was read in April, 1826.—See " Annual Register," 1826, and Domenech : " Histoire du Mexique," Vol II., p. 71.

sacked.* No man, as each day dawned, knew under what form of government the sun would go down in Mexico. He knew only that his life and his property were at the mercy of the strongest.

Nothing could have been more unfortunate for the early political discipline of the nation than that the first lawful election of a President, after the proclamation of the constitution of 1824, when Pedraza was duly elected by the constituencies, should have been upset by a military revolution when the *Yorkinos*,† as they were called, placed General Guerrero by force in the place of the constituted Chief of the State.‡

Santa Anna, as might have been supposed, was the leader and instigator of this constitutional outrage for he appears to have taken up arms at one time or another against every Government, or every Governor, that was established in Mexico, from the

---

* December, 1828.

† These *Yorkinos*, or New Yorkers, were a lodge, a branch of the Mexican Freemasons, introduced into Mexico for the first time in 1822, by Mr. Poinsett, the first accredited diplomatic agent of the United States in Mexico. Two years before, a number of lodges of the sect or order known as the *Escoces*, or Scotch, had become powerful instruments of party organisation The names are perpetually cropping up in the history of the country from 1820 to 1850. — See Demenech: Hist. du Mexique II., 44 - 46, 73 - 74, etc.

‡ It was on the 15th of September, 1829, that slavery was decreed to be non-existent and abolished throughout Mexico. The decree is signed by Guerrero. Cf. Baz. "Vida de Juarez," 31, 32.

sallying forth of Hidalgo from Dolores in 1810 to the return of Juarez to Mexico in 1867 ; a fifty years' record of revolution. In August, 1829, he had succeeded, in a spare moment of party neutrality, in expelling an army which had been tardily sent out from the Peninusla, under General Barradas, to bring the old Colony once more under subjection to Spain :* and at length, after five years' enjoyment in what may be called fighting at large, he accepted the post of President of the Republic in January 1833,† and relieved the monotony of office by proclaiming himself Dictator less than six months afterwards.‡

The Federal system was abolished; and the Governors of the States, now converted into Provinces, were made directly dependent upon the

---

* The Spanish fleet remained in Mexican waters for some time after the declaration of the independence of the Old Colony, and it was not until May 1st, 1825, that the ships of war lying off Vera Cruz were handed over by their crews to the Mexican Government.

The Fort of San Juan de Ulloa, in the Bay of Vera Cruz, which had held out as long as the fleet remained loyal to Ferdinand VII., was forced to surrender on the 21st of December, 1825, and thus the last remnant of Spanish rule in Nueva España was cut off.

† Alaman, minister of President Bustamente, dispossessed by Santa Anna in 1833, was one of the best and most statesmanlike of all the ministers or Presidents of Mexico before the days of Juarez.—See Domenech: " Histoire du Mexique," II., pp. 90-96.

‡ Domenech : Hist., II., 96-126.

central Government and absolutely under the control of the Autocrat at the Capital.

In no part of the Mexican dominions was this change more actively resented than in that vast territory to the north east of the Rio Grande which is comprised in the modern State of Texas; and from 1824 to 1836 was included in the old Mexican Province of Cohahuila.

Dissatisfied at once with the dictatorship of Santa Anna and with the Provincial Government at Saltillo, the inhabitants of this north-eastern Province, who were to a very large extent settlers and adventurers of Anglo-Saxon blood, who had found their way across the frontier from the United States by permission of the Government of Mexico, determined to assert their independence. A constitution was accordingly drawn up, somewhat after the Mexican fashion, by Colonel Austin,* a leading citizen, and maker of cities; and early in March, 1836, a Convention of Delegates from Texas assembled at Washington, where the absolute independence of the country was formally proclaimed, with the approbation of President Jackson.

The Mexican Dictator at once marched—rash and incompetent—into the rebellious Province, at

---

* After whom, Austin City, the capital of the State of Texas is appropriately named.

the head of a large army, and was not only defeated but taken prisoner at San Jacinto. Texas was immediately recognised as an independent Commonwealth by England and France, as well as by the United States of North America.

Santa Anna was detained as a prisoner of war from April 1836 to February 1837, when he returned to Mexico, and having been worsted in an attempt once more to obtain the Presidency of the Republic, he professed himself disgusted with public affairs, and retired into private life at Jalapa.*

From 1837 to 1845 the history of Mexico is at once confused and uninteresting.

Humbled as she was in 1836 by the defeat of her troops and the captivity of her President, the new Republic was exposed to the attacks of all comers; and the Orleanist Government of France took advantage of the opportunity to seek some cheap glory, by making an extravagant demand for compensation on account of some imaginary injury to French subjects; and a squadron under the Prince de Joinville and Admiral Baudin was despatched to Vera Cruz at the close of the year 1837, to enforce the demands which the Mexican Government pronounced entirely without foundation.

---

* He only received two votes out of 69! That he should have been allowed to depart in peace, or rather, to remain unmolested in Mexico, says a good deal for the long-suffering of his rivals.

One of the *gravamina* alleged was the destruction of the stock-in-trade of a French pastry cook, during some one of the hundred revolutions from 1810 to 1837.

For nearly a year the French fleet blockaded the gulf of Mexico, to the serious injury of foreign commerce ; and at length on the 27th of November, 1838, the Fort of San Juan de Ulloa was bombarded, and de Joinville landed some troops near Vera Cruz. Santa Anna, glad of the opportunity of some patriotic display of fighting, attacked the invaders on his own account, and received a wound in the leg, which rendered him lame for life.

But the French were, of course, successful in their warlike operations ; and the pastry cook received sixty thousand dollars for his tarts.*

To follow the chameleon-like changes of

---

* Ref.   Alison : "History of Europe," Vol. VI., pp. 28-29.

The French claims were known in Mexico as the *Reclamacion de los pasteles*.   The Convention, or Treaty of Peace after their Act of War—was drawn up by the intervention of Mr. Pakenham, British Minister at Mexico, and signed on the 9th of March, 1839, when the French withdrew their fleet, having obtained 3,000,000 francs in cash, as a satisfaction on all accounts!

Of the vigorous and repeated remonstrances of the English merchants ; of the loss and suffering occasioned by the action of the French ; of Lord Palmerston's apathy ; and of many cognate matters, a very full account will be found in the Parliamentary Blue Book ; Accounts and Papers, May, 1838 to March, 1839 (2) 399 and (18) 573.

Government in Mexico itself is a task alike unin-
viting and uninstructive. For many years scarce
a day passed without a *grito*, scarce a week without a *plan*, scarce a month without a *pronunciamiento*, not a year without a revolution.* But
everywhere and at all times was found the
inevitable Santa Anna.

The first stage of the long struggle for independence in Mexico may be taken to extend from
the Grito, or war cry, of Dolores (16th September,
1810) to the Coronation of the Emperor Yturbide
(July 21st, 1822).

The second period † dates from the appearance of
Santa Anna at Vera Cruz (December 6th, 1822) to
the dismemberment of the State by the Treaty of
Guadalupe Hidalgo (February 2nd, 1848). For
the most deadly blow that was struck at the new
Republic of Mexico came not from Royal Spain
nor from Imperial France, but from the sister
Republic of the United States of North America.
And one of the greatest and least justifiable acts
of national plunder that is recorded in the history

---

* " *Cada ano un gobernante ; Cada mes un motin*," are the
words of Señor Ignacio Rodriguez Galvan, quoted by Baz in
his " Vida de Juarez,"ᴸ cap. I.

† A very full and detailed " Treaty between Her Majesty,
(the Queen of England) and the Mexican Republick for the
abolition of the traffick in slaves," was signed at Mexico on the
24th of February, 1841, and is printed in the Accounts and
Papers, Parliamentary Blue Book, 1842, pp. 103-125.

of civilised nations was not the work of Kings or Emperors, legitimate or revolutionary, nor of semi-independent adventurers or buccaneers, but of the virtuous, the constitutional, and the exemplary Government of a neighbouring and a friendly Republic.

From 1837 to 1845 Texas, detached as we have seen from the Commonwealth of Mexico, had existed as an independent state.*

The inhabitants were chiefly of Anglo-Saxon blood. Eight years of home rule had only served to convince them of the value of union. And in 1844 when they, not unnaturally, sought to obtain admission into the North American Commonwealth, the Mexican Government, no less naturally, though perhaps not very wisely, protested. But the protest was utterly disregarded at Washington, where political combinations suggested a policy of annexation.

---

* By the Constitution of 1824, Mexico was divided into 19 States, of which Cohahuila was one of the largest. The present State of Cohahuila, from which Texas has been taken away, is only about 40,000 square miles. The capital is, as before the division, Saltillo, in the south of the State. The area of the present State of Texas is about 257,000 square miles. For an account of the areas of the United States which at one time were included in the Viceroyalty of New Spain, see *ante* p 10, and *post* pp. 41-3.

The total area of undivided Mexico, on the declaration of independence in 1824, is given on the authority of Fullarton's Gazetteer (1858) at 1,600,000 square miles.

Slavery, which was unlawful in New Spain, had flourished in independent Texas, and the addition of a new slave State to the American Union was favoured by a powerful party in North America.

Mr. Polk, an active and unscrupulous politician, on becoming President (March, 1845) took upon himself, in the Spring of the year, to order General Zachary Taylor with a small army to cross the Nueces River—the boundary between Texas and Mexico—and to occupy the western bank with his troops.*

Yet, during the greater part of the year 1845, negotiations were carried on between the Cabinet of Washington and President Herrera, which were as fruitless as it was intended that they should be. On the first of December, 1845, Texas was formally admitted as a State of the American Union, and on the 30th of the same month a revolution at Mexico drove President Herrera from power, and replaced him by the more vigorous and ambitious General Paredes.

Negotiations were now no longer continued, and an army was dispatched from Mexico by the new President, for the defence of his northern frontier.

---

* The Mexicans maintained that the river boundary was the Rio Grande del Norte, to the S.W. of the Nueces.

General Taylor was already in position. But political rather than strategic necessities compelled him to await an attack by the Mexican troops. " We were sent," says General Grant (Memoirs : vol. I., p. 68), " to provoke a fight, but it was essential that Mexico should commence it," in order that the war of spoliation, which had already been determined upon at Washington, should be proclaimed as a war of defence.* General Taylor's manœuvres were successful. A detachment of Arista's forces actually struck the first blow, and war was instantly declared. " Mexico " said the President in his Message, May 11th, 1846, " has passed the boundary of the United States, and shed American blood upon American soil ; war *exists* and exists by the act of Mexico herself."

The war was popular in the United States. Volunteers came forward in great numbers. A skirmish at Palo Alto, near the Rio Grande (May 8th, 1846), which was dignified with the name of a battle, was favourable to the Northern troops.

---

* Ulysses Grant served in this buccaneering expedition as a Lieutenant in the United States Army, and he has left in his Memoirs a vivid account of the attempts that were made to induce the Mexican troops to assume the offensive.

"I was bitterly opposed," says General Grant, "to the Policy of the annexation, and to this day regard the war which resulted, as one of the most unjust ever waged by a stronger against a weaker nation. . . . . Even if the annexation itself (of Texas only) could be justified, the manner in which the subsequent war was forced upon Mexico can not."—General Grant : Memoirs, Vol. I., p. 55.

And in the early Autumn a more serious victory was proclaimed on the taking of the fortified town of Monterey, in California (September 23rd, 1846), which led to the occupation of the Northern Provinces of Mexico by troops from Washington. Mexico, far from seeking—if she ever sought—to recover Texas, was hard pressed to keep an army in the field.

But the Northern Republic was not satisfied.

The exigencies of party strife, and the greed of further conquest, at once impelled the Government of the United States to send a fleet to blockade the undefended coasts of Mexico, and to order a prominent politician to march an invading army into Southern Mexico, that he might quarter his victorious troops in the ancient capital of Montezuma.

If General Wingfield Scott or his friends at the Capitol supposed that the expedition would be a mere *promenade militaire*, they were certainly mistaken. Yet, by way of effectually smoothing the way for the success of their arms, they were politic enough at this critical juncture to procure that Mexico should once more seek guidance and government at the hands of Santa Anna.*

---

* Santa Anna, who had, on 15th January, 1845, been impeached and arrested, remained imprisoned in Mexico till May, 1845, when he fled to Cuba, where he lived until his recall in August, 1846.

On the last day of July this hardy exile was permitted by the blockading forces to land at Vera
Cruz.   The necessary Revolution awaited his
arrival.   The Government of Paredes was overthrown, not by the Invader but by the Intriguer,
and on the 15th of September, Santa Anna, as President of the Republic, made his triumphal entry
into Mexico.*

On the occupation of the City of Mexico by United States
troops in 1847-48, he resigned his Presidency, and
begged leave of Juarez, then Governor of Oaxaca, for permission to reside at Tehuacan. This was refused, and he fled
to Jamaica. He was recalled in April, 1853, and ran away again
on the 9th August, 1854 (after Ayutla).

There is a very clear sketch of the character of Santa
Anna in an article by L. in *Frazer's Magazine* for December,
1861

" Like the limb which he lost in the defence of San Juan de
Ulloa against the French, and which was placed first under the
altar of the Cathedral at Puebla and afterwards thrown out
upon a dunghill, Santa Anna has been alternately idolised and
vilified

" Invariably unsuccessful in the field, he is considered as no
contemptible General, for it was invariably his practice never
to acknowledge a defeat, and to insist upon receiving an ovation
on his return to the capital after the most disastrous expedi-
tions !

" His chief source of strength," concludes the writer, " has
always been the thorough knowledge he possessed of his
countrymen "

The Mexicans of his day seem to have been as prone as
many other people to accept words for things.

A due and appropriate supply of words is indeed the chief
function of modern Party Governments.

* In July, 1846, the arrison of Vera Cruz, blockaded by a
North American Squadron, threw off their allegiance to the
Government at Mexico, and summoned Santa Anna from his
retirement at the Havannah. Such summonses were well

If the military preparations at the capital were scandalously deficient, it was scarcely to be supposed that any provision whatever should have been made for the defence of the distant Pacific ports, and of the great north-western territories of Mexico.

The immense districts of California, of Texas, New Mexico and Arizona, were already occupied by the invaders.

Of military capacity Santa Anna had absolutely none. His army was without organisation, without supplies, almost without arms.

The force that was maintained by the Government of Washington, was well armed, well led, and well provisioned.

On the 18th of February, 1847, General Scott landed at Sacrificios, some three miles to the south of Vera Cruz. And a few days later Santa Anna was handsomely beaten by the grateful Americans at Angostura.

Vera Cruz and St. Juan de Ulloa surrendered on the 28th of March. Santa Anna was once more

---

understood in Mexico, and proceeded, as a rule, from the person summoned !

Santa Anna, writing to a friend on October 11th, 1831, says, " My fixed system is *to be called (ser llamado)* like a modest damsel, who rather expects to be desired, than to show herself as desiring."—Mayer : " Mexico" I., 319.

The system of Santa Anna, and the modesty of the damsel are equally whimsical.

beaten near Jalapa. But failure seemed ever to render this fantastic personage more powerful and more popular than before ; and, invested once again with the functions of a Dictator, he was charged with the fortification and defence of the capital. But General Scott was rapidly approaching.

Puebla was occupied without striking a blow, and on the 15th of August, Mexico itself was formerly invested by the American Army.*

First at Churubusco and afterwards at Chapultepec, the Mexicans fought long and bravely. But they were defeated by the superior discipline and the superior armament of the invaders. For they fought as a mob, and not as an army.

Of their courage and of their incompetence, of their devotion and of their want of discipline, a distinguished general has spoken with the authority of an eye witness, and with the just appreciation of special experience.†

---

* The invaders, it must be owned, were a long way from Texas on the 15th of August.

† " The Mexican army of that day," says General Grant (Mem., I. 68), "was hardly an organisation. The private soldier was picked up from the lowest class of the inhabitants when wanted ; his consent was not asked. He was poorly clothed, worse fed, and seldom paid, and well nigh uninstructed in the use of the inefficient weapon with which he was supplied. He was turned adrift when no longer wanted. The officers of the lower grades were but little superior to the men." But General Grant speaks also in the highest terms of the bravery of these Mexican troops.

It is usually asserted that Santa Anna sold the position.

In any case, he was allowed to escape—when his presence was of no special advantage to the invader—unmolested and rich to the Havannah.* And when the foreign army had taken possession of the City of Mexico, it was found that the Dictator had already adopted his familiar policy of flight. [September 1847.] †

If the war with North America had been disastrous, the peace was more disastrous still. The country lay prostrate at the feet of the invader. And the price of victory was fixed at one half the territory of the vanquished. The whole of the Spanish Republic to the north of the Rio Grande, some of the fairest regions of the New World, was transferred to the United States.

---

* See "Apuntes para La Historia de la Guerra entre Mexico y los Estados Unidos;" Mexico, 1848, published by Manuel Payno ; 1 vol., with maps and plans ; p. 104.

† Between 1832 and 1853 Santa Anna acquired the supreme power and ran away from the country no less than six times.

He deposed Bustamante, November, 1832.
He deposed Gomez Farias, January, 1835.
He deposed Bustamante again, February, 1839.
He deposed Bustamante once more, October, 1841.
He deposed Paredes, August, 1846.
He deposed Arista, April, 1853.

And he finally ran away 9th August, 1855. He was deported by Bazaine, March, 1864. He landed again at Vera Cruz, and was deported by Juarez in 1867.

What remained was abandoned to the Government of Mexico.

It was as if Bismarck had drawn a line from Havre to Marseilles, and stipulated that, while the country to the west of the new frontier should thenceforth be known as France, the eastern districts should follow the fortunes of Alsace and Lorraine.

The Treaty of Peace and Partition was signed at Guadalupe Hidalgo, a village near Mexico, on the 2nd of February, 1848.

The United States, by way of indemnity for the territories acquired by them, agreed to pay a sum of fifteen million dollars; but a counter claim, on account of compensation to American citizens, was put forward *after* the signature of the Treaty, and the sum actually paid for the broad lands extending from South Eastern Texas to North Western California, was something over two millions sterling.*

The area of the Viceroyalty of Mexico, on the 1st of January, 1800, had been about 2,850,000 square miles. The amount abandoned by Charles IV. in that year was about 850,000 square miles.

---

* The counter-claim was finally settled at $3,250,000, which, deducted from the promised $15,000,000, leaves $11,750,000 or £2,300,000. See Domenech: Hist. II., 229-230.

The territories that were sold by his son Ferdinand, in 1819, included about 300,000 square miles.

But the Provinces annexed by the United States in 1848, amounted to close upon 1,000,000 square miles,* leaving the Mexicans with an area of not more than 750,000 square miles, or less than one third of the extent of the great Spanish Province but fifty years before.

California, indeed, as well as Texas, was in 1848 but sparsely populated. But within a year after the transfer to the United States, California became the El Dorado of the modern world, and the rush to the gold-fields made the old Mexican Province the most attractive State of the Union.†

And now that the pursuit of gold has given place to a more general development of the vast resources of the Pacific States of North America,

---

* Just 955,000 square miles passed under the treaty of Guadalupe Hidalgo. A *rectification of frontier* was negociated in 1853 between Mr. Gadsden and Señor Almonte, on behalf of Santa Anna; when a further 45,000 square miles of territory, known as the Mesilla, to the north of Sonora, was ceded for a further $10,000,000.

† California was admitted to full State rights in 1850. From 1800 to 1848 the population of Mexican California, including Utah, is said to have been about 16,000 souls. The census of 1850 gave 180,000; and that of 1853, 308,000. The census of 1892 gives to California alone a population of 1,210,000.

the city on the Sacramento river, still known by its Spanish name of San Francisco, has taken its place among the greatest commercial cities of the world, and ranks as an American seaport second only to New York itself.*

After the disastrous war and foreign occupation of 1847 and 1848, a Moderate Liberal Administration remained in power in Mexico. Santa Anna, shameless as he was, dared not return to the capital. The army was reduced and reorganised.† Herrera, who became President on the 3rd of June, 1848, was not only allowed to complete his four years of office ; but his successor, Arista, was constitutionally elected early in 1851. For

---

* In an admirable notice of Mexico in the supplement to the fourth, fifth and sixth editions of the " Encyclopædia Britannica " (six volumes) Edinburgh, 1824. San Francisco is said to have been also known as Port Sir Francis Drake.

The Saint has prevailed over the Knight in the now commonly accepted name!

† The Mexican army as reorganised in 1849 seems to have consisted of 5,200 men, with no less than 56 general officers to command them in chief, and a medical staff of 180 surgeons to attend to their wounds. – Mayer : *ubi supra* II., 127.

This strange disproportion between superior officers and fighting men has been remarkable at many other times in the Mexican army ; but it may be partly accounted for in 1849 by the fact that the Constitutional Government, wisely determining to reduce the army, found it easier to disband the common *soldiers*, who might possibly go back to labour in the fields, than to dismiss gentlemen with lofty titles, whose enforced idleness might be dangerous to order and good government.

nearly five years the country enjoyed the blessings of peace.*

And men began to speak of a young Indian lawyer, who, as Governor of his native State of Oaxaca, attracted the attention of all those who were interested in the peaceful and prosperous development of independent Mexico.

---

* A great number of the most eminent American writers who have written upon the subject profess themselves heartily ashamed of this war of plunder.

See for instance —

1 Personal Memoirs of U. S. Grant.
2 Ramona: Helen Jackson (1884).
3 A Study of Mexico: David Wells (1887).
4 Popular History of the Mexican People, by H. S. Bancroft (1888).
5 Face to Face with the Mexicans, by Fanny Chambers Gooch, (1888).
6 Mexico. By Susan Hale (1891).
7 The Formation of the Union : A. B. Hart (1892).
8 Division and Reunion (of the United States) : W. Wilson (1893).

There is a good description, with interesting statistics, of California and New Mexico immediately after annexation to the United States (in 1850) in Mayer's Mexico (Harvard, 1852), vol. II., book vi.

After this Note had been not only written but put into type, Mr. Goldwin Smith's new work, " The United States," came into my hands, and I am well pleased to find that my own views upon the invasion of Mexico by the United States are honoured by his approval.

" The quarrel," he says, " formed as striking an illustration as History can furnish of the quarrel between the wolf and the lamb, and is one which no American historian of character mentions without pain." (p. 211.)

He speaks also of the " hypocritical fiction of the ' Act of War' on the part of Mexico," and he bears testimony to the bravery of the " poorly armed Mexican troops." But Mexico, as he explains, " was avenged on her spoiler." (pp. 209—214.)

See also *The Academy*, No. 1119, Review by Mr. Seymour Long.

CHAPTER II.

BIRTH AND EARLY YEARS OF JUAREZ: 1806-1847.

The lofty Cordillera which traverses the American Continent from Alaska to Cape Horn; the far-famed Andes of the South, and the more familiar Rocky Mountains of the north; is known in Mexico by the name of the *Sierra Madre*.

To the south of the capital the range divides itself into two branches, skirting the Atlantic and the Pacific Coasts respectively; and enclosing in their giant embrace, ere they unite once more near Tehuantepec, the district that is known as the modern State of Oaxaca.

The country is wild. The soil is fertile. Well-cultivated valleys nestle amid lofty sierras. On the western slopes the vegetation is tropical; on the heights and table lands of the interior it is that of the temperate zone.

The streams that take their rise in the higher regions; the long *cañadas*;* the luxuriant vegetation

---

* Gorges

of the green slopes, the mineral wealth of the mountains ; the varied charm of the landscape in every direction ; all combine to make this southern State one of the richest and most picturesque in the rich and picturesque country of Mexico.   And in those distant and secluded valleys, fragrant with the odour of pine trees, there dwelt at the opening of the present century, the remnant of a great historic nation : still maintaining, amid their unconquered mountains, many of the old traditions, together with the ancient language of their race.

Long ages before the first Aztec set his foot on the soil of Mexico, before England became a nation on the breaking up of the Heptarchy ; further back in the dim and distant ages, when men dream that Atlantis may have bridged over the great chasm between the Straits of Gibraltar and the Carribean Sea, the powerful and ancient nation of the Zapotecs were lords of Central and Southern Mexico.*

Their immediate successors are said to have

---

* See Hubert Howe Bancroft : "Native races of the Pacific States of North America." London 1875. 6 vols., 8vo.—See especially I. 644-83.

But the entire work is full of most interesting details of this Zapotec Race, at all times one of the most remarkable among the early American Tribes or Nations.

Gentleness, affection, and frugality, according to the author, specially characterise the Zapotecs.

been the Toltecs, who are supposed to have descended upon Mexico from the ruder north, some six hundred years after the dawn of the Christian era.[*]

For unknown ages these Toltecs ruled in the land, until the country was overrun, invaded and conquered by the Chichimecs—who, in their turn, were subdued by an Aztec invasion—not more than three hundred years before the landing of Cortez and the Spaniards.

But, under the Toltec, under the Chichimec, under the Aztec, and even under the Spaniard, the Zapotec remained, defeated but never enslaved, supplanted but never exterminated—the boldest and the most vigorous of all the native races of Central America ; while the monumental relics of their bygone days still speak of an ancient and admirable civilisation that has been lost in the stress of ages.[†]

The most ancient historical records tell of the men of the Zapotec [‡] race as strong and well built,

---

[*]   All these invaders are traditionally supposed to have come from the north.

[†] See " Prehistoric America ;" by the Marquis de Nadaillac translated by N. d'Anvers, and edited by W. H. Dall, (Murray, 1885.) cap. VI.

[‡] The name of the Zapotecs is said (*Nature*, 25th December, 1880) to be derived from Tsapotl a " well-known fruit." Nadaillac, *ubi supra*, 362-3.

brave and often ferocious, with powerful frames and rugged looks ; and of their women as virtuous and well favoured, with delicate and finely cut features.*

The religious rites which the tribesmen still maintained at the time of the Spanish invasion, seem to have resembled those of the Aztecs, including the usual human sacrifices, and sanguinary rites and ceremonies for the propitiation of terrible and remorseless deities.

Their ruler was a semi-religious chief, a tyrant of remarkable sanctity and unquestioned power.

Their architecture and such manufactures as we know of, were of very high artistic and technical excellence.

" The monuments of the golden age of Greece and of Rome," says M. Violet-le-duc, "alone equal the beauty of the Zapotec Palace at Mitla."†

---

* There is an admirable Grammar of the Zapotec language published by the Government of Mexico in two volumes large 4to, 1886 and 1889, with a very complete bibliography of the whole subject of Mexican antiquities and ancient languages, especially those of the Zapotecs. The copy at the British Museum Library is classed 12,910 K. 11 and 12.

† An account of this wonderful building, with plans and sketches, will be found in Nadaillac, *ubi supra*, p. 364-369. Some jewellery which was dug up in 1875 at Tehuantepec, supposed to be of Zapotec workmanship, is figured at p. 369-371, cf. *Nature*, June 14th, 1879, and a number of works cited by Nadaillac.—See also Kirk Munroe, "The White Conquerors of Mexico." 1893.

E.

The glory of the Zapotecs has, indeed, long departed. Neither arts nor architecture are known to their modern descendants. But their virtue has at least been inherited; and their name and their nation has lived and still lives, honoured even in modern Mexico, as a tribe of bold honest mountaineers.*

Owing to some extent, no doubt, to the retired nature of the country, and to its physical configuration, modern civilization at the opening of the century had hardly made itself felt in their quiet valleys ; and the passing trader was the only link between the simple inhabitants, and the great world beyond the mountains. And thanks also to the independence of their secluded home, the Zapotecs of Oaxaca had never sunk, even under the masterful dominion of the Spaniards, to the level of many of the other Indian tribes, but had maintained, in spite of three hundred years of subjection to Church and State, a species of local independence. †

---

* The great work " The Antiquities of Mexico," edited by A. Aglio, and dedicated to Lord Kingsborough, by whose name the edition is always known, (1830), will of course be consulted. For San Pablo Mitlan in Oaxaca see vol. V., p. 253 *et seq.*

Vocabularies of the Zapotec language have been published by Antonio de Pozzo, J. de Cordova, and Chr. Aguano.

See also La Rousse : " Dict. du XIX Siècle," sub tit *Zapotècques ;* and A. von Humboldt : " Antiquities of Mexico."

† " The Zapotecs are still found (1874) in the cordilleras of Oaxaca ; where they maintain a position far more independent than that of any other Indian tribe. In the war of the Intervention, the regiments of Oaxaca were the terror of the Imperial army."-- E. Johnson : Mexico, etc., 1875.

The city of Oaxaca, chief town of the State of the same name, dominates a little valley on the slopes of Mount San Felipe ; and some thirty miles to the N.E. of the capital, beyond the town or pueblo of Ixtlan, and still further secluded in the recesses of the mountain, lies San Pablo Guelatao, a picturesque village of perhaps two hundred inhabitants, built upon the edge of a mountain lake, which, from the marvellous transparency of its waters, is known as the *Laguna Encantada*.

A few huts of sun-dried bricks, thatched for the most part with straw or reeds, a tiny church, and the ruins of a more splendid temple, erected long years before the coming of Cortez and the Cross, constituted the modest settlement. Fruit trees in profusion among the houses, and cultivated land in the valley beyond, attested at once the industry of the inhabitants and the fertility of the upland soil. And at San Pablo Guelatao, on the 21st of March, 1806, was born to Marcelino Juarez and Brigida Garcia, his wife—Indians both of the pure blood of the Zapotecs—a man child, who received at the village church the Christian names of Benito Pablo.*

Marcelino and Brigida were small cultivators, tilling their little fields. The childhood of their

---

* The *extrait de naissance* is given in full in Baz : Vida, pp. 22-23.

son Benito was that of an Indian peasant. At the age of three, indeed, he was deprived of both his parents ; and brought up partly by a grandmother and partly by an uncle, he was at the age of twelve years not only entirely ignorant of letters, but even of the Spanish language.

It appears that these children of the mountain enjoyed in the city of Oaxaca a reputation for honesty and hard work, something similar to that possessed by the modern Gallegos in Madrid or the Auvergnats in Paris; and in 1818 little Benito, sturdy and resourceful after twelve years of life and work among his native hills, made his way, alone and unassisted, from San Pablo to the capital, to seek some humble employment in the household of one of the citizens.

His elder sister had, it seems, already obtained some domestic service, and it is possible he may have intended to share her labours ; but he more fortunately found a home in the house of an honest bookbinder, one Antonio Salanueva, who had received the minor orders, and was attached to a confraternity of the Third Order of St. Francis at Oaxaca. The man and boy were mutually pleased with each other, and the young Indian, under the care of his good Christian master, promptly acquired the Castilian language, and gave proofs of an uncommon intelligence, as well as of uncommon industry. Benito, indeed, was no ordinary scholar; but Fray Antonio was no common Franciscan, and under his sympathetic care the orphan child of the mountains forgot none of the best traditions of his race and nation, and grew up from an honest servitor to be an honest student.

Education in Mexico at that time was still entirely in the hands of the clergy.

Mediæval Latin, Canon Law, Dogmatic Theology, and Philosophy, more or less according to Aristotle, comprised the utmost range of study that could be expected by, or permitted to, any student or scholar.

A strict censorship of the Press enabled the Bishops to exclude any modern works, not only from the schools, but even from the country.

Books indeed of any kind were rare, and were regarded with considerable suspicion. Knowledge was considered superfluous, if not absolutely unbecoming, in the laity.

The only career that was open to talent in Mexico, in the year of our Lord, 1820, was that which was afforded by the Church. A few Indians were annually permitted to enter the priesthood; and to these aspirants, the door of the seminary was open. And it was but natural that Salanueva should have destined his promising pupil for Holy Orders, and that as soon as he had passed through the primary school, and had profited by such supplemental instruction as the bookbinder was qualified to give him, he should have been entered as an exterior student at the ecclesiastical seminary of Oaxaca.

In the Spring of the year 1821, he commenced his new studies, and he followed the various courses with diligence and success for six years. But while Juarez was studying theology in Oaxaca, revolutions, good and bad, were rife in Mexico; and one of the immediate results of the new Constitution of 1824, notwithstanding the disturbances from which the country was suffering, was a strong impulse to education of every kind: and in 1826 an Institute of Arts and Sciences was founded by the local legislature of Oaxaca.

Juarez, aroused to new interests, and awakened to a new intellectual life, decided to transfer his studies from the old seminary to the new institute (1827). Two years afterwards he was appointed Professor of Experimental Physics in the Government College, and he continued reading, working, thinking, making ready, when the time arrived—to act. Pursuing his studies in various directions, even as he directed the studies of others, he obtained the degree of Bachelor of Law in 1832, and was admitted an advocate of the Supreme Court of the Republic on the 18th of January, 1834.

But political advancement had preceded these academic distinctions.

No thoughtful man in Mexico at that time could fail to take the keenest interest in political affairs ; no honest man could fail to assist, to the utmost of his capacity, in the peaceful development of his country.

In the early part of 1831, Juarez accepted the modest but onerous post of *Regidor del ayuntamiento*, or Judicial Secretary to the Municipal Council of Oaxaca.

In the next year he was elected by his native State to be their Deputy to the National Congress at Mexico, which met in August, 1832. The Congress was dissolved in December; when Santa Anna, after a brief campaign, once more made himself absolute ruler of the country. And Juarez, who hated intrigue and bloodshed, and loved hard work and peaceful study, both legal and scientific, withdrew himself cheerfully from the arena of political strife, and led, for the next ten years, the simple and uneventful life of a provincial lawyer.

But the interests of Mexico were not forgotten even in this quiet and happy retirement. And in 1836 he judged it to be his duty, as a provincial official, to protest against the *coup d'état* by which Santa Anna deprived Oaxaca, as well as the other federated provinces, of their independence and their old State rights, an outrage which led, as we have seen, directly to the secession of Texas, and indirectly, to the disastrous war with the United States.

For this protest, bolder than was looked for from a local governor, Juarez was arrested and imprisoned by the Dictator, or rather by Vice-President Barradas, one of those numerous lieutenants whom Santa Anna was able to engage at various times to do his bidding. But after a brief term of captivity, the undismayed remonstrant was suffered to return to the practice of his profession in his native State.

From 1842 to 1846 Juarez performed the duties of Civil and Revenue Judge at Oaxaca, being summoned only to the capital for a few months in 1844, when General Leon needed a man of uncommon parts to fill the office of Secretary to his Government.

In 1843 he had the good fortune to make the acquaintance of the beautiful Doña Margarita Maza, to whom, on the 31st of June of that year, he was happily married ; and who, by the simplicity of her life and manners, by her virtue and her understanding, and by her most uncommon culture, was a worthy, as she was ever a faithful, consort ; constant in adversity, modest in prosperity, at all times a true and devoted wife.

For ten years after the protest of Juarez in 1836, Oaxaca, like the other provinces of the Republic, remained at the mercy of the political adventurers at the capital; but after the revolution in August, 1846,* when General Salas took the place of President Paredes, before he himself was superseded by Santa Anna, the old independent State rights were at length restored; and a Junta of the principal citizens confided the executive government of Oaxaca to a triumvirate consisting of Juarez and his friends Arteaga and Del Campo. Sent up to Congress in December, 1846, as representative of Oaxaca in the new Assembly, and finding Santa Anna once more in power at the capital, Juarez maintained his accustomed independence, supported Gomez Farias, the Liberal Vice-President; voted for the law of the 11th of January, 1847, expropriating Church property to the extent of $15,000,000, to provide for the expenses of the war with America; and sought at least to make the best of a disastrous situation.

---

* General Salas overthrew President Paredes, August 4th, 1846.

Santa Anna overthrew Salas, August 20th.

On the 23rd December, 1846, Santa Anna, who had exercised the supreme power since the 20th of August, was formally elected President, with Gomez Farias as his Vice-President.

But the Bishops were too strong for the lawyers. The Clergy refused to part with their property. The House of Representatives was dissolved. The Vice-Presidency of the Republic was suppressed.* Santa Anna was invited—in the usual way — to re-assume the Dictatorship. Juarez, powerless at the capital, returned once more to Oaxaca, and, having been immediately elected Constitutional Governor of the State, he assumed office on the 27th of November, 1847.†

One of his first duties was to repress a *pronunciamiento* that had been organised in favour of Santa Anna, who was once more fleeing at the approach of danger : and to prohibit that expectant adventurer from entering, and vexing Oaxaca.

Santa Anna, thus foiled and disappointed, retired to his old quarters at the Havannah, whence he ceased not to assail Juarez with vituperation and calumny of every kind— the reward of honesty and success. But the determination, as well as the independence, of Juarez were sorely needed in his new Administration. In Oaxaca, as throughout the Republic in 1848, there reigned the utmost disorder and confusion in the body politic. The administration

---

* February, 1847.
† Which he occupied until 12th August, 1852.

of justice, the police, the finances, everything was
in a state of inextricable confusion. The old
order, such as it was, had passed away, and
nothing had yet been found to supply its place. The
local treasury was empty, the local forces were
mutinous, the local administration was hopelessly
corrupt.*

The first work of Juarez on entering upon his
office was to re-establish the Institute of Arts and
Sciences, which had been broken up by Santa
Anna; the second was the preparation and promulgation of a Civil and a Penal Code—the first
codes of law ever published in Mexico.

But the restoration and preservation of order
were at all times his peculiar care. For Juarez,
lawyer, student, purist, was essentially a man of
action, setting even the noblest programme a long
way below the most modest reality. In the course
of his five years of office he made few speeches,
but he made a great many roads; he made few
laws, but he paid off the State debt, which had been
increasing at the rate of $17,000 a-year; and he
accumulated a handsome surplus of over $50,000
in the exchequer. In a short time, the soldiers
were restored to discipline, and their officers to

---

* There is a copy of the Presidential speech of Juarez on
the opening of the Cortes of Oaxaca on the 2nd of July, 1848,
in the British Museum, with the book-plate and arms of
Maximilian, to whom the copy belonged.

obedience. The taxes were paid. Education was enormously developed. Justice was done to all.

With no violence, and with the least possible show of force, the State was efficiently governed.

The shootings and imprisonments, the confiscations and banishments, of former days, were absolutely unknown. The Commonwealth was not harassed. The State was governed by an indomitable will, ever averse from bloodshed or violence. Merciful at once by disposition and by policy, Juarez was able to display that gentleness which is the privilege of the strongest natures, and which was not inconsistent with the utmost vigour in emergencies and the most untiring watchfulness in daily administration.

Oaxaca, under this rule, became the model Province of the Republic, and its prosperity, its tranquillity, and its loyalty were admitted by the friends and the foes of the Indian Governor, whose name became gradually known throughout the length and breadth of Mexico, not so much as that of a brilliant administrator, but as that of an honest man.

CHAPTER III.

Dismembered Mexico.—1847-1857.

From November, 1847, to November, 1852, Juarez governed Oaxaca wisely and well. And for these five years, by a happy coincidence, the whole of Mexico enjoyed an amount of peace and prosperity that she had not known for more than a generation. But such halcyon days were not suffered to endure. At the end of 1852 the officers of the disbanded army, together with the leading bishops and the clergy, dreading the growth of liberal institutions, summoned the ever-ready Santa Anna to their assistance; and the Government was overthrown on his arrival from the West Indies, in April, 1853. Arista was driven out, and Santa Anna was proclaimed Dictator, with the title of Most Serene Highness.*

One of his first administrative acts was to

---

* This title is cited by a writer in the *Quarterly Review* (Vol. CXV.) as late as July, 1864, as a manifestation of the monarchical predilections of the Mexican people ; and *pro tanto* a justification of Maximilian's assumption of Imperial authority !

order the arrest of Juarez, (May 30th, 1853) who, without trial and even without accusation, was hurried off to the castle of San Juan de Ulloa, in the harbour of Vera Cruz; and imprisoned in a submarine dungeon of that fortress. One of the next acts of the Dictator was to provide himself with ready cash by the sale * of some 45,000 square miles of Mexican territory, known as the Mesilla, on the frontier of Sonora, to the United States, for $10,000,000; and the Jesuits † were restored by a Dictatorial degree before Santa Anna had been a month in power.‡

From his dreadful captivity in the Mexican Château d'If, Juarez was fortunate enough to make

---

* (30th June, 1854). Through the instrumentality of Almonte, his agent at Washington, of whom we shall have more to say later on. A considerable portion of this cash was, according to M. Leon de Montluc "Correspondance de Juarez," p. 10, divided between Señor Almonte, the agent, the bankers Lizardi, and one Arrangoiz, Mexican Consul at Washington, well known in later years as the Minister Resident of Maximilian in London, and the author of a work on the Mexican Empire, which will be quoted in a subsequent chapter.—See Domenech: Hist. II., 263–266.

† By Santa Anna, May 1st, 1853 (cf. Arrangoiz: "Mejico desde 1808 hasta 1867," tome II., p. 320). They were again suppressed by Comonfort in February, 1856.

‡ "During 1853 and 1855 Santa Anna," says the admiring Domenech ("Histoire du Mexique," etc., etc., Vol. II. pp. 253—4), "was Emperor of Mexico in all but the name." "Sa Cour aussi fastueuse que celle des plus grand Souverains de l'Europe, rappelait le luxe deployé dans certaines occasions solennelles à Rome, aux Tuileries et dans bien d'autre capitules." Santa Anna, Domenech, and Maximilian seem to have shared somewhat strange ideas of the attributes of Empire!

his escape, before the end of the Summer, on board an English sh┃ bound for the Havannah, whence he passed, almost penniless, to New Orleans; and there he devoted himself for nearly two years of exile, not to intrigue or lamentation, but to the study of English and Constitutional Law. At length, in February, 1855, the country had once more had enough of Santa Anna.* General Alvarez raised the standard of revolt in the Southern Provinces; and a plan, or proposed Constitution, of a liberal character, was promulgated at Ayutla, on the 11th of March, 1855, which obtained the support of all moderate men in Mexico.

Juarez hastened from New Orleans to take his share in the enfranchisement of his country, and landed at Acapulco in the early Summer of 1855, when General Carrera, a moderate politician, was elected ad interim President, and Ignacio Comonfort, a retired Colonel of Militia, was appointed Commander-in-Chief. Within a month (August 9th, 1855), Santa Anna, out-generalled and defeated in an engagement near Acapulco, fled according to precedent to Vera Cruz, where he embarked as usual for the Havannah.† The country

---

* Gutierrez de Estrada was sent to Europe by Santa Anna in July, 1854, according to Montluc, *op. cit.* page 10, to negotiate the *sale* of the sovereignty of Mexico, which he already found to be slipping from his grasp.

† August 16th, 1855. There is a strange regularity in the phases of Mexican disorder.

having been once more freed from his presence and his intrigues, the States General were convoked, in accordance with the plan of Ayutla, to meet at Cuernavaca; and on the 1st of October, the veteran Alvarez was duly elected President of the Republic, and was recognised by the Foreign Ministers within a few days after his nomination, (October 4th, 1855). Juarez, who had acted as Secretary or Registrar of the House of Assembly, was marked for high office under the new Government, and took his place in the Liberal Cabinet as Minister of Justice and Religion. The first measure for which he was responsible in this important position was one of extreme boldness, which at once drew down upon him the ill-will of the two most powerful classes in the country.

From the day of the Spanish conquest to the election of Alvarez, no *clerk* in Mexico was amenable to the civil tribunals, even for the crimes of murder or treason, but his offence was cognisable only by the ecclesiastical tribunals.* No military officer was punishable by the civil magistrate, but claimed exceptional consideration by a court-martial.

---

* The Mexican clergy were very irregular in their domestic habits, as the Abbé Domenech is forced to admit (p. 12), and it appears that the ladies who *kept house* for the priests were accustomed boldly to claim a similar immunity, and when they were unable or unwilling to pay their drapers and dressmakers, declined the jurisdiction of the ordinary courts.— See Lefèvre : " Documens Officiels," etc., tome I., p. 17--18.

As more than half the crimes committed in Mexico were the work of men calling themselves soldiers, and as more than a quarter of the landed property was in the hands of men calling themselves *clerks*, it is obvious that the administration of the ordinary law throughout the country was little better than a farce. Juarez, disregarding both the Bishops and the Colonels, abolished, by a stroke of the pen, the exclusive jurisdiction of both Ecclesiastical and Military Courts, and brought priests and soldiers under the general cognizance of the civil magistrates.

And one law for all men in Mexico was included among the franchises of the Republic.*

On the 12th of December, Alvarez resigned the supreme power to Comonfort, who was supposed to be somewhat less obnoxious to the clerical party. The Cabinet was reconstructed; Juarez was deprived of his portfolio, and sent back to his native State as Governor of Oaxaca.

A *pronunciamiento* heralded his arrival. But the rash promoters little knew the man with whom they had to deal; and in a few days the inevitable Colonel—on this occasion a certain Señor Villareal —soon found himself deserted by his troops, ridiculed by his supporters, and glad, after a few

---

* This law, known as the Juarez Law, was promulgated on the 22nd of November, 1855.

days of painful suspense, to crave pardon and life at the hands of the civil Governor (2nd of January, 1856).

The year 1856 was spent by Juarez in his peaceful retirement at Oaxaca, though he was in almost daily correspondence with his friends at the capital, where his influence was already consider- able, and where his friend and trusted companion, Miguel Lerdo de Tejada, succeeded in passing, by a majority of 71 to 13, in a sympathetic Chamber, the first law relating to ecclesiastical property in Mexico, which, though usually known as the Lerdo Act, was at least as much the work of Benito Juarez.

By the terms of the decree which was promulgated after the passing of this law, on the 25th of June, 1856, the whole of the immovable or landed property of the Church in Mexico, with the exception of the buildings devoted to public worship, was to be sold within a specified time by public auction, and the purchase money handed over to the ecclesiastical owners. The scope and policy of *The Reform*, as it was specifically called, was in no sense confiscation. It was not even disendowment.*

---

* The sales during the first three months after the issue of the decree were to be absolutely free of any tax or fee ; at the expiry of this period a Transfer Fee or Stamp Duty on sales of 6 per cent. *ad valorem* was to be chargeable — Domenech : " Histoire du Mexique," II. 292.

Neither the State nor any individual received a dollar of Church property. It was only a Law of Mortmain, the immensity of whose operations was due merely to the immensity of the territorial acquisitions of the Mexican Church.[*]

Indirectly, and in the future, no doubt the Staet would benefit, inasmuch as the vast estates of the clergy had been subject to no succession duties nor *Alcabalas*, which were, of course, to be payable on future transfers on death or sale, in the case of the new proprietors. But the change was impersonal, remote, and eminently reasonable. That the Mexican clergy, rich and independent, conformed but distantly to the apostolic ideal ; that the Bishops more especially, as great landowners, were of necessity too much concerned with their occupations of husbandry to have leisure for the performance of their religious duties ; this was admitted and deplored by every devout Catholic in Mexico.[†]

But the Bishops, as was only natural, did not

---

[*] Au fond des mille et un pronunciamientos dont se compose l'histoire mexicaine depuis un demi siècle, il n'y a pas eu autre chose en realitè que la lutte toujours renaissante du parti libéral, cherchant à briser la préponderance ecclesiastique, et du parti thèocratique dèfendant à outrance ses prèrogatives et son influence sèculaire.—Masseras : " Essai d'Empire," p. 17.

[†] Even by so devoted a daughter of the Church as the Empress Charlotte.

wish to part with their estates. A forced sale is never agreeable, and very rarely profitable.

The position of an ecclesiastical capitalist is far less dignified than that of a great territorial magnate.

And their Reverences, instead of displaying their title deeds, and making haste to avoid the six per cent. transfer duty that was imposed upon tardy transfers,* set to work to overthrow the Government.

The policy was sanctified by ancient and unchanging custom, and recommended by constant success. Yet the moment was not propitious for a new *pronunciamiento*, whether ecclesiastical or military. And the Bishops wisely awaited a more favourable opportunity for employing their strength and their activity.†

Meanwhile Comonfort, embarrassed as usual by civil war in the Provinces,‡ and by the extravagant

---

* *i.e.,* after the prescribed period of three months: not long in a dilatory country !

† The Mexican clergy, as a matter of principle, refused to accept the confession of any purchaser of ecclesiastical property, or even to grant him absolution *in articulo mortis.* How long this attitude was maintained, I do not know ; certainly until the end of the Imperial epoch. Upon the whole subject see Lefèvre, with his usual completeness of detail — vol. I., pp. 13-22. As to *l'absolution conditionelle,* granted as a compromise in certain cases ; and upon the general question see Gaulot, Max., 101, 104.

‡ It is idle to seek to follow the military operations of the time. Comonfort's greatest success was the taking of Puebla on the 25th of March, 1856. Miramon was taken prisoner in the following month, but soon slipped away.

pretensions of foreigners in the capital, was devoting his energies, heedless of the coming storm, to a revision of the Constitution,* a work which engaged the attention of the Chambers during the greater part of the year 1856; and no man in Mexico contributed more largely to the elaboration of this organic statute, at once by his legal and constitutional learning, his political moderation, and his practical experience of affairs, than the Governor of Oaxaca; and no man had greater cause for pride and satisfaction than Benito Juarez when, after hard upon a year of parliamentary debate and discussion, the new Constitution was promulgated, as it was, by presidential decree on the 5th of February, 1857.

A free press; freedom of meeting; equal civil rights; complete religious toleration; the abolition of special tribunals, of hereditary honours, of monopolies, of all unjust privileges; these were the leading features of the Constitution of 1857.

The legislative power was vested in a National Assembly, to be chosen every two years by an electoral college, in the proportion of one deputy to every forty thousand inhabitants. The President was to be elected for four years. The Chief Justice of

---

* Article 79. A copy of the Constitution will be found in the *Directorio Estadistico*, already referred to.

the Supreme Court, titular Vice-President of the
Republic, was to succeed, as of right, to
the supreme power, on the death or incapacity
of the President.

A decree expelling the Jesuits, also suggested by
Juarez, was promulgated about the same time
(June, 1856), and did not tend to make the Govern-
ment more popular with the clergy.

The foreigners became more aggressive than ever,
and on the 2nd of September, Mr. Lettsom, the
English Chargè d'Affaires, closed the Legation, and
broke off diplomatic relations with the Government, on account of some dispute regarding a
British Consul, Mr. Barrow. To bully the
Mexican Government was at this time considered
the correct thing at the British and French
Legations.*

The new Constitution was to come into force on
the 26th of September, 1857. The new President
was to take the oath of office on the 1st of
December. But before the Summer of 1857 was
far advanced, it had become evident that the
presence of Governor Juarez at the capital of the
Republic was well-nigh a necessity to the
Commonwealth. And neither the jealousy of
Comonfort, nor the fears of less liberal politicians,

---

* See, on this question generally, an article in *Fraser's
Magazine*, December, 1861.

nor even the entreaties of the citizens of Oaxaca, who implored him to remain at the local Government House, availed to keep Juarez away from his place in the Council Chamber at Mexico.

The new Congress met on the 8th of October; and it soon became apparent that the episcopal intrigues had already begun to bear fruit in Mexico.

In the city, the Chamber was rent asunder by faction. In the provinces, a dashing young General of five and twenty, Don Miguel Miramon, who had been taken prisoner by Comonfort after his victory at Puebla, and had contrived to escape, was once more abroad, at the head of a revolutionary force; while the more capable Mejia was supporting the cause of absolutism with equal vigour and success in his native mountains. Thus encouraged and supported from without, the Opposition in Parliament became more aggressive; and on the 20th of October the Ministry resigned.

A strong hand was needed in the National Palace, and Juarez was called upon to accept, in a new Cabinet, the portfolio of Home Affairs (*Gobernacion*) with the position of Chairman of the Council of Ministers. And when, just one month afterwards (November 18), Comonfort* was con-

---

* Comonfort, as the representative of the *Moderate* Party was elected by a large majority over Lerdo de Tejada, the candidate favoured by the extreme Radicals and the Clubs. Juarez was elected Vice-President by an almost unanimous vote.

firmed in his office as President, Juarez was nominated Chief Justice of the Supreme Court, and Vice-President of the United States of Mexico.*

But the reign of Comonfort was destined to be of short duration. Honest but vacillating, a successful revolutionary leader, a weak and un-certain Chief of the State, he was ill-qualified to withstand the varied influences, to master the infinite difficulties of his new position.† The appearance of the notorious Padre Miranda promptly brought matters to a crisis, and before the new Ministry had been a month in office, Comonfort was constrained to call upon Juarez‡ to join him in a " change of policy." The Vice-President refused. The President persisted.§ The country was once more threatened with revolution. Comonfort, dreading the extreme Radicals, yet seeking for the moment only to please the Ecclesiastical Absolutists, announced on the 7th of December that the new Constitution

---

* Mr. Lettsom, the British Chargè d'Affaires protested against the election.   I have not been able to discover why. —See " Mexico à Traves de los Siglos," tome V., p. 262, 4.

† " Correspondance de Montluc," p. 21.

‡ Whom, as his Vice-President and legal successor, it was peculiarly necessary to secure.

§ Juarez, according to Señor Payno, was the only man in Nov. 1857 that Comonfort did not dare to warn of his proposed *coup d'état.*

was to be reformed. But the victorious Bishops were not yet satisfied; and on the 17th one Zuloaga, who had been a croupier at a public gambling saloon, but who had assumed the title and rank of General in the army, issued a proclamation setting forth what was known as the Plan of Tacubaya, and marched at the head of his division upon the capital.

Comonfort, overawed by this display of ecclesiastical militarism, announced his adhesion to the new *Plan* (December 23rd, 1857) just three weeks after he had solemnly sworn allegiance to the new *Constitution:* and by way of showing his sincerity and zeal in the new cause, he gave orders for the arrest of Juarez.

This contemptible *coup d'état* was as futile as it was profligate. A counter revolution broke out at Vera Cruz. Comonfort again changed his mind, and Juarez and his companions were set at large after a few days' captivity.* But the Government was already broken up. The croupier and his employers were completely masters of the situation. Comonfort, who had pleased no one by his rapid changes of front, fled from the capital and from the country, and in less than a fortnight the victorious Zuloaga had been chosen and appointed Chief of

---

* January 11th, 1858.

the State by a new and so-called National Assembly, appointed and chosen by himself. The laws of June, 1856, were at once declared null and void. The ecclesiastical estates, the ecclesiastical courts, the ecclesiastical and military privileges, were declared to be fully restored.* With the entire wealth and influence of the Church to sustain him, with the entire army of Mexico at his command, Zuloaga, actively supported by the pious M. de Gabriac,† and promptly recognized by his sub-

---

* *Le lendemain des son installation.* Lefèvre, I., 26.

† That M. de Gabriac should have used his diplomatic influence to assist in the overthrow of the new Constitution and promote the success of this Ecclesiastical Revolution is, perhaps, not surprising.

A letter in his own hand to Lazaro, Archbishop of Mexico, sufficiently shews the extent of his services. This letter was left by the Archbishop in his palace at Tacubaya when Degollado took possession of the place in 1859; and found its way ultimately into the hands of M. Lefèvre, who has published it in his work, tom I., pp.35-36. It is dated 27th of February, 1858, and in it the writer seeks to obtain due credit for the success of his exertions in the recent revolution. The minister seems to have found something more solid than thanks by his diplomatic services in such respects, for in the course of his five years career in Mexico, he contrived to save and send back to France at least half-a-million of francs ; as is clearly proved by the punctilious Lefèvre : *op cit.* pp. 37-41.

But that the English Chargé de'Affairs should have suffered himself, even ignorantly, to have been led into an alliance with adventurers, lay or ecclesiastical, in overthrowing the Constitution, scarce twelve months old, is an unfortunate feature, which may be regretted, but should certainly not be concealed. That Juarez should make head against such a combination of forces seemed, no doubt, to all men impossible. They little knew the patient power of the Indian President.

servient colleague, Mr. Lettsom, assumed the title and authority of President of Mexico. Yet, however supported, and however recognized, the election of the croupier had been a nullity and a farce; for by a special provision of the new Constitution of 1857, on the abdication of President Comonfort, Vice-President Juarez had legally and *ipso facto* succeeded to his office. And Juarez was not a man to shrink from responsibility or danger.

In a subordinate position he had been ever loyal, zealous, devoted. Called suddenly to the supreme power in the State, when supreme power meant little but supreme peril, he set to work calmly and resolutely to accomplish the great work that it had been given him to do in Mexico.* And on the 19th of January, 1858, he assembled his Cabinet at Guanajuato, and announced his intention of defending the Constitution by force of arms.

---

* The States of Tampico, Cinaloa, Durango, Jalisco, Tabasco, San Luis de Potosi, Oaxaca, Guanajuato, and Vera Cruz remained faithful to the Constitutional Government. Montluc: Correspondance, p. 23.

CHAPTER IV.

Usurpation.—1858-1859.

The position of President Juarez, legitimate as it was, and unassailable on any legal grounds, was made light of by Zuloaga and his friends at the capital, where the Bishops and Absolutists were celebrating the New Year 1858, with rejoicings over the prompt success of their Revolution.

And young Miramon was in due time dispatched at the head of a numerous army, supported by the more experienced Commanders, Osollo and Mejia, to destroy the remnant of Constitutional Government in the Provinces.

But neither the Bishops nor the Generals, neither the Foreign Ministers nor the Mexican Absolutists, knew the power and determination of the man with whom they had now to deal.

Juarez, so far, had been spoken of only as an accomplished Jurisconsult, an industrious lawyer, a successful Provincial Governor.

The de Gabriacs and the Miramons little recked that they had entered upon a struggle, not with a timeserver like Comonfort, or even a swash-buckler like Santa Anna, but with the most patient, the most resolute, and the most capable man in Mexico.

Yet they may be excused for supposing that his position was desperate. To a man of even moderate ability it would have been absolutely hopeless.

The Regular Army was, of course, on the side of Absolute Power.

The forces at the disposal of Juarez were few in number, hastily recruited, without discipline, and well nigh without arms. And at the first encounter, which took place at Salamanca, between Guanajuato and Guadalajara, on the 10th of March, 1858, these raw levies, under the command of General Doblado, were completely defeated by the army of Miramon and Mejia; and on the same day Jalapa was occupied by their colleague, General Echeagarray. Vera Cruz, however, still held for the Constitutional Party; and an expedition sent to reduce that important seaport was repulsed with some loss by the townspeople; while Juarez was able for the moment to maintain his position at Guadalajara, whither he had retreated after the defeat at Salamanca (1st March, 1858). And it was at Guadalajara that he was the victim of an out-rage which was like to have changed the fortunes

of Mexico. The Colonel commanding the little
garrison that held for Juarez was one Landa, a
soldier of the worst Mexican type, who, after
renewed and particular assurances of his loyalty
to the Constitutional Government, had been entrusted with the special defence of the Palace; and
justified the confidence that had been reposed in
him, by announcing one morning [March 14th,
1858] to Juarez and his Cabinet, Ocampo, Ruiz,
Guzman, and Prieto, that they were his prisoners.
A condemned murderer, reprieved but a short time
before by Juarez himself, mounted guard upon the
captive Ministers, while Landa and his associates in
an adjoining apartment deliberated upon the fate
of the men whom they had betrayed. Embarrassed
by the very magnitude of their success, the paltry
traitors offered the President his liberty, if he
would send orders to his supporters in the city to
surrender their positions and abandon Guadalajara to the rebels. The proposition was rejected
with becoming scorn; and Landa, foiled in his
design, marched a file of soldiers into the room,
and gave orders for the immediate despatch
of his prisoners. Juarez, who just before the
arrival of the soldiers had withdrawn himself to
the other end of the room, moved forward as the
men were formed into line; and turned his
bright black eyes full upon the levelled muskets,

as the word was given to fire. The soldiers hesitated for a moment,* and then grounded their arms. Landa did not venture to repeat his orders ; and a small body of troops under a loyal commander, Miguel Cruz de Aedo, having at the moment forced their way into the court-yard, he gladly consented to negotiate. Negotiation with a man of his stamp had but one meaning, *Una fuerta cantidad* †—a good round sum, hastily collected by the loyal citizens, we are told, sufficed to satisfy his political aspirations ; and he was permitted to march off next morning at the head of such troops as admired or followed him.

But Juarez with the slender forces at his disposal was unable long to maintain his position at Guada-lajara, while his presence was most urgently needed at the important and loyal city of Vera Cruz.

In the beginning of April, accordingly, he made his way to the coast at Manzanillo, where he embarked with his entire Cabinet ‡ on board an

---

* Encouraged by General Prieto, a soldier born and bred. Baz. 138.

† $8,000 was the amount ; that being the utmost that could be raised in a few hours at Guadalajara. One Guillaume Augsburg, the French Vice-Consul, apparently an honest Alsatian, was of the utmost service in bringing these negotiations to a happy issue. "Mexico à traves de los siglos," tome V., pp. 290-296.

‡ Juarez signed himself, *Presidente interino Constitucional de la Republica.* He had named Degollado his Commander-in-

American vessel bound for Panama ; and continuing his journey without molestation, by way of Aspinwall and New Orleans, he arrived on the 4th of May at Vera Cruz, where he was received with the utmost enthusiasm by the entire population, and where he was soon after joined by his ever-devoted consort.

Meanwhile, the Absolutists were holding high holiday at the capital. The amiable Zuloaga had received at the hands of the Archbishop of Mexico the formal and specially-transmitted Benediction of Pope Pius IX ; Juarez had been as solemnly excommunicated,* and the Bishops and Generals were organising processions, negotiating loans, plundering foreign merchants, shooting domestic opponents, and generally making the most of their new opportunities in the distracted city of Mexico. Santa Anna, rejoicing at the prospect of further trouble, had expressed his willingness to be summoned for the salvation of the State, and had even organised a descent on his own account upon the undefended coast of Yucatan.†

But, if the rebel Government was in the utmost

Chief, February 24th. General Parrodi had been taken prisoner at Guadalajara.—See Baz. Vida, p. 140.

*Baz., Vida, p. 145.

† *Avec la garantie pécuniaire de Monseigneur La Bastida*, afterwards Archbishop of Mexico. Montluc : Corr., p. 24.

disorder, the Constitutional Government was in the utmost distress. The slender resources of Juarez were rapidly disappearing. M. de Gabriac and Mr. Lettsom had refused to recognise either him or his Government or his presidential rights, while Zuloaga and Miramon were playing at sovereignty in the capital. Yet, by a refinement of injustice, Admiral Penaud and Captain Aldham, commanding the French and English ships of war in the Gulf of Mexico, were now calling upon the defenders of Vera Cruz, not only to make good the amount of a loan that had been forced upon certain foreign merchants at Tampico by the inconsiderate zeal of General Garza,* but to hand over a substantial portion of the Customs' dues of Tampico and Vera Cruz to the creditors of their respective nations.†

A spirit of chicanery or a spirit of malice would equally have led the unrecognised President to refer the foreigners to their friends at the capital. But Juarez was too proud a man to resort to subterfuges. He was President of Mexico, whether

---

* On the occasion of his re-entry into Tampico after the flight of the Absolutists in August, 1858.

† The English Commander, Captain Aldham, R.N., shewed himself upon this, as upon all occasions, as friendly and as sympathetic to the Constitutional Government as was possible in accordance with his instructions. This distinguished officer afterwards died at Assiout, in Upper Egypt, 27th of February, 1878.

he was recognised or not.   The foreigners should have justice, as far as in him lay.   The demands of the French and English captains were held to be reasonable, and were accepted at Vera Cruz, even while the city was preparing to resist the attacks of the recognised usurpers from the capital.

And in spite of all difficulties, foreign and domestic, Vera Cruz remained loyal to the legitimate President of the Republic ; while at the city of Mexico, as the year drew to a close, the usurping President had long lost the consideration even of those who had set him up,* and had become a mere puppet in the hands of his Commander-in-Chief; until at length, on Christmas Eve, 1858, Miramon, flushed with his victories over Degollado and the Liberal forces at Atequiza and San Joaquin, quietly deposed the obliging Zuloaga and assumed the Presidency in his stead.†

---

* In July, 1858, Mr. Forsyth, the United States Minister, was ordered to break off diplomatic relations with the Government of Zuloaga.

Mr. Ottway, who had followed the lead of the French Envoy too closely for either British or Mexican advantage, was soon afterwards recalled by the British Government, and the abler and more sympathetic Mr. Mathew took his place at the capital.   See Lempriere: "Notes on Mexico," (1862) p. 43, and F. O. List. (1860).

† November, 1858.   On the 24th of January, 1859, after a reign of one month, Miramon once more gave place to Zuloaga, who after a week's government was again summarily ejected by his younger and more impatient rival. . . . . *Sans effusion de sang!*—Domenech: "Hist. du Mexique," Vol. II , pp. 308-9.

Thus, self-advanced to the supreme power, and recognised by the foreign ministers with the same goodwill that they had formerly shewn to his defeated rival, Miramon bethought him that it would be well, having overthrown his friend Zuloaga, to take some steps to overthrow his enemy Juarez, who was engaged in the honourable, but somewhat ungrateful, task of paying the foreign creditors—magnificently ignored at the capital—in his refuge by the sea coast.

Collecting, therefore, an army of some 7,000 men, with forty pieces of artillery, he marched out of Mexico, confident of easy victory, to reduce and occupy Vera Cruz.*   But Vera Cruz was prepared to receive him.

On the 29th of December, 1858, Juarez, in a stirring proclamation,† had called upon the inhabitants of the city to prepare themselves to resist the attack ; not only by collecting arms and provisions, by organization and work at the fortifications, but by the maintenance of strict and severe military discipline. Senor Zamora, appointed Governor of the city, ably and loyally carried out the President's wishes, and the utmost order prevailed at all times at the head-quarters of Constitutional Government, a noble and striking contrast to the

---

* Daran : " Vie de Miramon," p. 69.

† It is given in Baz, page 146.

universal license and daily plunder at the City of Mexico.

Upon purely military matters, Juarez was ever inclined to confide in his military advisers, but in matters of more general policy he shrank from no responsibility. Upon one point in particular he was now immovable. He would have none but Mexican subjects in the army that was to defend the constitutional rights of Mexico. Most of the military chiefs declared that it was necessary to enroll foreign volunteers. Officers as well as soldiers were ready and willing to serve ; adventurers of all nations, but chiefly fighting men from the neighbouring United States. Miguel Lerdo de Tejada, his faithful minister ; Zamora, the trusted Governor of Vera Cruz ; Francisco Zarco,* the ablest of his supporters in the Mexican press,

---

* Editor of *El Siglo XIX. (The Nineteenth Century).* "In vain the President was entreated ; in vain were proposed the most studied precautions to avoid any circumstances which might injure or impair the independence or the dignity of the Republic ; in vain the idea was combined with some other projects, joining it with the absolute necessity of colonisation, of making religious liberty effective, of maintaining after the victory an element of material force that would complete the pacification of the country. Juarez rejected all these ideas ; he had disagreements even with many of his friends. In his correspondence he always opposed the project, and, persevering in the struggle, events have shown that he was right. Thanks to him, the Republic overcame its oppressors without any other aid than that of her own resources and the intrepid efforts of her own sons. There exist a good many letters written by Juarez to prove our assertions."—" Juarez and Cesar Cantu," etc., (Mexico, 1885,) pages 16-17.

urged upon him the necessity of compliance. Juarez stood firm, and his firmness was severely blamed by his friends. But when, on the 11th of January, 1861, he was welcomed by the citizens, to the Presidential Palace at Mexico, he could say that his restoration was due exclusively to Mexican bravery and to Mexican devotion, and that in the heat and stress of three years of civil war, no drop of Mexican blood had been shed under his banner by a foreign hand.

Early in March, Miramon and his army took up their position before Vera Cruz. But the position was not long maintained. His guns failed to batter the walls, scarce worthy of the name of fortifications.* His troops failed to intimidate the defenders, exalted rather by devotion than by experience to the rank of a garrison. Juarez had never laid any claim to generalship. He was always the "President in a black coat." But he was in truth one of the best of commanders. Infinitely patient, yet absolutely determined, infinitely merciful, yet absolutely just, full of energy, full of resource, full of hope, he was ever the organiser of victory.

No great deeds of active heroism, no bold and dazzling strokes of policy, were done or to be done

---

* " La ville de Vera Cruz." writes M. Domenech, in 1867. in " Le Mexique tel Qu'il Est," p. 27, "is surrounded by low walls useless for defensive purposes, and too weak to resist the smallest bullet."

by him. But few soldiers and few Statesmen in modern times have more nobly stood their ground than the Indian lawyer, patiently and constantly striving to do his duty, unmindful of calumny and insult, undismayed by disaster, unchecked by disappointment, ever hopeful of brighter and better days, in the hour of his deepest distress.

Of all his Mexican rivals none stood more prominently forward than Miguel Miramon, a man who owes it to the happy accident of his death in the honourable company of his betters, rather than to any one action of his restless and profligate life, that his name is remembered beyond that of O'Horan or of Cobos, of Mendez, of Vidaurri, or of Robles—beyond even that of his brave, if misguided, companion Mejia.

Of Spanish parentage, but of French ancestry, claiming descent from a certain Marquis de Miramon, who is said to have fallen at the side of Francis I. at Pavia, Miguel Miramon was born in the city of Mexico on the 21st of November, 1831, and was thus barely six and twenty when he was called to the supreme command of the Absolutist army in the early days of the supremacy of Zuloaga.

Ambitious, rapacious, bloodthirsty, licentious, he shares with the atrocious Marquez the unenviable distinction of being the most impudent and the most unprincipled public man in Mexico. And the contrast that is offered by his life and character to that of his Indian rival is one of the most striking features in the contemporary history of their country.

The conduct by the young commander of his attack upon Vera Cruz was neither more intelligent nor more successful than his usual operations of war; and after six weeks consumed in fruitless endeavours to reduce the town, he was glad to raise the siege, and retire to the more sympathetic society of Padre Miranda and General Marquez at the capital.

Meanwhile, in the Provinces, the Liberal army had not been idle. In February and March General Degollado had occupied and garrisoned the important towns of Leon, Aguascalientes, Guanajuato, and Queretaro; and, at length, finding himself strong enough to march upon Mexico, he had actually occupied the suburbs of Tacubaya and Chapultepec on the 21st of March, 1859.

But precious time was wasted in demonstrations and consultations. Degollado was ever a poor soldier. The more vigorous Marquez was suffered to reorganise his shattered forces; and on the 11th of April the Liberal troops were defeated at Tacubaya, with the loss of all their artillery and munitions of war. Miramon, arriving on the ground fresh from his failure at

Vera Cruz, celebrated the victory by one of those acts of savagery so characteristic of his temper and of his policy.

The entire body of officers of the Constitutional army, who had surrendered themselves as prisoners of war, including seven surgeons, who were actually engaged in attending to the wounded, one General, three Colonels, three Captains, and a number of subaltern officers and civilians, were shot without further ceremony at Tacubaya, by the written orders of Miramon himself.* This act of assassination was approved of at the time by the military and clerical partisans of the Absolutist Government in Mexico, who welcomed the victors with shouts of " *Viva la Religion !* " But when, in later times and in foreign countries, the outrage acquired a somewhat remarkable notoriety, Miramon sought to throw the blame entirely upon Marquez. To distribute the blame between two such personages would be a difficult and a useless task ; yet I have seen a copy of the actual warrant signed by Miramon alone, with the motto "*Dios y Ley !* " added to the official attestation of his signature.†

---

* A simple monument to the *Martires de Tacubaya* has been erected in that charming suburb of the city of Mexico.

† Daran, the biographer of Miramon (Miguel Miranda, Rome, 1886), is at great pains to point out (pp 73-77) that the prisoners were shot by Marquez before the arrival of Miramon, that Miramon accordingly never could have ordered the

But if Miramon and Marquez had been successful after their kind, in the city of Mexico, the victors of Tacubaya did not venture to direct their steps against the quiet Indian lawyer at Vera Cruz : for the strength of these so-called Generals lay rather in assassination than in tactics, in plunder rather than in strategy;* and that important seaport remained untaken and unmolested. The surrender of the town and harbour of Mazatlan, on the Pacific coast, the taking of Colima, and various minor successes throughout the country, were counted, as the year advanced, as so many steps in the steady progress of Juarez. But none were so important, none surely so highly appreciated, as the great diplomatic victory implied in the recognition by the United States of his position as Constitutional President of Mexico, and by his public reception in his Presidential Palace at Vera Cruz, of Mr. M'Lane, the Envoy from Washington to the Court of Mexico (April 9th, 1859.)

The recognition of the Government of Juarez by that of the United States was, indeed, the severest

---

execution, and that the letter to Marquez was extorted by that *beau Compagnon*, ... *ex post facto!* an explanation as inherently probable as it is honourable to all parties concerned.

* The Absolutists in Mexico, who, flourishing aloft the sword of honour and the Cross of Christianity, employed more commonly in their active warfare, the pistol of the highwayman and the dagger of the assassin.

blow to the fortunes of the Absolutist party that they had yet suffered. And the extravagance of the misrepresentations that have surrounded the story is a fair measure of the chagrin that was felt by their supporters. Juarez, it was said, had sold an entire province, two provinces, the whole of Northern Mexico, the whole of Southern Mexico, to the United States. For this he had received nothing but a barren recognition. He had received four millions of dollars. He had received eight millions. He was to receive eighty millions. In any case his conduct had been base, wicked, foolish, unpatriotic, and entirely detestable; a striking and odious contrast to the simple dignity of Messrs. Zuloaga and Miramon at the capital. Thus the story was repeated and has ever been recorded with appropriate variations. The facts of the case would appear to be very simple.

As long before as 1846, Prince Louis Napoleon had published his pamphlet * upon the political and commercial advantages of cutting a canal through the narrow neck of Central America; and the Government of the United States, anxious to be beforehand in any scheme of inter-oceanic com-

* "Le Canal de Nicaragua," 1846. See also E. G. Squier: "Nicaragua," New York, 1850, and "Central America," London, 1856, as to the canal, and American views thereon.

munication by land or by water, had entered into a treaty with the actual Government of Mexico, reserving the right of transit from the Atlantic to the Pacific Oceans, in certain eventualities, for American goods and American citizens. And as a result of this convention, Mr. Webster* had obtained his *exequatur* as United States Consul at Tehuantepec and Huatulco. But nothing further was done at the moment. As soon as Juarez was fairly established at Vera Cruz in 1858, he had dispatched an Envoy to Washington, Senor Mata, to demand his recognition as Constitutional President of Mexico, and, if possible, to negotiate a loan in the United States. A Tehuantepec Company having meanwhile been formed by some northern speculator, it was but natural that the Government at Washington should seek to obtain from Juarez a formal confirmation of the treaty of 1850, and equally natural that the Mexican President should consent to do so, for good and valuable consideration. A loan of $4,000,000 was also fairly provided for, and might have been fairly granted, had it not been that the entire treaty failed to obtain the approbation of the United States Senate, and so

---

* Domenech : Hist. II., 231-2.

became a dead letter.* Thus, beyond the fact of his recognition by his powerful neighbours, Juarez neither gave nor took anything whatever. The loan remained a project. The rights of transit at Tehuantepec existed only as they were granted in 1850.

This, and no more, was the " M'Lane Surrender of 1859." But the recognition of President Juarez by the United States Government had, upon at least one occasion, a most important practical influence upon his fortunes. Towards the end of 1859 Miramon contrived to fit out and dispatch from the Havannah two gun-boats, the *Miramon* and the *Marquez*, to assist him from the sea board in his new attack upon Vera Cruz. But the American Commodore in the Gulf refused to recognize the cruisers as belligerents, and carried them off as pirates, to be judged by a prize court at New Orleans !

---

* Arrangoiz: II., 359-61 The convention between Juarez and Mr. McLane (1859), acting on behalf of the United States, for a loan of $8,000,000 (Domenech says $4,000,000), in return for certain rights as regards the carriage of United States goods across the Isthmus of Tehuantepec, was not approved by the United States Senate.

CHAPTER V.

RESTORATION :—1859-1861.

In the Summer of 1859, Juarez at length felt himself strong enough to legislate as well as to fight for the good of his country.

On the 7th of July he issued a long and elaborate proclamation, setting forth what may be called his political programme,* or plan of operations for the future ; and this most interesting State Paper should be read by everyone who would appreciate the statesmanlike qualities, the political knowledge, and the keen appreciation of the actual wants of his own country that ever distinguished the Indian President.

The mere preparation, indeed, of so far-reaching and so eminently practical a programme, at the time when he himself was shut up in a provincial fortress, and his capital had been long occupied by rebels, bears witness to the patient hopefulness of his disposition.

---

* See Baz : " Vida de Juarez," pp. 156-171.
The Presidential Address occupies fifteen of the large 4to pages of this valuable book.

The Presidential Address treated of—1, The dis-establishment and disendowment of the Roman Catholic Church. 2, The simplification of legal procedure, and the greater independence of the judicial power. 3, The extension and cheapening of education. 4, The systematic making of roads. 5, A general reform of the Finances, including the immediate abolition of the oppressive and old-fashioned Spanish *Alcabala*. 6, The encouragement of foreign commerce, by revision of duties and other measures. 7, The abolition of excessive pensions. 8, The establishment of a National Guard. 9, The sub-division of great estates, with a view to encouraging agriculture and establishing a peasant proprietary in the place of the existing population of labourers who were practically serfs. 10, The encouragement of the immigration of useful colonists. And, finally, 11, The establishment and subvention of railways.*

A few days after the appearance of this procla-mation, on the 12th of July, 1859, three laws or decrees, known as the New Reform Laws, were promulgated by the President at Vera Cruz.

By the first, the Church was completely disestab-lished and disendowed.

---

* The worst thing that could be said of the programme was that it was too complete.

By the second, marriage was declared to be a purely Civil contract.

By the third, the important duty of the Registration of Births, Deaths, and Marriages was taken away from the Clergy, and devolved upon Civil officers of the State. appointed for that purpose.

The Church was thus absolutely separated from the State in Mexico, and the ecclesiastical revenues finally appropriated by the Civil power. It was a bold step for a fugitive President.

It was the promulgation of the Lerdo Law that had induced the clergy to overthrow the Constitutional Government less than two years before. But they had taken very little by their success. For the scheme of Lerdo was Conservative in comparison with the sweeping decree of the man whom they had driven into exile.

The law of 1856 only forbade the ecclesiastics to remain proprietors. The decree of 1859 did not even suffer them to remain capitalists.

If Lerdo had chastised them with whips, Juarez was chastising them with scorpions.

Yet the mind of the Indian statesman was bent not on chastisement but on reform.

The new decrees were far-reaching in their scope. Monasteries, confraternities, and religious establishments of all kinds were suppressed or dissolved.

Nunneries were forbidden to receive any further novices, although all nuns actually professed were permitted to retain their property for their lives.

Compensation was to be granted to all existing holders of church property of every description.

Nor was any building, actually used for the performance of public worship, included within the scope of the decrees.

But in spite of these saving clauses, the Bishops must have been heartily disgusted with their folly in refusing to conform to the moderate laws of June, 1856. It was hardly to be expected that Juarez, with his back to the wall at Vera Cruz, should be more indulgent than Comonfort, in his good quarters at the Presidential Palace at Mexico.

Of the actual value of the Church property at the time of the promulgation of the decrees of 1859 it is supremely difficult to arrive at any certain conclusion; and the estimates range from ten million to one hundred million pounds sterling.*

* The number of Conventual establishments and religious houses in Mexico in 1844 is stated to have been 150, with a Monastic population of some 2,000 nuns and 1,700 monks.

But the secular or parochial clergy did not exceed 3,200 priests—"a small number," says Mr. Mayer, "to minister to the spiritual wants of a population of more than seven and a half millions—or 3,383 individuals assigned to the ecclesiastical charge of each priest, monk or curate. And yet among these men, the entire revenue of probably more than $90,000,000 of property was annually distributed or consoli-

I am myself inclined to estimate the actual worth of the property, both real and personal, even in a fair market, at a good deal less than is usually computed, while the actual selling value, in disturbed times, and with a very uncertain title for purchasers, would clearly have been something more moderate still.*

dated in a country from which they are constantly asking alms instead of bestowing them.

"The value of their churches, the extent of their city property, the power they possess as lenders and mortgagees in Mexico, where there are no banks, and the enormous masses of Church plate, golden ornaments and jewels, will swell the above statements and estimates of the Church's wealth to nearer one hundred millions than ninety millions, as computed by Señor Otero."—Mayer: Mexico, II., 133.

"Yet in order to bring up this ninety to the two hundred millions of dollars—or the *milliard* of francs—which Juarez is accused by French critics with having squandered by maladministration, another hundred million of dollars (1,000,000,000 francs is equivalent to \$200,000,000) has to be added as the estimated capital value of the contributions and other imposts which were laid upon the property of the country for the benefit of the clergy."

*   According to M. Gaulot, the entire immoveable or real property of Mexico amounted in 1849 to \$850,000,000, of which the Church possessed one third, or say \$270,000,000. The moveable or personal property of the clergy alone is further valued by the same author (as in 1860) at \$150,000,000. M. Gaulot certainly gives no authority for the former of these valuations, and a very doubtful one for the latter. Yet that a writer of his position should, in his carefully reasoned work, venture seriously to estimate the Church property in Mexico in 1859-1860 at \$520,00,000, or over £100,000,000, rather shakes my faith in my own modest calculations. Of this, at least, we may rest assured, that the amount of property held in Mortmain was of very great extent, and that whether in relation to the legitimate needs of the Clergy, or to the amount of free land in the hands of the laity, it was excessive. Gaulot: Max : pp., 103-5.

But, great or small, apprized at hundreds of millions,* or saleable at hundreds of thousands, the ecclesiastical estates and revenues were added at once and for ever to the national property of Mexico.

The reform may have been necessary. It may have been just. It was certainly a shrewd retort upon the rebel clergy. But the decree was not happily timed. For the denunciation and sale of the ecclesiastical property under a Government as uncertain in its operations and as restricted in its powers as that of Juarez, led to the infliction of the greatest possible amount of suffering upon the ecclesiastics,† whom it would have been wise to conciliate, and upon their devout followers, whom it would have been reasonable to consider ; while it was productive of substantial advantages to the State, under the Government of Juarez himself, so scandalously out of proportion to the injury inflicted,

---

* The author of the remarkable article on Mexico in the supplement to the " Encyclopædia Britannica," published in 1824 (page 373), says that at that time, the money capital, as distinguished from the real property, of the Church bodies in Mexico, amounted to £10,000,000, and that the money was lent out in small sums at a high rate of interest to landed proprietors ; and that the Spanish Government had tried in vain to possess themselves of this tempting hoard.

£10,000,000 is, say, $50,000,000, and between 1824 and 1859 the capital must have very largely increased.

† The future remuneration of priests was to be a matter of free arrangement between minister and people, without the interference of the civil power

that within less than two years after the nationalisa-
tion of property valued at hundreds of millions of
dollars, the Public Treasury was absolutely empty.

That the promulgation of this truly Radical
decree should have nerved the Bishops and Clergy
to renewed exertion on behalf of the Tacubayistas
at the capital, was only what could have been
expected under the circumstances. Yet as the year
1859 drew to a close, it became manifest that the
Puros, as the Constitutional Liberals came to be
called, were gaining ground—slowly, no doubt, but
surely—over the partizans of the Bishops and the
Bravos ; and the leaders of the declining faction
determined to seek assistance from beyond the
sea.

The Government of Juarez had been recognised,
as we have seen, by the Cabinet at Washington.
But the Government of Miramon, which was
established in the capital, and had possession of the
national archives, was treated by all the European
Powers as the *de facto* Government of the country.
The Bishops, moreover, had established friendly
relations not only at the Vatican but at the Tuileries.
And Don Juan Almonte, the honest broker in the
Mesilla sale, a personage of whom we shall
hear more in due time, in connection with the
French expedition, was dispatched by the
Tacubayista leaders to negotiate a treaty with

Spain. The negotiations were not long protracted; for Almonte's instructions were to agree to whatever conditions might be proposed; and on the 26th of September, 1859, a Convention was signed in Paris between the Mexican envoy and Señor Mon, on behalf of her most Catholic Majesty Isabella II.

The main feature of this Treaty was the recognition by the representative of Miramon of the claims of certain Spanish subjects, who had purchased Mexican bonds of the Internal Debt at something like ten per cent. of their nominal value, to have payment made to them at par, as if the depreciated paper, in which they had so rashly speculated, formed a part of the Spanish Convention Debt. The claim was preposterous. It had already been categorically rejected by Comonfort; and the Spanish minister had thereupon retired from Mexico.

Miramon, however, made no difficulties in the way of accepting the Spanish demands, as the price of Spanish support in Europe.*

And in virtue of this new Convention, Señor Pacheco, Envoy and Minister resident from Queen Isabella to the Court of Miramon, set sail from

* The bonds of the Internal Debt in the hands of these Spanish speculators had cost them about 12 per cent, and were by the terms of the treaty to be paid off at 100.

Cadiz, and arrived off Vera Cruz on the 23rd of May, 1860.

The city had not only been besieged a second time, but had even been bombarded by Miramon in the preceding March ; but the citizens had stood firm, the well-disciplined troops of Juarez had driven away the brilliant besiegers. Vera Cruz remained untaken, confident, and free.

Somewhat surprised to find that the President to whom he was accredited was not recognised at the chief seaport of the country, Pacheco asked permission of Juarez to land and proceed to the capital, a permission which was at once most courteously accorded. (June 1st, 1860.)

On reaching the City of Mexico, another surprise awaited the envoy, who was received, not by President *substitute* Miramon — these gentlemen were always very punctilious about their titles—but by President *ad interim* Zuloaga, who had on the 9th of May, 1860, re-assumed, by his own decree, the functions of President of the Republic, *vice* Miramon, appointed to the office of Commander-in-Chief, by the same unexceptional authority.

But the *Substitute* with the army in the provinces, was stronger than the *Interim* with the Bishops in the capital ; and on the 3rd of August the President *Interim* disappeared, and became a President *Fugitive*, to the great embarrassment of his particular friends; and in less than a fortnight afterwards (August 14th) the vivacious Miramon, installed once more in the Palace at Mexico, received the envoy Pacheco with the utmost pomp and ceremony at his Court.

The Foreign Ministers, M. de Gabriac and Mr. Otway, ever complaisant, were as ready to recognise Miramon as they had been to recognise Zuloaga; and they must have had hard work to keep pace with their changes of title.*

But Juarez remained President of Mexico.

Yet as the year 1860 drew to a close, and as it became apparent that the end of the struggle was rapidly approaching, the Liberal cause received a blow at the hands of its own supporters, which was more fatal in its results than any which it had suffered from the attacks of the most ferocious Absolutist. For it tended to impress upon European statesmen the necessity for intervention in the affairs of a country so regardless of all usages and traditions of public honesty and diplomatic convention.†

---

* Mr. Otway, indeed, who was supposed to have been too complaisant, was recalled in August, 1859; and was succeeded by Mr. Mathew, who maintained his position with dignity and credit for nearly two years, until May 25th, 1861.

† On the 24th of August, 1860, Lord John Russell had instructed Mr. Mathew, the British Envoy, to withdraw from the Court of Miramon, the " patron of outrage, spoliation, and atrocities " of every kind. But as Lord John would not

Up to that time the Government of President Juarez had shewed in honourable contrast with that of the robbers and cut-throats at the capital. No innocent blood had been shed. No private property had been appropriated. No plighted word had been violated. And now the days of their long struggle were almost accomplished. The hour of their triumph was at hand. Within four months Juarez was to make his public entry into the capital of enfranchised Mexico ; and it was at this supreme moment that General Degollado—"the respectable Degollado,"* as he was described, even after the event, by a judicious foreigner, saw fit to sully the fair fame of his President and of his Party, by an act of plunder worthy only of Miramon and Marquez.†

In the early part of September, 1860, a *Conducta*, or mule train, carrying specie of the value of some million and a quarter of dollars,

---

take upon himself to order Mr. Mathew to proceed at once to Vera Cruz, the Envoy retired in the non-official capacity of a diplomatic waiter on Providence, to Jalapa.

* Mr. Mathew to Lord John Russell, December 25th, 1860.

† In September, 1859, Marquez took forcible possession of some $600,000 at Guadalajara, "*parte de una remesa de fondos del comercio à los puertos del Pacifico.*" Arrangoiz,: II. 361. This is spoken of by Mr. Mathew to Lord John Russell, September 28th, 1860, (Accounts and Papers, etc.,) as "An act of common or uncommon highway robbery !" See also Domenech: Hist. : tom. II. p. 319.

for the most part the property of foreign merchants, was on its way from Querétaro to Tampico, under a guard or escort of the Constitutional forces of the country.   The money was being forwarded by the owners for shipment to Europe, and Degollado, jealous, no doubt, of the exploits of Marquez in a similar direction some months before, took upon himself to appropriate the dollars that were entrusted to his care, at the village of Laguna Seca (September 9th, 1860).   Doblado and Echeagarray signified their hearty approval, and many noble sentiments were expressed by these various worthies as to the duties of patriots, the honour of Mexico, the heroic self-sacrifice of gentlemen who preferred even to be falsely accused of misconduct, to the crime of allowing dollars to slip through their fingers, when dollars were needed by their country.

The appropriation of the bags of money, moreover, was spoken of by the Generals and their friends not as plunder, but an "occupation."

But Juarez was not a man to be misled by fine words.   And the moment the news of this impudent and still more foolish robbery was conveyed to him, he sent orders for the prompt restitution of the stolen property to the owners.

But bags of dollars do not as a rule remain

intact in the hands of those who patriotically occupy them ; and a great part of the cash had been already dispersed beyond recall or recovery, when the instructions from Juarez were received.

Four hundred thousand dollars, however, the property of certain English merchants, were recovered by the superior diligence of the English Minister;* and were by the good will of the somewhat repentant Degollado duly sent forward for shipment to Tampico.

But at the port of Tampico the Government of Juarez was as ill-served as it had been in the camp at Laguna Seca.

The English specie, though protected by the marks or seals of the British Legation, was seized before it could be sent on board the vessels in the harbour, by order of General Garza, at the instance of the French Consul, M. de St. Charles. An inquiry was then solemnly held as to the disposal of this re-stolen property, and the remaining dollars were at length handed over to certain merchants at Tampico for distribution, according to the order of a local judge. In fine, after the payment or retention of some very considerable fees for the officials concerned in this new conversion, about one-twelfth of the amount originally *occupied*, or about one-third

---

* Mr. Mathew was ably assisted by the British Consul, Mr. Glennie.

of that restored by Degollado to the English
Consul, seems to have found its way into the
pockets or ships of the rightful owners.*

In all this Juarez was not only blameless,
but he behaved with his usual probity and
judgment.

He gave immediate orders for the restitution of
all the money that could be recovered, as soon as
he heard of the outrage.

Two months later he issued a Presidential decree
providing special funds for the liquidation of the
unsatisfied claims.†

And lastly, within a month of his restoration to
supreme power at the capital, he instructed Señor
Zarco, his new Minister of Foreign Affairs, to con-
clude a final arrangement with the British
Plenipotentiary, which Mr. Mathew himself
characterized as fair and equitable.‡

But the impression conveyed in Europe was
entirely unfavourable. And although the British
Minister conducted his correspondence with the
Mexican Government with great moderation and

---

* Capt Aldham, R.N., to Mr. Mathew, December 7th, 1860.
" Accounts and Papers," etc.

† On December 17th, 1860, he signed a Presidential
Decree specially assigning certain property and revenue to
the repayment of this sum of money *eo nomine*. The decree is
printed in " Accounts and Papers," 1861, xv., p. 55. The restitution is said to be preferable *à tout autre paiement*

‡ Mr. Mathew to Lord John Russell, February 25th, 1861.

good temper, his remonstrances, vigorous and abundantly justified, were read in England with ignorant but not unnatural indignation. It is indeed scarcely a matter for surprise that foreign creditors six thousand miles away should be unwilling or unable to distinguish between the Constitutional responsibility of Juarez, the trickery of Garza, the backsliding of Degollado and Doblado, or the insolent and open plunder of Marquez and Miramon.

Mexico, at least, was called upon to suffer for them all. For if, thanks to the criminal folly of Degollado, the Constitutional Government of Juarez had been sullied by one single act of public plunder, the dying Government of Miramon surpassed all previous experience of administrative misfeasance, by the most notable outrage upon the comity of nations that is to be found even in the annals of revolutionary Mexico.

Finding himself, after three years of plunder, absolutely without resources either for the defence of the capital, or the usual provision for his own flight; with the Liberal troops at his gate, with his friend Jecker a bankrupt ;* and with no solvent or insolvent banker willing to lend him money even at the old rate of *eighteen hundred* per cent, Miramon,

---

* As to the issue of the Jecker bonds earlier in the year. See post Chapter VI.

upon the 17th of November, 1860, improving con-
siderably upon the procedure of the "respectable
Degollado," dispatched General Marquez with
three blacksmiths and a file of soldiers to the house
of the British Legation,* where they broke into the
strong room, and stole therefrom some three-quarters
of a million of dollars,† in specie, the property of the
English bondholders, which had been collected by
Juarez, and deposited for safe keeping with the
British Minister, in boxes sealed with his official
seal.‡

The Spanish Minister, Pacheco, specially
accredited, as we have seen, to the Government of
Miramon, used his utmost endeavours to prevent

---

* The news had just been received of the fall of Guadalajara, and the advance of the Liberal troops.

Mr. Mathew, when he had quitted the capital, and retired to
await the development of events at Jalapa (see ante, note
p. 103.) had left the Legation shut up : the strong room locked
and sealed ; the specie in boxes, marked and stamped with
his official seal.

† It must be remembered that these $660,000 stolen by
Miramon, from the British Legation had actually been pro-
vided by the Constitutional, but unrecognized Government of
Juarez.   Lefevre. I., 52.

There was a certain grim humour, in requiring him, before he
had been a month restored to power, *to pay it back !*

‡ $660,000 was the exact amount of the plunder.   The
coins were packed in boxes marked with the mark of the
British Legation and stored in a storehouse locked and sealed
up with the seal of the British Envoy.   There is a very full
and detailed account, with copies of all letters and other
documents relating to these robberies, both by Miramon and
by Degollado, in the "Accounts and Papers," Parliamentary
Blue Book, 1861, lxv pp. 1-56·

this astounding violation of all international decency, or even of common honesty; and he protested in the strongest language against the outrage—but in vain. The money was carried off; and was no doubt found useful by General Miramon in his subsequent retirement from Mexico. The Occupation, though certainly more impudent, was by no means as foolish as that of Degollado.

Upon the 6th of November., 1860, Juarez issued a Decree, under the Electoral Law of 1857, fixing the date of the election of a President and Vice-President for the following January, when the new Congress would also be chosen, to assemble, according to law, on the 19th of February.

The possible candidates, besides Juarez himself, were Comonfort, Degollado, Ortega, and Miguel Lerdo de Tejada.*

There was a fine boldness, no doubt, in this disregard of the present adversity, in the punctual fulfilment of constitutional obligations.†

But the reign of Miramon was drawing to a close.‡ And no acts of violence or recklessness availed to arrest the onward march of his oppo-

---

* Mathew to Lord John Russell, Dec. 30th, 1860.

† Suggestive of the old Roman spirit that prompted the purchase at a good price of the land actually occupied by Hannibal.

‡ M. Dubois de Saligny, the new French Minister, arrived in the city of Mexico on the 12th of Dec., 1860.

nents. The crowning victory of Calpulalpam, and
the fall of Guadalajara, on the 20th of December,
1860, left the road to Mexico open to the Liberal
army ; and on Christmas Day, the vanguard, under
General Ortega, entered the city without striking
a blow. Miramon, Marquez, and their disorganised
supporters indeed had already fled, and the restoration of Constitutional Government was celebrated
by an enthusiastic demonstration of public satisfaction and joy, on the first day of the New Year,
1861. Nor were these popular rejoicings sullied by
any manifestations of military insubordination or
civil disorder.*

It was on the 11th of January, 1858, that Felix
Zuloaga had raised the standard of revolution in
the city of Mexico; and upon the 11th of January,
1861, Benito Juarez, on his arrival from Vera Cruz,
made his triumphal entry into the capital of the
grateful Republic.

For three years he had struggled valiantly, he
had suffered silently, he had acted with infinite self-
restraint. And in the hour of victory he would have
entered his capital like a simple citizen, without
pomp, or glory, or display.†

---

* Mr Mathew to Lord John Russell particularly insists
upon this. It was indeed a noteworthy fact

† "President Juarez," writes Mr. Mathew at this time,
"is an upright and well-intentioned man, excellent in all

How much there yet remained to be done before Mexico could take her place among the nations, no man knew better than he. The men of Tacubaya, indeed, were vanquished ; but the community was yet divided. The State was bankrupt. The Commonwealth was disorganised. For the man who was to make Mexico into a nation, the task had scarcely yet begun.

Yet some public display or triumph was no doubt both prudent and politic ; and Juarez, who had steered the ship of State in her three years' voyage, through storm and tempest, through battle and breaker, was received with well-merited acclamation as he made his entry into the long-looked-for port.

But the vessel was battered almost beyond repair ; and the pilot, who had so steadfastly kept her afloat, was called upon without a moment's delay to convert the shattered hull into a staunch and seaworthy ship.

The best captain is not always the best ship-wright, but it was the hand of Juarez upon the tiller that had guided the vessel through the storm ; and it was the hand of Juarez in the workshop that alone

----

the private relations of life ; but the fact of his being an Indian exposes him to the hostility and sneers of the dregs of Spanish society, and even of those of mixed blood ! "— May 12th, 1861.—Mathew to Lord John Russell.

was capable of fitting her for the new voyages that awaited her.

The Indian was not the man to shrink from the task. But the task was rather rebuilding than repair. A Government so demoralised, an Administration so disorganised, a Society so shattered, a Commonwealth so impoverished, needed rather reconstruction than reform.

And as we may see from day to day in older and more peaceful countries than Mexico; to reform is often within the power of a commonplace enthusiast ; to reconstruct is reserved only for the greatest efforts of the most fortunate Statesmen.

But the impatient critics of the new Administration, and more especially the disappointed friends of the fallen usurpers, were not disposed to make any allowance for the inherent difficulties of the position. And from the very day of the return of Juarez, and before the country had, or could have, recovered from three years of demoralisation and disorder, while the Absolutists remained conquered, yet by no means suppressed, in every part of the country ; the foreign residents were loudly demanding peace and protection from an Administration which was hard pressed to maintain its own existence ; and the foreign creditors were still more loudly insisting upon the punctual payment of millions of doubtful dollars out of an absolutely empty Treasury.

The Presidential Elections were duly held in the month of January. The writs had been issued from Vera Cruz. The return was made at the capital of Mexico. Juarez, as may be supposed, was elected President by a large majority over his only rival, General Ortega, who was subsequently appointed Vice-President of the Supreme Court. (July 2nd, 1861.)*

The first work that had to be done in Mexico in that eventful January, 1861,† was to inspire citizens and strangers with confidence in the honesty, as well as the stability, of the Government. And yet the most honest of men is unable to make punctual payments when he himself is absolutely penniless.

" The Mexican Government," says Mr. Mathew, " has been accused, not without reason, of having frittered away the Church property, recently nationalised ; but it must be remembered that

---

* Miguel Lerdo de Tejada, at one time a candidate for the Presidency, had died in March, 1861. His brother Sebastian is a leading figure in the subsequent history of Mexico.

† The Chambers did not actually meet until May, nor was it till June 11th that the new President and Vice-President were formally installed.

Ortega soon after gave proofs of his loyalty, if not of his judicial competence, by a victory over the rebels at Jalatlaco (August 14th, 1861).

I

while forced contributions, plunder, and immense supplies from the Church and its supporters have enabled Zuloaga and Miramon to sustain the civil war for three years;* the Constitutional Government abstained from such acts, and have the sole robbery of the Conducta at *Laguna Seca*, which cannot be said to have benefitted them even from a pecuniary point of view, to answer for."

---

* "Their resources during this lengthened period were drawn from advances by individuals on Bonds for far greater sums, payable at the close of the war; and from the actual sale of a great part of the Church property at 25, 20, and even 15 per cent. of its value." Mathew to Lord John Russell, May 12th, 1861. "Accounts and Papers," *ubi supra*

The mode of payment for their ecclesiastical estates by the new purchasers was most unsatisfactory. "*Les bien-fonds*," says M. Gaulot (Max., p. 109). "*pouvaient être payés 2-5 en bons de la dette intérieure qui ne valaient que de 6 pour cent à 8 pour cent de leur valeur nominale, et 3-5 en Pagarés ou traites à 60 jours d'échéance Un agiotage enorme s'établit sur ces ventes, et la confusion la plus complète s'ensuivit.*"

"Since the Declaration of Independence, according to a Decree issued by them some time ago, anybody denouncing Church property has the right to purchase it on the following terms. 60 per cent. of the value of such houses or lands are to be paid in bonds of internal debt (which bonds are in reality only worth 6 per cent.), and the remaining 40 per cent., in 'pagarés" or promises to pay hard cash, at sixty, and even eighty month's sight These "pagares ' of course, were subsequently discounted at an enormous sacrifice, as the Government was pressed for money, and willing to pay any nominal value to obtain it without delay In this way $27,000,000 worth of Church property has been squandered in this city alone, and the Government, now without a sixpence, is endeavouring to raise a loan of a million dollars to pay the current expenses." Sir Charles Wyke to Lord John Russell, "Accounts and Papers, 1862," LXIV.

But such distinctions were very far from being known or regarded in England, or in any part of the Continent of Europe. The plundering of the Legation by Miramon was spoken of only as a Mexican outrage ; the atrocities of Marquez inflamed men, not against his Party, but against the Government which he was seeking to overthrow ; and the foreign creditors, set at nought by the Government of Zuloaga, neither knew nor cared to know that Juarez at least had never converted to his own use a dollar that did not belong to him, that his habits were simple, and his mode of life unostentatious, when they saw that money slipped through his fingers like water, and that the most tremendous confiscations led only to an empty Exchequer.

That Juarez himself was honest, not even his Mexican enemies ventured to question. That he had almost every qualification for a good governor, is now at least universally recognised : but he had no genius for finance, nor were any of his colleagues or subordinates apparently more skilful in the administration of this important department of state. The Nation, it was remembered, was not yet forty years old. A Minister of Finance is one of the maturest products of modern civilisation.

The immense estates of the Church, which

should have sufficed to provide for all the exigencies of the State, had been rashly and unprofitably dissipated. The Treasury of Mexico was as empty as the Treasury at Vera Cruz.

But whatever may have been the merits or demerits of Juarez as a financier, in one respect at least he stood immeasurably above every other man of his age and nation. Vengeance was foreign to his nature. Bloodshed had no part in his policy. His vanquished opponents were Mexicans. Mexico demanded, not their lives, but their labours in her service.

Fugitive at Colima, pent up in Vera Cruz, victorious at Guadalajara, supreme at Mexico, his policy had been always the same.

No man had been slain in cold blood by his orders during his three years' struggle for existence. The constant cruelty, the reckless military executions of his savage opponents, had provoked him to no reprisals.

It is the coward and the doubter who is most prone to cruelty. Juarez was ever brave and ever confident. Amid the merciless he was ever merciful. In an age of bloodshed he was ever ready to spare the lives of his enemies. And in this, at least, he imposed his own will upon all his followers.

"There has not," says the British Envoy, writing

to Lord John Russell in January, 1861, " been a single act of bloodshed or popular vengeance on the part of the successful party." *

It is not surprising, therefore, that a Decree of general amnesty should have been one of the first that was published on the return of Juarez to the President's Palace at Mexico. Marquez and Miramon, indeed, noted and shameless criminals, were most justly proscribed and outlawed. A few individuals, bitter and powerful enemies of the Constitutional Government, among whom were, unfortunately, no doubt, Senor Pacheco, the Spanish Envoy; the Papal Nuncio, titular Bishop of Damascus,† with one or two of the more violent

---

* "Accounts and Papers," 1861.

† ": The publication of the various Laws of Reform in the capital," writes Mr. Mathew under date, January 30th, 1861, " has been attended by the most violent opposition on the part of the higher clergy. . . . The most inflammatory appeals have been made by the Archbishop in the Cathedral. . . . Upon the promulgation of the Civil Marriage Act the Archbishop issued a Decree [copy enclosed of Decree and Manifesto] in direct opposition to the law, and refusing to withdraw it, he and some of the other Bishops have received orders to leave the country."
"Accounts and Papers," 1861, LIV., p. 56.
I have seen no less than five Pastorals of Archbishop Garza y Ballesteros ; all directed against Juarez *eo nomine* and denouncing him and his Decrees. They are dated respectively:
July 29th, 1859.
August 5th, 1859.
,, 12th, 1859.
,, 19th, 1859.
September 7th, 1859.

opponents of Liberal institutions, including Joaquin de Madrid, Bishop of Tenagra ; Clemente Munguia, Bishop of Michoacan ; and Pedro Barajas, Bishop of Potosi ; were requested to leave the country, and were furnished at their own convenience with a suitable escort to the coast.   It was not thus that the assassins of Tacubaya were wont to deal with their enemies in the day of victory.*

This magnificent lenity provoked the remonstrance of many hotheaded partizans ; and there were grave differences of opinion among the members of the new Cabinet, within a few days of the restoration, upon the question of an immediate return to Constitutional methods of Government.

The majority were in favour of a modified dictatorship.   The President would accept only the functions of a Constitutional Ruler.   Some of his Ministers saw fit to resign, but Juarez stood firm. The Cabinet was reconstituted.   The Constitution remained inviolate.   All the acts of the Assembly

---

The copy that I used came from the Library of Maximilian (sold to the British Museum by the Abbé Fischer.)   The Imperial *book plate* is still in the volume, and is *artistically* strange to say a very poor production.

* The Archbishop of Mexico (Garza y Ballesteros), and one or two of his suffragans were banished only after the publication of a Pastoral calling upon the parochial clergy of the diocese directly to defy the law, as to religious toleration and liberty, civil marriage, etc., in January, 1861.   The Archbishop died in Europe, and an intriguer of the name of La Bastida was, as we shall see, appointed to take his place.

at Vera Cruz were adopted or confirmed. Those of the Revolutionary Government at Mexico were formally repudiated.*

The Foreign Ministers returned to the capital, and were admitted to audience of the President. Mr. Weller, the Envoy of the United States, on January 30th, Baron Wagner, the Prussian Chargé d'Affaires, on February 3rd, and Mr. Mathew, the English Minister, on February 26th, were warm in their assurances of respect and good-will.

The delay in the demand of audience by Mr. Mathew arose from a protracted correspondence as to the national duty of restoring the money stolen by Miramon from the Treasury of the British Legation, and the admission of liability in respect thereof, which had been insisted upon by Lord John Russell, as a condition precedent to any recognition of the new Government. Juarez, however, not only undertook to pay the amount, but offered a handsome apology ; and on the day of the return of the English Minister and his suite to the violated Legation, the national flag was dis-

---

* Reams of constitutional disquisition have been written, and might be cited upon the legal aspects of the position. It may suffice at present to point out that there is a good deal to be said upon the subject. As far as purely domestic questions are concerned, the right of the new and Constitutional Parliament was undoubted. As regards the rights of foreigners, each individual case must be argued upon the merits.

played throughout the city, as a mark of special honour and welcome.*

M. de Saligny, who had succeeded M. de Gabriac, in Nov., 1860, as French Minister, alone was disposed to place difficulties in the way of the Administration,† while he connived at the escape of Miramon, disguised as a French naval officer, on board the frigate *Mercure*, off Vera Cruz. But nothing as yet seemed to indicate that the Constitutional Government, at length restored to power, would be hindered by any foreign nation from bringing back peace and prosperity to Mexico. And Juarez, heedless of the little cloud rising upon the eastern horizon, addressed himself manfully to the work of the regeneration of his country.

---

* The whole story is very fully told in the Blue Book "Accounts and Papers (Mexico)" 1861, vol. LXV., *ubi supra*

† M. de Saligny showed himself from the first—he had been appointed in succession to M. Gabriac at the end of 1860, and had arrived at Mexico on the 12th of December a partizan of the Absolutist Government ; and one of his first acts after the return of Juarez to the capital was an attempt to place some Mexican nuns under French protection, so as to enable them to evade the orders of the Mexican Government.

As to M. de Saligny's hectoring conduct as regards the Sisters of Charity, in one of whose houses a sum of \$42,000, abstracted from the National Treasury, had been fraudulently hidden, even before he had presented his credentials to the Government of Juarez, see Lefévre, I., 41-47. M. Lefévre was an eye-witness of at least a part of the transaction

As to the shelter accorded by him to Robles in the French Legation, from January to April, 1861, *ibid* pp. 50-51.

A list of the French and English Ministers Resident, or Chargés d' Affaires in Mexico, about this time, may be of interest.

ENGLISH.

Percy Doyle, to May, 1855.
William Lettsom (Chargé d' Affaires,) to May, 1858.
Loftus Otway, to August 1859.
George Mathew, to May, 1862.
Sir Charles Wyke, to November, 1864.
Hon. Peter Campbell Scarlett, to October, 1867.
Robert Middleton (Chargé d' Affaires) to December 21st, 1867, when diplomatic relations were finally broken off.

FRENCH.

Monsieur de Gabriac, August. 1855 to December, 1860.
Viscomte Dubois de Saligny, to November, 1864.
Marquis de Montholon. to June, 1866.
Monsieur Alfonse Dano, to August, 1867.

CHAPTER VI.

FINANCE.

Before anything could be done by Juarez or his new Cabinet to re-organise the battered framework of Government in Mexico: to reform the great departments of State, or to re-organize the collection of the taxes in the interior: Zuloaga took up arms at Iguala, and Mejia on the Rio Verde.

The storm was not yet spent, new troubles were at hand.[*]

In the month of March, the Liberal Party was deprived by sudden death of two of its most loyal supporters, Zamora, the Governor of Vera Cruz ; and Miguel Lerdo de Tejada, one of the most conspicuous and honoured members of the Cabinet of Juarez.[†] Ocampo, another of his ablest lieutenants,

---

[*] In spite of the hostility, not only of M. de Gabriac, but of M de Saligny, Juarez, on his restoration to supreme power—*pour faire preuve de bonne volonté à l'égard de la France*, chose M. de Montluc, a French citizen, to act as Consul General for Mexico in Paris.—"Correspondance de Montluc," p 57.

[†] He was at the time of his death a candidate for the Presidency, second only in popularity to Juarez himself, with whom he remained to the last on terms of close friendship.
Baz, Vida, 209.

was carried away from his own home by some supporters of Zuloaga, and murdered in cold blood by the orders of Marquez, on the 17th of June, 1861. General Valle soon afterwards fell a victim to the same ruffianism ; and General Degollado having been entrusted with a small force to seek and punish the assassins, was himself surprised and murdered. A price was put upon the head of Marquez, whose name was a terror to all honest men in Mexico, but he remained at large in the Provinces.

Yet the Government was never for a moment in real danger from any of these bandits and bravos. Zuloaga lost no time in following the example of his friend Miramon, and seeking safety in flight to the Havannah. Marquez, though a bold robber, and an undaunted assassin, was no soldier ; he was not even a Party leader.* Mejia alone remained to fight the battle of the fugitives.

But the greatest of all the difficulties that immediately beset the Government, was the impossibility of obtaining money. Not only was the Treasury empty, but the entire fiscal system was

---

* It was on the 4th of June, 1861, in consequence of the murder of Ocampo, that General Tomas Mejia was formally declared by the Assembly an *outlaw*, together with Zuloaga, Marquez and two or three others.

This must be remembered when considering the proceedings in June, 1867. Active association with Marquez was itself something in the nature of a crime.

disorganised. Public credit had ceased to exist. Reconstruction cannot be undertaken without funds. Seventy-seven per cent. of the Customs dues at Vera Cruz had been hypothecated to foreign creditors; and of the twenty-three per cent. that remained, very little found its way to the Treasury at Mexico.*

On the 27th of March, 1861, Senor Zarco, on behalf of President Juarez, made certain proposals with regard to the English claims, which were pronounced reasonable by the British Minister.†

But cash was scarce, the country was still unsettled; and on the 30th of April, 1861, Senor La Fuente was sent as a special Envoy to the Courts of Paris and London, to endeavour to obtain some reduction of the capital amount of the Public

---

* By far the greater part of the revenues of the country was derived from the import duties at the ports of Vera Cruz and Tampico, and of these no less than 77 per cent was already hypothecated at the time of the restoration of the Constitutional Government under Juarez in 1861.

27 per cent to London Bondholders.
24 per cent. "British Convention."
10 per cent to replace arrears.
10 per cent to replace money at mint of Guanajuato.
8 per cent. French Convention.
Mathew to Lord John Russell, May 12th, 1861.

† The Government further undertook, or rather proposed, to guarantee to the British subjects the fullest liberty of public worship in Mexico, an undertaking which was afterwards fully and loyally carried out

Señor Zarco's proposals are given in full in the Blue Book; Mexico, 1862, lxiv., p.p. 4-11.

Debt, or some delay in the payment of the interest.*

Very similar reductions or conversions have since been undertaken by many sovereign States, both in Europe and America; yet the suggestion that Mexico should compound in any way with her creditors, was treated in England, at least, with suspicion, in France with the utmost hostility.

The fact is that while most people in Europe were quite unable and others were quite unwilling to distinguish between the relative merits of the contending parties in Mexico, the Emperor of the French had already made up his mind to intervene in her affairs, and to impose a foreign Government upon the country.

And while Miramon, Almonte and the exiled Bishops were able to rouse the pious indignation of Roman Catholic Europe against Juarez and his friends, and to enlist the sympathy of exalted personages with a Restoration of clerical and absolute Government in Mexico, the Emperor Napoleon was able to induce the unsuspecting

---

* The utmost pains were taken by the representatives of the Absolutist Party in Europe to represent Juarez as an Indian savage, less civilized than Theodore of Abyssinia.

On the 14th of August, 1862—for instance—the Duke of Tetuan read aloud in the Spanish Cortes a letter which he had lately received from Zuloaga, stating that it was the intention of Juarez " to exterminate the entire white population of Mexico! "—" Cesar Cantu and Juarez," p. 8.

Statesmen of England and Spain to assist him in his ambitious designs of French aggrandisement in the New World.*

Yet it was absolutely necessary, in the interest of Mexico as well as that of her creditors, that some prompt arrangement should be made of the various debts and demands, that had now for so long, and for so many reasons, remained unsatisfied.†

But claims arising out of the robbery by General Miramon at Mexico, and the robbery by General Degollado at Laguna Seca, together with miscellaneous claims of British subjects, independent of arrears of interest due to bondholders, to say nothing of the various conversions of the various recognised debts, had so complicated what may be called the International financial situation that it was absolutely necessary that some special Convention should be negotiated between the Government

---

* The fact was concealed from the public in Europe that the greater part of the excesses charged against the Mexicans, more especially the breaking of the seals of the British Legation, had been committed by the very party that now solicited French aid to impose their despotic rule upon an unwilling people.

Ce qu'il y a de remarquable est qu'en France les impérialistes ont reproché au government de Juarez les atrocités commises précisément par ses adversaires, les insurgés retrogades Montluc · Correspondance, p. 62.

† The last arrangement was one that had been made with the Government of Juarez, by Captain Dunlop, of the English navy, in 1859, by which 25 per cent. of the Custom duties at Vera Cruz and Tampico were set aside for the English bondholders.

of Juarez and the Court of St. James's ; and a Minister Plenipotentiary, Sir Charles Wyke, was accordingly commissioned on the 30th of March, 1861, to proceed to Mexico for that purpose.* The instructions that were given by Lord John Russell to the new Envoy were to regulate, if possible, the financial situation, but above all things to assert that the policy of the English Government as regards Mexico was " a policy of non-intervention : " that " England desired to see Mexico free and independent, " and that, " notwithstanding the grievous wrongs which British subjects might have sustained at the hands of former Governments, the friendly feelings of Her Majesty's Government towards Mexico had undergone no change."†

---

* His instructions will be found in the Blue Book, 1862, lxiv. pp. 161 *et seq.*

† That the foreign merchants and residents who formulated all these claims, were themselves innocent and even exemplary in their treatment of the native Mexicans is a justification of a good deal of national indignation which will hardly be accepted by the readers of an article published in *Frazer's Magazine*, Dec. 1861, by an acute and very well informed Englishman. Of the foreign diplomatists—who conducted themselves as Viceroys, of the foreign officers—who conducted themselves as smugglers, of the foreign merchants—who organized *lucrative* pronunciamientos and shared the spoil of a despoiled Custom House with complaisant Governors, we may read with advantage in these impartial pages, and learn that even " the outrage committed by Degollado was not so entirely unprovoked as persons in this country may be apt to imagine," and that the Mexicans who were guilty of such and similar enterprises " were probably actuated rather by a rude theory of their own on the subject of justi-

On the 27th of May, Sir Charles Wyke, a somewhat less sympathetic negotiator than Mr. Mathew, had a long interview with Señor Guzman, who had succeeded Señor Zarco as Minister for Foreign Affairs. And that statesman sought rather to demonstrate the absolute impossibility of his Government paying away sums of money which they did not possess, than to suggest any reasonable settlement of so burning a question.

The English Envoy, astounded as he was at the disastrous and demoralized condition of the country, was rendered rather suspicious than sympathetic by the attitude of Señor Guzman ; and their negotiations were further embarrassed by the publication, on the 3rd of June, of a Presidential Decree, issued under the authority of the Assembly, which was then in full session, postponing all payments to creditors of the National Treasury for

---

fiable reprisals than by mere senseless hostility to foreigners, or rapacious desire for plunder."

It is also somewhat remarkable that among the Germans, represented by a not inconsiderable number of merchant traders, neither claims nor complaints were found.

See on this same subject Domenech : Hist. II. 341-344. " Dans mes dossiers j'ai des extraits des journaux de Mexico, révélant l'entrée en franchise pour le compte d'un ministre étranger que je nommerai—s'il le faut, de plus de deux cents caisses et ballots de marchandizes, destinées à un négotiant de la capitale."

The export of bullion was subjected to a tax of 8 per cent—" Pour frustrer le trésor," saystheAbbé, " les Anglais, possesseurs de la plupart des mines du Mexique, envoient cet argent á leur consuls pour l'exporter en franchise."

one year. The restoration of the bullion stolen from the British Legation was also postponed, and the letters of Sir Charles Wyke, in his correspondence with the Mexican Foreign Minister, began to assume a tone of severity and reproach, not unnatural under the impression that in this sequence of negotiations and decrees he had been falsely borne in hand.

It may, perhaps, be useful to give a brief summary of the Foreign debt * of Mexico at this crisis, and of the various means that had from time to time been devised for its repayment up to the 17th of June, 1861, the date of promulgation of the Decree by which the suspension of cash payments by the Government of Mexico was ordained.

The entire Foreign debt of Mexico stood on January, 1st, 1861, somewhat thus—

1. English bondholders (being the
      entire *Funded* debt of the ...
      country) $60,000,000
2. Spanish Convention, an *Un-
      funded* debt (with arrears of
      interest) and " Padre Moran "
      debt   9,000,000

---

* The history of the Convention debt of Mexico, with the text of the Conventions themselves, and the various modifications agreed to down to August 26th, 1861, will be found in the Blue Book, Mexico, 1861, lxiv. pp. 72-93.

K

3.   English Convention...   ...   5,000,000
4.   French Convention (not includ-
       ing claims for *penal* interest
       at 12 per cent.), estimated
       by Lefèvre [I. 64-65] at ...   190,850
                                          ———————
                                          74,190,850

5.   *Various claims (amounting, as
       will be seen, to more than the
       entire sum of the Funded
       and Unfunded debt !) say...   75,310,000
                                          ———————
                                          $149,500,850
                                          ———————

The British claims sent in to H. B. M. Consulate up to April 28th, 1861, amounted in round figures to $20,000,000, of which $16,500,000 was claimed by one house, Messrs. Manning and Mackintosh; the remainder, $3,500,000, by a great number of persons, claiming compensation for a variety of grievances.

---

* See Fenn on the Funds, 1860-63, p. 280.   But I cannot admit claims of any kind, however just, nor yet the Jecker Bonds, of which a full account will be given later on, as part of a foreign debt, funded or unfunded.

I have set down all these sums in round figures The interest and payment on account are calculated so differently by different authorities, that among all those whom I have consulted, and I regret to say they are many, no two agree with regard to any one sum.

I have to thank my kind friend, Mr. W. H. Bishop, for looking over these pages in M.S., a favour spontaneously offered, and much appreciated

The item " Plunder " is of constant occurrence, " Contributions," " Forced Loans," " Breach of Contract," " Robbery," " Assassination of husband " " Murder of Father," are among the most characteristic.

It is important in the first instance to distinguish between the *Funded* and *Unfunded* debt of the Republic.*   The former consisted of :

The 5 per cent. English loan of 1823,
    contracted at 55, and issued by
    Messrs. Goldsmidt, at 58 per cent.   £3,200,000
The 6 per cent. English loan of 1825,
    issued by Messrs. Barclay, at 86¾
    per cent.   3,200,000
    Arrears of interest   3,600,000

                  say   £10,000,000
                  or $60,000,000

No dividends were remitted to Europe on these loans between October, 1827, and April, 1831.   In 1831, when the arrears on the 5 per cents amounted to £18 15s. per cent., and on the 6 per cents to £22 10s. per cent., the coupons for these arrears were capitalized and exchanged for deferred bonds, to bear interest from April 1st,

---

* See Lefevre I., pp. 59-70 ; and Kozhevar, " Report on the Republic of Mexico," 1866, pp. 77-80.

1836.   The 6 per cent. deferred stock was issued at 75 per cent. and the 5 per cent. at 62½ per cent. An acknowledgment was given at the same time for half the coupons due from 1st April, 1831, to 1st April, 1836, and it was provided that bonds bearing interest from that date should be exchanged for the same on the same terms as the previous bonds.   This arrangement, however, was not fulfilled, so that the actual state of the debt on the 1st of October, 1837, was as follows :

5 per cent. loan of 1823, principal, funded coupons, etc.	£3,444,000
6 per cent. loan of 1825, do. ...	5,803,000
	£9,247,000
To be divided into	
Active Bonds	4,623,500
Deferred Bonds	4,623,500
	£9,247,000

There was, as may be supposed, some delay in carrying this arrangement into effect, and Messrs. Lizardi, who were charged with the conversion, caused further confusion by issuing over £750,000 of deferred bonds in excess of the authorised amount, on account of their claim for commission.[*]

---

[*] Kozhevar, pp. 84-86.

In 1846 the debt, once more converted, was recognised as amounting to £11,204,000.

Upon the outbreak of war between Mexico and the United States, in 1846, the Northern forces occupied Vera Cruz and Tampico ; and the payment of dividends upon the debt was once more suspended. In 1848 the war was terminated, as we have seen, on the conditions that Mexico should cede a large portion of her territory to the United States, and receive $15,000,000 (£3,000,000) as an indemnity. Upon this, the sterling bondholders agreed to accept a reduced rate of interest—3½ per cent. instead of 5 per cent.—on condition that a sum of $4,000,000 (£800,000) out of the American indemnity money, should be handed over to their representative in Mexico. There was a provision in the agreement securing original rights to the bondholders in case of non-fulfilment of the conditions stipulated.*

In 1850, a Mexican decree was promulgated reducing the interest upon the debt to 3 per cent. : while $2,500,000 (£500,000) of the American indemnity which actually, as we have seen, amounted to less than $11,000,000, was appropriated to the settlement of the overdue interest on the 5 per cent. debt. Under this decree of October 4th, 1850, the amount of the debt was ascertained as £10,241,650.

---

* See Introductory Chapter, page 42.

But beyond and entirely distinct from this Funded or Bond debt, both as regards origin, security, and mode of payment, was the Unfunded or Convention debt of England, Spain and France.

The *Spanish Convention* debt represented the amount of the public indebtedness of the Spanish Viceroys down to the 17th of September, 1810, fixed and recognised by the Treaty of the 17th of July, 1847, at $6,633,000.

The *French Convention* represented a capital sum of $1,500,000 recognised as due to certain French subjects in Mexico, and secured, by an agreement made in 1853, upon the Customs dues at the ports of entry.

The *English Convention*, or subsidiary debt had its origin in a loan of $200,000 made to the Government in 1840, by Messrs. Montgomery, Nicol and Co., in connection with a contract for the farming of the Tobacco Revenue to Don Benito Maceca, in 1839, and a claim of $50,000 by a Mr. Jamieson * " for advice rendered to the Minister of Finance ; " and on the 15th of October, 1842, Mr. Pakenham, British Minister at the Court of Mexico, signed a convention with the Mexican Government, under which these claims—recognised as amounting

---

* Kozhevar : " Report on the Republic of Mexico," 1886, p. 116. I hope Mr. Jamieson's advice was worth the fee !

to $250,000—were to be consolidated and paid off, principal and interest, by a percentage on the import dues at the Maritime Customs Houses of Vera Cruz and Tampico.

This convention, owing to the constant political disturbances, was never carried out. But fresh loans were made and never repaid. At length, in the more peaceful days of Aristas' Government, a new conversion was arranged and decreed.

In November and December of the year 1851, the British creditors met at the National Treasury, and it was agreed that the various claims, which had increased on all accounts to $4,984,910, should be treated as a consolidated debt, bearing interest at 3 per cent. for five years, and afterwards at 4 per cent., with a sinking fund of 5 per cent., which was afterwards increased to 6 per cent.

To provide for this, 12 per cent. per annum of the entire Customs Revenue, increased in December, 1852, to 15 per cent., and ultimately to 29 per cent., was assigned to the representatives of the bond-holders.

This Convention, known as the Doyle Convention, was signed by the British Minister, Mr. Doyle, on December 4th, 1851 ; and a subsequent arrangement by which the 4 per cent. interest was increased to 6 per cent., was signed on August 10th, 1858, by Mr. Otway, who had succeeded Mr. Doyle as

British Minister Resident, in the month of February of that year.

So far, it was the English creditors only who had taken action as regards consolidation and conversion; but within two days of the signing of the Doyle Convention (December 6th, 1851), the agreement known as the *Padre Moran* Convention * was signed on behalf of the Spanish creditors, whose claims amounted to only $983,000, by Señor Sayas, the Spanish Minister ; the securities and guarantees for payment being identical with those granted to the English bondholders.   And out of every assignment received from year to year, one sixth part was regularly handed over by the British to the Spanish agents.†

Between 1852 and 1861, the full amount of interest, as stipulated, was paid upon the Consolidated Fund of the British and the *Padre Moran* Conventions.

---

* An account of the Padre Moran Convention and the Spanish Convention is given in the same chapter of Mr. Kozhevar's very interesting work

† The payments on account of the sinking fund only were allowed to fall in arrear, and a vast number of claims for loss, damage to property, murder of relatives, and other misfortunes incident to the disturbed condition of the country were more or less honestly made upon the Government by individual foreigners,—claims which were rather postponed than rejected ; but never under any circumstances paid.   There is a list of " British claims of the small and most distressing class remaining undischarged in the Summer of 1861 " in the Blue Book, so often referred to. — LXIV, p. 23. " Accounts and Papers," June 27, 1861.

Yet, during the greater part of this time, not a shilling of interest was paid on the Bonded or Funded debt.* The distinctions must be carefully kept in view.

We have thus (dividing the liabilities of Mexico in another way) :

I.—ENGLISH.

				$
1.	Entire Funded Debt	...	...	60,000,000
2.	Convention Debt	...	...	5,000,000
3.	Claims for Compensation		...	20,000,000
				$85,000,000

II.—SPANISH.

				$
1.	Convention Debt	...	...	8,000,000
2.	Padre Moran Debt	...	...	1,000,000
3.	Claims	...	...	...	8,000,000
				$17,000,000

---

* See for Dunlop Convention, Lefèvre : Documents, etc. p. 96.
    Sketch of general debt .. .. .. pp. 97-105
    Jecker Bonds .. .. pp. 106-132
The Convention of February, 1859, was replaced by a new arrangement in July, and this again was superseded by the so-called definitive arrangement contained in Decree of 29th of October, 1859.

The new bonds were to bear interest at 6 per cent, and were accepted as 20 per cent. of their face value on account of taxes, duties, etc., and as regards payments to the clergy as 10 per cent.—This Decree is dated 30th of January, 1860.

III.—FRENCH.

		$
1. Convention Debt		300,000
2. Jecker Bonds		15,000,000
3. Claims		12,000,000
		$27,300,000

or again :

DEBT (FUNDED AND UNFUNDED).

		$
1. English		65,000,000
2. Spanish		9,000,000
3. French		300,000
		$74,300,000

CLAIMS.

		$
1. English		20,000,000
2. Spanish		8,000,000
3. French *		27,000,000
		$55,000,000

The agreements between Captain Dunlop, R.N., H M.S. *Tartar* ; Captain Cornwallis Aldham, R.N. ; and Señor Zamara, Governor of Vera Cruz under Juarez (January and February, 1859) are printed in a special Blue Book, 1861, LXV., p. 337.

* The French claims are collected and examined with his usual care by Monsieur Lefévre, tome II., pp. 170-222, where the names, dates, and amounts will be found fully set out.

The origin and history of the *Jecker Bonds* is even more remarkable than that of any other part of the Mexican debt as it existed in January, 1861. And as the settlement of this trebly scandalous loan was the main object or justification put forward for the French invasion of Mexico, it is as well that a certain amount of attention should be directed to the nature and development of the claim.

In October, 1859, the usurper Miramon and his friends and supporters were not only losing all hope of maintaining the struggle against President Juarez and the Constitutionalists in Mexico, but their Government, if Government it can be called, was absolutely bankrupt.

A certain Señor Peza, who was entrusted with the administration of the Finances, had issued in the course of the year 1858 no less than $80,000,000 of bonds, nominally for the purpose of *converting* the original debt, but really to obtain money on any terms. And his $100 bonds were dealt in at five, four, and even one half (50 centimes) per 100 !*

But even this was not the end. The Government was still absolutely without funds. Juarez was already at the gate.

---

* Montluc; Correspondance, Manuel Payno, Report, etc., Mexico, 1862.

And in this dire distress Miramon applied to a Swiss banker in Mexico, one Jecker, himself, as it turned out, on the verge of insolvency, for a loan on any conditions that he chose to name. " He who does not intend to pay," says the Spanish proverb, " is not troubled by the terms of his bargain."   And it was at length agreed by the high contracting parties that in consideration of what was practically an immediate cash advance to himself of six or seven hundred thousand dollars, the obliging Jecker should receive Government paper to the extent of $15,000,000, to be issued, sold, or dealt with by the Swiss bankers at their good pleasure.*

And the advance by insolvent Jecker to insolvent Miramon, at the expense of the Mexican nation, was spoken of not as a loan, but as a new conversion of the National Debt.†

---

* As a matter of fact a considerable number of these bogus bonds were used for the appropriate purpose of bribing those French adventurers who intervened some two years afterwards with the object of raising their price.

† In March, 1860, having paid to Miramon 3,000,000 francs or say $600,000, the house of Jecker received the 75,000,000 francs of bonds. Two months after, the house went into liquidation with 68,391,250 francs of the bonds in their strong box.   Kératry : " La créance Jecker," pp. 12-13.

The exact *modus operandi* of the Jecker *Conversion* will be found detailed in Lefévre, I., pp. 28-31

CHAPTER VII.

Agitation.—June, 1861—January, 1862.

On the 25th of June, 1861, Sir Charles Wyke wrote to his Government in England that nothing short of the employment of her Majesty's naval forces in a demonstration off the ports of Tampico and Vera Cruz would suffice to bring the Mexican authorities to reason.

The French—inspired by, or inspiring, Monsieur Dubois de Saligny—had already begun to speak of joint intervention. The Cabinet of Madrid had already been approached from Paris. Lord John Russell was hesitating in London.

And at this critical moment the Mexican Congress, moved by Señor Sebastian Lerdo de Tejada, and to the infinite regret of President Juarez,* saw fit to accept a motion, or resolution—

---

* Juarez, we must remember, was a Constitutional President. He had been formally installed in office on the 11th of June. His Government was carried on by an independent Cabinet, whose members were responsible to the Chamber; and this wretched Decree was supremely distasteful to him.

which, if not absolutely dishonest in fact, was supremely unfortunate in form—suspending cash payment on the part of the Government for two full years. Without a word of warning to any one of the representatives, national or commercial, of any foreign nation, without consultation with banker or agent, without even an intimation to Sir Charles Wyke, engaged in almost daily negotiations with a Cabinet Minister within a stone's throw of the Chamber of Deputies, this announcement of national bankruptcy was suddenly and shamelessly sent forth. (July 17th, 1861.)

No one, except perhaps Miramon and Marquez, the intriguers in France, or the rebels in Mexico, could even affect to be pleased by this disastrous Decree ; and no one was more indignant than Sir Charles Wyke, who felt keenly, and expressed, perhaps somewhat too warmly, the absurdity of the position in which he was placed by its rash and unexpected publication.

As to the folly of the Decree, as seen from the Mexican point of view, see " Mexico à traves de los siglos," V., pp. 467-8, and Baz ' " Vida de Juarez," chap. VII.

The President was, no doubt, constitutionally unwilling to publish his own dissatisfaction with the Chamber. But it was well known that on the 7th of September a resolution was proposed by 51 members calling upon Juarez to resign.

By way, presumably, of turning the motion into ridicule, 52 members proposed a contra-resolution—in a vote of confidence in the President, and nothing further was done with either.—" Mexico," *ubi supra*, p. 469. Baz. Vida : chap. VII.

His remonstrances * being entirely disregarded, he boldly took upon himself to suspend all diplomatic correspondence with the Government, whose proceeding was, he asserted, simply that of a thief. And his action was subsequently fully approved by the Court of St. James's.

M. de Saligny, the French Minister, took the still more decided step of demanding his passports, and actually breaking off his official relations with Mexico. Pacheco, the Spanish Envoy, had already left the country. It was *Mexico contra Mundum.* But Mexico, unfortunately, was in the wrong. And Sir Charles Wyke, in his despatches,†

---

* Addressed to Señor Zamacona, the Minister for Foreign Affairs.

† The words of Sir Charles Wyke's despatch are quoted in the " Annual Register " as a permanent record of the shameless wickedness of the Mexican Government. They form the text of an Imperialist article in the *Quarterly Review*, No. CXV.

I have seen them in French in half-a-dozen publications ; and, translated into Spanish, I have met with them not only in Spain but in Mexico.

It seems impossible to escape them. Written in haste and in very natural indignation, an expression of personal dissatisfaction at a state of things of which the full and real significance was hardly appreciated by the writer, Sir Charles Wyke's words not only influenced public opinion in England at a very critical juncture, but they have had a permanent effect upon the foreign estimate of Mexico and of Juarez, greater, perhaps, than has ever been produced by any similar means.

The following extract affords a fair specimen :—

" In the meantime Congress, instead of enabling the Government to put down the frightful disorder which reigns throughout the length and breadth of the land, is occupied in disputing about vain theories of so-called government on

accentuated her offences in vigorous but somewhat unbridled language, which produced a great and lasting effect, not only in England but on the Continent, where the Emperor Napoleon, then at the very height of his power and authority, made the most dexterous use of this opportunity to incite the Cabinets of London and of Madrid to undertake a joint expedition to Mexico in furtherance of his un-

---

ultra-Liberal principles, whilst the respectable part of the population is delivered up defenceless to the attacks of robbers and assassins, who swarm on the high roads and in the streets of the capital. The Constitutional Government is unable to maintain its authority in the various States of the Federation, which are becoming *de facto* perfectly independent, so that the same causes which, under similar circumstances, broke up the Confederation of Central America into five separate Republics, are now at work here, and will probably produce a like result.

" This state of things renders one all but powerless to obtain redress from a Government which is solely occupied in maintaining its existence from day to day, and therefore unwilling to attend to other people's misfortunes before their own. The only hope of improvement I can see is to be found in the small Moderate Party, who may step in perhaps before all is lost to save their country from impending ruin. Patriotism, in the common acceptation of the term, appears to be unknown, and no one of any note is to be found in the ranks of either party. Contending factions struggle for the possession of power only to gratify their cupidity or their revenge, and in the meantime the country sinks lower and lower, whilst its population becomes brutalised and degraded to an extent frightful to contemplate.

" Such is the actual state of affairs in Mexico, and your lordship will perceive, therefore, that there is little chance of justice or redress from such people, except by the employment of force to exact that which both persuasion and menaces have hitherto failed to obtain."— Blue Book, 1862, LXIV 35.

disclosed and long unsuspected designs upon that country.

Marshal O'Donnell assented without much difficulty.* Lord Russell more reluctantly acquiesced, stipulating as conditions precedent to any action in Mexico: I.—That the co-operation of the United States should be invited; II.—That the combined Powers should not interfere by force with the Government or in the internal affairs of Mexico.

Conditions on paper have never checked the progress of any adventurer. Lord Russell at the English Foreign Office dictated terms only for the greater glory of his diplomatic opponents. And thus, while despatches and protocols of the most unexceptional character, and telling only of the profound disinterestedness of the allies, were slowly passing between Paris and London and Madrid, no improvement was found either in the political or in the financial situation in Mexico.†

Juarez, as was afterwards but tardily admitted,

---

* Despatch to H. B. M. Minister at Madrid of September 27th, 1861, "Accounts and Papers," etc.

† Through the Autumn and early Winter of 1862, secret negotiations were actively carried on between Paris and Miramar, where Maximilian of Hapsburg, in return for present assistance, was preparing to accede to any terms that might be imposed upon him by the ambitious intriguers in Paris. A sum of no less than 8,000,000 francs in cash, to start with, was the amount agreed upon, and it was duly paid out of the first Mexican loan.

L

was at least doing his best. But the disorder of the country was so profound that no man could in weeks or months make any show of improvement.

The very foundations of society had to be relaid, before it was possible to commence the work of re-construction.

The news of the supposed attempt to murder the French Minister, who was said to have been fired at in the Legation on the 14th of August,* together with Sir Charles Wyke's renewed denunciation of the weakness and inefficiency of the Mexican Government, not only as regards finance, but in the maintenance of public order, created a painful impression in Europe. It was said that "the native Mexicans" had risen in great force near the capital, that "an insurrection of the entire Indian population was daily expected," and that Comonfort and Doblado, well-known Liberals, and old friends of Juarez, were independently "conspiring for the overthrow of his Government."

The French Minister had never been shot at. The Indian population did not rise. Both Doblado

---

* This supposed outrage was the subject of an immediate investigation by the Mexican Executive, and was pronounced to be an absolute figment, a diplomatic invention of M. de Saligny himself

and Comonfort retained their commands in the army of the Constitutional Republic.*

---

* On the 28th of June, 1861, Marquez, with a band of followers broke into the buildings of the celebrated Real del Monte Mines, stole all the money that he could lay his hands on, together with all the horses and such moveable property as he could carry away, and was hardly prevented from killing the miners, of whom 161 were Englishmen.

This outrage very properly excited the indignation of Sir Charles Wyke ; but it was hardly just, or even logical, that it should lead him to express his opinion that the Government of Juarez was " weak and tyrannical."

It is almost a matter of necessity to subjoin another extract from Sir Charles Wyke's own letters.

" It is very evident by the tone of these communications that they are now alarmed at the turn affairs have taken ; but their wretched vanity and pride will prevent them from taking any step to remedy the evil, and, therefore, I see no chance of the measure being withdrawn.

" Your lordship will thus perceive that it has become impossible any longer to suffer the illegal and outrageous proceedings of a Government which neither respects itself nor its most solemn engagements.

" It is only by adopting coercive measures that we can force them to give up a system of violent spoliation which in reality is nearly as prejudicial to themselves as to those foreigners who are so unfortunate as to have brought their capital and industry to a country so misgoverned.

" On the publication of the Decree, the British merchants resident here addressed a letter to me praying for my interference on their behalf, against the increase of duties on all foreign articles of consumption thus imposed upon them. I enclose copy of their letter, together with my reply thereto.

"As long as the present dishonest and incapable Administration remains in power, things will go from bad to worse ; but with a Government formed of respectable men, could such be found, the resources of the country are so great that it might easily fulfil its engagements, and increase threefold the amount of its exportations, not only of the precious metals but of those productions for which they receive British manufactured goods in exchange. Mexico furnishes two-thirds of the silver now in circulation, and might be made

But the news served its turn. And the well-founded report of the imposition of a tax upon capital (one per cent.) by a Decree of August 21st, 1861) from which the property of foreign merchants was not exempted, tended still further to exacerbate the feelings of the European creditors, speculators and enemies.

The banished bishops, the fugitive generals, the aspiring statesmen, the holders of Jecker bonds the hangers-on of Miramar and the Tuileries;

---

one of the richest and the most prosperous countries in the world; so that it becomes the interest of Great Britian to put a stop, by force if necessary, to its present state of anarchy, and insist on its Government paying what it owes to British subjects. The Moderate party which is now cowed by the two opposing ultra factions in the State, would then raise its head, and encouraged by adopting the measures I pointed out as necessary in my last month's correspondence, probably establish by themselves such a Government as we require, but without this moral support they fear to move, and hence the continuation of the deplorable state of things now existing.

" M. de Saligny, the French Minister here, has acted in concert with me throughout the affair, and although the interests he has to defend are trifling in comparison to ours, he has used even stronger language than I have, for he does not merely suspend, but actually breaks off all official intercourse with the Government, unless they rescind the Decree of the 17th instant.

" I have not the least hesitation in saying that unless Her Majesty's Government take the most decided measures for proving to this Government that it cannot thus act with impunity, British subjects resident here will remain defenceless, and their property be at the mercy of a set of men who disregard their most solemn engagements, whenever such interfere with either their caprice or rapacity."— " Accounts & Papers," 1861, lxiv., p. 21.

priests, financiers, adventurers, and devotees ;*
friends of the Pope and friends of Morny, with all
the military froth and scum of France in the later
days of the third Empire, all strove silently
together, greedy for Intervention and Plunder.

A military diversion, a review on a large scale in
the neighbourhood of the Havannah, commended
itself to the Spanish General Prim, and Lord
Russell,† protesting in precise despatches that
England would never be a party to doing any of
the things for the doing of which France alone
desired her co-operation and alliance, consented to
take part in an expedition, consisting, indeed, of
armed men in ships of war, but intended, as
explained to the ever-patient British public, to be
a demonstration, not of hostility, but of amity and
goodwill to Mexico.

The British public is always ready to accept
words instead of realities, if the words are printed
by Messrs. Eyre & Spottiswoode.

During the whole of the Autumn of 1861, Señor
La Fuente, the Mexican Envoy, had been doing his
utmost to prevail upon the European Powers to
consent to some re-arrangement of the National
Debt.

---

* "L'homme du bénitier, l'homme de l'agio."
Victor Hugo : Nox. iv.

† His patent as an Earl is dated July 30th, 1861.

Nothing would satisfy the Court of Madrid but the acceptance in its entirety of the Mon-Almonte agreement ; a bargain, as already set forth, so scandalously leonine in its character, that its ratification by a responsible Government in Mexico was obviously out of the question. The dismissal of Senor Pacheco was explained by the Mexican Envoy, with becoming expressions of regret, to have been a purely personal matter, and one in no way prejudicing the respect that was felt by the Government of Mexico for that of her Most Catholic Majesty. The claims under the Spanish Convention debt should be honoured as heretofore with the utmost punctuality ; a new Envoy from the Court of Madrid would be warmly welcomed by President Juarez at Mexico. But it was all to no purpose. The Spaniard would not move.

In France, as may be supposed, Señor La Fuente fared no better than in Spain. Proceeding to London, he was admitted to audience of Lord Russell, who treated him to a good deal of diplomatic circumlocution, but who paid no real attention to his proposals, to his suggestions, or his remonstrances.*

The Representative of the United States in London was more sympathetic, but no whit more useful than any of the European Ministers.

---

* Señor la Fuente's endeavours, as told in his letters, may be read in Lefèvre, I , 81-115. Lord Russell seems to have behaved with a good deal of disingenuousness.

The cause of Mexico was judged unheard. And England, whether from ignorance or mere ineptitude, added the weight of her influence to a scheme of transatlantic adventure, of which it is difficult to say whether it was more sordid, more shameless, or more extravagant.

On the 31st of October, 1861, a Convention* between Great Britain, France, and Spain was signed in London, wherein it was recited that the United Governments, " feeling compelled by the arbitrary and vexatious conduct of the authorities of the Republic of Mexico to demand more efficacious protection for the persons and properties of their subjects " . . . had agreed (1.) . . . " to dispatch military and naval forces sufficient to seize and occupy the several fortresses and military positions on the Mexican coast " . . . (2) " not to seek for themselves any acquisition of territory, nor any special advantages," and " not to exercise in the internal affairs of Mexico any influence to prejudice the right of the Mexican nation to choose and constitute freely the form of its government."

---

* The original draft of this Treaty of Alliance, prepared by Lord Russell himself, as it ran before its modification by the French negotiation, is printed side by side with the definite Treaty, by M. Lefèvre, I., 81-88. It is very instructive reading. The part played by Spain in the same negotiations will be seen on reading a letter from Señor Calderon Collantes, Foreign Minister at Madrid, printed by the same untiring collector, I., 89-98.

(3.) Three Commissioners were to be appointed to proceed to Mexico; and (4.)† the Government of the United States was to be invited to adhere to any Convention that should be executed.

The signature of the Convention rendered the august conspirators on the continent of Europe less reticent than before. It became necessary, indeed, to prepare the world for the development of the new phase of French restlessness. Strange rumours were permitted to make themselves heard as to the establishment of a Catholic Monarchy in Mexico, and of the desire of the Mexican nation to elect an Austrian Prince to the new throne that was to be established beyond the Atlantic.

As early as January, 1862, questions were addressed to the Court of Paris by the Spanish, the English,‡ and the United States Governments as regards the ultimate objects of the French intervention, and the French Foreign Minister replied from time to time in language more diplomatic than satisfactory.

---

* This last condition was made a *sine qua non* by the English Cabinet.

† Lord Cowley to Lord Russell, January 24th, 1862.

M. Thouvenel denied that "any negotiation had been pending between his Government and that of Austria with regard to the Emperor Maximilian."

On February 13th, Lord Russell intimated to the Austrian Government that the imposition of an Austrian Prince upon the Mexicans would be unfavourably regarded in England. But Lord John's intimations to foreign powers rarely led him any further.

While the English Foreign Secretary in Down-
ing Street renewed his protestations of academic
horror at the mere thought of intervention in the
domestic affairs of Mexico ; Monsieur Thouvenel
at the Tuileries, expressing his respectful admiration of such unexceptional theories of conduct,
found means to convey to Maximilian, to Miramon
and to de Saligny that the time for action was at
hand.

Meanwhile, towards the end of July, the Cabinet
at Washington, forewarned as to the French designs,
and supremely unwilling to see European troops
landed upon the shores of North America, proposed to the Mexican Government that the entire
foreign debt of the country should be taken over
by the Treasury of the United States,* upon the

---

* The United States Government was to pay 3 per cent. to
the bondholders ; Mexico was to pay 6 per cent. to the
United States ; a somewhat *leonine* contract.   Lord Lyons to
Earl Russell, Sept. 10th, 1861.   "Accounts and Papers," 1862,
lxiv., p. 56.

Juarez was accused by Marshal O'Donnell in a speech in
the Spanish Senate, Dec. 24th, 1862, of selling or desiring
to sell Mexican territory to the United States. -And the accusation has been repeated with some bitterness by the
Italian historian, Cesar Cantu.

O'Donnell was no doubt misinformed, possibly by Zuloaga,
who induced him at the same time to assert that Juarez was
"resolved upon the extinction of the white race in Mexico,"
and Juarez himself did not think it beneath his dignity to give
the story a categorical and official denial, which was
published in the *Diario Oficial* of Mexico, February 23rd, 1863.

Translation.]   February 22nd, 1863.
    To the Editor of the *Diario Oficial*.
My dear Sir,—I have just read in the *Monitor Republicano* of

pledge for the repayment within five years of the whole amount (say $72,000,000) of the provinces of Lower California and Sonora—a tract of country of some hundred and forty thousand square miles in extent.

It was not twelve years since President Pierce had acquired the Mexican Mesilla from the shameless Santa Anna, and now President Lincoln and his Secretary, Mr. Seward, would have com-

---

this date the speech of Marshal O'Donnell, President of the Spanish Cabinet, delivered in the discussion of the reply to the speech from the throne, and I have seen with surprise, amongst other inaccurate statements that he uses, in judging of the men and affairs of Mexico, the following remarkable words. " Juarez, as a Mexican, has, in my opinion, a stain which can never be effaced, that of having desired to sell two provinces of his country to the U. S. A ' This accusation, made by a high functionary of a nation, and on a solemn and serious occasion, in which a Statesman ought to be careful that his words shall carry the seal of truth, of justice, and of good faith, is an accusation of serious gravity, because it might be suspected that, by reason of his high position, he holds documents to prove his statements. Yet this is not true. Marshal O'Donnell is hereby authorised to publish the proofs which he may hold with regard to this matter. In the meanwhile my honour obliges me to state that Marshal O'Donnell has erred in the judgment he has formed of my official proceedings, and I authorize you, Mr. Editor, to deny the imputation which is so unjustly made against the chief magistrate of the State.

I am, Mr Editor,

Your obedient servant,

BENITO JUAREZ.

The whole question is fully discussed, with extracts from official documents, in a little work published in Mexico in 1885, under the title of "Juarez and Cesar Cantu," pp. 9-10 and 21, from which the above letter is taken as printed.

passed a further extension of their Southern frontier.

For, that Mexico should ever be able to repay the seventy-two millions of dollars, so temptingly offered by the honest broker, to say nothing of interest at six per cent., no one could for a moment suppose.

And the acquisition of Northern Mexico would have been something more to President Lincoln than the accession of so many hundreds of thousands of square miles of territory, or even the practical assertion of the Monroe doctrine as regards European intervention; it would have enclosed the seceding Southern States of the American Union between two fires, and prevented any support to the Confederate cause from a possibly sympathetic Mexico.

Yet, on the other hand, the discharge of the entire National debt ; a breathing time of five years to develop the resources of the country ; the infinite possibilities of a period of peace ; the removal of all possible excuse for European interference ; all these things were worthy of serious consideration in Mexico. Yet, after the fullest consideration, Juarez refused the offer. And a new proposal was made by Mr. Corwin, the Minister of the United States, who offered the Mexican Government a loan of nine or ten millions of dollars, repayable on easy terms, but always on condition of the mortgage of some portion of the Northern Provinces.

But in the meanwhile, assistance was found in an entirely unexpected quarter. Sir Charles Wyke, who had only technically suspended, and had not broken off, diplomatic relations, had turned over a new leaf in Mexico.

His attitude on his arrival had been somewhat unsympathetic. His despatches had been somewhat highly coloured ; and he himself had without doubt played unconsciously into the hands of the French. There was, unfortunately, nothing new in the position.

Left more to himself on the departure of M. de Saligny, and realising every day more fully the immensity of the task which lay before the Government, and the honesty of purpose of Juarez and most of his Cabinet, the English Envoy had invited Don Manuel Zamacona, the Mexican Minister of Foreign Affairs, to consult with him extra officially at the British Legation, if haply some arrangement could be suggested which should be satisfactory at once to England and to Mexico.

Authorised by Juarez, Zamacona gladly accepted the friendly hand that was stretched out to him by the Englishman.

And day after day, hour after hour, with infinite patience on either side, the negotiations were carried on.

That Don Manuel acted with perfect loyalty; that

Sir Charles acted with the greatest consideration, was admitted on either side. Neither zeal nor goodwill were wanting ; and, at length, on the 28th of October, 1861, the draft of a Convention was agreed to between the negotiators with regard to the English claims, which was pronounced by the English Envoy,* and subsequently by his chief in London, to be " highly satisfactory," and was certainly agreeable to the President of the Republic.†

And a promise was given by the Mexican to the English Minister that similar arrangements would be made for the settlement of the claims of the French and Spanish bondholders, which were of so

---

* Wyke to Lord Russell, October 28th ; Russell to Crampton, November 28th, 1861.

† Lord Russell's ultimatum of August 21st had been read by Señor Zamacona " with as much astonishment as alarm," and had compelled his immediate attention. The concluding words of this dispatch were indeed clear enough. " If these terms are not complied with you will leave Mexico with all the members of your mission." Thanks a good deal to the true patriotism and good sense of Señor Echeverria, who consented to accept the portfolio of Finance at the urgent instance of Sir Charles Wyke, the Convention was actually arranged.

The eleven articles are printed in "Accounts and Papers," etc., LXIV, 1861, pp. 129-134. The basis of the agreement had been the proposal made by the Government of the United States, that has been already referred to. And Sir Charles Wyke in his despatches bears witness to the constant loyalty of his colleague, Mr. Corwin, the Envoy from Washington.

much less importance than those of the English, and whose official representatives had withdrawn from Mexico.

Everything at length seemed to be settled. Señor Echeverria, a Mexican gentleman of independent fortune and of the highest honour, had been persuaded to accept the portfolio of Finance.

And the Convention, finally approved by the Mexican Cabinet, was actually signed on the 21st of November, 1861.

The English Minister had good cause for satisfaction. Foreign intervention was, of course, no longer to be expected. Mexico would have a fair chance of working her own way through peace to prosperity. The English claims had been fully admitted and fairly provided for. The interests of other nations had not been forgotten. The work of the Envoy was done, and well done.

On the 23rd of November, the Convention* recommended by the President was laid before the Chamber for their formal ratification.

---

* From this time forth Zamacona ceased to be a supporter of the domestic policy, or even of the future Presidential candidatures of Juarez. But Zamacona was never a rebel, and Juarez always treated his opposition as legitimate and entitled to all respect.

See Sosa: " Biografia de Benito Juarez," Mexico, 1884, pp. 25-27

The Chamber refused its assent. The whole fabric, so patiently and so hopefully reared, was destroyed in a single hour of folly.

Señor Zamacona resigned. Mr. Corwin withdrew the offer of his Government,* which had been the basis of the late negotiations, and the Senate of the United States subsequently confirmed his action.†

Sir Charles Wyke, deeply and naturally chagrined, demanded his passports, and prepared to withdraw from Mexico. Not one of them, as men of honour, could possibly have acted otherwise than they did. The Assembly, alarmed at the consequences of its rash and petulant action, saw fit to stultify itself still further, and now that it was too late, repealed the law of the 17th of July suspending all Government payments, and sought to cloak its folly by pompous and meaningless resolutions. But the time for resolutions, good or bad, was already past.‡

---

* The second offer of a small loan.

† Lord Lyons to Earl Russell, December 21, 1861.—"The Wyke-Zamacona Convention was, in the words of Mr. Seward, "a very proper treaty."

‡ The leader of the opposition to this Wyke-Zamacona Convention was Sebastian Lerdo de Tejada, younger brother of Miguel Lerdo de Tejada, who had died almost immediately after the return of Juarez to Mexico, in January, 1861, when he was actually a candidate for the Presidency. This Sebastian, after his victory in the Chambers, was called upon by the President, according to strict Constitutional principles,

On the 23rd of November, 1861, the Chamber repudiated Señor Zamacona's Convention. On the 5th of December the Spanish squadron set sail from the Havannah, and dropped their anchors three days later in the harbour of Vera Cruz.

Spain at this time was in a state of absolute peace with Mexico. No declaration of war had been, or was to be, made. No demand for redress or satisfaction was promulgated even by Admiral Rubalcaba. But, as he came within striking distance of San Juan de Ulloa, he cleared his ships for action, and called upon the fortress to surrender.

*The Mexicans, in pursuance of orders from

---

to form a Ministry in the place of that which had resigned in consequence of the hostile vote which he had obtained. But he refused. Yet he afterwards became the most faithful of Ministers. He left Mexico with Juarez on the arrival of the French, in April, 1863, was appointed Minister of Foreign Affairs in September, 1863, and shared all the peregrinations of the President from that day until his final return to Mexico after the execution of Maximilian on the 15th of July, 1867.

He was at all times a more bitter politician than his great chief, and is said to have used his influence against the grant of a pardon to Maximilian, which is at least highly probable.

He became President *ad interim* on the death of Juarez in July, 1872, and was elected President in the month of November following.

* The troops, consisting of 6,500 men, with 300 horses, were landed on the morning of the 15th. The fortress of San Juan de Ulloa, as well as the citadel of Vera Cruz, had been hastily dismantled, and the Spaniards took possession without striking a blow.

headquarters, whether wise or foolish, abandoned the castle, as well as the town, at the first summons. And Vera Cruz, evacuated not only by the soldiers, but by the citizens, was promptly occupied by six thousand Spanish soldiers.*

Meanwhile, on the 30th of November, 1861, the Envoys of the European Powers, greatly urged by the English Cabinet, had formally requested the Government of the United States to join them in their expedition against Mexico; and Mr. Seward on behalf of his Government (December, 1861) had categorically declined to do so.

---

* On the 13th of December, 1861, Sir Charles Wyke had demanded his passports and retired, regretfully, to Vera Cruz, on his way to meet his new colleague at Jamaica. On his arrival at the sea coast he found, to his great surprise, that the Spaniards were in actual occupation of the city, and he decided to await further instructions from his Government before quitting Mexico.

M. de Saligny had already begun to busy himself in preparing for the reception of the new Emperor, and took occasion to offer to the Mexican General Uraga, named by President Juarez to the command of the defending army of the east, a French title and military rank, if he would betray his charge, lead his troops against the existing Government, depose Juarez, and open friendly negotiations with France.

Uraga refused; and the French Minister afterwards denied that the interview had ever taken place; a denial which was at once necessary, diplomatic—and incredible.

On the 18th of December, 1861, Juarez issued a proclamation, or protest, expressed in dignified and temperate language. No molestation was offered to the Spaniards on the sea coast, but the utmost diligence was exercised in the fortification of the mountain passes of Chiquihuite, lying between Vera Cruz and Orizaba, on the road to Mexico. " Accounts and Papers," 1862, *ubi supra*, p. 152.

But, at the same time, the offer of an immediate loan of money which had been made to Mexico by the United States Government in October, 1861, and had formed the basis of the Wyke-Zamacona Convention of November 21st, 1861, was definitively withdrawn by the Senate.*

To consider what might have happened if the Mexican Chamber had not thrown over Juarez and his Foreign Minister in the matter of the Convention would be a vain and thankless task.

Would France have been baffled ? Would Spain have been satisfied ? Would England have been friendly ? Would America have been firm ? We cannot tell. Mexico, in any case, had thrown away her last chance. And the man who had the greatest cause for disappointment and chagrin, uttered no murmur of complaint, spoke no word of reproach, sought no abatement of responsibility.

On the contrary, seeing clearly that the time had come when Mexico might be called upon once more to face the foreigner in the field, Juarez, the man of peace and the man of law, set himself to organise

---

* "Accounts and Papers," 1862. pp. 116 and 143. The amount proposed had been $1,000,000, to relieve the more pressing necessities of the Government of President Juarez, without any stipulation as to the mode of disposal. The offer was now definitively withdrawn. It had been provisionally withdrawn by Mr. Corwin as before stated. See Lord Lyons to Lord Russell, February 3rd. 1862. "Accounts and Papers," *ubi supra*.

an army to defend his country, and to fortify the mountain passes of Chiquihuite, between Vera Cruz and Orizaba, on the road from the sea coast to the capital.

Yet his hopes lay rather in negotiation.

Sir Charles Wyke, once loudest among his denouncers, was now a trusted friend. The Chamber, abashed at the immediate consequences of its rash folly, was only too glad to allow him a free hand.

If he prepared for war, it was that his mind was most earnestly set upon the preservation of an honourable peace.

The occupation of Vera Cruz by the Spanish forces was speedily followed by the arrival of the French and English fleets. With the former came an army of some 4,500 men. The English did not send a single soldier, but a small force of 700 Marines was disembarked at the same time as the French troops, at Vera Cruz. The French Commissioner was, of course, M. de Saligny. The French Commander-in-Chief was Admiral Jurien de la Gravière. Spain was represented by the Prince de Reuss, better known to foreign readers as General Prim. And the interest of England was entrusted to Sir Charles Wyke, as Envoy Extraordinary, and Captain, now Commodore, Dunlop, who was in command of the ships and Marines.

CHAPTER VIII.

INTERVENTION.—JANUARY, 1862—APRIL, 1862.

Within two days * after the arrival of the Allied Commissioners, a pompous proclamation was issued by their instructions, setting out that their presence must be considered by the Mexicans not as in any way suggestive of war, but of peace; that they sought nothing but the honour and prosperity of Mexico; and that they had come partly to civilise their good friends the Mexicans, and partly to protect them against their enemies and aggressors.

Why they should have embarrassed themselves with powder and ball, on so peaceful and loving a mission, it was somewhat hard to understand; yet it very soon became apparent that the objects of the Allies were widely different in character, and that while the English and Spanish Commissioners would be contented with any reasonable settlement and

---

* January 9th, 1862.

guarantees as regards the vexed question of the debt, the occupation of Mexico and the over-throw of the existing Government were the least that would satisfy the French.*

At the very first meeting of the Allied Commissioners, M. de Saligny proposed to his colleagues the dispatch of an *ultimatum* of the most extravagant character, demanding :

1.—A payment of $12,000,000 on account of French claims *in general*.

2.—The assessment and payment of a further sum on account of other *special* claims.

3.—Payment of *all* claims under the Convention of 1853.

4.—The payment, *plena, leal y inmediata* of the nominal amount of the Jecker Bonds! $15,000,000.

5, 6, 7.—The payment of various indemnities, for various alleged injuries to French subjects.

8.—A payment of 6 per cent on all the foregoing.

9.—A French occupation of the most effective character, until the final payment of all present and future claims.

---

* M. de Saligny said to Mr. Louet, on his arrival with the French contingent : " My only merit is to have guessed the intention of the Emperor to intervene in Mexico, and to have rendered his intervention necessary." Gaulot, Rève., p. 29.

The terms of this remarkable note were no more acceptable to the Commissioners of England and Spain, than they would have been to Juarez himself. And M. de Saligny was persuaded, with the utmost difficulty, to agree to the dispatch (January 14th) in place of this *ultimatum*,* of a preliminary note of a temperate character, speaking, in vague language, of the necessity of a settlement of claims, and of the excellent intentions of the allies.

Day by day the Commissioners sat at Vera Cruz, and day by day their differences became more accentuated, as they awaited the return of the messenger who had carried their first summons up to the city of Mexico.

The treatment by the Mexican Government of this modified Collective Note was indeed a matter of supreme gravity and importance. The Chamber was fortunately not sitting. The decision rested absolutely in the hands of the President. And his answer was in the highest degree judicious and dignified. It set out (1.) that inasmuch as his Government was not only legally constituted, but was recognised and effective throughout the whole of Mexico, the " civilising mission " of the Allies,

---

* History certainly repeats itself. On the day that I was revising the MS. of this chapter, I read in the *Times* (July 23rd, 1893.) the French ultimatum to the Siamese Government. But Siam is not Mexico, and King Chulalongkorn is very far from being another Juarez.

however benevolent, was quite superfluous; (2.) that his Government was desirous of treating with the Allied Powers for the settlement of all debts and claims; (3.) that for the purpose of such a conference, the allied Commissioners, with a *guard of honour* of two thousand men, would be immediately received by the Mexican Authorities at Orizaba; and (4.) that under these circumstances it was hoped that the remainder of the *friendly troops*, whose presence in Mexico was now obviously superfluous, and calculated to irritate the Mexican people, would re-embark on board their ships at Vera Cruz.

By way of doing greater honour to the messengers who were entrusted with the delivery of this all-important note, Señor Zamacona, the ex-Minister and a *persona grata* to the English Commissioner, was instructed to accompany the party, which reached Vera Cruz on their return journey on the morning of the 29th day of January.

Strange things had happened since their departure, barely a fortnight before.

Miramon,* travelling under a false name and with a false passport, had arrived with a choice band of

---

* Miramon was in Paris in March 1861, admitted to audience at the Tuileries, and consulted confidentially by the duc de Morny. In November he was in Madrid, similarly honoured. In December we hear of him in New York. On the 27th he sailed for the Havannah. On the 13th of January 1861, he obtained a passport under a false name, and sailed in the s.s. *Avon* for Vera Cruz.

conspirators on the 27th of January in the English mail steamer—the friend, or the catspaw of de Saligny—with the avowed object of overthrowing the Government of Juarez.

Commodore Dunlop. commanding the British squadron, regardless of the protests of the French Commissioner, sent off a party of Marines, and arrested Miramon immediately on the arrival of the packet, on the charge of robbing the British Legation, and sent him back in a man-of-war to the Havannah.

It was obviously contrary at once to the letter and the spirit of the Convention of Alliance, and it would have been a scandalous abuse of their powers and presence at Vera Cruz, if an avowed conspirator against the *de facto* President of Mexico, with whom the allies were actually treating, were allowed to land in the country, and shelter himself under the guns of the allies, while he sought to compass the overthrow of a friendly Government.

Yet Miramon, as we shall soon see, was but the harbinger of a more august Pretender.

If the French Commissioners were angry at the arrest and deportation of Miramon on the 27th of January, they were made furious by the Note of Juarez on the 29th ; and Admiral Jurien proposed to his colleagues that Señor Zamacona should not even be received by the Commissioners, and that no answer should be vouchsafed to the President's letter.   More diplomatic counsels, however, were suffered to prevail, and a reply was ultimately agreed to, conveying, with formal expressions of friendship, and renewed asseverations of the civilising mission *(mision civilizadora)* of the Allies, the strange request that the foreign troops might be permited to shift their quarters, on purely hygienic grounds, to the high and healthy plateaux of the interior.

The answer to be returned by the Mexican President was obviously a matter of the utmost moment.   And Juarez decided boldly to adopt a policy which, if not, perhaps, justified in the result, was certainly at once honest, statesmanlike and prudent.

The Mexican Army was unprepared for war. The defences of the Chiquihuite might be carried by a *coup de main*.   In any case it was of the last importance that the foreign alliance should not be cemented by concerted and probably successful action against his forces in the field.*   He could scarcely hope to withstand the arms of three great European Powers as long as they stood shoulder to

---

* Prim had married a niece of the worthy Echeverria, who retained his portfolio of Minister of Finance in the Cabinet of Juarez even after the crisis of November 23rd, 1861.

shoulder. The breaking up of their alliance was the great object of his solicitude.

Of the good will of General Prim, of the loyalty of Sir Charles Wyke, he had no doubt. De Saligny he justly suspected of bad faith. But there was no reason for doubting the honour of the French Admiral. To treat the invaders as friends, as long as they maintained their professions of friendship, was not only good policy, but it accorded with the generous and straightforward nature of the Indian statesman.

He would offer them the best quarters that the country afforded. He would take no advantage of the difficulties created by their own action in landing their soldiers on his shores.

To guests, self-invited no doubt, it pleased him to play the part of the chivalrous host. Enemies, if enemies they should be, would find in him an equally chivalrous foe. Traitors at least he did not expect. And his reply* to the Allied Note was prompt and straightf .rward.

Regretting the vagueness with which the En-voys had explained or referred to the objects of their visit, while he accepted their renewed

---

* Written by the hand of Doblado on February 6th. Doblado was suspected of treachery. But Juarez, against the advice of his friends, did not hesitate to employ him in the work for which he was pre-eminently fitted to assist him. And his boldness was justified in the result.—Baz: Vida, 225-6.

assurances of peaceful and friendly intentions,* he suggested an immediate meeting of two chosen delegates, with the object of interchanging views by word of mouth, and if possible of concluding at least a preliminary agreement or Convention, in which case he would gladly consent to the cantonment of the friendly troops in the healthiest district in the Republic, awaiting a more extended and more formal conference.

The reasonableness of this proposal would have insured its immediate rejection by the French Commissioner, but that his Spanish and English colleagues insisted that an interview should take place as suggested; and General Prim was

---

* Sir Charles Wyke, says M. Niox, *op. cit.* p. 15, avait entamé des négotiations dans le but de ménager á l'Angleterre les avantages d'un protectorat formel, á la condition qu'elle prêterait son appui à Doblado, pour renverser Juarez.

And M. Niox actually has the effrontery to cite the despatches—Wyke to Russell, 23rd of February, 1862, Russell to Wyke, 1st of April, 1862, in support of this monstrous proposition.

The words used by Sir Charles Wyke are as follows ("Accounts and Papers," p. 67, February 23rd, 1862): "A Government representing the two principles that they, *i.e.*, Juarez and Doblado, now personify, affords the best reflection of public opinion to be found in this important country."

And nothing is more clear from this language, and from the context also, than that the British Minister, far from being guilty of the incredible baseness of seeking to overthrow *(renverser)* Juarez, was actually doing his best to promote union beween Juarez and Doblado, who, as a matter of fact, whether *propter hoc* or merely *post hoc*, remained true to his chief to the day of his death.

accordingly commissioned to meet the Mexican Envoy at the appointed place.

The honest and skilful statesmanship of President Juarez might claim its first victory over the trained diplomatists of Europe.

Upon the 19th of February, accordingly, General Doblado met the Prince of Reuss at Soledad, and received with satisfaction his assurances that the Allies had no desire to interfere directly or indirectly in the internal affairs of Mexico, least of all to impose any new Government, or form of Government, upon the country.

Upon these conditions and guarantees, the Foreign Minister, on behalf of President Juarez, invited the Allies to canton their troops in the healthy upland districts of the interior, awaiting the confirmation by their respective Governments of the Convention which was then and there drawn up, agreed to, and subsequently signed by all the Foreign Commissioners, and known as the Convention of Soledad.*

---

* "Seul l'avocat indien n'avait pas été parjure! Il avait pris la haute magistrature d'une république en convulsion, ruinée par la guerre civile. Chef d'un pays démoralisé, traversé par toutes les mauvaises passions qui cherchaient à le déborder, il aurait pu mieux faire peut-être, mais il aurait pu aussi faire plus mal. Sur lui est retombé de tout son poids le malheur d'un demi-siècle de fanatisme et d'anarchie! Il a eu le courage de porter le fardeau sans faiblir. Pour lui du moins, le mot de patrie a eu un sens."—"L' Empereur Maximilien," E. de Kératry. p. 6.

By the first article of this celebrated Treaty the legitimate status and authority of Juarez as President of Mexico was recognised and confirmed; by the last the Mexican flag was to be flown once more on the citadel of Vera Cruz, by the side of those of England, of France, and of Spain.

The diplomatic victory of Juarez was well nigh complete. But as far as the allies were concerned the President's permission was not granted a day too soon.

The deadly climate of the coast had already prostrated a large number of the foreign soldiers. Many had actually fallen victims to yellow fever and dysentery; many more were in hospital; nearly one-third of the entire force was *hors de combat*. Hostile operations would have been difficult with such an army, compelled, as a preliminary operation, to carry the fortifications of the mountain passes, and to escalade the heights of Chiquihuite.

Prolonged inaction at Vera Cruz would certainly have led to the loss of a great part of the army from disease. A repulse in the pass would have been at least equally disastrous.

Viewed in the light of subsequent events, it would no doubt have been more prudent on the part of Juarez, if not actually to declare war, at least to temporise. But bad faith was foreign to his nature and to his dealings ; and he looked to find at least common honesty on the part of the civilising nations who had come to regenerate his country.*

That the Convention of Soledad meant peace, both present and future, was the unhesitating opinion not only of the President, but of almost every man in Mexico ; yet, to provide for all contingencies, it was laid down in the fourth article : " That it may not be in the remotest degree believed that the Allies have signed these preliminaries in order to obtain the passage of the fortified places garrisoned by the Mexican army, it is stipulated that in the unhappy event of the negotiations being broken off, the forces of the Allies will retire from Cordova, Orizaba, and Tehuacan, and place themselves in the line that is beyond the fortifications."

It would have been difficult to have been more precise. Neither Mexicans, nor English, nor Spaniards, indeed, supposed for a moment that the

---

* Juarez, writing to an intimate friend, February 23rd, 1862, treats this celebrated agreement as definitive : "Como verá V. se salvan la independencia y soberania de la nacion asi como nuestras actuales instituciones, y por eso no he vacilado en aprobarlos. Creo que es lo mejor que podriamos conseguir atendidas nuestras actuales circunstancias.

"La reaccion queda definitamente desahuciada, pues ya no habrá intervencion en nuestra politica, que era su esperanza de vida.

"Me apresuro á comunicar à V. por extraordinario este suceso. . . . ."

Convention would not be ratified by their respective Governments. M. de Saligny may possibly have suspected the reception that would be accorded to it in Paris. In any case, President Juarez did not hesitate to confirm it in Mexico. And his formal Ratification was received by the Allied Commissioners at Vera Cruz on the 26th of February.

The French marched up country the same day, to take up their new positions at Orizaba, in the healthiest part of Mexico.

The Spaniards followed less promptly. Captain Dunlop, the English Commander, on his own authority withdrew his force of Marines from the country. As long as hostilities seemed probable or possible, this little contingent took its place beside the armies of Spain and France, on the deadly slopes of the *Tierras Calientes*.

But the Convention of Soledad, preliminary as a matter of course to an honourable settlement of all difficulties, left nothing for the British Marines to do in the Republic of Mexico. And they were promptly sent away to their own quarters at Bermuda.

It was not long before the French Envoys perceived the mistake that they had made; for whatever may have been the views of Admiral Jurien, M. de Saligny, at least, was well aware that they had been sent to Mexico not to make peace, but to make war, and if possible to draw their Allies into the conflict.

And now he had been compelled, at the risk of sacrificing a French army, to recognise the authority of the man whom he was seeking to depose, and to make a Convention with a Government which he was charged to overthrow. And his vexation was shown in a graceless attitude to his English and Spanish colleagues, and in his constant endeavours to aid the rebel Mexicans who were conspiring against the Government of the man whose diplomacy had been too good for him.

On the 1st of March, 1861, General Count de Lorencez, with reinforcements from France, disembarked at Vera Cruz,* and with him came Señor Almonte, an avowed conspirator against the existing Government of Mexico, the accredited agent of an aspirant Emperor, commissioned not only to promote Revolution, but actually authorised to bestow titles of honour in Mexico, in the name of Maximilian of Hapsburg.

---

* Captain Dunlop's explanations to his Government, and his justification of his conduct in arresting Miramon will be found in "Accounts and Papers, Mexico," 1862, lxiv., part III., 25-26, where we also read that had it not been for Señor Almonte's illness he would actually have received a passage to Mexico in a French man-of-war in company with General Lorencez.

Dunlop was said by Lord Russell to deserve the highest credit for his conduct.

F.O., June 5, 1862. Blue Book, *ubi supra*, Part III. 27.

And in spite of the dignified but vigorous remonstrance of the Mexican Government, followed by the urgent representations of the English Commissioners, Almonte was permitted to proceed to Orizaba, in the company and under the official protection of the French General in chief. At the same time Padre Miranda, "a man whose very name," in the words of an English diplomatist, "recalls some of the worst scenes of a civil war which has proved a disgrace to the civilisation of the present century," was welcomed by Admiral Jurien to his headquarters at Orizaba, where he lived and conspired under the shadow of the French flag.

The reception accorded to Almonte and his friends at length opened the eyes of the Allied Commissioners to the true nature of the French design upon Mexico ; and General Prim and Sir Charles Wyke, unable, after the fullest consideration, to see that non-intervention under the Treaty should be taken to signify a march upon the capital and the overthrow of the Constitutional Government, embarrassed the conspirators, French and Mexican, by obstinately treating a solemn undertaking not to set up any new form of sovereignty in Mexico as a reason for refraining from active co-operation with domestic outlaws and foreign intriguers in the overthrow of President Juarez.

This stupid subordination of the ideal to the real was, as may be supposed, most irritating to the French authorities at Vera Cruz, where Sir Charles Wyke cared nothing for M. Thouvenel in Paris, nor even for the feelings of his august sovereign, and where Commodore Dunlop,* in the happy absence of telegraphic communication with England, was entirely independent of Whitehall.

While the Councils of the Allies were thus divided,† Juarez judged that the time had at length arrived for protest on the part of the Mexican Government against their friendly harbouring of Mexican rebels ; and a Note, expressed in pretty plain language, was dispatched by Doblado to Vera Cruz.‡ The note was received by the Allied Com-

---

* Captain Dunlop commanded, with the title of Commodore, the British Fleet and Marines, in the absence of Vice-Admiral Sir A Milne, and acted as joint Commissioner with Sir Charles Wyke. Admiral Sir Thomas Maitland, in command of the British Pacific Squadron, had his headquarters at the same time at Acapulco.

† "La défense de nos nationaux, le désir de venger les outrages subis par eux, outrages dont il faut en justice accuser plutôt tout le Mexique que Juarez, tout cela n'était qu'un prétexte relégué d'avance au second plan de l'entreprise." "L'Empereur Maximilien," E. de Keratry, p. 10.

‡ The first serious step in the direction of dissolution was the independent action of Admiral Jurien de la Gravière, when he broke up his camp at Tehuacan, and ordered his troops to march, without consulting or even informing his Spanish and English colleagues. And while he afterwards expressed his formal regret, in answer to the indignant remonstrances of General Prim and Sir Charles Wyke, that Almonte and Miranda should have been permitted to accompany the French forces into the interior, he declined to withdraw his

missioners on the 7th of April, and considered by them at a special meeting on the 9th, when General Prim and Sir Charles Wyke contended that Almonte and Miranda should be requested at once to quit Mexico, and that every endeavour should be made to follow up the Convention of Soledad by a definite settlement of all financial differences in such a way as to hamper as little as possible the established Government of the country.

The French Commissioners refused to send away the conspirators; maintained that the best way to settle the debt was to march upon the capital; and reserved to themselves full liberty to interpret the language of the International Convention of Alliance in any way they chose.*

There was but one reply to such pretensions. The Spanish and English Commissioners declared that Joint Action was no longer possible, inasmuch as the French refused to be bound by the elemental conditions of Intervention; and they proceeded to withdraw their troops and ships of war from Mexico.†

protection from those gentlemen, who remained at the headquarters of the French army.

* A procès-verbal of the Conference, held at Orizaba on April 9th, 1862, is given in "Accounts and Papers," liv., 1862, p. 383 (114-127).

† "It is only just to say" (writes Señor Baz : " Vida de Juarez " p. 226), " that General Prim and his English colleague not only conducted themselves loyally in this matter, but they saved the honour of their Governments."

A Note conveying the intelligence of the dissolution of the alliance was received by General Doblado on the 12th of April, and on the same day his reply was dispatched to Vera Cruz to the effect that the Mexican Government was anxious to enter into a definite convention, at least with the English and Spanish Commissioners, whose "noble, loyal, generous, and considerate conduct is fully appreciated," as regards the settlement of all financial questions, and that the President solemnly protested against the action of the French as regards Almonte, Miranda, and other traitors and outlaws, and declared that their invasion would be resisted to the uttermost.

The Joint Intervention was at an end.*

The French flag alone flew on the fortress of Vera Cruz.

On the 12th of April, President Juarez issued a Proclamation to the Mexican people. The illegal and arbitrary conduct of the French, and their refusal to be bound by the fundamental conditions of the Triple Alliance, were calmly and dispassionately set forth ; the honourable conduct of the Spanish and English Commissioners was duly recognised ; and

---

* The English fleet was placed at the disposal of the Spanish Commander, for the conveyance of 1,500 Spanish troops, as he was not sufficiently supplied with transports, and the friendly powers retired without delay to the Havannah.

the Mexicans were urged to extend to every foreigner resident in their country—to the French as much as to any other stranger—the utmost protection and hospitality.*

But as regards the invaders there was but one word—War.†

Every Mexican between 20 and 60 years of age was called upon to take up arms for the defence of his country.

An admirable *Note* was dispatched to the French Commissioners, categorically protesting against their action.‡   The Chambers were summoned to meet within three days.   The Law and the Constitution were even in this supreme moment punctiliously regarded.

Meanwhile, the Convention of Soledad, accepted by President Juarez as signed by every one of the Joint Commissioners, was still binding upon all the parties to the agreement.

---

* "Una vez rotas las hostilidades, todos los extranjeros pacificos residentes en el pais quedarán bajo el amparo y proteccion de las leyes ; y el Gobierno excita à los Mejicanos à que dispensen à todos ellos y aun à los mismos franceses la hospitalidad y consideraciones, etc., etc."
This last sentence is eminently characteristic of Juarez, especially in that it was not a mere phrase, but a serious declaration of a policy which he fully and faithfully carried out.

† Le Gouvernement Constitutionnel soutiendra la guerre jusqu'á ce qu'il succombe.

‡ It is printed in Lefévre, pp. 230-233.

And it was not until the end of April that the replies of the European Cabinets were received at Vera Cruz.

*Sir Charles Wyke was informed by Lord Russell that " Her Majesty's Government entirely approved of the Convention of the 19th February ; " regretting only the use of the words " *regeneration of Mexico* " as suggesting even the possibility of an intention on the part of the Allies to " interfere in the internal affairs of " that country.

In Spain the Treaty was no less honourably accepted, and although a debate in the *Cortes* upon the conduct of the Government in so promptly accepting it was provoked by some of the extreme Clerical party, the action of Ministers was approved by a majority of 138 to 39.†

---

* Russell to Wyke, April 1st, 1862. "Accounts and Papers," 1862, No. 86. p., 1.

† In his article, or *Chronique Politique* in the *Revue Nationale*, of July 8th, 1862, M. Lanfrey compliments the Spaniards not only on their withdrawal from the alliance, but for the honesty with which they published the State Papers connected with the expedition ; papers which I regret I have not yet been able to see.

The entire object of the French, says M. Lanfrey, was a *simple recouvrement d'indemnité, un but si mesquin*, that Europe refused to believe in it, and credited the Imperial Cabinet with deep and magnificent schemes, which according to this acute *chroniqueur politique* existed only in their imaginations. M. Lanfrey, it must be remembered, was a bitter enemy of Napoleon III , but allowing for this, the entire article here referred to is well deserving of study It has been published among others written in 1860-65, by Charpentier, 1883, two vols., with a preface by L. de Ronchaud. Of this Edition, see vol. II. pp. 35-54.

In France the news had met with a very different reception. Not only had the Emperor refused to ratify the Convention; but Admiral Jurien de la Gravière was summarily withdrawn from Mexico, and the conduct of affairs committed to the more zealous and uncompromising hands of Monsieur Dubois de Saligny.

The mask was at length thrown aside; and in time it gradually became known that the people who had imposed upon themselves the duty, or friendly mission, of the civilising of the Mexicans, while refraining from interference, direct or indirect, with their domestic politics or institutions, intended to set up an Emperor of Mexico dependent upon the Emperor of the French; to conquer his empire for him by a French army; to overthrow the existing Constitutional Government of the country; * to restore the Bishops, with their friends Miramon, Marquez, and Padre Miranda; and possibly to accept a few hundred thousand square

---

* " En effet, la défense de nos nationaux n'a été jusqu'ici qu'un masque qu'il est temps d'écarter. L'archiduc va tout à l'heure paraître en scène. L'amiral a été désavoué parce que, agissant de bonne foi, il a failli ruiner un arrière projet dont il n'a pas reçu la confidence. La convention a été répudiée par la France, parce que celle-ci ne voulait pas, parce qu'elle ne pouvait plus traiter, liée qu'elle était vis-à-vis de Maximilien. Il ne s'agissait guère de nos réclamations financières pour le moment. La chute de Juarez était seule en jeu, et, pour renverser le fauteuil de président, il fallait que l'armée francaise pût entrer à Mexico les armes à la main."
—" L'Empereur Maximilien," E. de Kératry, 1867, p. 15.

miles of territory from the grateful Mexicans for the " restoration to the Latin race on the other side of the Atlantic of its ancient force and prestige."*

But one man stood between the Emperor Napoleon and the realisation of the great scheme, and that man was Benito Juarez. Ill-informed as was the third Napoleon, and mistaken as regards the conditions in Mexico, his great native shrewdness led him at least to grasp the cardinal fact in the situation, that the first object of the French policy must be the destruction of the incorruptible lawyer from Oaxaca.

And thus it came to pass that the Constitutional President and *de facto* ruler of the country was declared from the first a brigand and an outlaw, the one leader with whom the French authorities were categorically forbidden to treat.

The enormous weight of the Imperial authority in the year 1862 may now hardly be understood; and after a lapse of thirty years, a new generation hears of Europe hanging on the utterances of

---

* In January, 1862, Lord Russell was informed from Paris (1) That the French intended to send a reinforcement of 4,000 men to Mexico. (2) That the Archduke Ferdinand Maximilian would be invited by a large body of Mexicans to place himself on the throne of Mexico, and that the Mexican people would gladly hail such a change. "Accounts and Papers," pp. 146-148. Nothing, as yet, was said about French support or intervention.

Napoleon III. with the same conventional but un-realising belief as that with which it reads of Charles V. and the heroes of Pavia and the Gariglano trembling lest Europe should be over-run and subdued by the armies of the Ottoman Turk.* But before Lepanto, Solyman was the terror of Christendom ; before Sadowa, Napoleon was the arbiter of Europe ; and from Solferino to Sadowa one man alone was found to oppose the armies of the Colossus at the Tuileries—the bright-eyed lawyer of Oaxaca.

---

* Certainly after Mohacz (1526). Solyman the Magnificent died, as a matter of fact, in 1566, five years before Lepanto (1571), when the Turkish power was broken under his wretched successor, Selim.

CHAPTER IX.

War.—April., 1862—October, 1863.

One of the first acts of President Juarez, after the rupture of the alliance between the foreign invaders—with war and invasion hanging over his head—had been to authorise Doblado to negotiate a Convention with Sir Charles Wyke (April 28th, 1862), by which provision was made, admittedly abundant and even generous, for the discharge of the English claims.* The preliminaries were signed at Puebla, on the 28th of April, and the British Minister at once proceeded to the capital, where he arrived on the 11th of May, that he might

---

* The offer of a loan by the United States had been renewed to the extent of $11,000,000, and of this, $2,000,000 were immediately to be handed over to the British Commissioners, while all former provisions as regards the allocation of Customs duties to the payment of interest on the bonds were fully confirmed.

The convention was signed by Manuel Doblado, Hugh Dunlop, and Charles Lennox Wyke, at Puebla, August 28th, 1862.

pay a visit to the President.   Juarez, ever reasonable, consented to some further modifications in
the Convention of Puebla, which was then and
there ‚definitively signed by all the parties, and
transmitted to London for the ratification of her
Majesty's Government in England.*

This new act of recognition on the part of
England of the legality and efficiency of the
Government of Juarez—at a time when the French
army was actually supporting the *ad interim*
pretender, Almonte, self-styled and self-elected
President of the Empire—was another triumph
both for Doblado and for Juarez, and was bitterly
resented by the French and the other foreign
adventurers, both in Mexico and in Europe.†

---

* The Convention will be found in "Accounts and Papers,"
LXIV., 1862, part III., pp. 16-22 and 27-34.

† Lord Russell unfortunately was not able to shake himself
quite free from French influence, and he declined to ratify the
Convention of Puebla, as we are told, to the "very great
satisfaction of the Emperor."—"Accounts and Papers," *ubi
supra*, pp. 441 and 443.
It is only right to add that he gave two fairly sufficient
reasons for this refusal.   1. The non-ratification of the
United States Convention as to the loan upon which in was
founded (Seward: quoted by Lord Lyons to Lord Russell,
June 5th, 1862); and 2. The existence of a provision for
the payment of British claims, in that event, by the sale of
certain portions of Mexican territory, and the appropriation
of the proceeds to the satisfaction of the bondholders (Earl
Russell to Earl Cowley, June 19, 1862).
To judge his conduct with all possible fairness, it may be
said that he was not so much blameable for this refusal, as for
the poor and flaccid diplomacy which rendered it necessary.

In the meantime, the French Commanders and Diplomatists, without even waiting to learn if the Convention of Soledad had been ratified or repudiated in Paris, and while they were at least bound by the conditions of the document to which they had attached their signatures, took upon themselves to assume the offensive in Mexico, and to act regardless of treaties, conventions, and stipulations, in the development of their new plan of action.

If one clause in the Convention of Soledad had been, more than any other, clear and precise, it was that which provided that, in the event of a rupture, the French troops should retire from the quarters which they had been invited to occupy within the Mexican lines of defence, and should take up their old positions outside the fortifications.*

Yet, on the 18th of April, more than ten days before the Emperor's decision could have been received

He had been living for six months in a fool's paradise, supposing that he could alter, as well as disguise, the nature of things and of men by academic despatches. He had been deceived by France, he had puzzled England, he had pleased no man in Spain or Germany; and now he found himself suddenly called upon to open his eyes to what he might have seen six months before, and to choose between throwing over his Envoy or offending the French. That he contrived to do both, was only in accordance with the usual success of his diplomacy.

* See Domenech : *op. cit.* pp. 50-51, as to the great strength of the position at Chiquihuite.

from Paris, the French authorities took upon themselves to violate, in the most unblushing manner, this fundamental article of the recent Treaty, by refusing to evacuate Orizaba or Cordova, where they had been permitted to quarter themselves.   They even made a prisoner of Colonel Felix Diaz,* who peacefully presented himself to take over charge of the cantonments from the French Commander, [April 19th] and they attacked the small force of soldiers who lay awaiting his orders, about seven miles from Orizaba. Astonished at this unexpected action, the Mexicans retired, with the loss of five men killed and many wounded ; and this shameless opening of a shameful campaign is spoken of by more than one French writer as a brilliant feat of arms! †

The violation of the Convention of Soledad, by the very men that had signed it six weeks before, has called forth rather admiration than criticism in France.‡   Some feeble attempts, indeed, have been

---

* A brother of Porfirio Diaz, now President of Mexico.

† See Bibesco : " Retraite des cinq mille," Paris, 1872 ; an account by an eye witness of the operations before Puebla, and the subsequent retreat of Lorencez to Orizaba.   This Prince Georges Bibesco was the son of Prince Demetrini Bibesco, ex-Hospodar of Wallachia, the younger brother of the Hospodar Barbo Stirbey.   He was serving at this time, like so many other continental adventurers, in the French Imperial Army.

‡ "C'était donc le General Zaragoza et non le Général Lorencez," says the Abbé Domenech (Hist. III., 53) "qui manquait aux engagements de la Soledad." It is impossible for effrontery to go further than this.

made to defend it. General Lorencez was afraid of leaving his invalids in the hospital at Orizaba. General Lorencez did not consider himself bound by the signature of M. de Saligny, or of Admiral Jurien de la Gravière. Finally, and most truly, General Lorencez had too great a regard for the lives of his troops to abandon the admirable position in which he found himself. In a word, the Mexicans were savages—the French were a great and a noble people, whose mission of civilisation must not be hindered by ridiculous treaties.*

No faith in the days of Papal Supremacy was to be kept with those who questioned the authority of Rome. No faith in the days of Napoleonic aggressiveness need be kept with those who resisted the power of France.

On the 25th of April, the mail arrived from Paris, with the news of the repudiation of the Convention of Soledad, and with orders for Lorencez, promoted General of Division, to march at once upon Mexico.

Three days later, at Orizaba (April 28th), Almonte, the protégé of the French Army, proclaimed himself President, Supreme Ruler of the

---

* "Laissons l'Angleterre," says the Abbe Domenech in 1862 " le soin d'entraver notre mission réparatrice et féconde par sa politique égoiste anti-sociale et jalouse . . . placer le coton audessus des droits, *de la dignité des intérêts et de bien être de l'espéce humaine!* " L.' Empire au Mexique," 1862., p. 3.

Mexican nation, and Commander-in-Chief of the National Armies, and issued a magniloquent Proclamation calling upon his countrymen to welcome the " beneficial and civilizing influence of the illustrious Sovereign of France."*

Almonte had few followers, and no friends. But he asserted that Generals Zuloaga and Marquez, Mejia and Miramon, would probably flock to his protected banners; and that while the Mexican clergy were ready to bless, the Mexican people were ready to support, the French invaders.

Relying, it is possible, over much upon these magnificent assurances, and eager in any case for military glory which might justify the violation of the Convention of Soledad, General Lorencez lost not an hour in giving orders for that forward march, for which no doubt he had been already fully prepared; and by the evening of the 4th of

---

* The first expeditionary force, entrusted to Admiral Jurien de la Gravière, consisted of a regiment of Marines, a battery of Artillery, a battalion of Zouaves, and a squadron of Chasseurs d' Afrique, with some Engineers and miscellaneous troops; in all about three thousand men. The squadron numbered fourteen ships (steamers). Niox, chapter I. The brigade under the command of Lorencez consisted of 4,775 men ; and arrived at Vera Cruz the 8th of March, 1862 : and the total number of troops that marched under that General against Puebla, on April 27th, 1862, was 7,300. Niox, 133. From the arrival of the expedition, to the day that Bazaine assumed the chief command, 1st of October, 1863, Captain Niox calculates the naval forces at 20,312 sailors employed afloat, and 4,060 sailors and Marines engaged on shore. *Op. cit.*, p. 320.

May, the French Army, something over 5,000 strong, had arrived within striking distance of Puebla. The civil population had everywhere fled at the approach of the invaders. Zaragoza, the Mexican Commander-in-Chief, had so far made no resistance. Lorencez proposed to enter the city of Mexico early in the following week. Popocatepetl and Ixtaccihuatl were already in sight. The poet, who always accompanies such armies, was already preparing his hymn of triumph. A small fort—the fort of Guadalupe—which dominated the city of Puebla, was to be occupied the next morning.

At break of day the troops were under arms. But General Zaragoza was before them. And after a combat which reached its height soon after midday, and was prolonged until late in the afternoon, the French were handsomely beaten, with a loss of over five hundred men, leaving twenty five prisoners in the hands of the National troops (5th of May, 1862.)*

---

* These unsuccessful operations before Puebla are not regarded by the French as a defeat.

General Forey's proclamation, or general order to the troops, dated 28th of August 1862, commences in this characteristic fashion :

"SOLDATS !

"Un jour, vouz avez trop demandé à la Victoire, qui marche habituellement avec vos drapeaux, elle vous a fait une infidélité passagère qu'un ennemi dans sa presomptueuse forfanterie a exploité auprès des crédules et des ignorants, en

The news of this victory was received at the capital with the utmost joy. The well-deserved thanks of the President were conveyed to General Zaragoza and his able lieutenants, Negrete, Berriozabal, Lamadrid, and a young General who won his spurs on that glorious day, and who, as Porfirio Diaz, was destined to find undying honour among the great and good men of regenerate Mexico.

The Chambers resolved that all the officers and soldiers engaged in the battle had deserved well of their country. A subscription was opened to present Zaragoza with a sword of honour. The Government of Juarez was stronger than ever. But the Absolutist party made no sign;* Lorencez and his French army of civilisation, instead of continuing their march upon Mexico, thought it more prudent to retreat to the comfortable quarters at Orizaba, that had been placed at their disposal by the Mexican Government just three months before.†

---

pretendant qu'ils avaient vaincus les soldats de Magenta et de Solferino.

"*Non. Vous n'avez pas été vaincrus a Puebla ; et d'ailleurs* vous avez pris une noble revanche á Acalcingo."

This "*d'ailleurs*" is superb!

* If it be not an order by the Bishop of Puebla forbidding the administration of the last Sacraments to Mexican soldiers dying on the field of battle, inasmuch as they were under the ban of excommunication.

† On the 8th of May, the French troops turned their backs upon Puebla and the more distant capital, and never stopped

In his Proclamation of National Defence, the President had enjoined the greatest consideration to be shown to all peaceable French residents in Mexico. In his own action he went beyond this honourable advice.

The French prisoners that were taken at Puebla were sent back with safe conducts to their army at Orizaba ; their wounds cared for ; their medals and decorations restored to them ; and they themselves provided with money for their expenses by the way. It is not often thus that war is carried on, even by nations that pique themselves upon their chivalry and disinterestedness ! But Juarez was still spoken of in Europe as an Indian savage ; and the French, at the invitation and with the support of all the respectable inhabitants in Mexico, were supposed to be establishing a civilised and stable Government in his room.

Why they refrained so long from entering the capital where they were so ardently expected, no one in Europe seemed disposed to enquire.

The Emperor Napoleon, indeed, had with consummate skill contrived to make both the Spanish and the English Governments somewhat ashamed, not of their unhappy participation in his policy, but of

---

in their retreat until they had reached Orizaba, on the 19th of May, just one month after their violation of the Convention of Soledad.

their refusal to co-operate with him in its
development ; and thus Englishmen and Spaniards,
ignorant of the position in Mexico, and of the intentions of France as regards the country, were
chagrined, not at the folly of the exalted Statesmen by whom they had been betrayed into an
unholy alliance, but at the honourable and independent firmness of those humbler representatives
by whom that alliance had been dissolved. With
England and Spain thus muzzled, with Austria
flattered by the choice of Maximilian of Hapsburg,
and the Papal Benediction assured for a Catholic restoration; with the United States crippled and made
powerless by internal strife, the French had a free
hand in the New World. The star of the third
Napoleon, already exalted in Europe, was to rise
brighter and higher beyond the Western Atlantic.
And his first check was suffered to pass almost un-
noticed by Europe.*

The Mexican advocates of a Foreign Monarchy,
whose co-operation had been promised not only by

---

* A little book published by Dentu at the end of 1863, "La
France, le Mexique, et les Etats confedérés," is amusing reading if only for the curious unhappiness of its prophecies.

The Northern and the Southern States would *never* be
reconciled.

France would *never* quit Mexico ; but in alliance with the
Independent Republic of the Confederate States, would play a
great and enduring part in the New World ; "*et de notre
alliance avec le Sud sortira cetta grande rénovation sociale qu'a
poursuivie vainement l'Angleterre,*" p. 24.

Almonte,* but by Monsieur de Saligny, shewed no disposition to relieve the French at Orizaba. But they were by no means backward in reproaching the French Commander for his failure to proceed to Mexico. That brilliant General, Zuloaga, and his friend, General Cobos, had already fled to the Havannah, but Don Leonardo Marquez, who was left behind, was loud in his denunciation of the incompetence or apathy of the Count de Lorencez. Nor was M. de Saligny more sympathetic or less reticent in his officious condolences. Almonte and Miranda were almost actively hostile ; while the clergy of Guadalajara published a formal note or manifesto, dated and signed in the Sala Capitular de esta Iglesia Catedral (May 13th, 1862), protesting against the French occupation, and

---

* Almonte was a son of the patriot priest Morelos, and his name is said to have been acquired from the fact that his father, who had, according to the fashion borrowed from his opponents, named him Colonel at the age of ten, used on the eve of any exciting engagement to send him away *al monte* (to the hills) for safety. The origin of the man and of the name was thus almost equally irregular! But Almonte, like his father, was a person of some capacity, and though a rebel and an adventurer, must never be classed with such men as Marquez and Miramon.

On the 4th of June he had issued a proclamation from Orizaba, calling upon the Mexican nation to obey his behests (art. 1) ; and stating that any want of *affection* for his newly-established Government would be treated as a crime (art. 2).— See Lefevre, I., 247-250. He had proceeded to issue half a million of dollars in paper money, with a forced currency ; but on a contemptuous protest by Sir Charles Wyke, his French supporters had thrown over both Almonte and his bank-notes, and the issue came to nothing.

declaring for the Constitutional and Mexican Government of Juarez.

It was not all joy in the camp at Orizaba. To wards the end of May, General Douay arrived from France with a few hundred fresh troops ; but even this welcome assistance hardly sufficed to keep open the road between the French headquarters and Vera Cruz ; and had General Zaragoza been more vigorous or more fortunate, the French troops might have been driven out of Orizaba, if not out of Mexico, before the long-expected reinforcements had arrived. But if the national commanders were unskilful, the national troops were few and poorly equipped. Victorious armies are not created in a month by a Government without supplies, without material of war, and almost entirely without money.*

Yet, as month succeeded month, the Government of Juarez became more widely respected, his personal character more fully appreciated. And the General Count de Lorencez, virtually imprisoned at Orizaba, and favoured with the advice of de Saligny, of Almonte, and of Marquez,

---

* Juarez, indeed, showed himself almost the equal of Isabella the Catholic in raising and equipping new regiments. But Isabella was a great lady, and she commanded the support of the Church. Juarez was a despised Indian—excommunicate and anathema.

had abundant opportunity of taking a just view of the situation.

"1 am convinced," he wrote in the middle of June, " that we have no one in our favour. . . . . No one here desires a Monarchy, not even the reactionary party—the Mexicans would rather be absorbed by the Americans!" And again at the end of July: " There is not to be found in Mexico a single partizan of Monarchy; to reduce the people to submission a French occupation of many years will hardly suffice."

But the Emperor at the Tuileries was too blindly and too deeply committed to his extravagant policy in Mexico, to draw back after the first defeat. And on the 3rd of July, 1862, he wrote his celebrated letter* to General Forey, entrusted with the command of an army of thirty thousand men to restore the French fortunes beyond the Western Atlantic.†

---

* This letter is printed by many of the French and Mexican writers, and is too long for insertion here. It will be found in Domenech : Hist. III., pp. 91-93.

The letter certainly marks an epoch in the history of France as well as of Mexico.

† This notion of the aggrandisement of the Latin races is further developed by M. Michel Chevalier in his "Mexique Ancien et Moderne," 1863. pp. 492-505 ; where he maintains that the duty as well as the policy of France was to arrest the progress of Protestantism the world over.

This section of M. Chevalier's work is of much interest, as well as the last in his volume, entitled ".Comment nous

In the middle of September, General Forey arrived at Vera Cruz, and one of his first acts was to suppress the Government of Almonte, which had been constituted within range of the French cannon, in concert with the French diplomatists, by a simple advertisement in the local newspapers. To welcome Almonte in February was certainly not wise ; to insult him in September was scarcely wiser. But the insult was one more victory for Juarez in the President's Palace at Mexico. If Almonte was the chosen ruler of the Mexican people, then might the French intervention have found some shadow of justification. If Juarez was at once *de jure* and *de facto* Chief of the State, then the position of General Forey was that of a leader of buccaneers.

Early in September Zaragoza, the young Commander who had led his troops to victory at Puebla, fell a victim to the Autumn fever of the country ; and General Ortega was appointed Commander-in-Chief in his stead ; while Juarez, daily and hourly engaged in the raising and equipment of new forces, was at length able to put two

pourrons retrouver au Mexique la question Romaine, si nous tentons de le régénérér ! "

A pamphlet published in 1864 by Dentu, entitled " L'Empereur du Mexique," maintains that " L'Expédition du Mexique est la plus belle page," not only "du règne de Napoléon III," but, " de l'histoire contemporaire de l'Europe ! "

fresh armies in the field, under the command of his old friends and comrades, Comonfort and Doblado.

But even the raising of regiments to defend the fatherland did not interfere with the march of Constitutional Government.

The Autumn elections were held according to law in all districts not actually occupied by the foreigner ; and the new Chambers met at Mexico* on the 20th of October, three days before General Forey, in the first of a long series of magniloquent proclamations, published on his arrival at Cordova, announced his benevolent intention of " freeing Mexico from the demagogic tyranny of Benito Juarez, against whom, and not against the Mexican nation, he had come to make war." †

1863 opened sadly enough for all good men in Mexico.   Yet Forey, even with his enormous reinforcements, was compelled to restrict the sphere of his operations, if he would reach the promised goal ; and the French troops were withdrawn from

---

* The Presidential message : the reply of the House, under the able and patriotic Presidency of Señor Echeverria; and a special resolution of the Chambers, calling upon Juarez under no circumstance to dissociate himself from the nation which had elected him to defend as well as govern her ; will all be found translated into French in Montluc : Correspondance, pp. 139-155.

† Mexico, vol. V., p. 562.

Jalapa,* from Perote, and from the more important town of Tampico, which were all promptly occupied by the National troops.†

Four hundred black Soudanese, recruited for Napoleon by Ismail Pasha, for the more effectual civilisation of Mexico, were landed at Vera Cruz by the end of January, and Admiral Bouet treated the town of Acapulco to a three days bombardment, in consequence of the refusal of the Commandant to apologize for an article in a Peruvian newspaper *(El Chalaco)*, which he had not written, reflecting in some way upon the conduct of the French forces. On the 16th of January,

---

* Over 23,000 fresh troops had arrived from France.

In April—July about eight hundred arrived under various commanders :—

In April—July about eight hundred arrived under various commanders :—	800
In August — November, under Forey	22,320
	23,120
The troops under Lorencez had amounted to..	7,300
In all	30,420

See Niox, pp. 153-207.

† Writing to Montluc, his Consul-General in Paris, on the 22nd April, 1863, Juarez, entirely hopeful of the future, says :
" J'ai parfaitement compris que seule la force des armes ferait revenir l'Empereur sur ses pas, et lui ferait comprendre l' insanité de son entreprise, puisqu'il s'était obstiné à méconnaître la voix de la verité et de la raison. Aussi comprenant le péril imminent qui menacait la nationalité Mexicaine, le gouvernement prépara tous les moyens de défense dont il put disposer." Montluc : Correspondance, pp. 177-178.

Sir Charles Wyke demanded his passports, and retired with much regret from the capital.[*]

Meanwhile, Juarez was using every endeavour to strengthen the fortifications, not only of Mexico, but of Puebla. He passed a week [February 24th—March 4th, 1863,] at the latter city, cheering on the workers by words of counsel and encouragement; although Puebla, without ramparts or walls of circumvallation, remained to the last practically an open city surrounded by ditches and breast-works, protected chiefly by the neighbouring forts of Loreto and Guadalupe, and embarrassed with a miscellaneous throng of inhabitants, ill supplied with provisions, and defended by a garrison most insufficiently furnished with munitions of war. But slowly as the French advanced, General Forey at length felt strong enough to assume the offensive, and by the 29th of March—six months after his arrival in the country—he found himself at the head of some thirty thousand men, within striking distance of the city.

---

[*] In January, 1863, General Bazaine had laid hands upon one Floriano Bernardi, commanding an escort granted by the National Government to the Secretary of the United States Legislation and an American Consul ; and had ordered him to be shot. And in spite of diplomatic remonstrance the unfortunate officer was immediately put to death. " Mexico à traves de los siglos," V., p. 569.

This was neither very civilising nor very civilised, but it was only an earnest of far greater horrors to come.

An urgent request, conveyed by the Foreign Consuls, that the women and children should be permitted to leave the town, was promptly refused ; and on the 2nd of April the batteries of the invader opened fire upon the town of Puebla.

For two months the city held out.* But no relieving army appeared to raise the siege, and at length on the 17th of May, when the last cartridge had been burned and the last rations distributed, the guns were blown up, the small arms and military stores were destroyed, the National army was disbanded, and the invaders were informed that an undefended and famished city awaited their entry. The Mexican officers, who surrendered without further parley, were treated with the utmost military rigour, and were marched off, disarmed and on foot, under a strong escort, to the coast, for shipment to Europe. Porfirio Diaz, and one or two other officers of superior rank—one and all had refused to give their parole under the conditions on which it was tendered to them—

---

* On the 5th of May a truce for the exchange of prisoners disclosed the strange fact that the French prisoners in the hands of the Mexicans were more numerous, by some five and twenty fighting men, than the Mexicans who had fallen into the hands of the French ; and these unfortunate invaders were at once set free by Ortega, and sent back to General Forey without equivalent, or further bargaining as to exchange, in accordance with the policy dictated and ever maintained by Juarez himself.

made good their escape on the journey; but the remainder were promptly transported to France, where they were shown about the country as living tokens of the success of the French arms in Mexico.[*]

Puebla de los Angeles had been gallantly defended. But it was not to be supposed that the hastily-equipped levies and the inexperienced commanders of the National army should continue to hold their ground against the veterans of Magenta and Solferino, the picked troops and the chosen Generals of France.[†]

The city of Mexico was obviously untenable after the fall of Puebla. The President, careless of the effect upon his personal fortunes, refused to expose the capital to the horrors of siege and assault, and after due warning and every care for the safety of the peaceful inhabitants, he withdrew the seat of Government on the 31st of May, 1863, to San Luis Potosi.

On the 7th of June, General Bazaine, with the vanguard of the invading army, entered the city of

---

[*] As to the way in which they were treated in France see post pp. 248-9.

[†] According to Captain Niox, the actual number of officers taken prisoner at Puebla was 1,508, who had commanded 9,000 (or 11,000) common soldiers. Of these officers, 530 were actually shipped off to France.—Niox : p. 282.

The number of fighting men left in the city of Mexico after the fall of Puebla did not exceed 6,000.—Baz : Vida. p. 249.

Mexico, and three days later, General Forey, with Marquez and de Saligny, made a triumphal entry with the remainder of the French troops, accompanied by the Mexican partizans of the Absolutist and Clerical factions who found shelter under the flag of the invaders.

The French officers were quartered upon the citizens, and treated themselves with becoming liberality. General Forey, who lodged for three months in the Puente de Alvarado, ran up bills during that time to the extent of near fifty thousand dollars for his personal entertainment.* Marquez the assassin, Lopez the betrayer, and a friendly swindler of the name of Facio,† were all made Knight-Commanders of the Legion of Honour.

Proclamations now poured daily from the military printing press.

The entire property of those Mexicans who opposed the French intervention was formally sequestrated.‡

---

* The amounts are given in "Mexico à traves de los siglos," V., 589. One item, $4,200, is for flowers; another, $15,000, for looking-glasses. The entire amount is $48,427.

† "Qui passa en conseil de guerre pour détournements." Montluc, 211, and Domenech: Hist. III., 135 and 152-3.

‡ "Nous prenions," says the most indulgent of critics, M. Domenech (Hist. III., 96), "une allure de conquérants et non d'une armée expédiée pour aider les Mexicains a faire cesser l'anarchie et la guerre civile."

Courts-martial were established throughout the country, in which two French captains and one superior officer judged all questions—without appeal, and their sentence was carried out *dans les vingt quatre heures*.* The entire newspaper Press of Mexico was provisionally suspended until the appearance of an elaborate Decree, which permitted the editors to publish articles upon every subject, save only such as should have reference in any way (1) to the French occupation, or (2) to any officer in their army, (3) to Mexican politics, or (4) to any phase thereof, at home or abroad.

The ground having been thus carefully prepared, on the 16th of June, 1863, a National Assembly of thirty-five persons, chosen and named by the French General, was summoned to deliberate upon the affairs of the nation : while a triumvirate, consisting of Almonte, Salas, and Mgr. La Bastida, an ecclesiastical outlaw who had been created during his exile Archbishop of Mexico, was entrusted with

---

* Lefèvre, I., 320-326. As to the *flagellations et fusillades secrètes* to which the French boasted that they treated their Mexican opponents, see *L'Estafette*, a French newspaper published in Mexico, for August 4th, 1863, copied in Lefèvre, I., 336.

The Abbé Domenech no less pointedly says that the *Liberals* were treated in the same way as the *Thugs* in India, and that (195-196) " Les *Libéraux* sont les *Taugs* du Mexique ! " These were the people who had come *to deliver* the Mexicans from the cruelty of Juarez.

the executive power in the State, under the doubtful style of *The Regency*.

But all these gentlemen were soon made to feel that they were appointed merely to register the decrees of the French Commander-in-Chief.

The Archbishop, who in spite of military *Te Deums*, and even the French patronage of a solemn ceremony in the Cathedral on the Octave of Corpus Christi, was not at all satisfied with the disposal of ecclesiastical property, remonstrated, and was promptly dismissed.

The Mexican Press, both Trojan and Tyrian, was subjected to a strict and most effective censorship. The hard hand of the invader lay heavy upon the nation.*

On the 8th of July, 1863, a second Junta, selected with the utmost care by the French General, met to formulate a spontaneous national invitation to the Archduke Maximilian of Hapsburg, " or failing him, any other Catholic Prince indicated by the Emperor of the French," to come and reign over Mexico.†

---

* " Le moment était venu de déchirer le dernier voile. Sur l'invitation de M. de Saligny, aprés une entrevue á la légation. Almonte, Marquez, et le licenciado Aguilar posèrent du premier coup la candidature de l'Archiduc Maximilien sous le patronage des cléricaux."

† Article 4 of the Petition ran as follows : " En el caso que por circunstancias imposibles à prever el archiduque . . no llegase à tomar posesion del trono que se la ofrece la nacion

The invitation was somewhat more comprehensive than flattering, and was received with considerable disappointment at Miramar. But it was improved, or strengthened to order, before the close of the year.*

Meanwhile, on the 9th of June, Juarez and his Cabinet had arrived at San Luis Potosi; having been everywhere received by the population with the utmost respect and enthusiasm. Despatches had been sent to the Governors of the various Provinces, announcing the change of the seat of Government, and the most satisfactory assurances had been received from all those districts that were not actually occupied by the French. Constitutional Government was not yet dead in the Provinces of Mexico.

But in the city the intervention shewed itself supremely effective. The courts-martial, prompt and uncompromising, kept the population in excellent order.† French money was abundant. The troops were at least excellent customers. The Mexican Almonte proved to be an intelligent

Mexicana, se remite à la benevolencia de S. M. Napoleon III. Emperador de los Franceses, para que le indique otro principe catolico."

* " Maximilien ne pouvait prendre au sérieux l'offre d'une couronne par une commission qui tenait ses pouvoirs de M. M. Saligny et Forey."—Montluc: Correspondance, p. 217.

† Imprisonments: floggings: banishments: confiscations were of daily occurrence.

administrator, and was particularly successful in the department of finance.

In July, Miramon reappeared in the country, and after an interview with General Forey on the 29th of July, gave in his adhesion to the French cause. And his example was followed by many others.*

It needed, no doubt, considerable political honesty, or considerable political foresight, to maintain, almost at the point of the bayonet, and actually at the mercy of the confiscator, an allegiance to a fugitive President, and to a Government technically legitimate, but discredited, impoverished, and banished from the capital.

General Forey, indeed, was now absolute master not only of the city of Mexico but of the road to the coast at Vera Cruz ;† and the French fleet, whose arduous and thankless duties were at least

---

* Mejia had long before (April, 1862) pronounced himself a partizan of the intervention, or rather of Marquez.

Miramon is said, by his admiring biographer, M. Daran, to have been compelled by the French Marshal ; but it is doubtful whether Miramon was a personage whom any party would be very desirous of including in their ranks. Juarez, at all events, had given orders for his immediate arrest, whenever found, as an assassin and an outlaw.

† Vera Cruz, Tampico, and Acapulco being all in the hands of the Imperialists, Juarez derived his revenues chiefly from the customs duties levied at the port of Matamoros, which was not blockaded by the French fleet, as it served the Southern States for the export of their cotton ; all their own ports being blockaded by the Northern fleets.—Montluc : Correspondance, p. 176.

P

admirably performed, was able to carry out an effective blockade of the Mexican Sea frontier, which had been proclaimed by a French Decree of September 6th, 1863.

But on dry land little or nothing was done. Small parties of troops, indeed, harassed the country within a few miles of the city of Mexico, and the Free Companies that had been organized by the French under the name of *la Contra-guerilla*, murdered and plundered and burned throughout the whole of the temperate *plateaux* within reach of the French head-quarters.* Yet no forward movement was made in the direction of San Luis Potosi, where Juarez, the only enemy admitted by the French proclamation to exist in Mexico, was suffered to carry on the Government of the country without opposition.

----

* A little book published in Paris in 1868, "La Contre-Guérilla Francaise au Mexique," by Count de Kératry, is interesting chiefly in so far as it shows the way in which Mexico and the Mexicans were regarded by the French officers of even the highest class.

Their defence of their country against unprovoked invasion was treated as brigandage ; Mexican soldiers and officers were taken to be not only rebels, but highway robbers, to be shot down at all times, and in all places, without quarter or consideration.

The account that may be read on pp. 9 and 19 of a ball given by Bazaine, at Orizaba, is astounding in its naive hideousness.

A band of cut-throats was on the point of being organized, with French officers as leaders, to supplement the *legitimate*

And while the French fleet was harassed by their odious and inglorious duty on the coast, and the Contra-guerilla was harrying and exasperating the entire population in the mountains, the French regular army was content to rest on its slender laurels in the city of Mexico.

But this want of military vigour, or, possibly, this just appreciation of the political situation, on the part of the French Commander-in-Chief, was

---

warfare of Bazaine and Forey, by operations of frankly organized savagery.

"Le Colonel Du Pin demanda au Général ses instructions. On lui donnait pleins pouvoirs, il n'avait qu' à poursuivre à outrance les bandits et à purger le pays. Le bal continuait cependant ; au son des notes languissantes de la havanaise, les couples se croisaient sans cesse; parmi les belles Mexicaines qui s'abandonnaient à l'enivrement de la valse plusieurs eussent pâli si l'ordre tombé des lèvres du général en chef avait frappé leurs oreilles. Une contre-guérilla francaise venait en effet d'être décrétée, et peut-être y avait-il ce soir-là, dans les salons du ministre de France quelques chefs de guérillas travestis en galants cavaliers, dont les têtes souriantes en cette nuit de fête, devaient plus tard grimacer au bout d'une branche. "De Kératry," *op. cit.*, pp. 10-11.

"Cette bande d'aventuriers," says their admirer, "ignorait la discipline; officiers et soldats se grisaient sous la même tente : les coups de revolver sonnaient souvent le Réveil."

These were the troops—*fièrement deguenillés*, Francais, Grecs, Espagnols, Mexicains, Americains du Nord et du Sud, Anglais, Piémontais, Napolitains, Hollandais et Suisses, the runaways of every nation, slavers, beach combers, and filibusters—that were destined by France to regenerate the institutions of Mexico. (p. 13).

And this is how they are described by an enthusiastic French officer, writing to glorify this special phase in the intervention of his countrymen.

And his book of 332 pages is full of similar testimonials to the character of these French contre-guérilleros.

not appreciated in Paris. In twelve months
General Forey had marched no further than from
Vera Cruz to Mexico, after a detention of seventy-
two days before a feebly-fortified town ; and
in spite of his magniloquent proclamations, he
did not seem inclined to march any further.
Gratified accordingly, and justified *de par
le monde* with the title of Marshal, Forey was
recalled to France, and M. Dubois de Saligny
was instructed to accompany him. Bazaine was
appointed Commander-in-Chief of the French
expeditionary army.*

But public opinion in France had become somewhat hostile to an apparently fruitless intervention ;
and Bazaine was instructed to negotiate with any
Government that he could find in Mexico, except
that of Juarez.†

Yet, so far, it was the enemies of Juarez, rather
than Juarez himself, that had suffered in the
political strife in Mexico.‡

---

* Juarez remained *de facto* ruler of a great part of Mexico.

† Maximilian was disinclined to assume the purple at the
request of the Tuileries, and was chagrined at the hollowness
of the Mexican invitation.

The Imperial policy, in consequence, had undergone considerable modifications. Reference was even made to the
declaration of October 30th, 1861, as to the duty of non-
intervention !

‡ Marshal Forey handed over charge to Bazaine on
October 1st, and embarked on October 21st for France at
Vera Cruz.

The English and the Spanish, who had come to chastise him, had retired empty-handed, expressing their satisfaction at the honesty and rectitude of his policy.

The French, who had come to civilise him, complained that they had been deceived by the Mexican rebels, and had made little progress in the country.*

The Mexicans who had conspired to overthrow him, declared that they had been betrayed by the French.†

Saligny, who had neglected to leave Mexico with Marshal Forey, was ordered by a despatch of 28th, to quit Mexico, even if he should have already resigned his diplomatic functions, without another hour's delay, and without awaiting the arrival of his successor, M. de Montholon. M. de Saligny was said to be negotiating a rich marriage with a daughter of one of the clerical leaders, Señor Luz Ortiz. Montluc, p. 211.

The Emperor had apparently at length realised the true character of M. de Saligny's services.

* At the end of September, Bazaine had taken over charge of what was called the Regency. But he showed himself no more favourable to the pretensions of the clergy than his predecessor, and Archbishop La Bastida was removed from the Imperial Palace without much ceremony.

Yet no man knew precisely what to expect.

† A little book, published anonymously in Paris in 1864, by Dentu, "La question Mexicaine et la civilisation française," suggested a French *colonisation* of Mexico as the most satis-factory sequel to the *fait accompli* of the occupation (p. 28) —an occupation destined to give "de nouvelles splendeurs á notre politique, de nouvelles places de sûreté à nos flottes, de nouveaux débouchés á notre commerce." (p. 40).

"L'intérêt," says the author, sententiously, in another place, (p. 32), "est la conscience des nations!" This is at least *frank*.

As for individual enemies, Miramon and Miranda, Mr. Commissioner de Saligny, ex-President Zuloaga, Admiral Jurien, General Lorencez, Marshal Forey—all these worthies had come to Mexico with the object of overthrowing Juarez. They had called to their assistance an army of near forty thousand men. And now, after nearly two years fighting and proclaiming, they had all retired discomfited.

And Juarez was still President of Mexico.*

* On the 3rd of October, 1863, Maximilian provisionally accepted the Crown of Mexico. But he considered himself Emperor not only from that date, but from some earlier and Imperially indefinite period.

CHAPTER X.

MAXIMILIAN OF HAPSBURG.

On the night of the 18th of January, 1861, seven days after Juarez had returned victorious to the city of Mexico, an Indian runner made his way into the capital from the little neighbouring town of Tlalpam. He was the bearer of a secret missive from Marquez to the licentiate Aguilar—an old friend of Dictator Santa Anna—announcing to him that the hour had come for " organising reaction, political, social, and military ; " and offering him the post of President of the new Republic, of which Marquez was already appointed Commander-in-Chief with the motto or war-cry of *Dios y Orden* !

And, although neither Marquez nor his motto inspired the wily licentiate with entire confidence, he judged it expedient to accept, at least provisionally, the post. At the same time, the foreign correspondents of these self-appointed dignitaries, Señores Gutierrez de Estrada, Hidalgo, Almonte, and ex-President Miramon were busy on their own account in Paris, where they succeeded in exciting the active interest of the Empress, and afterwards of the Emperor of the French, in the cause of revolution in Mexico.

La Bastida, the intriguer of Yucatan, who, on the death of the exiled Ballesteros, had been made Archbishop of Mexico, was no less successful at Rome, and a plan was gradually matured between the Tuileries and the Vatican for the overthrow of Republican Government in Mexico, and the establishment of a pious prince of the great Catholic family of Hapsburg upon the throne of Montezuma.*

Warily, secretly, steadily, the project was matured. The Cabinet of Madrid, flattered by the French advances, was not unwilling to chastise their rebellious colonists. The British Foreign Minister, pedantic and ill-informed, was content to lay down the most unexceptionable principles as regards non-intervention, even while he was being cajoled by the more astute

---

* Certains prétendent que l'empire mexicain est sorti de la paix de Villafranca. Sans attacher grande importance à cette assertion, il est hors de doute qu à l'heure où Marquez organisait un soulèvement, le parti des émigrés mexicains, avec l'appui secret du gouvernement français dans le sein duquel prévalaient des sympathies espagnoles, offrait la couronne impériale à l'archiduc Maximilien, qui venait de renoncer à toutes charges dans son propre pays, pour se retirer à Miramar et se tenir prêt a toute éventualité.

diplomatists at the Tuileries into a joint invasion cf Mexico. And nothing but the independent vigour of the British Envoys, and the simple and straightforward dealing of President Juarez, had saved England from blind participation in a great crime.

For three hundred years the ineptitude of Right Honourable Administrators in London has been redeemed by individual Englishmen beyond the sea ; not merely by the Wellingtons, and the Clives, and the Dalhousies, but by thousands of unconsidered and forgotten worthies who have taken upon themselves the somewhat dangerous responsibility of upholding the honour of England abroad.

But if in January, 1862, the Joint Commissioners of the Allied Powers had been masters of the situation at Vera Cruz ; from the Autumn of 1863 to the Spring of 1864, Bazaine was the master of Mexico.* And the best that can be said for his Government was that it was effective. Taxes were paid. Private robbery was suppressed. French and even English money flowed into the country. Foreigners, if not always of the most desirable class, were encouraged to settle in the cities of the

---

* That is to say, of the *Capital*. It is unfortunate that there is only one word for the country and the city of Mexico in English, and more strangely still in Spanish.

The French as usual are more precise in their nomenclature, and distinguish *Mexico* from *Le Mexique*.

central plateau.   The purchasers of Church lands were confirmed in their possessions, even though it was necessary to dismiss all the judges of the Supreme Court by a stroke of the pen ;* and to involve the Government in a sentence of excommunication!

Santa Anna, who was naive enough to land at Vera Cruz in response to a Proclamation which set out that all good Mexicans, without distinction of party, would be welcomed by the Intervention, was summarily shipped on board a French corvette, and deposited at his usual retiring place at the Havannah.†

Sonora, indeed, was not colonized, but that was partly because Sonora still remained true to President Juarez. The French, it must be remembered, were masters of only a small part of the Republic of Mexico.

The dark stain, however, that lay, and will ever lie, upon their Intervention, and upon the character of Bazaine, is that of atrocious and cynical cruelty. Soldiers and civilians, officers and functionaries of the Constitutional Government were indifferently

---

* The Decree was dated 2nd January, 1864.   Domenech: Hist. III., pp. 136-7, 148, 151, 169-171.   See also Gaulot : Rève. 227-229, where the whole story of the Archbishop's conduct may be read in detail, with his dismissal, or retirement, the excommunications, etc., etc.

† March 12th, 1864, on board the corvette *Colbert*.

classed as bandits.   Quarter was rarely given by
the French troops, and of the prisoners that were
n ecessarily taken in the almost daily encounters
between French and Mexicans—the more important and loyal officers were usually shot in cold
blood, and the rank and file were alternatively
pressed into the service of Mejia and Marquez.*

The extraction of money, whether under the
guise of contributions to the expenses of the Intervention, or as fines for some supposed offence, was
the commonest cause of outrage.

In the larger towns, floggings, imprisonments,
outrage and confiscation were of daily and almost
hourly occurrence.   In the villages, not only the
property, but the life and honour of every Mexican
was at the mercy of the French soldiers ; and while
the smallest hint of disapproval was visited with the
death of the individual, the faintest show of opposition led to the destruction of entire communities.
And in the more open country the Contra-guerilla
gloried in the constant commission of outrages, of
which even the hints and suggestions that have
reached us through the sympathetic medium of
French narrators, are sufficient to fill us with horror
and indignation.†

---

* "Passés par les armes" is the French euphemism —the
phrase occurs in almost every page of contemporary memoirs.

† It is positively sickening to read of these atrocities. They

Meanwhile, in Europe, and even in Mexico, the cruelty of Juarez was daily denounced, and men were called upon to admire the self-sacrificing devotion with which " the heroes of Sebastopol and Solferino " were engaged in the civilization of a grateful Mexico!

Nothing was wanted to crown the fairy edifice but the appearance of the Austrian Archduke, to recline upon what he had been assured was " a bed of roses laid in a mine of gold."*

†Ferdinand Maximilian of Hapsburg, younger

---

will be found referred to, but not unduly dwelt upon, by all the Mexican historians; but I have derived my information rather from the mingled boasts and excuses of French writers. The fullest details, as usual, are collected by M. Lefèvre, I., 340-354 and 420-424, and II., 108-142. See also de Kératry and Gaulot, *op. cit.*

A long letter is printed by Domenech (Hist. III., 100-102), the most indulgent of critics of the Intervention, from which I quote one sentence. The letter was written by a trusty correspondent in Mexico to the Abbé himself, early in 1864 " Nos amis de l'intérieur. . . . les habitants des villes et villages occupés par les francais meurent de faim. . . . la misère est dans les familles qui maudissent l'intervention, par ce qu'elle leur apporte la faim, la misère et la ruine."

And this is the picture drawn by the hand of a friend !

See also de Kératry : " La Contra-guerilla " ; *passim.*

* Señor Gutierrez de Estrada, in his autobiographical sketch, entitled "Mejico y el arciduque Fernando Maximilian," Paris, 1862, says (p. 26) that as far back as 1840 he proposed the election as Sovereign of Mexico of some European Prince of good blood. . . . . *pero sin designarlo.*

† In 1862, according to Domenech (" l'Empire au Mexique," Paris, 1862), there were four candidates for the Mexican Throne — the Duc de Montpensier, the Archduke Maximilian, a Portuguese Prince, and a Prince—" Je ne veux pas citer des noms particulièrs," says he (133), " mais tout le monde sait

brother of the Emperor Francis Joseph of Austria, and son of the Archduke Francis Charles, was born at Schönbrunn, the 6th of July, 1832. Destined from his early boyhood for a naval life, he had, before he had reached his twenty-fifth year, visited almost all the countries of Europe and the neighbouring seas, and was reputed to be an intelligent as well as an amiable Prince.

In 1857 he married the Princess Maria Charlotte Amelia, daughter of Leopold King of the Belgians, and the Princess Louise of Orleans. Soon after his marriage he undertook a long voyage to the Brazils, and was entrusted on his return by his brother the Emperor, with the civil and military government of Lombardo-Venetia, in which he seems to have displayed more liberality than was entirely agreeable to the authorities at Vienna.

In 1851 he is described as tall of stature, slight of figure, with the blue eyes and fair hair of his house, refined in manners, gentle in disposition, naturally inclined to letters and the arts ; a poet and an author, as well as a

que dans la famille impériale de Napoléon il existe plusieurs princes reconnus par leurs talents, leurs intelligence, etc."

" Tous les hommes sérieux," says the author in another place (127), " sont d'accord sur la necessitéd 'etablir au plus tôt dans cette contrée la monarchie constitutionelle, etc."

That the Mexicans had anything to say to the matter never apparently suggested itself to this discreet politician.

sailor and a statesman, speaking six languages, hard-working, high-minded, ambitious. On the other hand he was weak, vain, restless, punctilious, ceremonious, unduly fond of magnificence and pageantry, wrapt up in the consuming fancy that he was born to absolute sovereignty. Versatile, frivolous, capricious, at once irresolute and obstinate ; inclined to study, but averse from trouble : earnest in the elaboration of petty details, ever shrinking from the solution of serious difficulties ; he was an unhappy mixture of the dilettante and the doctrinaire. And it would, perhaps, have been impossible to select among men of position and character, such as the Archduke undoubtedly was, a ruler so singularly unfitted to establish a new and stable form of government in Mexico.*

But Maximilian was on bad terms with his brother. He was overwhelmed with debt, dissatisfied with his present position, and unmanageable as regards the future. Extravagant, impracticable, ambitious, an Autocrat masquerading as a Radical, he had become an archducal and Imperial bore at Miramar, and his big brother at Vienna was glad to get rid of him, and find something for him to do, with a good salary, across the Atlantic.

---

* A list of the extravagant and absurd decrees published by Maximilian in the months of November, and December, 1865, for example, is given by his admirer, Arrangoiz, vol IV., pp.

Long before the month of September, 1861, when Sir Charles Wyke's letters were convulsing Europe and paving the way for European alliance and intervention, the French Government had already pitched upon Maximilian as the protagonist in the great drama which Napoleon III. would cause to be played in the Imperial theatre of Mexico; and as early as the 18th of September, the Emperor Francis Joseph, secretly consulted, had given his conditional consent to the employment of his brother by the French.*

64-66. The titles alone fill two 8vo. pages. The laws themselves—of 1865 only—were published in eight large octavo volumes! Domenech : Histoire, III, 346.

* For the first steps in the choice of Maximilian as Emperor of Mexico, and more especially as to the part played by Gutierrez de Estrada, who appears to have been hankering after a Mexican Emperor as far back as July, 1840, see Gaulot, " Rêve d'Empire," chapter I. The value as an authority of this book, and its two complementary volumes, " L'Empire de Maximilien," and " Fin d'Empire," to all of which I shall have occasion to refer in the course of this work, is chiefly in that the papers of M. Ernest Louet, Paymaster-General of the French Forces in Mexico, were placed in M. Gaulot's hands on the death of that officer, forming a collection of unique and quite exceptional interest, as may be gathered from the preface to the first volume. I must say also that M. Gaulot himself appears to me to marshal his facts with great fairness, and to have adopted generally a reasonable tone in discussing questions which have usually excited to an unfortunate extent the party spirit of French writers.

M. Gaulot has published his books to justify the French intervention in Mexico, to vindicate the character and proceedings of Napoleon III., and though I sympathize with him even less in the former than in the latter part of his task, I have always read his pages with pleasure and with respect.

The earlier and more secret history of these negotiations, the influence of the Archduchess Charlotte, of the Empress Eugénie, of Pius IX., and the parts that were played by the various priests and princes, Jesuits and great ladies, Mexican and French adventurers—all these things are outside the scope of the present work, and it must suffice to say that Maximilian of Hapsburg, forewarned and flattered, considered himself already as Emperor of Mexico, before even the alliance was signed (October 30, 1861) between the European allies, providing that none of them sought, or would under any circumstances seek, to interfere in the domestic politics of Mexico, or to impose any sovereign or sovereignty upon the people of that nation.

And it was as early as January, 1862, that he commissioned Señor Almonte, as we have already seen, to proceed to Mexico with the French army, invested with the powers and privileges of an Imperial Envoy.[*]

Mexican refugees, disaffected to the Constitutional Government, were summoned to the Court at Miramar, where the banished Bishops[†] were

---

[*] And with the right to promote and appoint officers in the Imperial Mexican Army, and even to confer titles upon Mexican subjects.—See *ante* pp. 176-7.

[†] The Archbishop of Mexico; the Bishops of Michoacan and of Oaxaca.

especially welcomed, and where an altar in honour of our Lady of Guadalupe, erected in the bedchamber of Maximilian, was displayed for their encouragement and veneration.

How Señor Almonte conducted himself, and how he was alternately set up and put down by the French in Mexico : how General Lorencez came and went : how, after a year's delay, General Forey at last reached the capital : and how a bogus Assembly resolved to offer a bogus Crown to the Austrian, or any other protected Prince—all these things have been already related.

The Deputation, or Committee of Invitation, left Mexico on the 18th of August ; arrived at Miramar on the 2nd of October, 1863 ; and was received on the following day by the Archduke. Their leader, or president, Gutierrez de Estrada, made a long speech, and laid the Crown of Mexico at the feet of the scion of Charles V.

Maximilian replied, *nolens imperare*, suggesting that a popular vote would alone justify him in accepting the proffered Throne ; and the Envoys, after some further discussion and consultation, proceeded from Miramar to Paris, to confer with the Emperor Napoleon. The obtaining of the popular vote in Mexico presented no difficulty to the master of twenty legions, and orders were at once transmitted to Bazaine, to the effect that a popular vote should be obtained.

The well-satisfied Envoys were content meanwhile to bide their time, as Maximilian privately assured them of his ultimate acceptance of the Crown. The confidence, indeed, was of no very extraordinary value, seeing that the Archduke immediately followed up his conditional refusal of the Mexican offer, by setting out upon a kind of Imperial and triumphal progress to the various Courts of Europe, accompanied by a Mexican confidant, in the person of Don Francisco Arrangoiz, a gentleman whose services in the matter of the sale of the Mesilla by Santa Anna to the United States had been somewhat too lavishly remunerated, and who was familiarly known to his friends and enemies as Don Gota de Agua.*

---

* The Mesilla Treaty had been negotiated by Almonte, as the representative of Santa Anna in the United States. The wily Dictator apparently distrusting one of the most truly honest of his supporters, dispatched Señor Arrangoiz in hot haste to Washington, with orders to Almonte to pay over the money to this new Envoy, which was accordingly done. But, whatever Almonte might have done with the money, it is certain that Arrangoiz appropriated a large share to himself under the name of commission, and allowed the bankers Lizardi & Co., to take a further $3,600,000 as their share of the plunder, leaving a very slender amount to be transmitted to Mexico. Called to account for the sum which he himself had converted, he professed it to be a mere drop of water, *gota de agua*, not worthy of consideration, and he was familiarly known as *gota de agua* to the end of his days, without forfeiting the esteem of any of his friends and admirers in Mexico. As a side light

His first visit, in January, 1864, was to Vienna, whence, after a brief sojourn, he proceeded to Paris, where he was received with the honours due to a reigning sovereign; and where two treaties were discussed and approved, and a number of financial and other questions of his Empire were arranged by him with his Imperial brother, Napoleon III., in March, 1864. From Paris he went on to London, where Lord Palmerston, to his great chagrin, received him as a simple Archduke; and after a visit to Claremont, he proceeded, by way of Brussels, to Vienna. But here a disagreeable surprise awaited him, in the form of a requisition by his Imperial brother that he should execute a solemn act of renunciation of his rights of succession to the ancient Empire of his ancestors, as a condition precedent to his acceptance of the shadowy diadem that was offered by the refugees of a distant Republic. And thus it happened that on the return of the Mexican delegates to Miramar, with the necessary popular vote in their portfolio, at the end of March, 1864, they found the

---

upon the financial morality of public men of his party and station, and especially upon the character of the *entourage* of the Archduke from the very first, this little story, the accuracy of which has never been questioned, (see Domenech, II., 260-269, and Gaulot, Rêve, 270) is sufficiently interesting.

Yet Juarez, who lived and died a poor man, is spoken of by the smiling recorder of Arrangoiz's good humour, as a rapacious and savage extortioner, who *sold Mexican territory to foreign nations* and put the purchase money in his pocket.

Archducal Court in the utmost confusion and distress.* Telegrams were flying backwards and forwards between Vienna and Paris, between Rome and Brussels and Trieste. Couriers with despatches arrived and departed at every hour. Friends were called in. Complaints were uttered—loud and long, and a dozen different resolutions were adopted in a single day.

Maximilian would never sign the suggested renunciation. He would sign it. The Pope should absolve him. His wife should plead for him. He would never give up his Austrian rights. He would never abandon his Mexican pretensions.†

At length, after a week of hesitation and lamentation, a solution was found, eminently characteristic of the temper and intelligence of the Archduke. If his brother would come to Miramar ‡ as the guest of the Emperor of Mexico, Maximilian would sign anything that was desired. A special train was accordingly got ready. Francis Joseph sped over the beautiful Sömmering at forty miles an hour; arrived at Miramar : saluted his *Imperial*

---

* They had expected to meet Maximilian at Vienna, but finding that he had suddenly left on the very day of their arrival, they followed with all speed to Miramar.

† Gaulot : Rêve, p. 284.

‡ According to M. Gaulot : Rêve (pp. 1-5)), the Crown of Mexico had been actually offered to and accepted by Maximilian two years before, on the 4th of October, 1861, at this same castle of Miramar.

brother ; and returned to Vienna the same day (April 9th) and in the same carriage, with the act of renunciation in his pocket, duly signed by Maximilian.*

And next morning the gratified Archduke signi-fied to the expectant deputation his definite acceptance of the Imperial Crown of Mexico, April 10th, 1863.†

Oaths were administered, *Te Deums* were sung, salutes were fired.   All the apparel of Empire was present.   And the young aspirant to a non-existent Throne proceeded at once to assert his sovereignty with the assurance of a reigning monarch.   He re-established the Sacred and Knightly Order of our Lady of Guadalupe, and gratified not only the worthy Estrada and the capable Mejia, but even

---

* The text of renunciation is given in full in " Mexico," p. 633.   It was at least characteristic of the temper and in-telligence of the Archduke, that as soon as he found himself —as he was foolish enough to suppose—firmly seated upon his Throne in Mexico (December, 1864) he disavowed the solemn renunciation which had given so much trouble, and announced that he had never legally divested himself, and would never part with his Austrian right of succession !—Domenech : III., p. 385.

† Monsieur Lanfrey, in October, 1863, pointed out pretty clearly the dangerous absurdity of Maximilian supposing that this so-called summons of the Mexican nation to assume a *trône sur un volcan* had any more solid basis than that of the power of the French army of occupation.

" L'archiduc n'a pas refléchi sans doute qu'il est plus facile aujourd' hui de donner un trône que de le garantir !   Qui lui rédigera ce bon billet ?   Et qui lui garantira ses garants ? "— Lanfrey : " Chroniques Politiques," as republished in 1883 ; tom. II.. p. 262.

the atrocious Marquez, with the decoration of the
Grand Cross. He appointed Ministers, with and
without portfolios, and commissioned Envoys, ordi-
nary and extraordinary. He dissolved the Mexican
Regency, appointed his wife Empress Regent of
Mexico ; and he finally sanctioned the issue of a
Franco-Mexican loan for eight millions of pounds
sterling, out of which he had been promised by the
Emperor Napoleon a *bonne main* of eight millions
of francs ! *

This last exercise of the sovereign power,
indeed, was that which chiefly commended itself
to his European friends and creditors ; while the
Convention, of which it was an important part, is
worthy of the attention of those who would understand the true nature of the conflict between
Benito Juarez and Maximilian of Hapsburg for
supreme power in Mexico.

This remarkable agreement provided in brief:
I.—That the expenses of the French expedition,
       fixed for the purpose of settlement at

---

* The contract for the loan had been actually signed in
Paris a month before. The decree of Maximilian for the issue
was dated Sunday, April 10th, the day of his assumption of the
Imperial title at Miramar There is no doubt that Maximilian was reduced to the utmost straits for want of money.
" Le château de Miramar, criblé d'hypothéques, était, disait-on,
à la veille d'être saisi par ses créanciers ! " Lefèvre : I., 313.

A very sympathetic account of the manner of life led by
the Archduke and Archduchess at Miramar will be found in
Lady Burton's life of her husband, 1893, vol.II., pp. 19-20.

275,000,000 francs, should be a charge upon the Mexican Exchequer. That seventy-six millions should be immediately handed over to France, in bonds of the new loan, the whole to bear interest at the rate of 3 per cent.

II.—That of the remaining 199,000,000 francs, 25,000,000 francs should be paid off in each year in cash (to be paid by Mexico to France) on account of principal and interest.

III.—That all future expenses of the French occupation should be paid exclusively and directly by Mexico.

IV.—That the French army of occupation should be gradually reduced to 25,000 men, to be paid for by Mexico at the rate of 1,000 francs per man per annum ; and that the supreme command of all troops in Mexico, Mexican as well as French, should be given exclusively to French officers.

V.—And that, in addition to all the old claims formulated by the French Commissioners in January, 1862, the Mexican Government should indemnify all French subjects for all loss, damage, or injury which they might in any way have sustained in connection with, or in consequence of, the French expedition; and that a Commission should sit in Mexico within three months for the hearing and disposal of all claims.

Verily, the little finger of the Austrian defender was thicker than the loins of the French assailant. The demands of de Saligny were as nothing compared with the concessions of Maximilian.*

---

* The secret articles had reference to the adoption of the anti-Mexican policy of Forey, as proclaimed 11th of June, 1863, the grant of a concession to Fould and other French bankers for the foundation of a National Bank (Baz : "Vida de Juarez," 253) ; and the reduction in the number of French troops in Mexico, then admitted to be 38,000, to 28,000 in 1864, 25,000 in 1866, and 20,000 in 1867. The cession to France of Sonora and other districts in the north of Mexico was a still more secret branch of the Imperial Convention, which was not even committed to writing.

The whole question of the cession of the Province of Sonora supposed to be as rich as California – to France by Mexico, as part of the consideration for their Imperial bargain, is exceedingly obscure, and is only indirectly of interest in a biography of Benito Juarez. A number of documents chiefly those which would tend to throw full light upon the matter, and compromise the exalted huxters, have been stolen from their place in the Mexican archives; and perhaps the best information and references available will be found in Lefèvre, II., pp. 90-108.

But in every book upon the subject of the French intervention, some more or less puzzling reference will be found to Doctor Gwin and the colonization of Sonora.

The question is no doubt involved in much obscurity. The facts would seem to be, (1.) that Napoleon intended that one of the most striking triumphs of the French intervention in Mexico, should be the acquisition of a large slice of territory in the New World; (2.) that the cession, under the guise of a colonisation, of Sonora was provisionally agreed upon before the departure of Maximilian; but that no reference was

Yet, in addition to the avowed objects of this singular Convention, there were, after the good old mediæval fashion, certain secret articles, not perhaps in themselves more disgraceful than those which were announced to Mexico and to the world; but more strikingly characteristic of the nature of the bargain, which France, acting upon a weak and ambitious adventurer, was seeking to foist upon a people with whom neither Napoleon nor Maximilian had the smallest concern, and who were in absolute ignorance of the entire transaction. The whole story, indeed, recalls rather those facile dispositions of sovereignty in the Middle Ages, when all-powerful Roman Pontiffs were used to fling crowns and sceptres from one favourite to another, than a diplomatic Convention in everyday Europe towards the close of the Nineteenth Century.

---

made to the subject in the Convention of Miramar for reasons of high policy ; (3.) that the difficulties attending the establishment of the Archduke in Mexico interfered with the realization of the project, until the success of the Federals in the United States made the acquisition of territory on their frontier by a European Power, a matter of supreme difficulty ; and (4.) that Maximilian, having by that time learned to hate the French, persuaded himself that he had never really intended to give up any Mexican province to his Imperial brother at the Tuileries, and paid no attention to the schemes of Doctor Gwin, or the claims of his august protector.

See also two letters of the Emperor Napoleon to Bazaine : dated September 12th, 1863, and December 16th, 1863, printed in Gaulot : Rêve, pp. 167-169 and 215-216.

CHAPTER XI.

A Sham Empire.—May, 1864—August, 1865.

On the 29th of May, 1864, Maximilian of Hapsburg and his brilliant train set foot on the shores of the promised land at Vera Cruz.[*]

In spite of an expenditure of a hundred and twenty thousand dollars, his reception by the inhabitants was frigid in the extreme; and after a visit to Orizaba and Puebla, and the shrine of our Lady of Guadalupe, he made his public entry into the city of Mexico on the 12th of June. Proclamations and receptions, *Te Deums* and distributions, shows and ceremonies—of these there was no lack, but of popular welcome on the part of Mexico, of

---

[*] "On dut payer les habits de certains notables, comme nous avions déja payé des fleurs sous les pas des français á leur entrée dans Mexico."—Kératry, 28.

The poor Archduchess was moved to shed actual tears of vexation at the coldness of the reception. Mr. Corwin, the American Envoy, left Mexico in May, 1864, on hearing of the expected arrival of Maximilian, *on temporary leave of absence.* The Ministers of the other powers were instructed to welcome the new Emperor.

solid statesmanship on the part of Maximilian, there was no sign nor symptom.

The first care of the new Emperor had been to pay a visit to Rome on his way from Miramar to Vera Cruz—not that he might secure the good offices and practical co-operation of the Pope in the all-important question of the Mexican Church ; but merely that he might receive the personal blessing of Pius IX.* And the rest of the voyage had been devoted to the solution of weighty questions of Court etiquette, and the preparation of rules for the administration, not of the country, but of the Palace.   To reign gracefully, this was the chief concern of Maximilian.

Mexico, according to Bazaine and the French historians, was already conquered. Juarez, if not actually slain, was dispossessed, discredited, practically, if not technically, an exile.†

---

* For an account of the voyage and of the interview between the Archduke and Pope Pius IX., at Rome, on the way, see Gaulot : Maximilian, Chap. I.   See also " La Cour de Rome et l'Empereur Maximilian," (pp. 1-11), where it is said that *aucune négotiation relative aux affaires religieuses du Mexique* was undertaken. Anything so practical was foreign to the temper of the Archduke, who was engaged upon the preparation of his celebrated Manual of Court Etiquette.

" Ce code formait un volume de 250 pages et reproduisait, dans leurs formules les plus méticuleuses, les règles, observées a la cour d'Autriche. L'empereur y attachait un tel prix que, même pendant le voyage qu'il entreprit brentôt après, les épreuves durent lui être envoyées d'étape en étape," Masseras : " Essai d'Empire," 35. Domenech, III., 180.

† As a matter of fact, Doblado died in harness at

Every city in Mexico, it was glibly asserted, with the exception of one or two distant towns, had given their allegiance to the *Intervention*; a convenient word, which to the French signified Napoleon, to the Austrians, Maximilian ; and whilst to the Mexicans it may possibly have suggested some future state, conceivably better than the actual condition of things, practically signified in the immediate present, the French Provost Marshal and the tender mercies of the Contra-guerilla !*

As a matter of fact, in spite of all his difficulties, Juarez was still recognised, in the Summer of 1864,

---

Zacatecas, April 22nd, 1864, of fever, due to exposure to various hardships, and General Urraga remained faithful until August, 1864, when the Government of the Emperor looked most promising, and the fortunes of Juarez seemed well nigh hopeless.   He had even sent his wife to the United States for greater safety.   Comonfort was dead ; one more victim of the inevitable Marquez.   Juarez was left well nigh alone.

There is a good account of the operations of the Mexican army of the North from 1864 to 1867, by Don Juan de Dios Arias – Mexico, 1867, 1 vol. pp. 730, with numerous maps and plans, well drawn, well coloured and neatly mounted on linen, It is entitled, " Reseña Historica de la formacion y operaciones del ejercito del Norte."

* "Un francais avantureux, le colonel du Pui, après avoir fait campagne en Chine était venu au Mexique, et guerroyait à la tête de la contre-guerilla.   Traitant *indistinctment tous ses adversaires comme des bandits,*' says M Gaulot, at once a patriotic and an honest apologist of the French intervention, this gentleman highwayman had acquired " une universelle réputation de cruauté."   Gaulot : Max., 311.

See also Kératry : " La Contre Guerilla," *passim*.

in the provinces of New Leon, Coahuilla, Tamaulipas, Chihuahua, Sonora, Cinaloa, Colima, Guerrero, Oaxaca, Tabasco, Chiapas, and Jalisco,* while a French army of over 30,000 men, assisted by some 20,000 Mexican soldiers, was employed during the whole of 1864 in gaining continual and important victories over the Constitutional forces that were supposed already to have ceased to exist.

But Maximilian, pleased with his new plaything, set to work vigorously to perform all the ceremonial duties of royalty, and to scatter the money that was, or might be, at his disposal with a lavish and fatuous hand. The ex-consul Arrangoiz was named Minister Plenipotentiary in London, with a salary of £8,000 a-year. The Spanish intriguer Hidalgo was gratified with a similar post and a similar salary in Paris. Marquez was sent with a splendid mission to Constantinople!

The trusted Mexican supporters of the new régime, on the other hand,† were removed from

---

* See Mexico : V., p. 642.

† His most trusted adviser, virtually Grand Vizier of Mexico, was Monsieur Eloin, a Belgian engineer, who knew nothing about Mexico, who hated the French, and whose greatest talent was that of a singer of comic songs. Gaulot : Maximilian, 38-39.

The way that Marquez was *provided for* at the same time is almost the only act of Maximilian which looks as if he had any sense of humour : for that monster of cruelty was sent

their posts; and even Mejia, who was not only the most faithful, but the only really capable General among the Mexican officers on any side, with the single exception of Porfirio Diaz,* narrowly escaped dismissal.

Even the Bishops were estranged—not by any anti-clerical policy, but by the absence of any policy whatever.† The Archduke's visit to Rome had resulted in nothing more solid than a Papal Benediction. The Catholic Emperor had not even suggested a Concordat for his Mexican Church.

Almonte, the most capable and perhaps the devoted of the partizans of the new régime, most who had presided over the Council of Regency during a trying year with such success that he had been able to hand three hundred thousand dollars of savings to the Archduke on his arrival, was

---

upon a diplomatic mission to the Ottoman Empire, to obtain a Firman from the Sultan for the establishment of a Mexican Convent of Nuns at Jerusalem. " Mexico," (Longmans, 1865). p. 20.

Miramon was about the same time sent to Berlin " to study Fortification." Gaulot : Maximilian, 96.

* And he was brought up, like Juarez, as a lawyer.— Kératry.

† Neither the Ecclesiastics nor those who had recently acquired their property were satisfied, conciliated, or even considered. See Domenech: Hist., III., pp. 108-181, and ante p. 235.

" Le règlement des biens de main morte restait toujours en suspens. La cour de Rome n'avait pas encore consenté à se prononcer."– Kératry, 63.

relegated to the ridiculous position of Master of the Ceremonies ! *

Nor did the new Sovereign succeed in conciliating any class or party in Mexico, Ecclesiastical, Liberal, Absolutist, National, or even French. Sincerely believing that by consenting to reign over the Mexicans, he had done them an honour which called rather for their gratitude than for any further services on his part, he was collecting butterflies and beetles, classifying rare plants and deciphering ancient inscriptions, while the gravest questions of policy and of administration remained untouched, or consigned to the portfolios of procrastination.†

A doctrinaire and a pedant, the Archduke would neither devote himself to the practical but troublesome task of creating a Government, nor suffer any of his subordinates or Ministers to act independently of his interference. He took credit for rising at five in the morning, and harassed his secretaries till nightfall with a parade of business ; and when evening fell, nothing had been added to the work of the regeneration of Mexico, but

---

* Gaulot : Maximilian, 40-41.
As to the Archduke's neglect of Gutierrez de Estrada, who was left in France, rewarded with a despicable *order* ; and the appointment of Fernando Ramirez Minister of Foreign Affairs, see Gaulot : Max., 50-58.

† Masseras, 46-47.

the further complication of questions already complicated, and the establishment, it might be, of a new Order of Mexican chivalry.*

His vacillations between a useless Liberalism and an offensive Absolutism; neither summoning a Parliament nor grasping in his own hands the reins of Government ; neither trusting nor dismissing his French allies: alarming the Church without relieving the State ; vain, extravagant, incompetent, and volatile ; he devoted his narrow intellect to questions of precedence and of etiquette, the amount of lace on a courtier's coat, or the due marshalling of the ladies of the bedchamber when the Empress went to mass at the Cathedral.†

---

* Among the other orders and decorations instituted by Maximilian was the *Order of Constancy*, of which the insignia were only to be granted to those who had served *fifty years* in the army ! If military service under a recognised Government was *subauditur*, it is hard to say when this half century was to be taken to begin !

† "Placé en face d'une situation où l'activité la plus éclairée chez le chef du pouvoir aurait amplement trouvé son emploi dans la seule tâche de diriger les ministres, il avait attiré à lui le gouvernement tout entier. Son cabinet particulier accaparait les questions les plus considérables comme les plus minimes, les projets d'importance vitale comme les derniers détails de routine administrative. Lui-même accumulait sur son bureau les dossiers par centaines, les confondant dans un pêle-mêle où les plus essentiels et les plus urgents disparaissaient sous les plus futiles. Le perfectionnement du code d'etiquette, l' ordonnance d'une cérémonie, le règlement d'un cortège, la création de l'ordre de l' Aigle Mexicaine, ou de l'ordre de Saint Charles, l'installation du théâtre de la cour, la tenue correcte des équipages et des livrées l'occupaient facilement des semaines entières. Puis venaient la botanique

In a country as yet without industries, his attention was chiefly set on the choice of a body of
hallebardiers unequalled in beauty and stature, for
the service of his new Palace.   In a country as yet
without roads, many days and many dollars were
spent in the elaboration of a State carriage more
gorgeous than anything that was to be found in the
stables at Schönbrunn or Madrid.

From a country, the immensity of whose foreign
debt, even before his own vast concession of
indebtedness, had provoked the indignation and the
intervention of Europe, he received four hundred
thousand pounds sterling for his yearly support,
to say nothing of immense sums spent upon
more enduring or less personal objects of his
folly.*

Every morning something over £1,000 sterling
in Mexican gold coin, ceremoniously disposed
upon a gilt salver, was handed to Maximilian in his

---

et l'archéologie, pour lesquelles il lui prenait des accès de
passion intermittente." Masseras, 47.

* The amount allowed to the *privy purse* of the Emperor
and Empress was fixed at $1,700,000, or say, £340,000 per
annum.

But the independent expenses of the Court were enormous.
From April to August, 1864, $319,670, say £65,000, was spent
upon carriages and horses, liveries and harness, and such like.
For the establishment of a Court Theatre $75,000 was gaily
allocated at the time when Mejia was unable to move for want of
a few thousand dollars.   He afterwards occupied Matomoras
without striking a blow, September 26th, 1864. Masseras, 47-49.

R

cabinet, while £100 was similarly laid before Her Majesty the Empress.*

It is impossible to conceive of royalty under a more grotesque, or a more sordid light ; albeit there is a kind of old-fashioned child's fairy-story simplicity in this daily delivery of spoil. †

The resources thus strangely devoted to the support of a sham Empire were provided, not so much by the taxpayers of Mexico, as by the investing public of England and France. Maximilian lived and reigned on borrowed money. And the borrowing was reckless in the extreme.‡

On the 25th of March, 1864, a contract was signed by Mr. Glyn, of the great banking house of Glyn, Mills, and Currie, for the issue in London and in Paris of a Mexican Loan. The amount, fixed at the respectable sum of £8,000,000 sterling, was afterwards increased by a stroke of the pen to £12,365,000.

Subscribed   at   the   price   of   63   per   cent,§

---

* Masseras, 411.

† We feel inclined to wonder if this fantastic Emperor "counted out his money" while his consort was in her parlour with the bread and honey before her,

‡ Kératry, 79-81-3.

§ The loan was ill-received both in Paris and London, and the French bankers suffered, according to M. de Kératry, for their devotion to the Emperor and to his Finance Minister, Monsieur Achille Fould. The Six per Cent. Anglo-French loan of April, 1864, was for a nominal sum of

this larger amount should have produced over £7,500,000 sterling in specie, to be dealt with by the Mexican Chancellor of the Exchequer; but, as usual in such cases, a good many millions of francs had to be subtracted, before the dollars were piled up in the Treasury at Mexico. And it is probable that no more than one million sterling of this immense issue, found its way directly into the Mexican Exchequer. Of the nominal amount of £12,365,000, indeed, less than two-thirds or, say, £8,000,000, was destined for Mexico in any shape or way.* The remaining £4,365,000, which constituted a new charge upon the Mexican Finances, was surreptitiously added by the creation of a supplementary bonded debt of 110,000,000 francs, handed over in the form of bonds, precisely similar to those of the authorised issue to the French Government, partly on account of the expenses of the war in Mexico, and partly to provide indemnities for French subjects in that country.

£12,365,000, producing at 63 £7,790,000, issued in bonds by Glyn, and in Paris by the Credit Mobilier.

At this time there was an estimated annual deficit of £2,600,000 on an estimated revenue of £3,300,000!—Fenn : on the Funds, 1867, 354.

* This £4,365,000, added to the legitimate amount of £8,000,000, makes up the sum of the actual issue to £12,365,000, See Lefèvre II., 144-147. This £12,365,000 was disposed of much as follows :

Meanwhile, Juarez, hardly considered by the glittering triflers at Chapultepec,* was patiently biding his time in the North. Yet the Autumn and Winter of 1864 brought nothing but disaster to the National forces; and the seat of Constitutional Government was constantly moved further and further north of the ancient capital ; and the territory that acknowledged the supremacy of Juarez was daily growing smaller and smaller,

		£
Handed direct to the French Government in bonds, as explained above		4,365,000
Difference between par and price of 63 on 8,000,000 francs		2,140,000
Retained by the Commission in Paris out of the balance, for the payment of further interest to Bondholders, chiefly French		2,600,000
Pay of French troops in Mexico for one year, (see Lefèvre, II., 149)		1,000,000
	Francs.	
Cash to Maximilian as agreed ..	8,000,000	
Debt on Palace of Miramar ..	1,500,000	
Belgian Legion	1,800,000	
Austrian Legion	2,500,000	
Francs 13,800,000		550,000
Expenses of issue, printing of bonds, commission to financial houses, brokers, and others ; discount allowed for payment in advance, etc. ; and bonds unissued—(Lefèvre: II., 149-150 ; Gaulot : Max., 138,)		710,000
Received by the Treasury at Mexico		1,000,000
		£12,365,000

* Maximilian had established his Palace and Court in the beautiful suburb and park of Chapultepec. The Castle stands on rising ground four miles to the S.W. of the capital.

like the dreadful prison chamber created by the sombre imagination of Balzac.[*]

On the 7th of June, 1863, the same day that Bazaine had led the vanguard of the French army into the Mexican capital, the President and his Ministers had entered upon their functions at San Luis Potosi, and Juarez had taken the opportunity of issuing a manifesto protesting, as a matter of form, against the French invasion, and calling upon all good Mexicans to take up arms at once for the maintenance of Constitutional Government and for the defence of Mexican Independence. Assurances of loyal support had poured in from every part of the country. And for some time the Government of Juarez appeared as well established at San Luis as it had formerly been at Mexico.

In the beginning of September, 1863, the President's Cabinet was remodelled. General Doblado, who had held the portfolio of Foreign Affairs, was replaced by Sebastian Lerdo de Tejada ; Comonfort remained at the War Office ; and a young lawyer, Don Jose Iglesias, became Minister of Justice and Religion. But neither Juarez nor his supporters could hope to withstand the well-armed and well-organized forces of the

---

* In " La Peau de Chagrin."

French invader, when, after the departure of Forey, the Intervention became somewhat more active than before, and Bazaine, preparing for the reception of a new Emperor, had occupied in quick succession Querétaro, Morelia, Guanajuato, Leon, and Aguas Calientes in the course of November and December, 1863.

Nor was it only at the hands of the French invader that the National forces were doomed to suffer defeat.

On the 24th of November, 1863, Negrete was out-generalled and beaten, not by a French Marshal, but by the little Indian, Thomas Mejia, one of the bravest and most capable Generals of Mexico, and San Luis itself was threatened by his rebel forces.

Comonfort, surprised at the head of a small detachment by a body of troops under Marquez, was butchered in cold blood before the end of the same month.*

And at length, on Christmas Eve, 1863, Mejia succeeded in taking possession of San Luis Potosi, whence the President, with the other members of the National Government, were forced to flee in haste to Saltillo, in the far North-East of Mexico.

---

* At San Miguel de Allende, 11th of November, 1863. The disgrace of his murder is shared by Marquez and Mejia.

Madame Juarez and her children had already been sent further north for greater safety.   Juarez himself, anxious to remain at his post to the very last moment, owed his safety, it is said, to the promptitude and courage of his devoted servant, Juan Udueta.*

Arriving at Saltillo on the 9th of January, 1864, he found that General Vidaurri, Governor of New Leon and Coahuila, had actually offered to surrender those important provinces to the French. Without troops ; for he had left every available soldier with Negrete and Uraga to make head against the advance of the invader ; almost without guards; but accompanied by his little Cabinet and a few secretaries and faithful followers, Juarez lost not a moment in pushing on to Monterey. The Governor, surprised by this rapid movement, was unable to organise an armed resistance : and his uncertain troops, encouraged by the arrival of Juarez himself, declined to rebel at the bidding of their commander. Vidaurri, dismissed and vanquished without the firing of a shot, fled to Mexico, where he was welcomed by Maximilian ; and Juarez took up his quarters with his entire Cabinet in the picturesque and loyal city of Monterey.

---

* He had served the President as a coachman from his landing at Vera Cruz in 1858, and he continued in his service until his master's death in 1872.

It was here that a small party of his friends, headed by Doblado, despairing of the Republic, and not unnaturally disheartened by the reiterated assurances of the invaders that the only Government with which they could not treat was that of Juarez—waited upon the President, and requested or suggested to him, that he should abdicate his supreme power in favour of General Ortega (January, 1864). The suggestion found no favour in the sight of Juarez, or any member of his Cabinet ;* but Doblado remained loyal to his old chief, until his death some three months afterwards† deprived the National party of a most capable if not an entirely trusted officer.

Juarez meanwhile maintained the even tenour of his way; and in these trying times, when every dollar was needed for the actual necessities of the defence, and when dollars were few and hardly obtained, he was not unmindful of absent friends. The officers taken prisoners at Puebla in July, 1863, to the number of 543, who had refused to take the new oath of allegiance tendered by Forey, had been shipped off to France by their captors; and they were lodged in various inland towns, isolated

---

* Lerdo de Tejada's answer is given in Baz : Vida, p. 263.

† Monsieur Gaulot : (Rêve, 266,) says that Doblado retired to the United States in May, 1864, taking with him *an immense treasure,* and that he died in exile in the following year. I believe my account to be the correct one.

one from another, and hardly provided with the means of subsistence.*

Various attempts were made to induce them to sign declarations recognising the new Government of Mexico. But a large majority refused to transfer their allegiance to the invader. And, in order to provide adequately for the support of these loyal countrymen, Juarez himself, harassed fugitive as he was in Mexico, contrived to procure and dispatch to France over a hundred thousand francs.†

Until the 15th of August, 1864, the President was able to maintain his position and his Government at Monterey; but the ever-advancing French drove him once more to seek a more northern asylum, until at length, on the 12th of October, 1864, he halted at the remote provincial capital of Chihuahua; while Madame Juarez, yielding to the entreaties of her husband, took refuge with her family in the United States.‡

---

* Some of these unfortunates were reduced to a subsistence allowance of £4 a month, out of which they had to pay for their own lodgings.—Lefèvre, I., 331-333.

† " Mexico ; " V., 645-7.

‡ On the 31st of July, 1864, Maximilian, to the great annoyance of his French advisers, decreed the cessation of the blockade on all the coasts of Mexico.

On the 30th of August, 1864, Bazaine received at the hands of Napoleon the well-deserved bâton. His army was judiciously augmented, and for the time being, the French influence was strong in well-nigh every part of Mexico.

General Negrete, whose army had been cut to pieces by the French some months before, joined his chief at Chihuahua, and having been appointed Minister of War in the place of the unfortunate Comonfort (September, 1864), was entrusted with the command of a new army raised and equipped by the untiring energy of Juarez, even as he himself was driven from city to city by the ever advancing tide of invasion. The Indian statesman would, in one respect at least, have gained the applause of William of Orange, in that, being no soldier, but a " President in a black coat," he made no pretence of commanding his armies, and entrusted the conduct of military operations entirely to his Generals in the field. But as a raiser of armies under the most constant and apparently overwhelming difficulties, he is almost without an equal in history. His military commanders were no doubt frequently incompetent, his Indian troops poorly equipped; and that they should have been so constantly unsuccessful when opposed to the trained and seasoned troops of Imperial France, is a result hardly to be wondered at. But as each army was defeated and broken up, Juarez was found to have equipped another, ready to take its place for the defence of his country.*

---

* By a somewhat singular coincidence, at the end of the year 1864. the number of troops at the disposal of President

Negrete, in the Spring of 1865, succeeded in retaking not only Saltillo, but Monterey; but by some military blundering, he contrived to lose both those important positions, as well as his entire army, ere he presented himself once more before the most patient of Presidents, at Chihuahua. *On n'est plus heureux à notre âge; Monsieur le Maréchal*, said the most courtly of Monarchs to his defeated Marshal of France.*

Yet a fine phrase was easy enough when nothing

Juarez and that of those charged with his destruction was about equal. According to Niox, the invaders were,

French	35,000
Belgians	1,500
Austrians	6,500
	43,000

And I take from Lefèvre, I., 392, the following estimate of the number of the Constitutional forces.

In the Province or State of Jalisco	10,000
,, ,, ,, Oaxaca	9,000
,, ,, ,, Nuevo Leon ..	5,000
,, ,, ,, Durango ..	2,000
,, ,, ,, Vera Cruz ..	2,000
,, ,, ,, Puebla	3,000
,, ,, ,, San Luis ..	5,000
,, ,, ,, Tamaulipas ..	2,000
,, ,, ,, Zacatecas ..	2,000
,, ,, ,, Michoacan ..	1,500
,, ,, ,, Guanajuato ..	1,500
	43,000

* Marshal Villeroi, after Ramillies, May, 1706.

menaced the Crown or dignity of Louis XIV., nor abated a jot of the splendour of Versailles.

Juarez, on the contrary, threatened in person as well as in Government by the victorious column that pursued the defeated Negrete, was compelled once again to retire.* And after a rough journey, he turned to make his last stand on the very northernmost frontier of his country, at a place that was appropriately known as *Paso del Norte*, at a distance of over eleven hundred miles from the City of Mexico.†

---

* 5th of August, 1865.

† Now, no less appropriately, named Ciudad de Juarez, the frontier station on the through line of railway (Mexican Central) from New York to the city of Mexico.

It may afford some idea of the change that has passed over the country in eight-and-twenty years to note that the express train leaving New York at 10.0 p.m. on Monday, crosses the frontier at Ciudad de Juarez at 7.0 p.m. on the following Friday, and arrives at the city of Mexico at 7.0 a.m on the next Monday, after a run of 1,225 miles (1,970 kilometres) of Mexican railway in thirty-six hours.

CHAPTER XII.

PLAYING WITH FIRE.—AUGUST, 1865—OCTOBER, 1865.

From August, 1864, when Bazaine was rewarded for his zeal and his success with a Marshal's *bâton*,* to June, 1865, when he married a Mexican wife, French influence was at its height in Mexico, both at the Court and in the Provinces.†

Yet Maximilian was by no means satisfied with his position; ‡ and as early as February, 1865,

---

* On the 1st of October, 1864, a new French journal, devoted to the policy of the Intervention, and subsidized by the French to the extent of 150,000 francs per annum, appeared in Mexico. It was called *L'Ere Nouvelle*, and was edited by an accomplished journalist, M. Emmanuel Masseras, whose "Essai d'Empire " I have constantly consulted with advantage in the course of my own work. The contract between him and Marshal Bazaine and M. de Montholon is given by Gaulot: Max, p. 90.

† In March, 1865, Bazaine took upon himself to banish from Mexico a certain Father Allean, on suspicion of being a friend of the Papal Nuncio! Gaulot: Maximilian, 135-136. Juarez himself had never ventured to take such liberties with the Clergy.

‡ See translation of a letter written in cipher from the city of Mexico, January 5th, 1865, in Gaulot: Maximilian, 155.

he had actually contemplated abdication. Money was already scarce; procrastination was already common : and the settlement of the Jecker debt, so earnestly desired by his friends at the Tuileries, appeared to be as far off as ever. * For Maximilian, now that he was fairly established on the throne, showed a considerable aptitude for the postponement of disagreeable claims.† But he was at length given so very clearly to understand that no further delay could be permitted, that after endless negotiations and subterfuges, a Convention, known as the Corta-Bonnefons Convention, was signed in April, 1865, by which the amount of the Jecker debt, reduced by about 40 per cent. to a trifle over $5,500,000, was to be paid off at the rate of $1,000,000 a year, in something over five year and a half.

The Mexican Government was at this time hopelessly insolvent ; and Jecker contrived to

---

* M. Lefèvre consecrates an entire chapter of his first volume (cap. xiv. pp. 164-185) to the history of the *Créance Jecker* : the Swiss nationality of the banker ; the mode of issue of the bonds ; with many interesting and piquant details, which must be exceedingly unpleasant reading to the friends of M. Dubois de Saligny .   .   . et Compagnie.

† The Budget of the Mexican Empire, as prepared in June, 1865, by a French financier, shews an ordinary expenditure of no less than $205,000,000 or over £40,000,000 sterling. The Revenue calculated upon the most hopeful basis could not exceed £30,000,000, leaving a minimum annual deficit of over £10,000,000 sterling.

obtain a modification of the Convention of April by another agreement, which was signed in August of the same year, under the terms of which he consented to a still further reduction of the amount to be recovered, to $4,500,000 payable immediately in cash, by two instalments, in August and December. A bill for the first moiety of $2,500,000 was immediately drawn upon the Commissioners of the Mexican Loan in Paris, and was duly met at maturity; but a second draft for the remaining $2,000,000 was dishonoured, and formed the subject of a claim by French Jecker against the French Government, after the fall of Maximilian; a claim which, it is needless to say, was entirely disregarded in Paris.

The net result, therefore, of the French intervention, as far as it was undertaken to enforce the payment to Monsieur Jecker and *his friends* in France of $15,000,000 by the Mexican taxpayers, was ultimately the payment of $2,500,000 to Monsieur Jecker himself, by certain French financiers in Paris.

The secret history * of the Jecker claim forms no

---

* Jecker was naturalized a Frenchman at the solicitation of the Duc de Morny, March 26th, 1862.

See also Lano: "Secret d'Empire," and "Diary of an English Resident in Paris," vol. II., pp. 67-70, where the true reason for the French intervention in Mexico is found—or sought--in a Court intrigue about a box at the Opera!

part of the biography of Juarez ; and yet some slight acquaintance with the subject is necessary to enable us fully to realise the nature and extent of the forces against which the Mexican President was called upon to struggle. The bribery of the Duc de Morny by Jecker and his friends ; the coercion of Napoleon III. by his irrepressible step-brother ; the naturalisation of Swiss Jecker, who at the time of the intervention could not even claim to be a French subject ; these things should at least be referred to. They may be studied in the secret history of the Tuileries Nor is the end of the unhappy banker unworthy of a passing notice.

Having rendered himself, by his proceedings in Mexico,* liable to criminal prosecution after the fall of Maximilian ; and having lost all his influence in Paris on the death of Morny in 1865, Jecker was at length reduced to writing a threatening letter to the Emperor Napoleon, on

---

* On the 3rd of November, 1858, Juarez had issued a Decree from the Palace of Government at Vera Cruz, cautioning all persons, Mexicans and foreigners, against lending any assistance in money, munitions of war, or otherwise, to the revolutionary leaders in Mexico ; and decreeing moreover, that any person so lending should forfeit *ipso facto* the money or goods so lent or provided, and should further be liable to prosecution for the recovery of a penalty of double the amount or value of the loan, or other assistance. [Kératry, 17.] The remembrance of this Decree was not encouraging to Monsieur Jecker, as regards making good any claim for repayment or compensation from the Constitutional Government when it was restored in Mexico.

the 8th of December, 1870, stating that he would publish the correspondence and papers that were in his possession with regard to the Imperial intervention in Mexico, unless he was paid by the Emperor.   The letter was found, with other secret papers, on the sack of the Tuileries, and Jecker himself was shot by the Communists as he was stealing out of Paris, on the 26th of May, 1871.

It was against such men as these : the Jeckers, the Mornys, the Miramons, the Bastidas,* the Napoleons, the Maximilians, and the less distinguished adventurers of two continents, who flattered and plundered them, that Benito Juarez, almost forgotten in his northern retreat, was found to fight in Mexico.

But at Chapultepec and at the Tuileries, the trumpet was bravely blown for the delectation of fools.

In September, 1865, a new Mexican loan for £10,000,000 was launched in Paris, in bonds or

---

* According to Griscelli, "Crimes Politiques de Napoleon III.," (Paris, 1873), pp. 55-59, it was Monsignor La Bastida, afterwards Archbishop of Mexico, who negotiated the secret Convention between Jecker and Morny.   It is only fair to Monsieur Jecker to add to all that has been said and cited, that he has published a long and elaborate defence of his conduct in the *Revue Contemporaine* of January 15th, 1868.
I have read the article with much care, but with little satisfaction.

obligations of 500 francs, issued at 340, with a lottery or drawing, with rich prizes, devised to attract the Mexicans, who were understood to be devoted to gambling. But the net was spread in vain. The Mexicans—gamblers or otherwise, failed to subscribe ; and although the new loan was combined with a scheme of converting the loan of the previous year, already at a serious discount, and, although the entire administrative power of the French Empire and a powerful syndicate of bankers, supported by M. Fould, was devoted to the placing of the bonds among the French provincials, the issue fell very flat, and before the end of 1866 the bonds were quoted on the Exchanges of London and Paris at a nominal $18\frac{1}{4}$ per cent. of their *par* value.

Nor did any very large number of dollars find their way into the Mexican Treasury ; and the Empire was once more bankrupt, within a twelvemonth of the issue of the loan.

The French army of occupation had been guilty, almost from the time of their arrival in the city of Mexico, of many and great atrocities : not the spasmodic cruelties of an ill-disciplined

---

* The 1864 Loan had declined at the same time to $12\frac{1}{2}$
The secret history of all these Imperial stock-jobbing operations will be found in Kératry ' La Créance Jecker," pp. 106-153.
See also Lefèvre ; II , pp, 156-170, where the matter is still more fully developed by extracts from the Imperial correspondence,

soldiery, but the organized tyranny of military Governors, irresponsible and arbitrary, chagrined at the poor success of their operations in the field. Courts Martial were the only tribunals recognized in the country, wherever the National flag had ceased to fly. The capital, under the eye of the Commander-in-Chief, was governed with an uncompromising vigour. In the provinces the vigour was still more pronounced. Houses and even villages were plundered and burnt, as a matter of military discipline. The lives and honour of the peaceable inhabitants were everywhere at the mercy of some choleric captain on the spot.* The Contra-guerrilla had more than the savagery, without any of the redeeming patriotism, of the guerilleros.

But for all this Bazaine was more blameable than Maximilian, and local commanders like General de Champagny were perhaps more blameable than

---

* By a decree issued as early as 20th June, 1863, the whole of Mexico was placed under martial law, and so remained virtually until the restoration of President Juarez.—Lefèvre, I., 315 ; and II., 243-5.

The massacres at Tlacotalpam (July 30, 1864), Amatlan Huanchinango (August, 1864) ["Mexico; V." pp.658-660] were only exceeded in horror by that of Concordia—whose name is more easily recalled! (11th nf February, 1865) (*op. cit.*, p. 696).

These are only one or two out of the many hundreds.

The celebrated Courts Martial, first established by Castagny, 25th of January, 1865, were so *effective* that Bazaine refused to countersign the Imperial Decree of October 5th.—Kératry, 84, Mexico, 694-6, and *post* p. 264.

Bazaine. Mexico, to the French soldiery, who were not likely to have been influenced by sentimental proclamations, was an enemy's country. The climate was trying ; the occupation was unpopular ; the National troops, patiently maintaining an unequal contest against the overwhelming forces of the invader, were always spoken of as rebels and brigands. That houses should be plundered and towns burnt, that prisoners should be shot and defenceless citizens murdered and outraged, was not extraordinary. But that the system* which produced these horrors should be accepted and perpetuated by the foreign usurper says as little for his heart as for his head. †

Yet all this was as nothing to his conduct in October, 1865.

---

* As a specimen and a certain indication of the savagery with which the war was waged by the French against the Mexicans, whom they came to civilise, I am able to give *totidem verbis* a general order issued by Bazaine to all the officers of his army on the 11th of October, 1865:

"Je vous invite à faire savoir aux troupes sous vos ordres que je n'admets pas qu'on fasse des prisonniers. Tout individu, quel qu'il soit, qui sera pris les armes à la main, sera mis à mort. Aucun échange de prisonniers ne se fera.

" BAZAINE."

It is scarcely possible to believe that such an order is genuine' yet I have copied it from the appreciative pages of Monsieur Duvernois, where it may be read, with the Editor's apologies, on pp. 364-370.

† According to M. Faucher de Saint Maurice, author of a very eulogistic little biography of the Archduke, pleasantly written, but poetry rather than history, under the title of " Notes pour servir," etc., Quebec, 1889, (p. 49), the favourite motto of Maximilian was the English, *Take it coolly !*

By that time, not only any man of sense, but any man of only average folly, would have perceived that the Empire was a failure ; any man of only average vanity would have realized that he was not wanted in Mexico. An acquaintance of a year-and-a-half had not rendered Maximilian's Government more popular.* An army of sixty thousand men had not been able to drive his modest rival out of his country. While he received the measured homage of lords in waiting, and was admired by maids of honour ; while he lavished the money that was collected by foreign bayonets, on the gratification of each passing whim, Juarez, without a Court and without an ally, remained President of Mexico.

Yet beyond the fact that Maximilian was singularly and pre-eminently unfitted for the position in which he had placed himself, and that he had neither legal nor moral right to be there at all, his faults, up to October, 1865, had been rather faults of omission than of commission ; of incompetence

---

* " A la fin de 1865, le trésor Mexicain s'épuisait déjà, et la mauvaise gestion financière provoquait un accroissement de déficit qui d'ailleurs n'eût jamais pu être comblé par le contrôle le plus sévère, car les recettes, eussent-elles été regulierement perçues ne dépassaient pas 90 millions de francs, tandis que, sans parler des amortissements les dépenses engloutissaient 150 millions au moins. Pourtant jamais le besoin d'argent ne s'était manifesté plus impérieusement." Kératry, p. 88.

rather than of wickedness, of weakness rather than
of blood-guiltiness.

Had he abdicated his pinchbeck Crown, as he is
said to have desired, in the Summer of 1865,*
he might have been blamed as a poltroon, or he
might have been lauded as a hero—a Reputation is
that which no man can foretell—but he would have
quitted Mexico with the self-satisfaction of an
honest man.

What he actually did was something very
different. Believing, or affecting to believe, that all
resistance to his authority was on the point of
extinction, and anxious to give the *coup de grâce* to
such resistance as might yet endure, he prepared
and published a Proclamation and a Decree † by

---

* Mexico, 763.

† It is always stoutly maintained by the apologists of
Maximilian, as the only possible justification for this sanguinary Decree, that the Archduke at least honestly supposed that
the whole of Mexico was already subject to his Government,
and that none but brigands were left to oppose him and his
civilization.

But in a very interesting little book, published at Rome, at the
end of 1867 : "Rapporti della Corte di Roma col governo Messi-
cano," publishing for the first time many original letters and
documents, I read in a confidential letter from Maximilian to the
Holy See, under date 29th of June, 1865, not only that the
greater part of Mexico refused to accept his government, but
that he knew it, and complained bitterly to the Pope of his
hard and helpless condition :

"*Bisogna dirlo francamente* " says he, in the opening of this
letter, "*che la nostra situazione militare è delle peggiore*" .. And after
enumerating in detail the various cities that were still in open

which it was ordained that every soldier or officer, or any man belonging or appertaining or attached in any way to the forces of the National army, or any other person who might give them warning, notice, or counsel, or should give or sell them horses, arms, or food, should, on falling into the hands of the French or Imperial Mexican commanders, be put to death within twenty-four hours.* The whole of Mexico, with the exception of the partizans of the usurper, was condemned to death. The religious wars of the Sixteenth Century in Europe can hardly supply a parallel in reckless contemplation of slaughter.

The apologists of Maximilian have endeavoured to lay the blame of this wicked and foolish Decree upon the Ministers who accepted it, rather than upon the Autocrat who propounded it ; and Maximilian himself, in his defence before the Tribunal at Querétaro, sought to cast the entire responsibility of its enunciation upon Marshal Bazaine ; and of its execution upon his French officers.† A plea under such circumstances must not be too nicely criticized. Yet the responsi-

---

revolt, and the list is a long one, he concludes his review of the situation thus : "*Dal Norte non pervengono fiu notizie, di modo che la posizione militareé lo repèto, assai cattiva.*"

* Procurando que el reo reciba los auxilios espirituales.

† Mexico, 727.

bility is purely that of the Emperor himself. The draft of the Decree exists, and it is in his own handwriting.[1]   Bazaine disapproved and declined even to countersign the Proclamation.[2]

---

*   Kératry, 84

Yet Arrangoiz (IV 17-24), elaborately contends that Bazaine was entirely to blame.

† According to Lefèvre, II , 240: the draft which he has seen is not in the Archduke's handwriting.

‡ The refusal of Bazaine, indeed, was not suggested by any considerations of mercy, but simply in that, not being one of Maximilian's regular Ministers, his signature would have been superfluous, if not impertinent. The Courts Martial, moreover, were in full swing No quarter was given, as we have seen, by the French in the field ; and the grant to Mexicans of such enormous power of slaughtering other Mexicans appeared to Bazaine to be bad policy No action of the French would render the Archduke so unpopular in Mexico as the proceedings of his Mexican supporters. And French cruelty in the eyes of a French Marshal like Bazaine, was a much more reasonable and respectable thing than Mexican cruelty, even when suggested by an Austrian Archduke

Yet, according to M. Gaulot (" Maximilian," 277), Bazaine, in a confidential letter to the Minister of War in Paris, makes use of words which would seem to invest him with a certain share in the responsibility of this odious edict. " S. M.," says he, " s'est enfin decidée *sur mes conseils* à donner une preuve de fermeté qui a fait un bon effet parmi les conservateurs."

" Mais quant á la forme choisie par Maximilien," continues M. Gaulot himself (*ib.*), " le Marechal n'y fut pour rien."

" La *fermeté* de Maximilien " was indeed a poor thing !

It may perhaps fairly be noticed here that on the 7th of August, 1866, a year after the Decree, and when the fortunes of the Empire were desperate, Maximilian proposed to *declare the whole of Mexico in a state of siege* ; and that he was only prevented from this astounding act of savagery by the remonstrances of Bazaine! His letter and that of the humane Marshal will be found in Kératry, 152-157.

One single individual was withdrawn from the scope of this edict of death.   Not Lerdo de Tejada, nor yet Porfirio Diaz, not even the President himself. But in case Vicente Riva Palacio should fall into the hands of the army, wrote the Imperial Secretary to Marshal Bazaine, let him be brought at once to Mexico.   "*This is the only exception* that his Majesty for special reasons proposes to make to the execution of the Decree of October 3."*

The belief in the truth of statements on account of their *impossibility* is one of the lost theological arts or mental exercises of the middle ages.   But when we are gravely told that Maximilian's reason for the fulmination of this dreadful decree was to predispose the mind of Juarez to recognise his Government, and induce him to accept the post of Chief Justice of the Supreme Court † under the Empire, we are tempted to wonder that people can find anything strange in the creations of Mr. Gilbert and Mr. Lewis Carroll.   Whether the suggestion is more valuable as a sample of Maximilian's methods of Government, or of the fatuity of those who would explain them, is somewhat hard to say.

---

* Letter of November 16th, 1865, Military Secretary to Bazaine.

Kératry, 319-320-—Mexico, V., 735.

† Kératry, 83-4

The making of the decree itself; the exception of one favoured foe from the universality of its operation; the reasons that were suggested for its issue; the excuses that were made for its execution; each and all are marked with the same brand of folly and wickedness, leading, as they needs must, to disaster and disgrace.*

It is a common device in Oriental fiction, an one familiar to every reader of the Biblical story of Esther, for a judicious Sovereign to present to an unsuspecting evil-doer some hypothetical case of iniquity, and desire to be advised as to the punish-

---

* It is commonly said that this sanguinary edict was directed only against persons found by the French or Imperialist troops with arms in their hands. This would have been sufficiently comprehensive, yet the scope of the Decree was far greater. "All those," runs the opening section, " who may belong to armed bands or associations *(reunions)* not legally authorized, whether they proclaim any political pretext or not, and whatever may be the number of those who form the band, their organization and the character and denomination which they may assume, shall be judged in military fashion by the Courts Martial, and on being found guilty, even if only of the fact of belonging to the band, shall be condemned to death, and executed within twenty-four hours from the time of sentence "

My translation is somewhat bald. I have desired only to make it literal.

It is further worthy of notice that on the 4th of November, 1866, over a year after this Decree had been in force, it was replaced, after mature consideration by Maximilian, by one hardly less sanguinary; and the order transmitted on the 5th of February, 1867, by the Archduke to *Mon cher Miramon* as to the disposal of Juarez as soon as he should be taken, is more than sufficient to show the disposition of the so-called Emperor, even when Bazaine was far away. See Lefèvre, II., 290-295.

ment that should be meted out to the culprit. But
Maximilian of Hapsburg little recked, when he
decreed the death of every man who opposed his
Government in the free Republic of Mexico, that
he was signing his own death-warrant. It was no
shaft forged by Juarez that struck him down at
Querétaro. It was the weapon that he himself had
fashioned.*

The Decree of October 3rd, 1865, was not long
suffered to remain a dead letter. On the 13th of
the same month the Imperialist General Mendez †
surprised and defeated the Constitutional forces
under General Arteaga, at Santa Anna Amatlan,
near Tancitaro; and a number of prisoners fell
into his hands. Their high rank and military position induced Mendez to refer the case to headquarters,
where as Maximilian afterwards maintained, the
Decree was interpreted with *benignity*, before
carrying out the new decree. And the result
was the execution, or rather the murder in cold
blood, at Uruapan, on October 22nd, 1865, of
General Arteaga, Brigadier-General Salazar, and
Colonels Diaz Paracho, Villa Gomez, and Perez

---

* Technically, no doubt, he was tried and condemned to
death under the law and decree of February, 1862, but he
would hardly have been indicted under its provisions but for
his own action in October, 1865.

† Mendez had only the rank of Colonel at the time. See
Lefèvre, II., 267-9

Milicua, with a number of officers of lower grade. No reference to this exploit was permitted in any of the Mexican newspapers. Mendez was rewarded with a step in the Army, and the command of a Brigade.* The civilization of Mexico had indeed been commenced in good earnest.

Yet some Belgian prisoners in the hands of the Constitutional army, who had been treated with the utmost consideration by their captors, were moved to address a remonstrance to the Emperor upon his violation of all the laws and usages of civilized warfare, inasmuch as it might expose them to reprisals. But reprisals were never permitted by Juarez or his Generals. Yet no one at the Imperial Court seems to have had sufficient sense of humour to be struck by the difference between the procedure of the refined and refining

---

* The remonstrance of Mr. Bigelow, the United States Minister, to the French Foreign Office, provoked only a scornful refusal to be responsible for the acts of the Emperor of Mexico. "Mexico." 735.

M. Gaulot, in his elaborate apology for Bazaine and Maximilian, is very severe upon those writers who "donnant dans un don-quichottisme un peu naif, ont gémi sur cette legion de patriotes exposés à être fusillés dans le vingt quatre heures." "Maximilian:" 280-282.‌ "L'Empire," says he, "a essayé au Mexique ce que la royauté a fait en Algérie, ce que la Republique a executé à Tunis et à Tonkin." This defence appears to me even more *naïve* than the indignation of his opponents. Is the man, moreover, so very simple who prefers Don Quixote to Bazaine?

foreigner and that of the savage and unspeakable barbarian. If Maximilian was not the most unscrupulous of usurpers, he was certainly the dullest of doctrinaires.

CHAPTER XIII.

Paso del Norte.

At the end of 1865 the fortunes of Juarez had fallen to their very lowest ebb. His patience alone was not exhausted. Hope yet remained in the well-nigh empty box. Porfirio Diaz, his most trusted General, had been besieged at Oaxaca by Bazaine in person, at the head of a numerous army. The town had fallen; and the Commander, after a gallant defence, had been taken prisoner and imprisoned in a fortress at Puebla.[*]

In other places the National troops had suffered serious, if less striking, reverses; and at Paso del Norte, on the very brink of the river which divided his territory from that of the United States, Juarez was making his last stand.

By the end of the year, the army of the Intervention had been increased to an effective of not less

---

[*] He refused to give his parole, and was fortunate enough to make his escape after a few weeks' captivity. Marshal Forey expressed his opinion in the French Senate that he ought to have been shot. Kératry, 58.

than seventy-two thousand men,[*] while the National forces, scattered, harassed, and disorganised, could hardly be said to constitute an army at all. It was the master-hand of Juarez alone that held aloft the torch of National life in Mexico.

At this moment the country was threatened with a new danger, a deadly peril from within. The Presidential powers with which Juarez was invested under the Constitution, in January, 1861, expired on the 30th of November, 1865; and pending a new election, the supreme authority would, under ordinary circumstances, pass into the hands of the Vice-President, Chief Justice of the Supreme Court of Mexico.

Juarez himself had succeeded in this way to the Presidential chair on the flight of Comonfort. Yet the general conditions were widely different; for Comonfort in 1859 was a rebel and a fugitive; Juarez in 1865 was well-nigh the sole representative of National authority and National defence in the country. He had, moreover, been specially

---

*	Mexicans	35,500
	Belgians	1,500
	Austrians	6,500
	French	28,500
	Total troops	72,000

Kératry, 92.

invested by the Chambers, in April, 1863, with the supreme power in Mexico, until the foreigner should have been driven out of the country ; and it was obvious, not only to him, but to all his friends, that a Presidential election, although it would certainly have led to his own re-election to office, might possibly have been productive of dangerous divisions, or unfortunate political complications, and would certainly, under the existing circumstances of the country, have been a piece of pure constitutional pedantry.

Accordingly, at Paso del Norte, on the 8th of November, 1865, Juarez issued a Decree* formally postponing the new Presidential election until a more convenient season.

It is hard to see how he could have acted otherwise ; and his action has been criticised only by a few of the more jealous of his enemies, and a few of the most impracticable of doctrinaires. Had Maximilian taken advantage of the opportunity to summon a Parliament, and submitted his own claims to supreme government to the representatives of the nation—however elected—he would have seriously embarrassed Juarez, and he could hardly have failed to strengthen his own position both in and out of Mexico.

---

* The Decree is printed in full by Domenech : History, III., 368-9.

That in a country like Mexico, and under circumstances like those in which Juarez then found himself, only two men should have been found to make anything like a protest against his action, when so admirable an opportunity presented itself for pronouncement and defection, is itself one of the most remarkable facts in the situation. It was General Ortega, a man who had begun life as a travelling mountebank, and as a capable soldier, had been advanced to high honour by Juarez, who saw fit at this juncture to challenge his right to a retention of power. And a *pronunciamiento*, of somewhat an antiquated type, was planned by him against the President, or against his new Decree.

Ortega, however, found neither sympathy nor assistance in Mexico; his projects were sternly repressed in the United States ; and his intrigues led to nothing but his own confusion, and the desertion of his solitary supporter, General Ruiz,* to the camp of Maximilian.

The demeanour of Juarez, in these trying times, was in the highest degree characteristic and

---

* General Ruiz took advantage of this opportunity of changing sides; but he was alone, or almost alone in his action.

Sebastian Lerdo de Tejada was, in this as in other cases, the most faithful supporter and the boldest adviser of President Juarez.—See Domenech, III., 367-370.

admirable. Hunted, like some wild creature, to the very confines of his territory; outlawed, not only by the usurper in Mexico, but by every Government in Europe; without money, without credit, and at length actually doomed to death; the inflexible President maintained not only a calm, but even a well-satisfied demeanour; doing all that was humanly possible to maintain his Constitutional Government in Mexico, with the least appearance of effort; never complaining, never reviling, awaiting with a cheerful hope the dawn of a happier day.

His establishment at Paso del Norte was, as may be supposed, of the simplest; and yet the social obligations of his position as President of Mexico were never forgotten; and the ball that was given in honour of the anniversary of Mexican Independence, in the autumn of 1865, was attended not only by many of his friends in Mexico, but by some visitors from the United States to the North of the Rio Grande.

" We have seen many entertainments in New York," says one of his American guests, "some under the most favourable auspices, but we must in justice declare that we have seen none which surpassed the Mexican President's ball at El Paso * . . . .

* " New York Catholic World," Vol. XVI., No. 92, Nov., 1872, p. 283.

There may have been more glare, more glitter, more diamonds; but not more good taste, nor more elegance, nor more refinement, nor more genuine good breeding and good humour." . . . . . . After supper the President sat for over an hour chatting pleasantly with the American ladies in the simplest Spanish he could devise. " No one, "says the appreciative guest, " could have imagined, as they saw him laughing and chatting gaily away, that he had on his shoulders all the cares of a tottering government and of an empty treasury."

He would have been a bold man who, on that September night, would have prophesied that in less than eighteen months Maximilian would be a fugitive in a provincial town, and that in less than two years Juarez would be sitting in his Palace in the ancient capital of Mexico.

His guests, delighted as they were with the President and his reception, dared not harbour any such anticipations.

One personal trait that is recorded by the same American visitor, is too characteristic of the true nature of Juarez to be passed over in silence. When the toast of American Independence was proposed by the Mexican President, a tray was produced "generously loaded with excellent champagne": and the attendant in his hurry to open the wine, to which he was, no doubt, but little accustomed, allowed almost the entire contents of one bottle to discharge itself full in the face of Juarez himself. Juarez looked at the poor peon—" whose swarthy face grew sickly pale, and who seemed about to sink to the ground with terror and confusion "—neither in sorrow nor in anger. He took no notice whatever of the incident, but went on talking cheerfully as before. Such an accident, happening to most men, would have been laughable in the extreme. " It did not seem to us," said the stranger, " to place Juarez in a ludicrous position at all; his self-command was so perfect, his dignity so thoroughly preserved." *

It is an easy and a self-satisfying task to point out, in the workings of Divine Providence, the development of our own notions of the due apportionment of rewards and punishments in this world. Yet as to judge thus justly is surely superhuman, let it be sufficient for us to say as a simple historical fact, that after the 3rd of October, 1865, the position of Maximilian became steadily more and more impossible in Mexico,† and that the fortunes of Juarez, reduced by the end of the year to their lowest depth of abasement,

---

* " Catholic World " *in loc. cit.* p. 281.

† La crise du dénouement commença avec l'année 1866. Masseras, p. 66.

were destined soon afterwards to enter upon a new era of prosperity.

The efforts of generations of Alfonsos and Ferdinands in old Spain were devoted during nearly eight hundred years, from the rout of Covadonga to the fall of Granada, to what was known as the Reconquest, *la Reconquista*, of Spain.

Reduced by the end of 1865 to a hands-breadth of territory in the extreme north of the Republic, less important than the ancient kingdoms of Oviedo and the Asturias, Juarez, in little more than a year-and-a-half, accomplished the *Reconquest* of Mexico.

It is sometimes asserted by those who would minimise the credit that is due to the " Indian Savage " for his steadfastness in misfortune and adversity, that he was ever secretly supported by the United States. But this supposed assistance was rather negative than positive. It was not that Juarez was loved, but that Maximilian was hated, at Washington. And at the close of 1865, Mr. Seward actually undertook a journey to the West Indies in order to negotiate with the evergreen Santa Anna * at Saint Thomas. At the

---

* " Et dont l'ambition," says M. Gaulot [Max., 317-318] " aiguisée par la rancune et le désir de vengeance accepterait avec enthousiasme le rôle qu'on lui destinait." How the negotiations came to nought I have never been able to learn.

same time General Logan refused the post of American Minister at the Court of Juarez, and Mr. Campbell, who soon afterwards accepted the Mission in his place, neglected, or feared, to present his credentials at the Wandering Court of the President. In all this there was but little of support, or even of encouragement. But the negotiations with Santa Anna came to nothing.* Juarez was able to bide his time. And Mr. Campbell's credentials were ultimately presented to the President, installed in his Palace at Mexico. So much for the trials and troubles of 1865.

With the Spring of 1866 came a change in the National fortunes. The Emperor Napoleon, weary of the fruitless struggle on behalf of the ungrateful and fatuous Archduke, and chagrined at the failure of all his hopes of French aggrandizement in the New World, † announced on the opening of the Chambers (January 22nd, 1866), that " inasmuch as the Mexican Empire was already consolidated, and its opponents had no

---

* Gaulot : Maximilian, 320.

See further as to Santa Anna at St. Thomas, Report of Lieutenant Gaston de Béarn, printed in the same work, pp. 246-251.

† Mr. Goldwin Smith, " History of the United States," 1893, p. 292, suggests that Napoleon had views even more ambitious than the acquisition of territory within the limits of Mexico, and may have even contemplated the recovery of Louisiana.

longer even a leader "—the presence of Juarez was conveniently ignored—the French troops " having accomplished their mission " would shortly retire from Mexico.   And on the 6th of April (1866) his Foreign Minister, M. Drouyn de Lluys, addressed a note to the Mexican Government, announcing that the withdrawal of French troops would commence in the following October, to be completed before the end of 1867.

Maximilian, overwhelmed at first by the fatal news, promptly proceeded to persuade himself that the threat would not be carried into execution; and as we are told by an eye-witness, at the end of a week no trace remained of the anxiety that was caused by the French despatch.*

The mere suggestion of a French retirement would have nerved any ruler of average intelligence to take some thought for the defence of his position, when the foreign supporters should have abandoned him.   But nothing was done, even at this eleventh hour, to organise a Mexican Army.† To inspire the existing troops with zeal, with con-

---

* In March, 1866, Eloin was sent on a secret mission to Austria, and Almonte was entrusted with a less equivocal embassy to the Court of the Tuileries.

† Masseras, 72.

A convention was signed at Mexico, June 26th, 1866, for the investigation and settlement of British claims, by a mixed commission. Nothing, as far as I can learn, ever came of it. See " Accounts and Papers," 1867, LXXIV., p. 501.

fidence, with military pride, or even to subject them to military discipline, was a task not only beyond the power, but beyond the vision of Maximilian.

Recruiting for the Imperial Army was only carried on by means of a press. Indian labourers, carried off by force from their farms or their villages, were added to the scourings of the jails throughout the country.[*]

The troops so recruited were poorly paid, and that only by forced loans exacted by the local commanders, to the ruin of the peaceful inhabitants. The provincial treasuries were plundered,[†] not only by Imperial Mexicans, but by the Imperial foreigners.[‡] If government be the maintenance of law and order, then assuredly in the Autumn of 1866 there was no Government in Mexico.

Yet Maximilian, when he was not wandering about the country, was working almost night and day at Chapultepec. Plans were elaborated. Commissioners were appointed. Reports were submitted. Minutes were written. Decrees were promulgated. But no business was ever done.

---

[*] Kératry, 141.

[†] Plaçant les citoyens dans la necessité d'émigrer pour ne pas être victimes de telles vexations. Lacunza to Bazaine, 28th of April, 1866. Cited in Kératry, 100-104.

[‡] Les hommes de la légion autrichiénne forcaient à Puebla la caisse de la Douane pour se payer l'arriéré de leur solde. Masseras, 83.

In June, 1866, the Imperial Treasury was actually bankrupt. At the beginning of July, the port of Matamoros, where Mejia had held good with great tenacity for twenty months, fell at length into the hands of the Liberal forces, and Mejia, with the few tattered soldiers that still followed him, was glad to escape by ship to Vera Cruz.* There was but one course open to Maximilian, and that was abdication. The courage or ambition of his consort, it is said, stayed his hand; and within a fortnight after the receipt of the news from the North, the Empress Charlotte† embarked at Vera Cruz on a desperate mission to the Tuileries.‡

Upon the personal and political results of her most unhappy journey it is not necessary for us to enlarge. Our place is with Juarez in Mexico.

---

* " Mexico," V., 753.

† When the Empress Charlotte undertook her ill-fated mission to Paris, there was actually not enough cash in the Treasury to provide for the expense of her journey, and it was necessary to appropriate some of the money set apart for the drainage of the lakes, held in reserve in case of sudden inundation of the capital.

‡ On July 13th. Kératry, 149.

CHAPTER XIV.

RECONQUISTA.

From June, 1866, the tide of reconquest steadily set in from the North. The French were concen‑ trating their troops, previous to re-embarkation. As they evacuated one post after another, the National forces reoccupied the cities or fortresses, in most cases not only without resistance, but amid the hearty acclamation of the citizens. The Mexican Imperialists, or those who had been counted as such, one by one returned to their allegiance, and either took service in the National armies, or became merged in the civil population. The persecution of his Mexican opponents formed no part of the policy of Juarez. Bloodshed, save on the field of battle, was not permitted to the Constitutional leaders.

On the 17th of June, the President was able to move his seat of Government from Paso del Norte to the more important town of Chihuahua ; on the 26th of July he was found at Monterey, and on the 3rd of August at Saltillo.

Maximilian, after the departure of the Empress, fell a prey to more interested and less scrupulous advisers.

The origin of the Abbé Fischer, one of the evil influences of the last days of the Empire, is involved in considerable obscurity. A German, connected in some left-handed way with the Royal family of Wurtemberg, Fischer seems to have made his first appearance as a Texas colonist in 1845. Afterwards a lawyer's clerk, then a Californian goldseeker, he at length abjured his Lutheran faith, took Orders of the Church of Rome in Mexico, and succeeded in getting himself appointed secretary to the Bishop of Durango. Dismissed from this post on account of a scandalous intrigue, he contrived to introduce himself to Maximilian, by whom he was sent upon some backstairs mission to Rome ; and soon after his return from the Vatican he took his place as nominal Private Secretary to His Majesty --in truth the hidden director of the affairs of Mexico. And the hand of this Court priest is possibly to be seen, when Maximilian, taking advantage of the absence of Bazaine in the provinces, suddenly called upon two officers on active service in the French Army, General Osmont and General Friant, to accept the portfolios of War and Finance in the Mexican Imperial Cabinet. *

---

* It appeared to Marshal Bazaine. (see the letter quoted in Gaulot : Fin, 130-131,) to be a *manœuvre* "pour entraîner

The appointment was no doubt [*] well calculated to embarrass the French Government.
And the objections that were necessarily urged
by Marshal Randon, the Minister of War in
Paris, to the employment of the French Generals
in the civil Government of Mexico, gave the Archduke the opportunity for much peevish complaint
and expostulation. Yet the manœuvre was scarcely
worthy of the occasion.

To seek to force the hand of Louis Napoleon,
beset as he was with difficulties both in Paris and
at Washington, was neither generous nor politic;
but to seek, to fail, and to lament, was simply
detestable. It is not thus that Empires are
established.

The wisest thing, perhaps, that Maximilian could
do, or did, about this time, was to pack up his
valuables, and send them off to Vera Cruz, for
embarkation on board the Austrian *Dandolo*. But

la France malgré elle, à reconstituer le rôle de l'intervention,
ou même pour lui susciter des embarras."

It was, in truth, a stroke of policy in which the Archduke
is seen at his worst, with the hand of a Court Jesuit, and the
heart of a second-rate attorney.

  [*] The appointment of MM. Osmont and Friant was announced on the 25th of July.

Bazaine's remonstrances and Maximilian's insistances lasted
until the middle of September, when instructions were
received from Paris, to the effect that the officers must choose
between French and Mexican service. It was then that the
Archduke threw himself into the arms of the Reactionary
party. Gaulot: Fin, 159-163.

the sight of the well-laden *fourgons* wending their way down to the coast was not re-assuring to his starving supporters in Mexico.* Abdication was obviously in the air.

On the 26th of September, already tired of the French toys for which he had so loudly cried not two months before, he dismissed his entire Cabinet, and summoned a new set of Ministers to the Palace, drawn from the ranks of the Ultramontane or Reactionary party, and controlled by the all-powerful Abbé Fischer.†

September passed away and brought no relief. The new Ministry was no more successful, and was, if anything, less popular than the old. And in October came the news that the Archduchess had quarrelled with the French Emperor, and that her reason was at least gravely affected. Maximilian, overwhelmed by the cruel tidings, fled, at two o'clock on the morning of the 21st of October, secretly and almost alone, from

---

* Masseras, 85-87. Kératry, 202-210.

† The appointment of the two Frenchmen had not involved either Bazaine or Napoleon in the desired embarrassment ; and Maximilian abruptly dismissed them and threw himself into the arms of their bitterest enemies.—Gaulot: Fin, 130-131 and 158.

The nominal chief, or President , of this new Cabinet, was Teodosio Lares, a violent reactionary "qui passait avec raison pour l'âme damnée de Mgr. La Bastida." Gaulot: Fin, 158. Kératry, 103.

the capital, leaving his astonished Ministers to offer their resignations to the departing Bazaine.* For Maximilian had, at this time, not only resolved upon abdication, but he had virtually abdicated, and he informed Marshal Bazaine in a most confidential letter of his progress and of his plans.

The story of the flight from Mexico; the hesitation at Orizaba; the sudden re-appearance of Marquez and Miramon; the temptation of Eloin; the mission of Castelnau; † the wiles of the Abbé Fischer; the conference of notables; and the half-hearted and completely insane return of the Archduke to the capital—all this may be read, in the fullest details, in the sympathetic pages of M. de Kératry, M. Masseras, and M. Gaulot. And it is a terrible exposition of vanity and of irresolution; the history of a man no less obstinate than irresolute, ‡

---

* Bazaine not only refused to accept their resignation, but he even induced them to withdraw it. Masseras, 92.

† I have said nothing about the mission of General Castelnau, of which the importance is rather French than Mexican; although in a life of Maximilian the subject would be of the utmost interest. I am afraid, as it is, that the great attraction of the story of Maximilian's own fall may have led me to dwell more upon some details than is quite justifiable in a biography of Juarez. I can only say in extenuation, that I have not only constantly checked myself in the progress of my work, but that I have cut out a great deal in the course of revision.

‡ —— Nec jam revocabile damnum . . .
Eventu rerum stolido didicere magistro.
Claudian, contra Eutrop: lib. II. 489.

the victim of evil counsellors, of evil principles, and of superlatively evil fortune.*

Pushed on when he might have stood in safety, held back when he was rightly struggling to advance, trusting only in those who were unworthy of confidence, flouting all good advisers ; he showed like the incarnation of the weakness of humanity striving in vain against the great world forces which his presumption had raised up in his path. †

On the tenth of November, Miramon and Marquez disembarked together at Vera Cruz : ‡

---

* See a letter from Eloin to Maximilian, stating that the Austrians were loudly demanding the abdication of the Emperor Francis Joseph, and were ready to welcome Maximilian as Emperor ; referred to in Masseras, 101, and Kératry, 218, and printed in full in the Appendix to Kératry, 320-322.

† General Douay, in his confidential reports addressed to a friend in France, and submitted privately to the eye of Napoleon at the Tuileries, speaks at this time of the blind folly of Maximilian, " un des princes les plus idiots et plus imbéciles." . . . . and of " son entêtement qui ne peut que le mener á une chute ridicule."—Letter of 27th of October, 1869, in *cit*. Gaulot, Fin, 188-9.

‡ Miramon and Marquez were associated in so many villainies from 1857 to 1867, that it is hardly surprising that each one should seek to excuse or palliate his own conduct at the expense of the other. The *Times* correspondent in Mexico in 1867, who should have known better, writes of " Marquez, the brother of Miramon."—*Times*, 17th of August, 1867.

Maximilian is said to have declared almost with his dying breath that Marquez was the greatest blackguard in Mexico (Clément Duvernois, " L'Intervention Français," p. 934 ; Daran: "Miguel Miramon," p. 252), and he was probably not far

one from his Asiatic Nunnery, the other from his Prussian School. The last act of the tragedy was about to open, and the dark figures of these two storm-birds take their places once more upon the scene.*

In the meantime, almost from the day in May, 1865, that the war of Secession had come to an end with the capture of Jefferson Davis, Mr. Seward had been urging the Emperor Napoleon to withdraw his troops from the soil of the great northern continent of America.

The *States* indeed, once more *United*, had now nothing to fear from the action of the French in Mexico; yet the presence of a European army on their frontier was distasteful to the Government of Washington. Diplomatic representations of ever increasing vigour were constantly conveyed to the Tuileries; and the French Emperor was well

---

wrong. He escaped the death which has cast a faint glamour of respectability upon Miramon. It is said by M. Daran(p. 251) that " de l'exil il redigea des libelles outrageants pour la mémoire Miramon." It is just what might have been expected of him !

* An incident that occurred in November, 1866, is worthy of passing notice.

"An attempt, benevolent in the intention, but highly irregular in the execution, was made by the United States Commandant at Brownsville, on the North-East frontier, to assist General Escobedo in the reduction of the Mexican town of Matamoros, separated from it only by the breadth of the river, and led to a practical demonstration of the National policy of permitting no foreigner to intervene even as a friend in the domestic affairs of the country."—" Mexico" V., 795-7.

content to announce the withdrawal of his army before the end of 1867.

But in November, 1866, it was obvious that a crisis* was impending in Mexico. The French Army was already on the move. The abdication of Maximilian was virtually announced. And at this juncture, two special envoys, Mr. Campbell and General Sherman, were dispatched from Washington, formally accredited to Juarez as President of the Republic, with instructions to await the development of affairs in Mexico.†

The appointment of Mr. Campbell, indeed, had been actually made some time before. But he had not thought fit to proceed to his destination. The inclusion of a distinguished General in the new Commission added much to its special importance, and the Envoys were enjoined to use their good offices as regards the establishment of an effective National Government, upon the expected departure of Maximilian. Juarez, no doubt, was to be recognised, as he had always been recognised, by the United States, as the Elect of the Mexican nation. But the instructions to the Envoys were as vague as they were comprehensive, and would

---

* Mr. Seward had failed to make anything of his negotiations with Santa Anna ; but it was said that he was at this time inclined to favour Porfirio Diaz rather than Juarez as a candidate for the Presidency of Mexico.

† Kératry, 226-234.

U

have justified negotiations with the retiring French, if not with the retiring Emperor.

At the end of the last week of November, 1866, the frigate *Susquehannah* arrived off Vera Cruz. Bazaine was sounded as to the reception that would be accorded to the officious visitors. The attitude of the Marshal was courteous, if not actually inviting.* But before the Envoys had decided to land, the most astounding intelligence was received from Orizaba.

Maximilian had changed his mind. He would not abdicate. He would conquer Mexico for himself; the more easily, he said, as the French, who had so long thwarted him, were about to take their departure from the country. Padre Fischer had promised him money. Marquez had promised him troops. Miramon had promised him victory. Bazaine might go, as soon as he chose—Maximilian would remain in Mexico.

On the 26th of November, he had summoned a solemn conference to meet at Orizaba, when the Mexican people, represented by eighteen particular adherents of Maximilian, resolved, by a majority of two ! (10 to 8) to request him to continue to reign.

Such conferences might have been good enough,

----

* " Le Maréchal répondit que le Général Sherman serait acceuilli par lui avec toute la distinction due à son haut grade, et avec la plus franche cordialité." Gaulot · Fin, 211.

before his arrival, to deceive others ; but that after the experience of nearly three years in Mexico, he should summon a conference to deceive himself, passes the common measure of folly. *

On the 1st of December, accordingly, after four day's hesitation, a proclamation made known to the city and to the world that the good of Mexico rendered it necessary that Maximilian should retain the supreme power, until such time as he should see fit to summon a National Assembly.† The National Assembly, as may be supposed, was never summoned ; but Maximilian's proclamation rendered the presence of the Envoys on the coast of Mexico superfluous, if not ridiculous, and the *Susquehannah* steamed slowly back to New Orleans.‡

---

* Gaulot : Fin, 203-205 ; and Domenech : Hist. III., 400-409.

† "A compter de ce moment" says Monsieur Masseras, p. 114, "c'en été fini . . . les envoyés americains n'avait plus dès lors que repartir."—ib., p. 119.

‡ One of the very numerous projects which are said to have about this time suggested themselves to Maximilian [according to M. de Kératry, 233-4] was the summoning of a Parliament. It is strange indeed that neither he nor any one of his so-called Liberal supporters should have thought of this before ; more especially as Juarez, hunted as he was in distant parts of the country, had never had an opportunity of summoning a Congress since the day on which he was entrusted with exceptional powers on the approach of the French, by the Parliament then sitting, in the Spring of 1863. Under these circumstances, Maximilian could have more effectively called his assembly the States General of the Nation. . . . and he could no doubt have had the members elected as he liked. [See also Kératry, 278-80.] A Parliament in 1864 might have gone far to establish his rule.

All this time, Juarez and the Constitutional troops were advancing ever nearer the goal. The area that still acknowledged the Empire was growing smaller and smaller. The tide of foreign invasion had already flowed away. The waters were drying up from off the face of the land, and the tops of the mountains were beginning to appear, as the floods were abating over Mexico.

Tampico had been re-occupied on the 7th of August, and Tuxpan on the 20th of September. The western ports of Guaymas and Mazatlan soon followed, with La Paz and Durango, in November, and on Christmas Eve the important city of Guadalajara,* second only in population to Mexico itself, and within three hundred miles of the Imperial Palace at Chapultepec, became the southern limit of the government of Juarez.

Nor was it only to the north of the capital that the rising tide engulphed the slender possessions of the usurper.

The important city of Oaxaca, so lately occupied by Bazaine himself, capitulated on the 31st of October to General Porfirio Diaz, who found himself once more at the head of a division; Jalapa was evacuated by its Austrian garrison at the

---

* After a battle fought and won by Colonel Parra, December 20-21, 1866. The inhabitants, without distinction of politics, were treated with the usual clemency of those who obeyed the orders of Juarez.

summons of General Alatorre on the 10th of
November. Perote was recovered on the 4th of
January, 1867, and Juarez, passing rapidly through
Durango, arrived on the 22nd at Zacatecas, on the
high road to the city of Mexico.

Everywhere the country was reoccupied, rather
than re-conquered, amid the acclamations of the
inhabitants. The cities surrendered, for the most
part, without striking a blow. The Imperial troops
hastened to enroll themselves under the banner of
the Constitutional Republic. The military commanders, amid so unanimous a display of National
feeling, did not even venture, on deserting the
Imperial colours, to indulge in the conventional
and time-honoured luxury of a *pronunciamiento*.*

The new administration, organised almost from
day to day, in the name of Juarez, was recognised
and obeyed by all, and worked with as much regularity as if it had never been interrupted† by the

---

* "Une tentative," says M. Masseras, 140-141, "faite
par le Géneral Ortega pour revendiquer la Présidence en vert u
d'une argutie légale avortait dans le ridicule, et se dénouait
prosaïquement par l' arrestation du malencontreux prétendant
resté l'unique partizan de sa propre candidature, phènomène
sans exemple dans les annales des pronunciamentos."

† This statement is not my own, with the exception of
the last few words, but a literal translation of Masseras,
p. 140. No foreigner in Mexico had better opportunities of
judging justly on the matter than he. His language struck
me as being very remarkable.

transitory intervention of any French or Austrian authority.

But we may not linger on the threshold of disaster.

On the 12th of December, 1866, Maximilian turned his steps once more towards the capital, drifting,* rather than marching to his doom. The friction between the French and the Imperial authorities was already extreme. The new Minister of Finance declined to recognise the receipts of the French Customs Surveyor at Vera Cruz; and called upon importers to pay their duties† twice over. Bazaine arrested the Chief of Police in the city of Mexico, and wrote to justify his conduct to the Archduke. Maximilian returned to the Marshal his own letter, unread, with an offensive note from the Abbé Fischer.‡

It was but a poor triumph over the departing ally.

On the 5th of February, 1867, the tricolour was hauled down on the flagstaff of the Palace of Buena Vista, and the French troops turned their faces to-

---

* Six weeks were occupied in this journey of one hundred and twenty miles!

† Masseras, 145.

‡ In connection with the arrest of a certain Garay, supposed to be a representative of President Juarez, and certainly furnished with a safe conduct by Bazaine. The editor of the Government newspaper *La Patria* was also arrested. Masseras, 146-8.

wards France. With bands playing and colours fly-ing, with drum and trumpet and all military pageant, Bazaine led his army through the streets and the great square of Mexico. With no feelings of grati-tude nor of kind regard towards the departing foe, the citizens knew not what they might expect in their place; and the French regiments marched out of the city through an uncertain and a silent crowd. Yet should one house at least have extended to them a grateful farewell.

But in the Imperial Palace every window remained tightly closed, as though a funeral pro-cession was in the streets. Maximilian, at this supreme moment, forgot what he owed to the man who had so long and so faithfully served him, who had protected his Government, and had actually paid his bills.

He forgot, moreover, what he owed to himself, as a Hapsburg, if not as a host—as an Austrian gentleman, if not as a Mexican Sovereign.

And Bazaine, with his ever faithful troops, rode out of Mexico, without show or token of merest conventional leave taking.* The army departed without aide-de-camp or escort, without a stirrup

* "A la fin du mois de Janvier, 1867, l'armée francaise en pleine retraite, s'allongeait comme un ruban d'acier sur la route poudreuse de Mexico à Vera Cruz." Kératry, 295.

cup, without a salute, without a complimentary riband of honour.*

The cross of Guadalupe may not have been a very precious decoration, but it would have been a token of gratitude and goodwill. And the refusal to grant so very cheap a favour was but one sign among many of Maximilian's singular perverseness as a politician; and of his singular paltriness as a Prince. The blood of the Hapsburgs flowed very thin in the veins of this unhappy descendant of so many Emperors.

Before the afternoon of the 5th of February was well spent, the last Frenchman had marched out of Mexico on his way to Puebla. And by six o'clock in the evening the walls and buildings were placarded with posters, on which the affrighted citizens read that the Government of the city had been assumed by Leonardo Marquez.

Miramon had quitted the capital on the 28th of December at the head of a considerable body of troops, and having surprised a small force under Colonel Antillon, at Zacatecas, just a month afterwards, he had dispatched a magniloquent report, speaking of his expectation of capturing Juarez

---

* How the Abbé Fischer prevented Maximilian from even extending to the departing soldiers the *promised* honour of a decoration, may also be read in the confessor's own most insolent letter addressed to General Osmont, and printed by M. de Kératry, pp. 298-300.

and his entire Cabinet in the course of a few days.

Maximilian, excited at the news, lost not an hour in writing to his General, specially charging him * to cause Juarez, Lerdo de Tejeda, Iglesias, Garcia, and Negrete to be *tried and condemned* by a Court Martial, as soon as they should be taken prisoners; and extending his recommendations generally to all civil functionaries, judicial, financial, cr ecclesiastical, who might fall into his hands.

These amiable instructions were happily not carried out, for the simple reason that, before they were received by Miramon, that General had been completely beaten by the Constitutional forces under Escobedo, and had only escaped with his life by abandoning his entire army to the enemy at San Jacinto (February 1st).† And among the spoils of war that fell into the hands of Escobedo was the very latest letter from Maximilian, which furnished President Juarez with the most unimpeachable evidence of the Archduke's benevolent intentions with regard to himself.

Meanwhile, the Imperial authority was reduced to the precarious possession of four or five towns,

---

* "*De una manera muy especial.*"—" Mexico á traves de los siglos," V., 815.

† The shooting of the French prisoners after the battle has given rise to considerable controversy. Taking them even to have been deserters, they might more advantageously have been sent after Bazaine.

and the doubtful allegiance of five or six thousand
soldiers.   The troops were recruited by raids upon
the passers-by in the public streets.   The Treasury
was replenished, not only by forced loans and forced
gifts, but by night attacks by the police upon the
strong-boxes of the merchants and shopkeepers.
" It was thus," says an intelligent eye-witness, himself a Frenchman, " that promises solemnly made
and more solemnly reiterated, were realised under
the Empire in Mexico." *

The open pillage of individuals by the Imperial
Government can hardly be believed or realised
without special study, and the enquiring reader
must be referred to the pages of M. Masseras, himself an eye-witness, and to the more *categorical*
chapter of M. Lefèvre.   The Foreign Ministers
protested in vain.   Even the proceedings of Miramon
in former days were as nothing to those of the
Imperial officers in 1867.   " *On voit*," says one
writer, " *des cavaliers arrêtés en pleine rue, et forcés
de délivrer leur monture : trop heureux quand ils n'étaient
pas emmenés à la caserne avec elle*." Women and
children were shut up by the police in their own
houses, without food or water, until their husbands
and fathers had ransomed them by a payment in
coin. †   A daily contribution, varying from £120 to

---

* Masseras, 142.
† Masseras, 188-9.

£1, was exacted by similar methods from every householder in the city.* The Foreign Ministers, who protested against these exactions, narrowly escaped arrest.†

And yet Europe, hoodwinked by Napoleon at the Tuileries, and unenlightened by intelligent reports from Mexico, believed that a gentle and statesmanlike Emperor was still engaged in the noble duty of protecting the Mexicans, whom he had succeeded to some extent in civilising, from the atrocities of an Indian bandit of the name of Juarez.

By the end of January, 1867, the Constitutional forces in Mexico had been brought up by the ceaseless vigilance of Juarez, to very respectable proportions, and consisted of some five and forty thousand men, fairly armed and disciplined— disposed somewhat as follows throughout the country.‡

Under Porfirio Diaz	13,000
„ General Alvarez	9,000
„ „ Rivera	4,200
„ „ Carbajal	4,600

---

* The commercial house of Barron was plundered in one day of 100,000 dollars, that of Bergstein upon another day was mulct in 150,000 dollars. Masseras, 214.

† Masseras, 200-201.

‡ I have followed Lefèvre, II., 367.

Garrison of Mazatlan	... ...	600
,, Guaymas	... ...	350
.. Aguascalientes	...	375
,, Tampico	... ...	450
In Michoacan, Sonora, and Sinaloa...		2,700
In Querétaro, Guanajuato, Puebla, and Jalisco	...	10,000
		45,275

It was a wonderful result, after nearly three years of supposed extinction.

At five o'clock in the morning of the 13th of February, Maximilian once more stole away* or rather was hustled out of the capital of Mexico. He had sent a certain Monsieur Burnouf to treat with Porfirio Diaz, whose army was threatening the city, even while he was seeking the special advice of his own Minister Lares, within the walls. And the Imperialists, judging that it would be eminently advantageous for them, if not for the Empire, that so very uncertain a chief as Maximilian should be removed from the capital, suggested that his presence would be of greater value in some other

---

* He carried off with him all the money upon which he could lay his hands. The Treasury contained just 47,000 dollars, say £9,000. He left it absolutely empty, trusting to O'Horan to replenish it by the accustomed methods.

place.* The ever-devoted Marquez would accompany him, and the governorship of the city should be confided, during the temporary absence of Don Leonardo, to a certain O'Horan.†

Thus Maximilian, escorted by some fifteen hundred men, abandoned the capital, and rode at full speed to Querétaro almost at the same moment that Juarez, moving steadily to the southward in his patient progress to victory, established the seat of his Government once more at San Luis Potosi.

On the 19th of February, 1866, twelve hundred long miles‡ had separated the President at Paso del Norte from the Prince at Chapultepec.

On the 19th of February, 1867, but forty leagues intervened between the Palace at St. Luis and the fortress at Querétaro.

Within a week of the flight of Maximilian from the capital, the city of Puebla was finally evacuated by the French, who were suffered to retire, uninterrupted, but hedged in on either side by the National troops, as they marched along the well-known road, by way of Orizaba and

---

* The history of this curious intrigue will be found in Masseras, 172-174.

† And the citizens had no great cause for congratulation at the change.

‡ Over 1,200 by road : about 1,100 as the crow flies. See Map.

Cordova, to embark on board their ships at Vera Cruz.

Up to the last moment Bazaine expected and hoped that Maximilian would once more change his mind, and would retire with the French army to Europe, and he even sent a mounted escort back from Vera Cruz, in case he should be actually on the way, not forty-eight hours before his own final embarkation.

But the Archduke was riding a very different road, the end whereof it was not given to him to discern.

CHAPTER XV.

PORFIRIO DIAZ.

The noblest and most conspicuous figure, after that of Juarez himself, in the closing scene of the great tragic farce of Mexican Empire, and the definite triumph of the National Constitutional party, is that of Porfirio Diaz.* And for him, the loyal and trusted lieutenant of Juarez when his fortunes were at the lowest, the wisest and noblest of his counsellors in the day of his triumph,† it

---

* Porfirio Diaz was the candidate for the Presidency on the abdication of Maximilian, who was favoured by Bazaine. In Paris, Ortega was preferred. Juarez alone was *nefandus*. At Washington it would seem that Diaz was the *persona gratissima*. Kératry, 246-48.

† "It was generally believed," writes Prince Salm-Salm: Diary, vol. I., p. 314. "that the Emperor would not have been shot if he had fallen into the hands of Porfirio Diaz, instead of those of Escobedo." I give this bit of contemporary gossip merely to shew the high opinion universally held of the clemency of General Diaz. For Escobedo was by no means cruel. And he actually offered to allow Tomas Mejia to escape after his surrender. Mejia refused to take advantage of the offer, unless Maximilian was permitted to go with him. Escobedo's power did not extend so far. Mejia thus died at least

has been happily reserved to rule over a united and a respected Commonwealth, and to be known the world over as the President of a peaceful and prosperous Republic.

Born, like his great chief, in Oaxaca, in September, 1830, Diaz, like Juarez, was an Indian, a lawyer, and an honest man. Ready alike with sword and with pen—a counsellor and a man of action, like the ideal grandee of old Spain, Don Porfirio was found ready, on the defection of Comonfort in 1858, to put aside his lawyer's gown; and at a time when good generalship was more needed than the best of advocacy, and loyalty was more precious than law, he accepted the command of a Regiment in the National army.

Throwing himself heartily into the great struggle for the maintenance of Constitutional Government, he distinguished himself as a military commander, at once by his skill and by his judgment, in the revolutionary war of 1858-1861. With a large share in the victory at Puebla in 1862; counted among the heroic defenders of the same city in 1863; escaping, by a bold stroke for liberty, the banishment of his fellow prisoners to France after the surrender; entrusted with the command of an

---

like a man of honour. But it is not likely that Escobedo had much to say to the President's decision in confirming the sentence of the Court-Martial as regards Maximilian.

army in the November of the same year ; besieged at Oaxaca, which surrendered only after a heroic defence to Bazaine in person at the head of an overwhelming force in February, 1865, Porfirio Diaz, again imprisoned, and again, as before, refusing to give his parole to the French Commander, succeeded once more in escaping (Sept. 20th, 1865), and now, as the end was approaching, he found his natural place at the head of the army entrusted with the all-important duty of occupying the capital.*

But, before Mexico could be threatened, it was necessary that Puebla should be reduced.   For

---

* The amount of ammunition handed over by the French to the Imperialists in the City of Mexico alone, was 35,000 projectiles (shells, cannon balls, etc.), with powder equal to 300 rounds for each gun in position, and 500,000 cartridges. See official reports in Kératry, pp. 305-6.

Puebla was left even more richly provided. Vera Cruz, from its situation, most richly of all.

" What you have to give to the cat," says an old Spanish proverb, " you may as well give to the mouse." All this material of war passed promptly into the hands, not of Maximilian, but of Mexico. According to General Diaz, the retiring Bazaine offered to sell him 4,000,000 copper caps, and to hand over to him, not only the cities evacuated by the French—which was quite unnecessary—but the persons of Marquez, Miramon, and even Maximilian himself. Baz., Vida: quoting letter of Porfirio Diaz, pp. 279-280.

This might have seemed incredible in 1867, especially to European readers, but who is the man to-day, in any country, who would set Bazaine's honour above the word of Porfirio Diaz ?

" I am able to affirm," says Prince Salm-Salm (I. 18) " that Bazaine offered Porfirio Diaz to deliver [the city of] Mexico into his hands, as the General told us so himself in November, 1867: but Diaz declined, adding that he hoped to be able to take the city himself."

Puebla, alone among the cities of Mexico, had not on the departure of the French immediately declared for the Republic, but had been dominated by the quasi-Imperial troops of Mejia and Marquez, to whom the immense stores of war material that had been left by the French rendered it a stronghold of the very last importance. But the city which had baffled the French army in 1862, and only fallen after a two months' siege in 1863, was occupied by a brilliant *coup de main* on the morning of the 3rd of April, 1867, when Porfirio Diaz, at the head of the National army, entered the city without the loss of a loyal soldier or the molestation of an unarmed citizen."

---

* Not the slightest disorder accompanied the assault on Puebla; such was the spirit of discipline and moderation with which General Diaz had succeeded in inspiring his subordinates. Whatever may be the merits of the taking of Puebla as a feat of arms, as an example of discipline it has few parallels in history. " The Republic of Mexico Restored," by James White, 1867, p. 17

Three weeks before, at Tlalpam, the savage Imperialist, O'Horan, had shot Vicente Martinez and thirteen companions, taken prisoners, without form of trial - October 7th, 1866. Such things should be known and remembered in order fully to appreciate the moderation and restraint of those who obeyed the orders of Juarez. It is often enough from ignorance that the critic "*Dat veniam corvis, vexat censura Columbas.*"

The highest and most important testimony is borne to this constant clemency, not only on the part of Diaz, but of all the Generals who followed the instructions of Juarez, by Monsieur Gaulot, by no means a favourable witness, who says (Maximilian, 297), with regard to the giving up of no less than seven Belgian officers, and 180 soldiers, after the battle of Tacambaro, " *il eût été facile au Général Riva Palacio de prendre*

Within a week after the surrender, a rash attack by Marquez was brilliantly repulsed, and the *Lieutenant of the Empire*[*] ran away with all speed to take refuge within the walls of Mexico, leaving the remnant of his army to follow or surrender as they chose. And Porfirio Diaz, pursuing at his leisure, sat down before the expectant capital on the 12th of April, 1867.

His objective was not glory, but peace. And he announced that if the city gates were opened to his Constitutional forces, the lives and property of the citizens should not only be regarded, but protected by his troops. Among the respectable inhabitants

---

prétexte de l'éxecution d'Arteaga et de Salazar pour venger. . . . comme Mendez avait vengé. . . .

Cette générosité est d'autant plus belle de sa part que le decret du 3 Octobre, venait lui même de le mettre hors la loi."

See also still more striking proofs in Kératry, pp. 290-294.

A little book, in English, printed at Mexico in 1867, by James White, is full of interest and local colour.

As to the atrocities committed by the French, "a history of calumny, of blood, of cruelty, of injustice and of barbarity of which France is ignorant, and which Europe could hardly believe," from the very day of the violation of the Treaty of Soledad, the author bears striking testimony ; as well as to the extraordinary moderation and humanity of the Constitutional troops, who were ever urged by Juarez, not only to refrain from reprisals, but to set a noble example of generosity. His facts speak for themselves, pp. 13-20. They are too numerous to quote well.

* Marquez, having virtually run away from Querétaro, had arrived at the capital on the 25th of March, armed with a letter from Maximilian, conferring upon him absolute power, and the fine-sounding title of *Lieutenant of the Empire*.

there was but one opinion as to the course to be pursued. And even the foreign Envoys, departing from their usual reserve, consented to add the weight of their remonstrances to the general expression of opinion.*

But, as usual in such circumstances, the worst counsels, rather than the best, prevailed. Marquez and the Abbé Fischer, Lares and Tabera, O'Horan and Vidaurri, sought, in a desperate resistance, to postpone, if but for a few days, the wreck of their own desperate fortunes. And Porfirio Diaz, patient to the last, refrained from the assault which would have made him triumphant master of the city; preferring even the possible dangers of delay to the shedding of Mexican blood.†

The General was accused of incompetence, of cowardice, of treachery; a hundred disgraceful reasons were assigned by his enemies for his inactivity before Mexico. The ill-disciplined troops under his own command murmured long and loudly. His conduct was denounced to Juarez. But Juarez was the very last man to think evil of a subordinate, or to interfere with the discretion of a Commander-in-Chief.

---

* On the first appearance of his troops within hail of the walls, every decent man in Mexico would have taken refuge under his standard. J. White, *ubi supra*.

† "Cette génereuse fermeté," says M. Masseras, 196., "ne fut ni sans difficulté ni sans mérite."

In patient resolution, moreover, General Diaz was hardly inferior to the President himself, and General Diaz had made up his mind to sit still.

He would never, even in the very last necessity, let loose a victorious army upon the defenceless citizens of the capital of his country.*

On the 19th of February, Maximilian had made what was called, with that strange want of any sense of humour which never deserted him in good or evil fortune, a " triumphal entry " into Querétaro.

Two divisions of the National army, that of the North, under Escobedo, and that of the South, under Corona, were then marching upon the town. Separated by many leagues of intervening country, they might have been attacked and haply defeated in detail.

But no attempt was made to check the onward course of either one or the other, nor was anything done to fortify, or even to provision, the town in which the Emperor had chosen to make his last stand.

---

* He saw, too, with the keen eye of an accomplished soldier, that there was little danger in delay. Querétaro, the last abiding place of the Empire—Vera Cruz may hardly be counted—was, by the middle of April, 1867, virtually in the hands of the besiegers, and untenable, save by a General very different from those who held chief command in the city. Mexico could wait upon Querétaro.

Disputes for precedence between Miramon and Marquez were grandiloquently composed by a declaration that Maximilian was his own Commander-in-Chief. But the Archduke commanded nothing, not even himself. He did nothing. He foresaw nothing. And on the 14th of March, after four weeks of delay, he found himself shut up by the united army of the advancing Generals who had at length brought their scattered forces together before the town.

On the 22nd of March, Marquez was sent to Mexico for reinforcements. That he did not return to Querétaro could surprise no one, except perhaps, the man who sent him.

Miramon, relieved at his absence, talked of sorties, and awaited the favourable moment for a profitable defection.*

There was, indeed, one General with the Archduke in Querétaro. But the counsels of Tomas Mejia were uniformly disregarded by his Sovereign.

Meanwhile, the unhappy Mexicans of Querétaro,

---

* If anyone doubts Miramon's treachery at the last moment, let him read Prince Salm-Salm's Journal, Vol. I., more especially, pp. 122-123-125-133.

Whether he was too slow at the end, or whether Lopez was too quick for him, or whether, as is more probable, Maximilian was not betrayed at all, but fell a victim to his own obstinacy and folly, is a question on which every reader of the contemporay memoirs is entitled to form his own opinion.

besieged in form by their own National troops, were in fact at the mercy of the Imperialists. Their store-rooms and their warehouses, their shops, and even their dwellings were exposed to daily pillage. Maximilian's garrison must be fed, even if the townsmen should starve.[*] Maximilian's troops, moreover, must be paid ; and the humbled citizen must be persuaded by the lash, cr mcre dreadful instruments of extortion, to cpen his little hoard to the vain and pitiless usurper.[|] When all else was abandoned, the Archduke retained his favourite power of issuing decrees. Every man in Querétaro between the ages of 16 and 60 was to enroll himself in his army. Food of all kinds, money, stores, everything was to be abandoned to his Staff. Rules, regulations, conditions, and above all, punishments were prescribed and insisted upon with his usual minuteness of detail.[‡]

At length, after infinite indecision, a general sortie was ordered for the 10th of May. But the

---

* See Lefèvre, II., 382-385.

As to the extent of the famine and the misery endured by the citizens during the siege, see Gaulot : Fin, 291-293.

† The best authorities for the siege of Querétaro, in addition to those already cited are :—

    1.—" Querétaro " par Albert Hans, (Dentu, 1868).

    2.—"Les dernières heures d'un Empire," par le Général Avellano.

    3.—Basch : " Souvenirs du Mexique."

Masseras devoted an entire chapter [*op: cit.* cap. X.] to the subject.

order was almost immediately withdrawn. The sortie was deferred till the 13th. Maximilian was engaged in the work of granting decorations, and found himself embarrassed as to the due apportionment of such honours. Whether the Italian Minister, who was far away in the City of Mexico, should receive the Cross of Guadalupe or the Star of the Mexican Eagle, indeed, was too weighty a question to be resolved at a single sitting. The grant, like the sortie, was postponed, * But the undecorated defenders of the town were already on the verge of starvation : the troops were worn out with delay.

But when the 13th came, the sortie was again postponed. On the 15th, it was finally declared, Maximilian would march out of the city, to conquer, to die—or to escape.

But the sands of his vacillation were at length running out. And after three years of postpone-

---

* " Besides this, the Emperor dictated to me the following distributions of decorations. Baron Magnus, the Commander's Cross of the Order of the Eagle ; his Chancellor, Mr Scholler, the Cross of the Order of Guadalupe ; Dr. Basch, the Officer's Cross of the same ; Captain Pawlowski and Lieutenant Koelich, of the Hussars, the Cross of the Guadalupe Order, and General Prince Salm-Salm, the Commander's Cross of the Order of the Eagle. At the same time, he told me that he intended to decorate the Italian minister, Curtopassi, but *he did not know yet which Order he would give him !* and said he *would tell me on the 14th*, when he expected to see me again " See " Diary of Prince Salm-Salm," vol. I., pp. 267-8.

ment, the inevitable end surprised him, as it ever surprises the unready.

As the summer's day was dawning on Querétaro, on the 15th of May, 1867, and the wearied garrison were asleep in their quarters, * Escobedo advanced boldly upon the position that had become no longer tenable; and Maximilian, unprepared for action, and uncertain to the last whether to fight or to fly, gave himself up as a prisoner into the † hands of the Commander-in-Chief of the besieging army, expressing the hope that his blood alone might be shed, to atone for the faults or the misfortunes of his followers.‡

---

* "Tout le monde dormait d'un profond sommeil." Juan de Dios Arias : *op. cit.*, 224-233. Lefèvre, II. p. 393.

† " When we stepped out of the door to go over the plaza to the quarters of the Hussars, we were stopped by soldiers of the enemy. Involuntarily I raised one of the Emperor's revolvers, but he made me a gesture with his hand, and I dropped it. At the same moment, Lopez stepped from among the enemy, and at his side was the Liberal Colonel, Don Jose Rincon Gallardo. The latter recognised the Emperor, but turned to his soldiers, and said : 'Que pasen, son paisanos '— They may pass, they are citizens. The soldiers stepped aside, and we passed ; the Emperor, Castillo, Pradillo, and myself in full uniform, and secretary Blasio. It was obvious that it was not intended to capture the Emperor, but to give him time to escape. The whole proceeding was so astonishing and striking that I looked enquiringly up to the face of the Emperor." Salm-Salm, vol. I., page 193. Gaulot : Fin. 296.297. I.

‡ His words are said to have been on giving up his sword :—*Si se necesita una victima, aqui estoy yo. Espero que mi sangre sea la ultima que se derrame en bien de este pais.*

If Maximilian was really ready to die for his friends or for

The betrayal of Maximilian and of Querétaro to General Escobedo by a certain Colonel Lopez has long been an accepted article of belief, not only by the admirers of Maximilian, among whom the devoted Prince Salm-Salm* speaks at least with the authority of an eye-witness, but by M. Masseras and M. Gaulot, and most of those who have written upon the contemporary history of Mexico.†

Mexico, these words are sufficiently noble. But if, as is usually asserted, he had no thought of suffering death, and was satisfied that he would be permitted to return to Europe *on parole*, they become somewhat too *stagey* for a true Hapsburg.

But the exact words that are said upon such exciting occasions are rarely accurately recorded, and Maximilian may be judged fairly enough by his own actions.

And see the letter of Escobedo to Juarez, dated Querétaro, May 16th, 1867, in which the Commander-in-Chief says :

" He informed me that his sole desire was to leave Mexico, and that he hoped an escort would be placed at his disposal to conduct him to the port at which he should embark."

* The defence of Lopez, being a translation of a pamphlet, published by him, entitled " The Capture of Querétaro ; " with the reply by certain field-officers, prisoners at Morelia, are all given in vol. II. of Prince Salm-Salm " Diary in Mexico," pp. 178-283. And in most of the authorities cited, the question is more or less fully discussed. I am by no means inclined to consider the " betrayal " to be an historical fact.

† The witnesses, moreover, do not agree among themselves. " I do not believe," says Prince Salm-Salm (Diary, etc , vol I , pp. 214-15), who is one of the most convinced advocates of the theory that Lopez betrayed, or desired to betray the city, " that Lopez intended to deliver the *Emperor* into the hands of the Liberals.   .   .   .   he endeavoured to save his life and earn at the same time a good round sum of money.   The *Emperor frustrated all his calculations*

For everyone who may fully credit his narrative, the whole question of the treachery of Lopez is set at rest by the statement officially made by Escobedo himself, in his note or memorandum* of July 8th, 1887, addressed to President Porfirio Diaz, and published in all the Mexican journals of the day.

According to this authoritative statement, Lopez was the Envoy, and not the betrayer, of Maximilian—the confidant, not of Escobedo, but of the Archduke. On a careful review and consideration of the many conflicting versions of the events of the 14th and 15th of May, 1867, I am inclined to think that that of General Escobedo is by far the most reasonable. But it is perhaps hardly worth while to pursue the subject any further in this place.

Juarez, at least, was by no means anxious that so embarrassing a prisoner should fall into his hands at all; and he would have been inclined to pay, if he had wished to pay at all, not for assistance in arresting him, but for connivance at his escape from Mexico.

One of the most remarkable inherent weaknesses in the corruption of Lopez theory is, that although

---

and arrangements to save him by his refusal to conceal himself in the house of Señor Rubio. . . . . an action . . which he considered to be against his dignity!"

* It is reproduced as a species of State Paper in "Mexico à Traves de los Siglos," V., 838-844.

various sums of money have been mentioned as the price of blood, all large, some enormous ; no one has ever suggested how or when the money was found.

Gold pieces were certainly not so plentiful at Querétaro in May, 1867, as that thousands could have been picked up, as it were, unobserved, and handed over to passing traitors, as sums of fabulous value are disposed of by tragedy kings upon the stage.

The fact remains, and it may suffice for us to know that Maximilian was taken prisoner in the open, surrounded by his faithful officers, at the head of an army of 8,000 men ; and that Querétaro was occupied by Escobedo's troops, after a somewhat commonplace assault. [*]

No less than 15 Generals, 20 Colonels, [†] and 375 officers of lower rank, with nearly 8,000 men

---

* Masseras, (p. 249), who is always reasonable, puts it as low as £4,000. I have seen £10,000 given as the amount.

† There is a good account of the operations of the army of the North from 1864 to 1867, and of the siege of Querétaro from a military point of view, as well as of the trial of Maximilian, by D. Juan de Dios Arias, entitled *Resena historica de la formacion y operaciones del Ejercito del Norte. Mejico,* 1 vol., 1867.
There is a very inferior military history by ex-Captain Schrynmakers, of the Belgian Legion, Brussels, N.D., a work abounding, if not in errors, at least in *suggestiones falsi.*

‡ Mejia to Escobedo, 21st of May, 1867. Lefèvre, II., 413. General Ignacio Mejia, Minister of War at this time in the Cabinet of Juarez, must not be confused with General Tomas Mejia who had just been taken prisoner.

of the rank and file, were taken prisoners, together with the Archduke, at Querétaro. Lopez can hardly have betrayed them all. Poor Tomas Mejia, ill as he was, offered, as Maximilian was actually on the point of surrendering, to cut a way for him through the surrounding enemy. But the Archduke unbuckled his sword, and all was over. Whether Lopez was or was not feed by Escobedo, the man who betrayed Maximilian was none other than Maximilian himself.

CHAPTER XVI.

JUSTICE.

The first plea that was tendered by the captive Maximilian was strangely characteristic of the man, and added one more to the many reasons that he had himself provided for uncompromising treatment on the part of the Constitutional Government. He was not, he said, Emperor of Mexico at all. His Abdication had been signed, and hidden away, more than two months before. He was an Austrian Archduke, unhappily present in Mexico, and he demanded to be conducted to the sea coast, that he might return to his own country.

The document that he so tardily referred to, which was in effect found among his papers, had it even been published on the day that he had signed it, was not in any sense an act of abdication. It was a species of political testament prepared for publication only in the event of the death or captivity of the testator, and by its provisions, Maximilian, far from abdicating his sovereignty to the lawful Government of Mexico, named a *Regency* of three persons, Marquez, Lares, and Lacunza, to take his place at the Imperial Palace; "and thus," says so indulgent a critic as Monsieur Masseras, "having maintained his authority up to the very moment at which it was no longer in his power to exercise it, he delegated his functions to the irreconcilable enemies of the Constitutional Government of the country! "*

It is hard to conceive of a political expedient more disingenuous, more feeble, or more futile.

---

* This act of abdication would, perhaps, have been considered *smart* on the part of a Yankee attorney of the less scrupulous order ; but it was hardly worthy of a descendant of Charles V.

It may possibly have been inspired by the Abbé Fischer!

To show how little real importance Maximilian attached to his so-called abdication, even after he had so reluctantly made it public, it is somewhat characteristic to note that in the second week in June, when he was planning his escape, in counsel with the Foreign Ministers, he proposed to decorate them all with the Grand Cross of his Imperial Mexican Orders.— Masseras, p. 316.

"Though his powers were now at an end (this was on the 28th of May), he ordered Blasio to make out the patents from the date of the verbal appointment, viz., May 14th. He made me Grand Officer of the Order of Guadalupe. He also made my wife Lady of Honour of the San Carlos Order, which had been instituted by the most excellent Empress Carlotta. He said he would have made her 'palastdame' of the Empress but that it was an impossibility, as the document had to be signed by the Empress herself. General Castillo, Colonel Pradille, Dr. Basch, and others were also decorated." —Diary of Salm-Salm, vol. I. page 236.

Escobedo, however, assured the Archduke that his protest and his papers should be forwarded to the President; and in the meanwhile he was confined in the Convent of La Cruz and treated in a manner which, as he himself expressed it, "in no way violated the customs of civilised nations."

His doctor, his private secretary, his chamberlain, Prince Salm-Salm, and other officers of his Staff and of his household were permitted to share his captivity.

Señor Rubio, at whose house he had judged it beneath his dignity to take refuge, on the morning of the 15th of May, was permitted to supply the Archducal table with choice food.

On the 20th, a new arrival brought new hopes to the prisoner at Querétaro.

Born in New York, of French parents, not many years before, Mademoiselle Agnes Le Clerq had

This was nearly three months after the signature of the so-called abdication, and a fortnight after it had been actually made public.

Maximilian, at least, considered himself in no wise bound by a document which had been prepared merely to embarrass his enemies.

* See the telegram forwarded by Maximilian to Vienna.

Escobedo has been accused of undue harshness to Maximilian. It would be well to remember that, under the existing law, that General would have been fully justified in ordering him to be shot within twenty-four hours of his capture, "upon a simple proof of identity."

This, moreover, was the treatment reserved for Juarez, the constitutional ruler of the country, by special order of Maximilian to Miramon, conveyed but a few weeks before.

married Prince Salm-Salm when he was serving in the ranks of the Federal army in the United States, and had followed him to Mexico when he took service under Maximilian, in the Summer of 1866. Her beauty, her grace, her wit, her zeal rendered her at once one of the most interesting, and one of the most effective of the friends of the captive Archduke, between the time of his surrender and his execution. Had Maximilian himself been endowed with only half her energy, or a quarter of her intelligence, he would never have found his way into Querétaro; or, being there, he would certainly have found his way out.*

Inspired by the presence of this most amiable aide-de-camp, Maximilian, before any reply had been received from the Government at San Luis, consented to face the position ; and arrangements were made at once for his defence and for his escape.

On May 24th, nine days after the surrender, a dispatch from the supreme Government at San Luis was received by General Escobedo, ordering him, as Commander-in-Chief of the National army, to summon a Court-Martial for the trial of Ferdinand

---

* Her diary, written in English, is appended to that of her husband, published by Bentley, two volumes, 1868 ; and the vignette portrait of the Princess herself, which forms the frontispiece to the second volume of this work, suggests at least a young lady of exceptional grace and beauty.

Maximilian of Hapsburg, Miguel Miramon, and Tomas Mejia, under the Law of the 25th January, 1862. The document, drawn up obviously after the fullest and most mature deliberation, set forth under various heads the reasons that rendered such a procedure necessary. The three persons affected, having been taken prisoners with arms in their hands, were liable under article 28 of the Law of 1862, to be executed as rebels after the simple formality of identification : but the Government had decided that a full and public trial should be allowed to them.*

Wi h regard to Maximilian himself, he was accused for that

(1) He had invaded the country without right or claim, and " had been the principal instrum nt of that iniquitous Intervention which had dur ng five years afflicted the Republic with crimes and calamities of every kind."

(2) Tha' l e had further called in the subjects

---

* The law of anuary 25th, 1862, had been passed not only before Maximilian had come to Mexico, but even before he had accepted the invitation at Miramar. And an agent of the Constitutional Government, the Licenciado Don Jesus Teran, actually warned him at Miramar of the dangers that he ran in seeking to overthrow the existing institutions of the country. See Memorandum by Mariano Riva Palacio and Rafael Martinez de la Torre, Mexico, 1867.

The copy in the British Museum Library of this interesting has inscribed upon the fly leaf the almost equally interesting words—S D. *Augustin Fischer, de su at'mo Euldi 'a. Orte '.*

of foreign nations, Austrians and Belgians, at peace with the Republic of Mexico, to aid him in his unrighteous warfare.

(3) That he had overthrown the Constitution and free institutions of the country.

(4) That he had unjustly and illegally disposed of the lives and liberties of the Mexicans.

(5) That he had promulgated a barbarous decree prescribing the assassination of such Mexicans as should defend the independence and institutions of their country.

(6) That he had given effect to this decree by numerous sanguinary executions.

(7) That he had authorised the destruction of many Mexican villages and towns by his soldiers, more especially in the Provinces of Michoacan, Cinaloa, Chihuahua, Coahuila, and Nuevo Leon.

(8) That he had permitted and encouraged foreign troops to slay thousands of Mexican subjects.

(9) That he had, when the foreign army had retired, continued to employ Mexican rebels to sustain his usurped power by every means of violence, depredation, desolation and death, to the last moment ; and he had pretended to divest himself of this usurped authority only when he found himself deprived of it by actual force.*

---

* Nothing was said about the savage instructions conveyed

With regard to Miramon and Tomas Mejia, it sufficed to say that they were both actually outlaws, rebels, and leaders of rebels, prominent among those Mexicans who had welcomed the foreigner, and had desolated their country during four long and dreadful years.

Against the five-and-thirty Generals and Colonels of minor importance; against the three hundred and seventy-five officers of lesser degree, who had fallen into the hands of the National forces at Querétaro, no indictment would be preferred.*

It was necessary only to make an example of the most powerful offenders. What was sought at San Luis, was not vengeance, but peace.

The Law of 1862 prescribed that death should follow conviction within the space of twenty-four hours; but nowhere was there any desire to hasten the end.

Colonel Azpiroz, appointed public prosecutor

---

by Maximilian to Miramon, as lately as the 5th of February, 1867, with regard to the prompt execution of Juarez and his Ministers when they should be taken captive.

There is no trace of personal vengeance in the conduct of Juarez throughout the whole matter.

The indictment is studiously temperate, and is very far from being an exhaustive *acte d' accusation*.

* That is, of course, not under the law of 1862.

A certain number of the superior military rebels were sentenced to various terms of imprisonment, as ordinary defaulters. They were pardoned, for the most part, as the country became tranquillized towards the end of the year.

ad litem, was instructed by the General Commanding to undertake the examination of the prisoners before the summoning of the court. After three days the indictment or act of accusation, was formally drawn up, and copies were supplied to the prisoners.

Maximilian now requested that he might be defended by counsel ; and after a reference to the President, a further delay of ten days was accorded for the preparation of the defence, while special * instructions were transmitted by telegraph to General Porfirio Diaz to permit the Archduke's messengers to enter the besieged city of Mexico, and to allow the advocates whom he had chosen to pass through his lines, on their way to consult with their august client at Querétaro. But the respite had been demanded, not that the Archduke might prepare an impossible defence, but that he might make good his escape from captivity.|

---

* The Princess Salm-Salm had in the boldest and most energetic manner travelled as far as San Luis, and had had more than one interview with Juarez himself, whom she describes as " a man a little under the middle size, with a very dark-complexioned Indian face, which is not disfigured, but, on the contrary, made more interesting, by a very large scar across it. He has very black, piercing eyes, and gives one the impression of a man who reflects much and deliberates long and carefully before acting. He wore high old English collars, and a black necktie, and was dressed in black broad-cloth."—" Diary of Princess Salm-Salm," pp. 30-31.

† On the 19th of May the Princess arrived at Querétaro ; and set out some days afterwards for San Luis, where she

A long memorandum, drawn up by Maximilian himself, was submitted to Escobedo, and by him forwarded to the seat of Government at San Luis. And at the same time the Prince and Princess of Salm were devoting all their intelligence and all their zeal to making ready the way for the flight of the Imperial captive.

It is distressing to read that, even after all that had happened, the Archduke's design was not frankly to quit the country : but to take refuge at Vera Cruz, " whence he intended to treat with Juarez," while Messrs. " Miramon and Mejia were busy in the country ! " *

---

again was admitted to interviews with the President ; and after the desired respite had been accorded, she returned once more to Querétaro.

* " If an escape could be effected," says Prince Salm-Salm, " we were to go next to the Sierra Gorda, from thence to the Rio Grande, and thence to Vera Cruz. In that city the Emperor expected to find more than a million dollars in the Treasury, and as the Mexicans had no fleet to prevent it, we could procure provisions from Havana, and troops from the State of Yucatan, which was in favour of the Emperor. Thus we might be able to hold out for at least a year, whilst Miramon and Mejia were busy in the country. A year is a very long time in Mexico, and the cause of the Emperor might again take a favourable turn."—" Diary of Salm-Salm," vol. I., page 264.

Miramon and Mejia *busy in the country* for another year, suggests a dreadful prolongation of bloodshed and suffering. And after all the parade of abdication and retirement to Europe, the entire programme is sufficiently disgraceful.

" Maximilien," says M. Masseras, " attendait pour s'y joindre, le résultat d'un pronunciamento tenté sur la còte par l'ancien dictateur Santa Anna." Masseras : 362.

But, whatever his ultimate design, by Sunday, the 2nd of June, everything had been prepared for his escape,* and the escape was to be effected that very night.

Maximilian, although he had "refused to cut off his beautiful beard,"† in order to disguise himself, had bribed his immediate guards, and had signed bills for a large amount for the corruption of their commander, payable only upon his own safe arrival in Europe—whither he did *not* intend to proceed! Everything was ready. His friends were compromised; the guards were unwatchful; the doors were open, the horses were saddled, the escort armed; and at five o'clock in the afternoon, the Archduke sent for his trusted chamberlain, and informed him *that he would not escape that night.*‡

Santa Anna, as a matter of fact, was taken prisoner by the Commander of the ss. *Tacony*, an American ship of war, in the gulf of Vera Cruz, on the 7th of June, 1867; and was ordered to quit the country. Making another attempt at invasion soon after, he fell into the hands of the Mexican authorities, and was mercifully dealt with by order of Juarez, the capital sentence being commuted to one of simple banishment.

* President Juarez had granted a respite (Salm-Salm, I., 240), and would himself have been well content that the Archduke should make his escape.

† Salm-Salm, IV. p. 239.

‡ As to the willingness of the Mexican authorities that Maximilian should make his escape, and as to the constant and characteristic fatuity of the Archduke in failing to take advan-

" Had a thunderbolt," says Prince Salm-Salm,
" fallen at my feet, I could not have been more
aghast. I implored the Emperor, almost on my
knees, not to postpone his escape ; " as " such a
favourable opportunity could never occur again."
But it was all in vain. Without reason, without
motive, without excuse, but that of his own
obstinate indecision, Maximilian drifted feebly to
his death.

On the 4th of June, at midnight, Baron Magnus,
with the counsel for the defence, Don Mariano
Riva Palacio, Don Rafael Martinez de la Torre,
and Don Eulalio Ortega, arrived at Querétaro,
together with M. Hoorickx, the Belgian Chargé
d'Affaires, and M. Forest, in the place of M.
Dano. And they were joined two days later by M.
de Lago, the Austrian Minister, more particularly
interested in the fate of an Austrian Archduke.

On the morning of the 5th, the advocates
conferred with their client and his local lawyer,
Señor Vasquez, in the Convent Prison ; and a
request for further delay to elaborate a defence
was directed by them to San Luis. The answer
was favourable. A postponement for nine days

---

tage of their benign attitude, see the " Diary of the Princess
Salm-Salm," 1868, vol. II., pp. 60-62 and 79-80.

*   What a very happy name for an advocate – *Eulalio !*

was granted. Juarez, at least, would precipitate nothing.

After further consultation, it was agreed that Don Rafael and Don Mariano should proceed at once to San Luis to conduct what may be called the political or *ad misericordiam* part of the case ; while Don Eulalio and Señor Vasquez should remain at Querétaro, and occupy themselves with the more regular judicial defence.*

On the 13th of June, at 8 o'clock in the morning, the Court-Martial assembled in the Iturbide theatre at Querétaro.†

Miramon and Mejia appeared before the tribunal.

---

*It is, perhaps, needless to give any fuller account of the numerous plots and plans for the escape of the Archduke, not only in May, but even in June, of which the Princess Salm-Salm was the moving spirit. Her husband, in his published diary, so often referred to in this and the preceding chapter, seems to think that the Belgian and Austrian Ministers were lukewarm in their assistance, and that they virtually spoiled the plans of escape.

Masseras [chapter 13] on the other hand, gives it as his opinion that they acted with great discretion, and would have compromised themselves, without saving the Archduke, if they had done as the Princess desired.

" Cette clairvoyance et cette énergie sauvèrent probablement les diplomates d'un grand danger," p. 321.

In any case, their schemes became known to the Commander-in-Chief, and they were all put into a travelling carriage and politely turned out of Querétaro on the 14th day of June, while the Court-Martial was still sitting.

† The Court was composed of a Lieutenant-Colonel as President, with six Captains as ordinary members. It would certainly have been more dignified if the tribunal had been composed of Generals, at least, in a country where Generals were so common.

Maximilian was unwell, and did not attend, but his defence was conducted by his counsel with the utmost zeal and vigour. Their speeches were at once bold and eloquent. Yet legally there was little to be said. The law was plain. The crime was patent. The only hope was at San Luis, whither the most urgent telegrams were constantly being dispatched.

Upon three separate occasions the uncompromising Foreign Minister, Sebastian Lerdo de Tejada,* granted interviews to the professional and officious defenders of Maximilian at San Luis Potosi. Their arguments and their entreaties were listened to with the utmost attention. But the reply was invariably the same. The prisoners would be treated according to law.†

---

* "M. Lerdo was the right hand of M. Juarez, and enjoyed, not only his perfect confidence, but had also the reputation of being a great politician. He does not look at all like a Mexican, for he is fair and has blue eyes. He is a very refined gentleman, and most exquisitely polite." -" Diary of Princess Salm-Salm," p. 84.

† On the 14th of June, the legal guilt of Maximilian being apparent to all, and practically admitted by his zealous and devoted advocates, they sought an interview with Señor Lerdo de Tejada upon the question of the exercise of the prerogative of mercy after the inevitable sentence.

The reply of Señor Lerdo was eminently just (Memorandum *ubi supra*, pp. 64-68) and may be thus summarised :

1.— Maximilian could not be trusted. His unstable nature, moreover, offered no guarantee that he would not be made the tool of other and more vigorous politicians.

Meanwhile, in the hall of audience at Querétaro, the eloquence of the advocates induced the court at least to waver; but at eleven o'clock at night on the second day of the trial (June 14th), their finding was published and recorded.

The facts allowed but one verdict, and that was, *Guilty*.

The law allowed but one sentence, and that was, *Death*.

On the morning of the 15th of June, a telegram was dispatched from Querétaro, in which Baron Magnus, the Prussian Minister,* craved the favour of three days further delay. Escobedo, who had already ratified the finding of the court, took upon himself to violate the law and suspend the execution, awaiting the reply from San Luis.

Once more the reply was favourable. The delay was accorded as desired.

A carriage was placed at the disposal of Baron Magnus in the evening of the 16th, and in the early morning of the 18th he arrived at San Luis.

2.—His pardon would thus cause the utmost confusion and political uncertainty in the country, which needed, above all things, *finality*.

3.—His release would be an encouragement to Europe, which had so poor an opinion of the Mexicans and of their institutions, to undertake a fresh intervention on his behalf.

* The Austrian, rather than the Prussian, Minister would seem to have been a more natural intercessor or envoy.

A final respite of three days had already been accorded by Juarez. But the Envoy was warned that it must be the last. The execution of the sentence was not only an act of simple justice, it was necessary to the peace of Mexico.[*]

But Baron Magnus was not the only intercessor for the life of the Archduke.

Upon the 14th of June, the Princess Salm-Salm had been requested to leave Querétaro. And she had taken advantage of the opportunity to proceed to San Luis, and make a final appeal to Juarez himself.

The President received her once more with his usual simple courtesy. "It was eight o'clock at night when I went to the Palace of M. Juarez," says the lady, "and he consented to see me at once He looked pale and suffering himself. Our interview was painful[†] in the extreme."

It were unkind to reproduce the record of grief

---

[*] Even M. Domenech sees in these repeated respites a desire to save Maximilian's life, and he blames the United States Minister, above all others, for his apathy and clumsiness in expressing the wishes of his Government, which he feels sure Juarez would have gladly taken the opportunity of gratifying. Domenech: Hist., III., pp. 431-434.

[†] "Juarez . . . had tears in his eyes: he said in a low sad voice : 'I am grieved, madam, to see you thus on your knees before me, but if all the kings and queens of Europe were in your place I could not spare that life. It is not I who take it, it is the people and the law, and if I should not do its will, the people would take it and mine also.'"— "Diary of Princess Salm-Salm," p. 82.

—torn from its sympathetic setting in the diary of the Princess. The wife of Miramon, leading in her hands her two little children, was also admitted to audience, and the behaviour of Juarez, even in the eyes of the disappointed and heart-broken suppliants, was found to be considerate and even tender ;[*] but as President of Mexico, he could return but one answer to their prayers.

Yet when the visitors had retired, human nature asserted itself in the Palace, and the inflexible President completely broke down. He retired to his own room, and would see no one nor transact business of any description for three entire days.[†]

On Thursday, the 19th of June, the last respite had expired.

The National army paraded at daybreak outside

---

[*] As to the dignified and considerate courtesy of Juarez and his Ministers, even in the first flush of victory, to those who felt and expressed themselves most bitterly against him, see "Diary of the Princess Salm-Salm," vol. II., pp. 30-33 and 77-80.

Her visit to Juarez in July, from the time when the President gave her his hand, and led her to a seat, to when " he gave me his arm and accompanied me through all the rooms to the head of the staircase, and dismissed me with a low bow," is very happily described.

Some days later a second interview was accorded to the Princess, and " although I had planned the escape of the Emperor, Juarez received me in his usual manner. . . His whole manner impressed me with the idea that the escape of the Emperor would not have been disagreeable to him."

[†] Salm-Salm, II., 83.

the walls of Querétaro, and the convicted prisoners, Maximilian of Hapsburg, Miguel Miramon, and Tomas Mejia suffered the extreme penalty of the law.

CHAPTER XVII.

JUDGMENT.

If ever the dread precept that " Whoso sheddeth man's blood by man shall his blood be shed," is to be judicially interpreted ; if ever the execution of political criminals is justifiable for the common weal, then surely Maximilian of Hapsburg was justly punished for his offences in Mexico.

Let it be granted that he was mistaken in the true nature of his summons to a strange empire—and mistakes in such exceptional circumstances are not far removed from crimes—his eyes must surely have been opened, had he taken the pains to see, before he had been three months in the country. But instead of retiring from a position so obviously false, both as regards the French and the Mexicans, a position in itself productive of constant blood-shed and suffering of every kind, this Austrian adventurer, maintained only by French bayonets, took upon himself to decree the death of every loyal and patriotic Mexican who should oppose him or his foreign supporters.[*]

The ordinary usurper supplants only a monarch, less worthy perhaps than himself; but Maximilian supplanted an entire Constitution: not by his bravery in the field nor by his skill in the Council Chamber, but as the figure-head of the invading army of a nation that owed him no allegiance.[†]

From October, 1861, to May, 1864, the Archduke was an ignorant intriguer. From May, 1864, to October, 1865, he was a most incompetent intruder; but after October, 1865, he was merely the accepted leader of a Revolutionary Party, without even the poor justification of Mexican nationality; a man less capable than Santa Anna, less devoted than Yturbide, more destructive than those forgotten adventurers who, three hundred years before the voyage of the *Novara*, had sailed from Europe for the Gulf of Mexico, and had fought for their own hands against all and several, under the uncompromising shadow of the black flag.

---

[*] "*J'ai vu avec plaisir*," writes Maximilian himself under date August 17th, 1865, "*que le nombre des troupes françaises allait augmenter, c'était de toute nécessité pour améliorer la situation militaire . . . et faire sortir Juarez*" Domenech: Hist III., 307.

[†] Even Bazaine was forced to call attention to the *mesures extrèmes* adopted by Maximilian . . . *pour prolonger l'agonie d'une situation impossible.* Report, cited in Gaulot: Fin, 130-131

That Juarez might have earned the applause of foreign nations by a display of misplaced clemency, is very probable.* But Juarez was the last man in the world likely to be influenced by such considerations in his conduct of public affairs.

Merciful as we know him to have been, at once by disposition and by policy, averse at all times from bloodshed, with no base or revengeful feelings in his nature, it would no doubt have been to him an immense personal gratification to have spared the life of his defeated and humbled adversary.

For an Indian lawyer to pardon a suppliant Archduke, would have been a fine bit of theatrical triumph, that a man less simple and less single-minded than Juarez, could hardly have consented to forego. But as long as Maximilian lived, it was clear that there could be no peace in Mexico. His doom had been pronounced by the law. The law should take its course.†

---

* "Juarez a certes perdu une grande occasion d'étonner l'Europe par un acte de clémence, signe caractéristique des forts, qui l'eût réconcilié avec les cours de l'Europe : mais à coup sûr cet acte de clémence n'eût pas sauvé la vie á Maximilien, et l'eût coûtée à Juarez. Qui connaît le pays et ses passions sauvages arrivées, ces derniers temps, au paroxysme, n'en peut douter un instant."—Kératry, 38.

† "Un debil generosidad se hubiera interpretado como una cobardia, hubiera sido una burla sangriente de las leyes, y dejando sin castigo la traicion y sin venganza las victimas que sacrificó el Imperio, habria consagrado con toda injusticia la supremacia de los reyes sobre los pueblos."—Baz, 283.

It is sometimes a mark of the truest greatness to refrain from action, and to accept the supreme responsibility of non-interference. A cruel, a hasty, or a revengeful man would have ordered the execution of Maximilian, as Maximilian had ordered the execution of Juarez, within twenty-four hours of his capture.[*] A weak or an unprincipled man would have given himself the cheap satisfaction of pardoning him. Juarez was content simply to do his duty; and the foreign reader who, without the dreadful burden of his responsibility, or the disquieting solicitations of his emotion, is content to-day to judge him, will hardly be found to say that he failed.

But the Archduke was not the only man who suffered death at Querétaro. The victims were three in number.

That Maximilian should die was but strict justice. That Miramon should die was but righteous judgment. The man who may fairly challenge our sympathy was the little Indian, Tomas Mejia, a man who was no politician, but a dashing General of Cavalry, no assassin, but a brave and a not unsuccessful soldier, whose devotion to a bad cause had led him into actual rebellion, and who

---

[*] Instead of the possible twenty-four hours, Maximilian was granted a period of five weeks to prepare his defence.

was worthy to die in better company than that of Miramon.*

Let us, at least, waste no sympathy upon the dead Maximilian, however much we may pity his wretched career. Let us turn to another and far more agreeable figure, of the man who lived, and still lives to serve his country.

The conduct of Porfirio Diaz, encamped before Mexico, had been worthy of all praise. From the middle of April to the middle of June, his patience had been proof against all the solicitations of friends and rivals. Within the city, the inhabitants of all political parties awaited his entrance as a deliverer from famine, from pillage, and from the savage who oppressed them in the name of Maximilian— Leonardo or Leopardo Marquez, Knight Com-

---

* "Don Tomas Mejia was a little ugly Indian, remarkably yellow, of about forty-five, with an enormous mouth, and over it a few bristles representing a moustache. He was a thoroughly reliable, honest man, devoted to the Emperor, a very good General of Cavalry, and well known for his personal bravery. Before an attack, it was his habit to take a lance from one of his soldiers, and rush with it, among the first, on the line of the enemy. Some years ago he took Querétaro from the Liberals. On his entering the city, its last defenders fled to the first story of the Town Hall. Mejia appeared in front of it, at the head of his Cavalry. Lance in hand he rode up the steps, and in the large hall made the Liberals prisoners, and then rode to the balcony welcoming, with a hurrah, his victorious troops."—Diary of Salm-Salm, I., pp. 38-39.

Escobedo, as we have seen, *ante* p. 303, offered to assist Mejia to escape; and he refused as his Emperor could not be saved with him. The trait is characteristic and worthy of honourable mention and memory. See Arrangoiz, vol. IV., 314.

mander of the Legion of Honour, and Grand Cross of the Order of Guadalupe.

For the horrors of the siege of Mexico were the work, not of the besieging army, but of the besieged tyrants in the city, Marquez, Vidaurri, O'Horan, and the Abbé Fischer. The news of the surrender at Querétaro, which had been officially conveyed to these pseudo-Imperialist leaders within a few hours of the announcement of Maximilian's so-called abdication, was studiously concealed from the inhabitants. False news of Imperialist successes was, on the contrary, invented and inculcated by Marquez and his companions. The departure of the advocates and foreign Envoys from Querétaro, as it could not be concealed, was ingeniously misinterpreted. The illusion, indeed, was boldly kept up. On the 15th of June, the joy bells were rung from all the city churches, and a public proclamation bade the citizens prepare to welcome the coming of the Emperor at the head of his victorious army. Within forty-eight hours, O'Horan, anxious to steal a march upon Marquez, had made his way disguised into the camp of the besiegers, and offered Porfirio Diaz to give up to him, not only the city, but Marquez himself; and, at the same time, Marquez, taking advantage of the absence of O'Horan, laid hands upon all the gold pieces in the Treasury, and stole a very decided march upon his colleague, by making his way not only out of the city, but out of Mexico ; and retiring for good, with the cash in his valise, from an ungrateful and impecunious country.*

The death of Maximilian and the flight of his Imperial Lieutenant† relieved the National Government from all further opposition, and on the 21st of June, at break of day, the army of Porfirio Diaz marched into the city, and took peaceable possession of the capital of Mexico. Yet even this supreme victory was marked with the accustomed moderation of the victor, and the delighted ‡ inhabitants were not even permitted to salute their deliverers with cheers, lest a counter demonstration should mar the harmony of the day.§

---

* He turned up some weeks after at the usual trysting place, the Havannah. How he got there has never been told.

† Marquez.

‡ Masseras, 382-3.

§ We are all familiar, says Mr. White, with the events of the siege of the city of Mexico, and can never forget while we live the pleasurable surprise at being relieved from the tyranny of a monster by the entrance of General Diaz, whose chivalrous care for our safety exceeded our most sanguine hopes. James White: " The Republic of Mexico Restored," 1867, p. 20.

The following extract from the report of M. Lago, to his Government at home, and dated Mexico, June 25th, 1867, is not likely to be highly coloured.   The entire report is cited

Great waggons loaded with bread that had been specially baked the night before, followed the advancing columns. The welcome food was distributed with order and decorum. The weak were served before the strong. The sick were provided for before the more vigorous citizens. The most perfect order was maintained in the ranks of the victorious army. Not a drunken man was to be seen in the streets. The introduction of the favourite *Pulque* was forbidden during three days. For acts of plunder or personal violence the prescribed punishment was death. But the public peace remained absolutely undisturbed.

So vigorous a repression of military license is almost unexampled in the history of conquered cities, and the utmost credit must be given to the General Commanding, for the great-hearted humanity of his intentions, and the firmness and ability with which he carried them into action. But we must not forget that the man who had ever

---

by Domenech : Histoire, III., 433-439. " Le 16 au soir, nous arrivâmes, après un voyage pénible, á Tacubaya, on nous apprîmes que le Général Marquez ne songeait nullement á rendre la ville, mais qu'il continuait á dépouiller et á torturer les habitants de la manière la plus éhontée . . ."

The exasperation in the Liberal army was so great that it was proposed to put to death all the superior officers in the city, European as well as Mexican, as soon as it should be taken.

How they were saved by Porfirio Diaz aud Juarez we have already seen. Cf. Domenech, *ubi supra*.

prescribed clemency to vanquished opponents, and set his face resolutely against the shedding of Mexican blood, was Benito Juarez, once more directing the Government of Mexico from his modest Palace at San Luis.

And to Juarez, as was only natural, the ultimate disposal of the actual garrison that was found in the capital, Mexicans and foreigners, was immediately referred.

His answer was not long awaited. The entire body of soldiers and subaltern officers were dismissed unpunished—the foreigners to quit the country, the natives to return under supervision to their own homes.

The disposal of the superior officers, not only those who had been taken in Mexico, but the unsentenced prisoners of Querétaro, presented greater difficulty. Yet was no unreasonable delay suffered to retard the general return of confidence throughout the country.*

On the 15th of July, Juarez made his public entry into the capital;† and his first duty was that of disposing of the prisoners. Porfirio Diaz, the first General of the Republic, Vicente Riva Palacio, a

---

* The temper of the people was somewhat uncertain. Masseras, 391-3. Baz, 288.

† The return of Juarez to the capital was celebrated, *more Britannico*, by a great public dinner, with plenty of speeches at dessert. Baz, p. 288.

soldier and a statesman, with many other less distinguished counsellors, were supposed to be in
favour of a complete amnesty. Lerdo de Tejada,
the most intimate friend and companion of the
President, was known to be inclined to greater
severity.

Within a day or two after his return to the
capital, the policy of Juarez was made known, and
it was essentially a policy of mercy.

The foreigners, both soldiers and civilians, who
had been sentenced to various terms of imprisonment, were to be permitted to take their departure
from Mexico before the end of the year. The
Mexican officers of superior rank, already in
custody, were to be released, from time to time,
as the circumstances of the country might warrant. With the exception of the rebel tyrants
of the capital, Vidaurri and O'Horan, traitors at
once to Maximilian and to Mexico, no man paid
the price of his treason with his life.*

The Foreign Ministers, whose equivocal conduct
in Mexico had rendered them somewhat nervous
as to the reception that awaited them, on the
return of the " Indian Savage," were treated with
all the consideration that was due to their position ;
and were, after a decent interval, diplomatically

---

* Baz : Vida, 284-5.

furnished with their passports, and provided with the usual escort to Vera Cruz.*

That men who had been accredited to a usurper, condemned and executed as a rebel, should continue to be received as *persona grata* at the Court of the legitimate ruler of the country, on his return to power : this was what no one could expect. And no one, as a matter of fact, appears to have expected it in Mexico.

---

* Mr. Middleton, the English Chargé d'Affaires, did not leave Mexico until December ; and then not on account of any action of the President as regards himself, but by order of Lord Stanley, in consequence of a dispute about the status of a Consul. See " Accounts and Papers," 1868. Masseras, 391-3, and post p. 351.

CHAPTER XVIII.

CONCLUSION.—JULY, 1867—JULY, 1872.

The time had now come when Benito Juarez could safely resign into the hands of those who had granted them, the great and exceptional powers with which he had been invested just fifty months before.

The position was unique. For the history of these four years of tempest and of trial was without parallel in the annals of nations.

Eighteen hundred and sixty-two had seen an English fleet, a Spanish fleet, a French fleet in Mexican waters; an invasion undertaken by three great European powers, with all the forces at the disposal of the most aggressive military nation in the world, and followed by a usurpation countenanced by all the politicians of Europe, and supported by the capitalists not only of Paris, but of London.

And the object of all their efforts had been the

overthrow of President Juarez, the constitutional ruler of Mexico.

Eighteen hundred and sixty-seven saw a very different sight in Mexico. The British fleet had sailed away. The Spanish troops had retired. The French army of 60,000 men, two Marshals of France, with all their proclamations and declarations, with all their gunpowder and glory, the Austrian contingent, the Belgian volunteers, the cosmopolitan Contra-guerilla, Maximilian of Hapsburg, with his ancient traditions and his modern theories, with his foreign loans and his domestic magnificence : all these things had absolutely passed away, rolled up like a scroll that is cast upon the fire, scattered like the small dust that is driven before the wind. And the object of all their attacks, the foe of five years' endurance, a quiet Indian gentleman with gleaming eyes and a scar across his unclouded brow, stood forth to give an account of his stewardship to the nation that had trusted him so long.

The account was not hard to render ; not a stone of a Mexican fortress, not an inch of Mexican territory had been lost in his hands. The foreign invader had been driven out. Their led-captain had been executed. Mexico was at length united and free.*

---

* As a contrast, we can cite what occurred after the colossal war between France and Germany. France lost

On the 14th of August, less than one month after the return of Juarez to the capital, the writs went out for the election of a new Chamber and a President of the Republic.

The usual grumblers asserted that the delay was excessive, and complained too that certain provisions with regard to the mode of voting were not sufficiently democratic. The action of the President was, however, fully approved by the electorate, who accepted the new regulations, and returned a Chamber of moderate complexion, with Juarez as President, and his trusty Lerdo de Tejada as Vice-President and Chief Justice of the Supreme Court of Mexico.*

The Chambers met on the 2nd of December, when Juarez had already constituted his new Cabinet, which included Lerdo de Tejada, who

---

Alsace and Lorraine, was obliged to pay to Germany an indemnity of five thousand million francs. Italy in her war had to cede Nice and Savoy to France. And this has happened not alone in Europe. We have seen in America what Peru has lost in her war with Chili. Mexico alone, without signing a treaty, without granting away any right, without even listening to the terms of the invader, saw the war ended without making any sacrifice, either of her honour, her dignity, or her independence, or of the integrity of her territory. And although this has happened before our own eyes, there are still persons who believe, or pretend to believe, and say that Juarez intended to cede to the Americans a portion of our national territory. "Juarez and Cesar Cantu." (Mexico, 1885), p. 21.

* Porfirio Diaz was also a candidate, and stood third at the poll.

took the portfolio of Home and Foreign Affairs ; José Maria Iglesias, that of Finance ; General Ignacio Mejia, that of War ; Señor Martinez de Castro, that of Justice and Education ; and Señor Blas Bulcaral, that of Agriculture and Commerce.

The army, reduced to an effective of only twenty thousand men, was divided into five great commands: the first division under Porfirio Diaz, the second under Escobedo, the third under Corona, the fourth under Regules, and the fifth under Alvarez, consisting each of not more than four thousand soldiers.

This wise and most politic reduction was not likely to be popular with the immense mass of officers who had fought on one side or another during the last ten years, and who, without sufficient private means for their support, were unfitted by the very fact of their past career for solid and useful work ; and during the whole of the year 1868, risings and sedition upon a small scale retarded the peaceful settlement of the country. But the palmy days of the *pronunciamiento* were passed and gone ; and Juarez, ever maintaining his old policy of firmness in administration and generosity in punishment, was able to meet the Chambers at the end of the year with assurances of the satisfactory, if somewhat tardy, progress of the country towards domestic peace and prosperity.

Yet, in the important cities of Puebla and San Luis Potosi, serious risings called forth all the vigour of the Administration ; and it was over two years before order was so firmly established as to justify the announcement of that general pardon which was at once the joy and the justification of the restored President.

To give anything like a detailed account of the not untroubled history of Mexico, from the beginning of the year 1868 to the death of Juarez some four years later, would be impertinent in every sense of the word. Most of the characters are still alive. Many of the events are still among the vexed questions of contemporary politics ; and yet none of them are of any commanding importance abroad. Suffice it to say, that under the just and vigorous government of Juarez, Mexico progressed slowly but surely, even though the progress was not always apparent at the time. The Mexican Railway, from the capital to Vera Cruz, which had been projected in the time of Maximilian (1864), and had remained in a state of suspended animation during his reign, was restored to life by a new charter in November, 1867, and was encouraged by the grant of further privileges in November, 1868.

The Telegraph system was largely developed. The Post Office was reconstructed. Every department of State was rendered less costly and more efficient than before.   In the Treasury only, a new order of things could not at once be instituted. Juarez was himself an indifferent financier. Nor in a still vexed commonwealth, deprived * of European assistance and foreign credit, was it to be expected that chronic bankruptcy should be succeeded by immediate financial prosperity.   The country, impoverished by fifty years of revolution and five years of struggle against a powerful invader, was unprovided with the funds that are one of the necessaries of modern progress.

Juarez had assuredly no reason to love or to trust the foreigner ; yet it is one of the most apparent shortcomings of his policy that it failed to obtain for his country the advantages of that public national intercourse with the Governments of friendly powers, which are possessed by most of the civilised countries of the world.   Without the aid of any foreign nation, and in spite of their ignorant hostility, Juarez had conquered his foes,

---

* In December, 1867, the Government having declined to hold any official communication with the agents of those powers who recognised Maximilian as Emperor, Mr. Middleton, the British Minister, acting on instructions from Lord Stanley, broke off all diplomatic relations between England and Mexico, closed the Legation, and carried off all the archives, etc., as well as his staff and Consul Glennie to Europe *via* New York. " Accounts and Papers," 1867, lxxiii.
See also Note at conclusion of Chapter XVII, p. 345.

and had showed the world that Mexico was able to stand alone. But something more was needed for the happiness and prosperity of the country than the mere defeat of the invader. [*] And that was just what could hardly be attained without the co-operation, the good-will, and the confidence of other nations.

But, within the bounds of the Republic, Juarez

---

[*] French writers, in their eagerness to blacken the character of the man whom they were unable to defeat, represent Juarez as a monster so grotesque, that Art as well as probability is set at defiance in the creation, while any resemblance in the picture to the real man is no more to be found than it was sought in the painting. See Domenech · Hist. du Mexique, volume III., *passim*.

One extract may possibly serve as a sample of many similar passages.

" Juarez," says the Abbé Domenech, II., 359, "est le type de l' incapacité la plus notoire. . . . . . le vrai Zapotéc, ennemi des Mexicains, n'ayant aucune notion de la legalité (350) . . . . . l'excés personnifié des mauvaises passions, de l'ignorance, et du manque de patriotisme. . . . . . .

" Si Miramon a rougi le doigt du sang de ses compatriotes, Juarez a mis tout le bras ! (359). . . . .

" Juarez, dont le nom, moins le talent rappellent ceux de Robespierre et de Marat." II., 296.

One writer, indeed, rises superior to the prejudice of his countrymen.

"Que serait-t-il advenu de l'œuvre entreprise par Napoléon III.," says Monsieur Gaulot. " si le souverain choisi par lui pour l'executer eût possédé les mêmes qualités que Juarez, ayant une égale ambition ? Cette pensée hanta plus d'une fois l'esprit de l'Empereur des Français, et l'impatience dut le gagner quand il sentait s'émietter une puissance qu'il avait crue forte et qu'il avait espérée victorieuse." - Gaulot : Maximilian. p. 300.

And, to be quite just, there is plenty of ignorant abuse and vilification of Juarez to be read in English books and newspapers at any time between 1859 and 1869.

did all that man could do to consolidate, to compose, to construct; and by October, 1870, he was able to give a practical assurance of the success of his Government, and an earnest of his confidence for the future, by the issue of the decree of final amnesty, in which all his foes, domestic and foreign, were freely included.

Two months later he was struck down by a blow more cruel than any that had ever been dealt him by Marquez or Miramon, in the death of his wife Doña Margarita Maza de Juarez; and the Mexicans showed their respect for his sorrow by a display of general mourning, unprescribed and unsolicited, —a spontaneous expression of national sympathy and affection.

In the same month, December, 1870, the Presidential election once more took place, and Juarez was again returned at the head of the poll by a considerable majority over his competitors; * but inasmuch as none of the candidates had obtained an absolute majority of the entire number of voters, the Congress decided the question on October 12th, 1871, by decreeing that Juarez was duly

---

* The numbers were as follow :

Juarez	-	-	-	-	5,837
Diaz	-	-	-	-	3,555
Lerdo	-	-	-	-	2,874

12,266

elected ; and on the 1st of December, 1871, he re-assumed the Presidential powers by virtue of this Parliamentary mandate. The reign of law, how-ever, had not yet been fairly established in Mexico ; and the decision of the Chambers was violently challenged, not by the defeated candidate himself, but by some of his more impetuous supporters, who plunged the country once more in an aimless and profligate civil war.

But before the close of the conflict the great President had gone to his rest, in a world where haply ingratitude is unknown, and virtue and simplicity are welcome guests.

It was a custom of Juarez to walk every after-noon with his daughters in the *Paseo*, or public promenade of Mexico. And upon the 18th of July, 1872, his absence was remarked and commented upon. In the evening it was known that he was ill. Dangerous symptoms were mani-fested during the night. From early dawn enquirers of every rank presented themselves at the doors of the Palace. The President's condition rapidly became critical. Without in the city men went sadly, and spoke under their breath, craving for news of the President. Within his chamber, throughout the long Summer day, the sick man suffered violent pain : his breathing was difficult : the heart was gravely affected.

Surrounded by his children and other members of his family, he sought to distract their attention from his own sufferings by cheerful and encouraging conversation. But one loved face was wanting in the sick room. Doña Maria was no longer there to minister to the last wants of her husband. And as the end drew near, the dying man called for her portrait, which was brought in from an adjoining room ; and after one last fond look upon the image of the wife who had gone before him, he folded the bed-clothes about his face, and peacefully gave up the ghost.*

The funeral obsequies of the dead President were in keeping with the simple dignity of his life. The coffin, with no further inscription or title than the letters B. J., and placed in a modest car, was conveyed to its last resting place by the faithful servant, Juan Udueta, who had followed his master's fortunes in all his wanderings, who had driven his carriage as he retired by successive stages from Vera Cruz to Paso del Norte; and from Paso del Norte to Mexico.

Five thousand of all that was best in the city and country followed in a mournful procession. The streets were deeply lined with silent and respectful spectators ; but of the false glitter and conven-

---

* 20th of July, 1872.

A A—2

tional pageantry of a State funeral there was no trace nor token.

The great President lies by his wife in the Pantheon of San Fernando; and an effigy of white marble has been raised to mark the spot for the admiration of future ages.

For sixty years the life of Benito Juarez was distinguished by many and rare virtues. Yet in nothing was it more specially remarkable than in its perfect consistency.

As the Indian apprentice, as the earnest student, as the hard-working advocate, as the single-minded politician, as the patient exile, as the moderate reformer, as the indefatigable Chief of the State, he was ever the same simple, honest, dignified Indian gentleman.

At one time in a palace, at another in a dungeon; now threatened by all Europe, now supreme in Mexico, to-day an international outlaw, on the morrow the arbiter of Imperial fate; the confiscator of untold riches, honourably poor to the day of his death, after hard upon fifteen years of office—no man with whose works and ways we are so intimately acquainted was so little puffed up by success, so little cast down by failure, through a long and eventful life.

His career was as varied and as exciting as that of a hero of Oriental romance. His character was as simple and as constant as that of some old-fashioned village worthy in England. Truly and honestly vigorous as a ruler and as a judge, he detested cruelty in any form; and he feared neither friend nor foe.

He disliked pomp. He despised parade. He coveted no man's riches. His greatest pleasure in life was not in war, nor even in politics, but in the society of his wife and children.*

A student rather than a soldier, he waged the greatest and the most successful war that his country had ever known, without putting on a uniform or even assuming a military title.

In a country where Generals were more common than soldiers, he remained, like Castlereagh, distinguished by the undecorated simplicity of his black coat.†

As regards personal appearance, Juarez was short in stature, of a powerful frame, with small

---

* There were born to Juarez and his wife nine sons and three daughters, of whom two boys and three girls died in their childhood.

The eldest daughter married D. Pedro Santacilla, a Cuban of refinement and culture; a younger sister found a husband in Don Delfin Sanchez, the great Mexican railway contractor.

The eldest son, Benito, is a distinguished member of the present Mexican Legislature, and sits, not for Oaxaca, but for the fourth division of the city of Mexico.

† " Huia de toda clase de honores oficiales, y en medio de las mas bulliciosas fiestas se lo veia solo ó bien acompañado à su familia."—Baz : Vida, p. 316.

hands and feet, and with the black eyes, the dark*
skin, and the strongly marked features of his
race.†

His manner was frank and open, his bearing
simple and dignified. Calm and deliberate in all
his movements, and in all his actions, he ever
possessed and displayed the quiet and sustained
vigour that belongs to exceptionally strong
natures.

Unrestrained, and even communicative, upon
matters of no public moment, he was reserved in
the extreme as regards all matters of State.

Expansive in his family circle and among his
intimate friends, he was grave, but ever courteous,
in his intercourse with strangers.

Above all things, he was cool and self-possessed
at the approach and in the actual stress of
danger.‡

---

* Señor Baz: (Vida, cap. VIII,) speaks of him as of a
lymphatico-bilious temperament.

† The portrait which serves as a frontispiece to this
volume has been carefully copied from a sketch most kindly
sent to me by the President's eldest son, Señor Don Benito
Juarez, of the City of Mexico, as giving a fair representation
of the personal appearance of his great father.
The copy, as far as I can judge, has been admirably
made, and will, I hope, satisfy those who may have the
advantage of having personally known the President.

‡ The calmness with which he faced the soldiers' muskets
in the Palace at Salamanca, April, 1857, was not greater than
that with which seven years earlier, April, 1850, on hearing that
the garrison of Oaxaca had fired upon their officers, he had
hastened, unarmed and unprotected, to face the rebels, and in

Simple in his personal habits, abstemious in eating and drinking ; an early riser, needing at all times but little sleep, he blended to an uncommon degree the characteristics of the student with those of the man of action, and he enjoyed * a measure of bodily health which is given to few— whether in the library or in the field. Hardy and vigorous, yet disinclined to active exercise, tempe- rate, sober, chaste, he did his work not in the Senate hall, nor on the battle field, but in the study. For even in the pursuit of his profession Juarez was a juris-consult rather than an advocate; deeply read in constitutional law, and an ardent admirer of our English institutions and polity.†

His favourite relaxation was History. His fa- vourite author was Tacitus; and among the papers that he left behind him is an annotated collection of maxims from the works of that great master of

the midst of a hail of bullets had compelled them to surrender to his authority. When Marquez was threatening the capital at the end of June, 1861, the military commander of the city took flight and disappeared ; Juarez, by his coolness and resource, restored confidence after a day of panic, which was nigh to have led to another Tacubaya. Mexico, V. 462-6. Baz : Vida, cap. VII.

* He is said by Baz to have had only one illness during the whole of his life, which confined him for a single day to his bed, until his last and fatal seizure.

† Juarez could not speak English, though he could read works published in that language. A number of his letters, written in excellent French, may be read in the " Correspon- dance de Juarez et de Montluc," frequently referred to in these pages.

language, translated in hours of ease and leisure, into his own vigorous Castilian.   He has also left behind him, in his own handwriting, a detailed account, or   record, of his   many journeys : *(Cuenta exacta de mis gastos y viajes)*, and a still more interesting collection of estimates of the characters of those personages with whom he had been brought in contact : *(Un juicio sobre las personas mas notables que habria tratado.*—Baz : Vida, p. 315.)

The collection of maxims is rather an indication of taste than a work of public or general importance, and the publication of his personal and political reminiscences is no doubt judiciously postponed until the actors, whose works and ways he must have severely if justly criticized, have disappeared from this mortal scene.

But the work of his life was not the pursuit of letters, nor the making of laws, nor yet the organization of armies.

It was not even that he withstood the usurper, and that he freed his country from her many foes.

The undying glory of Benito Juarez is that, undaunted by fierce opposition, undismayed by constant danger, unshaken by enormous temptations, he set Law above Force in Mexico.

FINIS.

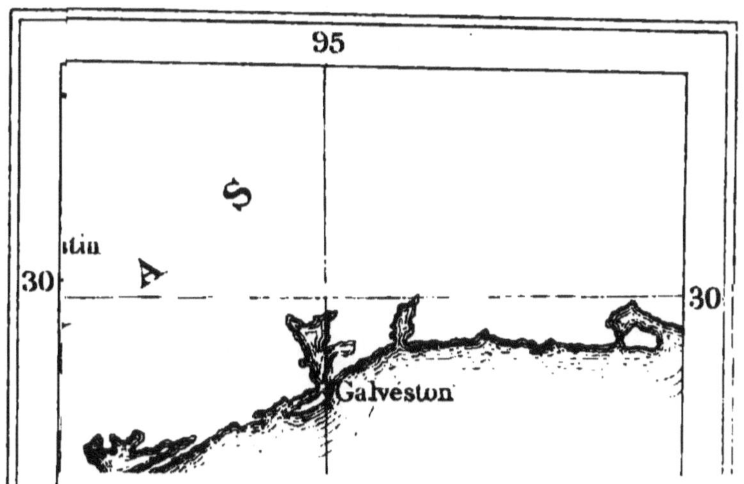

95
30
30
S
A
stin
Galveston

INDEX.

———

A.

B.

E.

F.

G.

H.

of Arts and Sciences, 59; imprisoned in San Juan de
Ulloa, 62; exile at New Orleans, 63; returns to
Mexico, 64; abolishes ecclesiastical and military
courts, 65; his Reform Laws, 66-67; opposition of
Bishops, 68; new Constitution, 69; Vice-President
of the Republic, 70 and 72; Minister of Home Affairs,
71; imprisoned by Comonfort, 73; assembles his Cabinet
at Guanajuato, 75; legitimate President, 76; military forces
of, 77; Landa attempts his life, 78; leaves Guadalajara,
79; excommunicated, 80; recognises French and English claims, 81; loyalty of Vera Cruz to, 82; organises
defence of town, 83; refuses foreign volunteers, 84, a
" President in a black coat, ' 85, contrasted with Miramon, 87; reception of McLane, 89; accused of selling
National property, 90-92; his programme of July 18th,
59 and 93; ecclesiastical laws, 95-96; an unskilful financier, 98, 114-115-116, and 351, admits Spanish Minister
to Mexico, 101; probity and honesty of his Government,
103; decree of restitution in Laguna Seca case, 104-7
fixes new elections, 109; re-enters Mexico, 110; difficulties of administration, 111-112; re-elected President, 113,
hatred of cruelty, 116-117; banishes certain Bishops, 118;
recognised by European Ministers, 119; opposition of M.
de Saligny, 120; re-organisation of administration, 122;
slanders upon, in Europe, 125-6, 146, 154, 220, and 352,
declines loan from United States, 155; authorises Zamacona to confer with Sir C. Wyke, 156-7; approves Convention, 158; organizes defence of Mexico, 162-163, his
answer to Allied note, 166-7, honest treatment of Allies,
169-70, 173-4, and 217; proposes Conference 71, confirms Convention of Soledad, 172-175; remonstrances
as to Almonte, 177-8; negociates treaty with France
and Spain, 180; declares war against France, 181;
thwarts Napoleon III., 184-5; new Convention with
England, 186-7; thanks General Zaragoza, 193; his
treatment of French prisoners, 194; is especially denounced by French, 200; fortifies Puebla, 202; retires
to San Luis Potosi, 204-208; the common enemy, 214,
loyalty of Sonora to, 218-232; true nature of his conflict
with Maximilian, 230; an unconsidered exile, 235;
recognized by 12 provinces, 236-7; his administration in
the North, 244; manifesto of June 7th, '63, 245; re-
models his Cabinet, 245; at Saltillo and Monterey, 247
and 282; retirement suggested by Doblado, 248; remits
cash to prisoners in France, 249; a raiser of armies, 250;
at Chihuahua, 251 and 282; number of his forces, 251;

P.

ber, 1862, 200; Maximilian neglects to summon, 291;
new election, 1867, 348; meets, 349; confirms Presidential
election, 353-4.

Paso del Norte.— (Now Ciudad de Juarez), Juarez at, 252;
Decree of, 272; Court ball at, 274-5; Juarez at, 282.

Pasteles, Reclamacion de los.—32.

Payno.—Señor, quoted, 72.

Pedraza.—Presidential candidate, 27-28.

Penaud.—Admiral, commanding French Fleet, in Mexican
Gulf, 81.

Perote.—Evacuated by French, 201.

Peza.—Señor, issues bonds for Miramon, '58, 139.

Pierce.—President, purchases the Mesilla from Santa Anna,
62 and 154.

Poinsett.— Mr., American Minister in Mexico, 28.

Polk.—Mr., President of United States of America, 35.

Popocatapetl.— In sight of French troops, 192.

" President in a Black Coat." - Juarez called, 250.

Press Law.—Under the Intervention, 206-7.

Prim.—General, Prince of Reuss, approves of joint intervention, 149, 170, 172.

Prisoners.—French, taken at Puebla, 194.

Proclamations.—Numerous French, 205.

Programme.—Political, of Juarez at Vera Cruz, 93-5.

Pronunciamientos. - Number of, 2.

Provinces.—Mexican, acknowledging Juarez, 236-7.

Puebla —Taken by Comonfort, March, '56, 68; French not
conquered at, 193; besieged by General Forey, 202;
Bishop of, order regarding excommunicate soldiers, 193;
surrenders, 203; Mexican officers at, 203-4; evacuated
by the French, 301; occupied by Diaz, 306; risings at,
350.

Q.

Quarterly Review. - Article cited, No. CXV., 13, 143.

Queretaro.-- Maximilian retires to, 301; siege of, 311-17; false
news from, 340.

R.

S.

U.

V.

END OF INDEX.